The
Lines
Between
Us

Books by Amy Lynn Green

Things We Didn't Say
The Lines Between Us

The Lines Between Us

AMY LYNN GREEN

BETHANYHOUSE

a division of Baker Publishing Group
Minneapolis, Minnesota

© 2021 by Amy Lynn Green

Published by Bethany House Publishers
11400 Hampshire Avenue South
Bloomington, Minnesota 55438
www.bethanyhouse.com

Bethany House Publishers is a division of
Baker Publishing Group, Grand Rapids, Michigan

Printed in the United States of America

Library of Congress Cataloging-in-Publication Data
Names: Green, Amy Lynn, author.
Title: The lines between us / Amy Lynn Green.
Description: Minneapolis, Minnesota : Bethany House Publishers, [2021] |
Identifiers: LCCN 2021015482 | ISBN 9780764237171 (trade paper) | ISBN
    9780764239373 (casebound) | ISBN 9781493433834 (ebook)
Subjects: GSAFD: Christian fiction. | Suspense fiction.
Classification: LCC PS3607.R4299 L56 2021 | DDC 813/.6—dc23
LC record available at https://lccn.loc.gov/2021015482

Scripture quotations are from the King James Version of the Bible.

This is a work of historical reconstruction; the appearances of certain historical figures are therefore inevitable. All other characters, however, are products
of the author's imagination, and any resemblance to actual persons, living or
dead, is coincidental.

Cover design by Jennifer Parker
Cover image of smokejumpers and airplane courtesy of the Forest History
Society, Durham, NC

21 22 23 24 25 26 27   7 6 5 4 3 2 1

To my grandparents,
Bob and Edna Shelenberger and
Ray and Marian Green.
Thank you for the legacy of faith.

Prologue

FROM GORDON HOOPER TO DORIE ARMITAGE

November 25, 1941

Dear Dorie,

When a girl asks a fellow to write to her, is one day after leaving too soon to send the first letter? I bet it is.

But honestly, Dorie, it isn't fair. Whenever I try to study, my mind drifts back to the time we spent together last week. The way you fired back witty replies before I could catch a breath. Your laugh that sounded like sleigh bells. That easy smile of yours I caught aimed at me across the table more than once during the turkey dinner.

Something must be wrong with me. George down the hall's got a record playing "Blue Skies," so Frank Sinatra crooning about being in love must be affecting my mood.

If you're smart, you'll crumple this up and tell Jack to give me a good talking-to. Lucky for me, he's a pacifist now too and won't deck me for sending his sister a love letter. (Probably.)

Doris Armitage, what have you done to me? I used to be a

no-nonsense college man, with dreams of a career and a stock portfolio and making it in the world better than my father did. Now all I can think about is you.

Speaking of fathers, I hope yours doesn't read this. I got the sense from the way he scowled at me that he didn't appreciate my visit. This letter probably wouldn't help.

Listen, even if I'm wrong, even if your request for me to write you was simply one friend to another, I'd love to hear from you anyway. Just have pity on a fellow and put me out of my misery—fast.

Yours in hope,
Gordon

FROM DORIE TO GORDON

November 29, 1941

Dear Gordon,

A love letter? Gosh, Gordon, I barely know you. At least other than the stories Jack's told about you this past year.

Still, I've written a few love letters in my day, though none to a college man who's got all kinds of pretty co-eds swarming around him. Meanwhile, I'm just a mechanic's daughter you met hours away in the-middle-of-nowhere Pennsylvania.

Missing you desperately.

Darn this typewriter! I'm awful about writing things before thinking them through, and it's just such trouble to use the correction fluid that I suppose I won't bother.

As for Daddy, don't worry about him. You know how fathers are. Besides that, he didn't like Jack coming home with new ideas after his first semester away. He's always hoped Jack would take

8

over his auto shop and thinks college classes are a bunch of hooey invented by city folks to steal money from homegrown people like us. You shouldn't let him get to you.

By which I mean . . . you should write again, soon and often. Start now, if you like.

Dorie

P.S. I'm glad Jack brought you home for Thanksgiving. You didn't talk about them much, but I suppose your family will steal you away for Christmas, won't they?

FROM GORDON TO DORIS

December 2, 1941

Dear Dorie,

Do you know, I actually whooped aloud when I got your letter? The fellow at the post office must've thought I was plain nuts, but I didn't care.

You wrote back! To me! I must've read that page five or six times just to make sure I didn't mistake your meaning.

I don't care what you call these letters—I want to know everything about you, Dorie. What you like and dislike, who you admire, what you're afraid of, what you dream about.

I promise I'm normally a rational fellow. President of the campus debate society, member of a Friends congregation, business student, and construction worker during the summers.

But right now, all I am is the happiest man in the United States of America. Maybe the world. Nothing could take away this soaring feeling inside of me, almost like I could jump off a roof and fly.

9

I'm headed to classes, but I had to get this in the mail. Write back soon.

Yours,
Gordon

P.S. Yes, I'm planning to go to Syracuse for Christmas at my uncle's house. But if I take the train, I can duck out at the Allentown station stop, even if it's just for an hour or two. Will you be there? I checked the schedule—I should be there on December 19 at 4 PM.

FROM DORIE TO GORDON

December 5, 1941

Dear Gordon,

It makes a girl blush to have someone go on so about her.

So please don't stop. I'm awfully pale, and as Daddy insists that "no daughter of mine will wear makeup while under this roof," blushing is the only way to improve my complexion.

I'd love to meet you at the station on the 19th. I'll be wearing my red silk scarf. I can only assume you liked it, the way you stared at me the last time I wore it. Gosh, I love train stations, don't you? The adventure of travel, the thrill of a journey. You never know what might happen.

In the meantime, best of luck with your exams. I'll keep this short so I won't distract you from your studies.

Or maybe I've already done that. The world looks—I don't know—happier and brighter right now, doesn't it? Like nothing bad can really happen, or if it does, it won't reach us. I hope you feel it too.

It's a delicious sensation, being above the world. I'm not sure
I ever want to come down.

> *Yours,*
> *Dorie*

RADIO BROADCAST FROM THE NEW YORK NBC NEWSROOM ON DECEMBER 7, 1941

President Roosevelt said in a statement today that the Japanese have attacked Pearl Harbor, Hawaii, from the air. Stay tuned for further updates.

IN THE DECEMBER 8, 1941, *PHILADELPHIA DAILY NEWS*

1500 CONFIRMED DEAD IN HAWAII
US DECLARES WAR
Senate–82–0
House–388–1

FROM DORIE TO GORDON

December 10, 1941

Dear Gordon,

War, Gordon! All this talk about it for years, and now we're finally getting involved. Everyone here is talking about joining up. Some of the farmers will have to stay behind, of course, but I'm sure we women will fill open jobs. Naturally I'm glad to do it—if Daddy will let me. He made me stop wearing overalls and boots at age eight, and I'm not sure even the war effort will convince him to let me back into them at twenty.

Have you and Jack talked about enlisting yet? Or will you wait until you graduate?

I know both of you went on about peace after dinner one night, but surely you can see this isn't some political stance. When I read about what Hitler's men are doing in France . . . well, it makes my blood boil. Not to mention the awful news from Pearl Harbor.

My friend Carrie and her sweetheart are getting married next week, before he enlists, just to have a few months together first. I've thought about it and want you to know I'm willing to wait for you if you go overseas. After all, it's the girls at home that keep our men fighting for victory.

Please write to me. Better yet, call. You have such a deep, steady voice. I miss hearing it in times like these.

Yours,
Dorie

Application For
Conscientious Objector Status

GORDON HOOPER

December 14, 1941

The following is my appeal for exemption from military service on the basis of my moral objection to war. As a university student in Philadelphia, the city of brotherly love founded by pacifists, I hope to find sympathy for my convictions.

As evidence that this is a long-held belief, I've been attending a Friends (also known as Quaker) assembly, one of the historic peace churches, since I was eighteen. I'm prepared to appear before the draft board and explain how Jesus' teachings leave me no choice but to reject all kinds of violence.

When I was young, I used to delay bedtime by begging my mother to tell me a story about Clara Hooper, her great-grandmother, a Quaker abolitionist who sheltered enslaved men and women on the Underground Railroad.

I remember huddling under my blanket near the radiator at eight years old, imagining myself as one of those fugitives, heart pounding in fear, back sore from hard labor and whippings, feet cut from nights stumbling through the woods. And there was Clara, standing inside the farmhouse door, with her soft-spoken "thees" and "thous," her kettle of soup simmering over the fire, and her quiet, unshakable commitment to peaceful resistance of a great evil. Almost every refugee who came through her door made their way safely to Canada.

When I was eighteen, I applied to legally change my surname to hers, rather than keep the name of my late father.

I tell you this because I want you to know: I am not only an idealist who can't imagine looking his fellow man in the eye and taking his life by force. I am also the great-great-grandson of Clara Hooper. I have a legacy behind me, and I hope to leave one after me.

Please give me the freedom to choose what that legacy will be.

Gordon P. Hooper

FROM GORDON TO DORIE

December 19, 1941

Dear Dorie,

You weren't at the station.

At first I thought the snow delayed you. Then I wondered if your father tried to keep you from coming, or if you'd bummed a ride from someone with an unreliable car, or even if you'd forgotten.

Eventually, after I wore out a groove in the platform hoping to see you coming over the hill, I had to get back on the train home to New York. That's where I'm starting this letter.

Jack told you, didn't he? That I'm going to apply for conscientious objector status, I mean.

That's why I wanted to see you in person. How else can I explain what I believe? You assumed I'd leap at the chance to fire bullets through men who have the misfortune of living in a country ruled by a madman.

It's not right, Dorie. I can't read the New Testament and find a way to justify killing or any violence, and now . . . well, now's my chance to live it out. Even though it's hard.

One of my professors told me I should start the paperwork, since the process to prove my sincerity can be intensive. If I'm drafted and approved as a conscientious objector, I'll be assigned with the CPS—the Civilian Public Service—till the end of the war.

I don't know how often, if ever, they approve furloughs in the CPS. From the sound of things, they want to make things as tough as possible for the COs to avoid getting an influx of lazy men who don't like the idea of overseas duty. That means my only contact with you might be through letters until this terrible war is over.

I hope I can make you understand. If you have questions, I'm happy to answer them. Below is my uncle's address in Syracuse so you can write or even call if you want. I'll pay the long-distance charges. We can work through this, I know it.

Have a wonderful Christmas, and remember as you sing "Silent Night" that I truly want the world to "sleep in heavenly peace."

Yours,
Gordon

FROM DORIE TO GORDON

December 22, 1941

Dear Gordon,

Your only contact with me will not be through letters. It will be in your memories.

How can you think I'd be interested in a relationship with you after this? Our country is fighting for survival, and you wonder what Jesus would do? Of course he would want you to fight!

If that was all, maybe we could say good-bye as friends. But you dragged Jack into pacifism with you. He's back for Christmas, and it's been days of long arguments, cold silences, and angry outbursts—at the holidays, no less, when all I wanted was for everyone to be happy.

Daddy served with distinction in WWI. We still have the saber from our Civil War ancestor, Robert Armitage, mounted over the fireplace. Now it's Jack's turn, and all he can talk about is flimsy arguments about peace in a world that's gone up in flames.

You can have your Inner Light or Sermon on the Mount or

15

whatever you call it. I'll have justice. If I were a man, I'd be down at the recruiting station this minute. Then maybe the neighbors would stop talking about how disgraceful it is for Jack to join the conchies.

Mother's always told me I'm too impulsive. Well, maybe she was right. I should have known better than to chase after some city slicker I knew barely anything about.

We live in different worlds, Gordon. Mine is the real one, and yours is some idealistic fantasy where everyone loves their neighbor and no one has to fight for freedom. It took a declaration of war to wake us up to that, but I'd rather know now than keep pretending.

Good-bye, Gordon. I hope the CPS treats you and Jack well— safe, coddled, and far away from those who are sacrificing for the ones they love.

Dorie

CHAPTER 1

Gordon Hooper

December 31, 1944
Three Years Later

Seems to me that if you have to ring in another year of war, you might as well do it parachuting into a wildfire.

That's what I'd thought, anyway, answering Earl Morrissey's crack-of-dawn call to pile into the Ford Trimotor with Jack. An hour later, fingers numb under hand-me-down leather gloves in the December cold, I was having second thoughts.

Thoughts like *I bet the others are eating breakfast right now.* A nice tall stack of Mrs. Edith's pancakes. No butter—rationing hit even the Forest Service—but plenty of maple syrup, pooling over the edge onto the plate.

Not the two of us, though. No sir. We sat crammed in the back of a flimsy plane that lofted us across the forests of Oregon. I could feel the seeping cold of the metal bench beneath me, even through my scratchy long johns and thick canvas pants.

I glanced over at Jack, the padded shoulders of his uniform giving him a hunchbacked look. Puffs of white breath curled out of his mesh-masked helmet, like a dragon had decided to try out for the local football team. "Nervous?" he shouted over the engine's roar.

I shrugged, figuring that even my Friends meeting back home would agree that wasn't a lie, strictly speaking. My hands wandered to the ripcord for the emergency chute strapped across my chest, a tiny thread of a lifeline if the worst happened.

"Get ready, boys!" a voice near my ear hollered, the unmistakable Nicholas Tate, a longtime ranger and our spotter. He gestured to the doorless opening near the back of the plane.

I'd crouched atop the practice tower dozens—no, hundreds—of times at our training center in Missoula, Montana, waiting for the starting gun of a single tap on the shoulder. After that, I'd gone on seven real fire jumps, four the summer of '44, three the year before. But those had ranged from May to September, so I'd never seen snow from the air before, clotting the ground between trees and dusting the coniferous branches far, far below.

At the sight, crooning strains of Bing Crosby wafted through my mind—*"I'm dreaming of a white Christmas."* I shook my head to get rid of them.

Another Christmas away from home had come and gone for those of us in the Civilian Public Service. We'd roasted a few chickens back at our remote Oregon spike camp, far from glazed ham dinners, neighborhood carolers, department store displays, and pretty girls in red scarves waiting at train stations.

Where did that come from?

It was the nerves of the jump, that was all. Who knew where Dorie Armitage was now? She never wrote, not to me, not even to her own brother. We'd said our good-byes three years ago and never looked back. While some of her words still stung, I knew in my heart that she was right about one thing, at least: We'd both been young and foolish to think we were in love, until the war interrupted our daydreams.

I clipped myself onto the static line that would inflate our parachutes and crouched by the door, ready to fall into nothingness. My eyes found the clearing we'd be aiming for.

Take a look at that postage stamp. It would get bigger the closer we got to it, I knew—as long as the wind currents Jack had tested with drift chutes held.

As long as my parachute opened.

As long as I didn't get swept off course and into the trees.

As long as the hundreds of things that could go wrong didn't.

Earl Morrissey's words echoed in my head, delivered with the authority of a district forest ranger and his usual piercing look up and down the line. *"As smokejumpers, you run toward the fire, even when every instinct screams at you to run away from it. That's true courage, men."*

I'd signed up for that, applying to this program, and for two dry seasons, I'd plummeted through the air toward blaze after blaze.

But that didn't mean I had to like it.

I flinched when a hand touched my shoulder, but it wasn't the tap of our spotter, the signal to leave the plane behind. The hand rested there instead. I swiveled to see Jack, his dark eyes reassuring through the opening in the helmet.

"Hey," he said. "We're in this together, Gordon. It'll be all right."

I took in a deep breath. "Thanks."

He clapped me on the back, then moved himself in line in front of me. That was Jack for you. Always willing to go first.

"Ten seconds till drop!" Nick boomed.

I crouched, every muscle tense, my mouth dry as underbrush in July, staring down through cold, thin air.

Just a two-person crew for a small lightning fire. So far, it hadn't even crowned, the smoke rising from burning underbrush rather than the treetops themselves. After we jumped, Tate would have the pilot circle around and drop equipment, food, and sleeping bags, in case we needed to spend the night. An easy job.

I tried to tell that to my stomach, but it wasn't listening.

Back when the Wright brothers first took off at Kitty Hawk—they were pacifists too—there were plenty of churchgoing Americans who declared that if God had wanted men to fly, he would have given them wings.

Mr. Tate's hand came down on Jack's shoulder. *Tap.* Jack disappeared out the mouth of the plane into the sky. I shifted forward to the door.

I've never been sure about that, but I am pretty certain that even if it was God's idea for men to fly, it was the devil's idea for them to fall.

Tap.

My body reacted on instinct, sprung like a wound tin toy, launching me out of the plane, feet first, arms crossed. For a few terrible seconds, I plummeted toward the earth.

It came a moment before I'd braced myself for it: the sharp jerk of the harness as the parachute bloomed above me like a silk mushroom. *Breathe. Come on, Gordon. It opened. You're all right.*

As usual, the training they'd drilled into us at Missoula played in my head over and over, like the tunes at the cheap bar in town with only a few records to spin on the jukebox. How to maneuver the chute, where to keep my eyes, how to brace myself for an easy landing. Some of the men talked about the float to the ground like it was a pleasant, drifting dream. I always nodded along. It was easier to pretend I wasn't terrified every time I saw the tips of pines and cedars pointing toward me like spears, the whirl of cold air against me almost as terrifying as the whiffs of uncontrolled smoke in the distance.

Those same feelings rushed over me as the ground came nearer, winter bald and dusted with snow. This time, though, I landed without incident, standing on shaky legs.

I waved the red signal streamer from the pocket on my lower left leg to let Mr. Tate and the pilot know I was all right, then rolled my silk chute with practiced hands. Unlike the military, who'd had to start using nylon after Japan cut off our supply of silk, the Forest Service took good care of their expensive materials. For a man who made $2.50 a month for CPS labor, the $125 silk chute was like giving an urchin a royal robe, and I meant to take good care of it.

"Come on, Gordon!" Jack called, a few yards away, already sniffing the air. No compass or map for him—he oriented himself by his nose, since we rarely landed close enough to a fire to see smoke from the ground. "Let's get this taken care of and start an early dinner."

I snorted. "Someone's optimistic." The position of the sun told me we still had a few hours till noon, but this wasn't a city fire, with a shiny fire engine and hydrants to stop the blaze.

No, the only way to stop a fire out here was to suffocate it. Find the Pulaskis and shovels the spotter had parachuted down, then use them to dig a trench wide and deep enough that, without grass or underbrush to catch, the fire wouldn't have fuel to keep itself roaring. Sometimes we had to cut down trees, haul water in from a stream, or toss loose dirt over smoldering patches, but most of our time was spent digging the fire line.

Once we'd hiked to the fire's perimeter, I slammed my Pulaski into the earth, driving a furrow like the hand of God divided the Israelites from the Egyptians, so the plagues and the Angel of Death couldn't cross over. This far, and no farther.

The fire could rage all it wanted, but it wasn't getting more of the forest today. Not if I could stop it.

I let slip a groan as I set down my pack to take a swig from my canteen, slowly rolling my shoulders in a stretch. As always, it felt like the fire had gone out of the underbrush and straight into my muscles.

Eight hours of backbreaking work had clocked us in well within the 10 AM next-day containment goal the Forest Service used as their baseline for a job well done. Jack and I had taken two short breaks for our K-ration meals, the same dried stuff the troops ate on their missions, but then it was back to the unending digging of the fire line.

Two-man fires felt different than the blazes that called out our full eighteen-man crew or the infernos that requested jumpers from base camp and several of the spike camps combined. No mules to haul supplies and water, no cook assigned to rustle up grub over a makeshift wood stove, not as much camaraderie to pass the time. Still, it was better to be stuck here with Jack than someone like Shorty Schumacher, who could talk a fellow to death.

"Come on, Gordon," Jack called back, his flashlight bobbing in the murky twilight, ahead of me as usual. "Another half mile, that's all, and we'll be out of here."

"Another half mile, and I'll die of exhaustion," I grumbled.

Jack laughed and forged ahead. "Don't be stupid. The bears would get you first."

Too much energy to be real, like one of the black-capped chicka-dees that flitted around us during morning exercises, taunting the smokejumpers who needed to work so hard to be able to fly. Even in college, Jack had been that way, the handsome athlete everyone was drawn to, with the same winning smile as his sister, though they didn't share any other features.

Just a few steps behind him, I managed to push my aching body forward.

On most jumps, we stuck around overnight and in the morning walked the breadth of the burned area, checking for pockets of hot coals to smother. We kept an eye out for snags—trees still standing upright, but with their roots burned out from under them. "Silent killers," Morrissey called them, and he'd seen his fair share in three decades of forestry work.

Tonight, though, the midwinter sun set early and temperatures dipped below freezing. Morrissey had ordered us to report when the blaze was extinguished, then hike the few miles to the road and let the lookout who had spotted the fire come back to check for damage. A small blessing, anyway.

Once we'd made it to the highway, we radioed in our location and huddled within sight of the road. It wasn't long before we heard the rumble of an engine, and a dull-colored truck rounded the bend in the distance.

"Now, that's service for you." I elbowed Jack and pointed out the truck. "Roadside pickup."

He grinned and pinched his nose. "Sure, just like garbage collection back in Philadelphia."

After a long day's work, we sure didn't smell like a Macy's perfume counter. Not to mention Jack was just as broad-shouldered as me, so it would be a sardine-and-shoehorn fit inside the truck's cab. *But at least it'll be warm.* When had I last felt my toes, numb as chunks of ice even while wrapped in government-issue wool socks?

Inside, the ranger, who looked like he could have started in the forestry department under the *first* President Roosevelt in 1905, introduced himself as Arthur Calhoun and offered us slabs of jerky wrapped in wax paper. "Made 'em myself," he bragged, lurching onto the road.

I gave it the old college try, biting off a chunk. Back home, I'd never been much for food you had to gnaw like a beaver. Then again, back home, I'd never seen a beaver outside of a zoo. Now, though, the salt and hickory of the meat tasted better than the sweat and smoke I'd tasted the rest of the day. "Thanks for the pickup, Mr. Calhoun," I managed around the mouthful.

"Just doing my job." Our driver gunned the engine and rocketed down the road, making me jostle into Jack. "It's four hours or so to Flintlock Mountain, so best get comfortable. Been years since I drove all night like this. Normally, I'd tell 'em to make you wait through the night in those sleeping bags they drop in, but it's a chilly one, no mistake." Mr. Calhoun grunted. "Can't get a moment's peace, even in winter, I guess."

Next to me, Jack leaned forward. "About that. Isn't it odd that we had a blaze so long after fire season?"

I kept myself from rolling my eyes, but only barely. Leave it to Jack to care about probability when all I wanted to do was sleep. He'd be finishing up his training to become a top-notch high school calculus teacher if it wasn't for the draft.

"Don't know that I'd call it odd," Mr. Calhoun said thoughtfully. "Sure, we don't get much lightning this season, and things are wet enough with snow that they don't usually catch. But for every usual, there's an unusual, y'know?"

But Jack wouldn't let up. "Last year we had one winter fire in the whole state of Oregon. Morrissey told me this was the fourth fire report in the past six weeks."

"Like I say, these things happen sometimes." Mr. Calhoun took a turn I thought would send us into the snowy ditch, but righted us jerkily. "Now tell me, did you boys get a deferment for the smoke-jumping, or were you 4-F, some old injury or the like keeping you back in the States? If you don't mind my asking."

I glanced uneasily at Jack. Usually, forestry employees had heard about the conscientious objectors working fire duty, but every now and then, the farther away we got from the base camp in Missoula, we'd find someone who didn't know.

Here we go again.

"Something like that," Jack said, at the same time that I said, louder, "Neither, sir. We're with the Civilian Public Service."

"With the what, now?" Before we could explain, Mr. Calhoun twisted to look at us, swerving wildly across the blessedly empty road. "Hold on, you're not some of those conchies, are you?"

"Yes. We are."

Mr. Calhoun swore, swinging his eyes back to the road. "I don't believe it. *Conchies*. In my truck. That's some nerve you've got, dodging the draft."

I clenched my teeth. I'd heard it all before. Shirkers, cowards, bums. As if we weren't making any sacrifices. The truck's cab seemed to shrink, like there wasn't quite enough air for all three of us.

"It's not draft dodging," I said, trying to keep my voice even and rational. "We've chosen to serve our country in a non-combat role because we don't believe anyone has a right to take another man's life."

"Huh. Tell that to Hitler."

I bit back a smart reply and waited for Jack to help me out. Two against one, we could make a strong enough case that Mr. Calhoun would leave us alone.

But Jack only shrugged, suddenly withdrawn. "It's between us and God. Just a matter of conscience."

Mr. Calhoun snorted. "Like blooming heck it is. If everyone was like you, why, we'd all be wearing swastikas and humming Germany's national anthem right now. Or Japan's, for that matter."

I had a standard comeback for that, and it came out quick and sharp. "If everyone was like us, there wouldn't *be* any wars."

For a moment, I thought Mr. Calhoun was going to dump us on the side of the road to walk the hundred-odd miles back to the Flintlock Mountain District. But he kept the battered vehicle on course, even speeding up, like he couldn't wait to be rid of us.

"Puh," he huffed. "That's an excuse if I ever heard it."

I felt a sharp pain and realized I'd formed my hand into a fist, fingernails cutting into my palm. *Calm down. Breathe in deeply. Let the anger go.*

I wouldn't be like my father. I *wouldn't*.

Slowly, I let my fingers relax, one by one. "I know it seems strange, Mr. Calhoun, but we've done a lot of thinking." I shifted to face Jack, prompting him out of his unusual quiet. "Right, Jack?"

But instead of answering, Jack faced the truck's window, as if he could see anything between the frost-laced glass and the darkness.

He's tired, that's all. Both of us were. This wasn't the time or the place for a debate.

"Just doesn't seem right," Mr. Calhoun muttered. Despite the large bundle on the dash, he didn't offer us any more jerky.

In the cold silence that now reigned in the cab, I felt my smoke-reddened eyes droop shut.

New Year's Eve. Almost 1945. Three years since Pearl Harbor.

We were doing the right thing. Of course we were. And if that meant building fences, digging trenches around dozens of fires, and arguing with old rangers until this crazy war was finally over, so be it.

I just hope the end comes soon.

CHAPTER 2

Dorie Armitage

January 5, 1945

The buttery tones of Frank Sinatra's big-band brass poured into the chilly Seattle night as my friends and I strolled toward the gymnasium that hosted the USO New Year's dance.

Hearing it made my foot start to twitch. It had been too long—ages, really—since I'd been to a proper dance, not just an impromptu spin to Bea's jazz record collection with others in the Women's Army Corps.

"Come on, girls," I said, motioning them forward. Violet was gawking at the line of uniformed men, and Bea patted her hair nervously. "We're already late."

As we got closer, I saw something that gave my stomach a quick-and-dirty gut punch. *Well, if that's not trouble, I don't know what is.*

Flanking the door like a tank gunner was an older woman whose face, beaming as she greeted the military men filing inside, froze when she saw us.

"Dorie . . ." Violet whispered uncertainly from behind me, apparently spotting the same obstacle.

I kept my posture straight and proper anyway, reaching into my uniform pocket to produce the tickets I'd gotten at the PX.

"Three for the dance," I said, smiling and leveraging my famous Armitage charm.

"I'm sorry, but you can't come inside," the woman said firmly. *Mrs. Coleridge*, the name badge pinned to a dark formal dress declared.

Behind me, Bea coughed uncomfortably, and Violet shrank back like she was trying to disappear.

I sighed. Apparently, this was going to be up to me.

"I understand we're a little late," I said, hoping I sounded caramel-smooth and confident. "It took longer than we expected to get ready for the party."

Mrs. Coleridge's eyes flitted to my khaki WAC uniform.

Well, of course we didn't have a choice of clothing to slow us down, once we heard that only military personnel in uniform would be admitted to the dance. But because it was a dress-up occasion, I'd put on red lipstick, secured my wild hair into Victory rolls with an artillery belt's worth of hairpins, and polished my shoes with saddle soap.

And here we were, after all our pains, still not quite good enough.

"Your lack of punctuality is not the issue," Mrs. Coleridge explained as if we were bobby-socked thirteen-year-olds. "You see, the only women permitted to attend the dance are our *civilian* hostesses."

"Oh," Violet said, her voice rising an octave. "We didn't know. That is, no one told us."

Mrs. Coleridge nodded in a motherly way to acknowledge her simpering. "I do apologize for the inconvenience."

I slid back the tickets and studied them, as if looking for fine print. "Gee, and here I thought the USO was open to members of the armed services. Which we are."

"Let's *go*, Dorie," Bea whispered with a tug at my sleeve. Her upper-crust upbringing strictly prohibited making, as she called it, "a scene."

But I say every good story has a few scenes.

Mrs. Coleridge was just like all the other people who disapproved of my choice to join the Women's Army Corps—my neighbors, my family's minister, my parents. Jack, who only knew because Mother had blabbed. Gordon Hooper, if he knew or cared, which he wouldn't, because I'd unceremoniously dumped him after a five-letter courtship.

None of them had been able to stop me, and a middle-aged woman wrapped in black crepe and rosewater sure wasn't going to now.

I craned my neck to look past her into the gymnasium, transformed with festive draperies and paper lanterns and filled to bursting with servicemen and demure young ladies in dresses of every color but khaki. Max and some of his buddies from the Transportation Corps were probably already inside.

"You have five times the number of men here as women," I observed. "We'll be helping even out your numbers."

Mrs. Coleridge didn't flinch, and I noticed that she had a layer of face powder crusted in the wrinkle grooves around her eyes and mouth. "I'm sorry to disappoint, but rules are rules, Miss . . ."

"Hightower. PFC Nora Hightower." It was the name I always gave when it looked like there might be trouble, just in case someone decided to report me.

Not that I set out to cause trouble. It just . . . well . . . followed me.

"You see, our junior hostesses went through a rigorous application process—"

"We did too." And an IQ test, a physical, a typing exam, and on and on, simply to prove ourselves. I'd scored near the top in all of them, and aced the driving test too.

"—and these young women are not even allowed to step out with one of the men on a date, much less . . ." Her voice trailed off, and her cheeks reddened under the face powder.

So *that* was it. "Much less what, Mrs. Coleridge? What do you think we WACs do, anyway?"

"Dorie . . ." Violet's voice, less scared now and more with an edge of warning.

Which I ignored. "Filing medical records?" I suggested innocently. "Driving shipments of supplies from base to base? Directing an air traffic control tower? The members of the Women's Army Corps work to free up the servicemen you seem so enamored with."

Ever so slightly, the smug smile on the woman's face faded. "I'm sure that's true for the majority. But you can't deny that rumors are started for reasons."

"Eleanor Roosevelt said that rumors about the WAC's loose reputation were part of a Nazi-inspired slander campaign to undermine the war effort." I clucked my tongue, shaking my head at the notion. "Surely you wouldn't want to participate in such a thing as a patriotic American citizen."

I heard Bea suck in a gasp, but otherwise only the strains of "Swinging on a Star" broke the silence.

You know those high-noon duels in B-movie Westerns where the sheriff and the desperado stare each other down before pacing away to shoot? That's what we did, Mrs. Coleridge and I, and for a second I wasn't sure whose hat was white and whose was black.

Then a baritone "Hey, what's the holdup?" alerted us to a group of army boys who were eager to get inside to dance with the respectable junior hostesses.

I glared at them, but Mrs. Coleridge smiled over my shoulder, her voice sweeter than a melted Milk Dud. "One moment, please." Her eyes returned to us. "Run along now, ladies."

Turning away without wiping that smug smile off the woman's face was the hardest thing I had done in a long time. As we trudged back to the street leading to the fort, Bea was saying something about being too tired to dance anyway, but I wasn't listening. My mind was already spinning through ways to sneak in, and I couldn't help but give one glance back at the men who had stolen our place in line.

Wait. Was that . . . ? I took another look, and even in the twilight, it was obvious that one of them was a black man. And what's more . . . I squinted at his uniform, and there it was, glinting silver on his shoulder: the brand of command. An officer.

My, my. Poor Mrs. Coleridge is having an eventful evening.

"Come on, Dorie," Violet said, tugging at my arm. "We can play bridge back at the barracks."

I waved her off, motioning her to be quiet. As if a card game could be half as interesting as this.

"I'm sorry." Mrs. Coleridge's stentorian voice boomed across the distance between us, right on cue. "But the USO club for *colored* servicemen is at the YMCA on East Olive Street."

Her meaning—and firm stance blocking the door—couldn't have been clearer. But the officer was either playing dumb or really was, because all he said was "I see. Are they having a dance tonight too?"

I edged closer, approaching from the side and leaving Bea and Violet behind, close enough to hear Mrs. Coleridge huff, "I don't know the schedules of the other branches. But your kind aren't permitted in this one, private."

"Lieutenant, ma'am," he corrected mildly. "First Lieutenant Vincent Leland."

So I'd been right about the uniform. Usually officers didn't dignify the enlisted men's USO clubs with their presence.

"As you might have heard me say before, rules are rules."

"I did hear. Thank you for letting me know how things stand. Which way to East Olive Street, if you don't mind?"

She pointed to her left, and I think she would have gestured in any direction, so long as it would get rid of the latest inconvenience on her strained nerves.

"Thank you, ma'am. You have a good evening." He stuck his hands in his pockets and walked where she'd indicated, not whistling a jaunty tune, but not storming off, either.

I can't tell you what made me run a few steps after him, but suddenly there I was, calling out, "Wait!"

Lieutenant Leland turned slowly, removing his hands from his pockets like I might be the police accusing him of pickpocketing. "Piano hands," my mother would have said. She was always despairing of mine, which couldn't even span a full octave.

Now, this close to him, I couldn't think of a thing to say. He was handsome, with a neatly trimmed moustache and a strong jaw. "Looks like we've both been kicked out of the club."

"It seems we have."

Unlike all the black people I saw in movies, he didn't speak with a Southern accent and had no trace of a sunny smile pasted on his face. There was a hardness to the mouth under his trim moustache, no matter how mild the words that came out of it.

I was too curious not to ask. "Did you really expect to get in?"

He didn't meet my eyes exactly, but he gave a tired smile. "Not really. I just came from Fort Benning, Georgia. Down in the heart of Dixie." He drawled the last part. "I only wanted to see if Seattle would be more of the same. Should've guessed."

"There *is* probably a back door, you know. To the gymnasium."

Now he looked at me, but not with amusement the way I'd hoped. More like he thought I needed a one-way escort to the loony bin.

That expression faded to a flicker hidden behind a stoic politeness. "Listen, private . . . "

"Armitage," I supplied.

"PFC Armitage." He repeated the name slowly, frowning, and for a moment, I worried that he'd heard me use my other, false name at the door and was going to ask about it. But instead, he shook his head. "I'm an army officer, here on special invitation to get a job done. Not to cause trouble."

A special invitation. He might as well have lit an electric marquee with a giant arrow to direct my curiosity.

"You do what you want," Leland continued. "But me . . . I'm going to wait to dance till I'm invited in."

I glanced at the white soldiers streaming into the gymnasium, where Mrs. Coleridge paused her ticket taking to glance suspiciously at us. "You might be waiting a long time."

"Yeah, I might." He nodded slowly. "Now, if you'll excuse me, from the way that lady is looking at me, I shouldn't be seen talking to you, so . . ." He tipped his cap at me. "Good evening."

With that, he continued down the street, whether toward East Olive or back to the fort, I couldn't say. But not before I saw the glint of something else on the lapel of his uniform: a pair of silver wings.

But that didn't make sense. There weren't any black paratroopers . . . were there? Almost all of the black troops who had come through Fort Lawton were in the service corps—supply drivers, facility guards, and mess stewards—or else in their own segregated units. They certainly didn't fly planes, much less jump out of them.

"Dorie!"

My name came out shocked and slicing, and I turned to see Bea advancing on me, her expensive leather shoes tapping against the pavement and Violet trailing behind her. She looked meaningfully

THE LINES BETWEEN US

after Lieutenant Leland. "You don't know when to leave well enough alone."

I shrugged off her concern. "I'd hoped he could help."

"Help with what?" Violet asked.

"Boost me up to the windows, of course. That is, if the back door's locked."

Violet looked about ready to pass out on the sidewalk. "You can't be serious."

"Dorie, we can't—" Bea huffed and crossed her arms. "You know it's not going to end well."

My eyes went from the glow of light and music inside the gymnasium to the shadowed alleyway beside it.

"We've made sacrifices for our country too," I reasoned. "It's not right, turning us away."

Bea shook her head. "That's all well and good, but they've made it clear they don't want us here."

To that, I smiled. "That's only because they haven't seen us dance."

In the military, sometimes you got used to falling into line. Obeying commands from Captain Dora Petmencky, the officer in charge of the Fort Lawton WACs. Abiding by the speed limit in the army motorcade vehicles. Standing up as straight as an over-starched shirt for morning roll call.

Other times, you found yourself clambering onto a garbage can to climb in a gymnasium window.

By some miracle, I managed to avoid spraining my ankle or tearing my hosiery, and after I let Violet and Bea in through the back door, we stole down the hallway toward the gymnasium, peeking out at the crepe banners, the swing band in the corner, the table weighed down with punch and doughnuts.

"Wait until this song ends," I instructed, "and hustle right in there. Try to find a partner as soon as possible." From the looks of the long stag line around the fringes, that shouldn't be a hardship.

"But what do we do if—?" Violet began, but the concluding brass flourish of the latest number cut her off.

This was our moment. I'd already done a quick reconnaissance to find a likely group of fellows and strode up to them. Bea and Violet could follow if they liked. This close to Puget Sound, we all knew what sink or swim meant.

"Hello, boys," I said in my best sultry voice as I came near the group of soldiers, and a private with slicked-back hair was already turning toward me when I heard a "Hey, Doris! Glad you made it."

I turned to see Max, as close to a "buddy" as a gal could have on base and a real mechanic besides, not just someone who ducked into the transportation corps because it seemed like an easier job. He always showed up on time and carried an Italian-English dictionary in his back pocket to communicate with the prisoners of war who worked in the garage.

Yes, a stand-up guy, Amos Maxwell, though a poor fox-trotter, I found out only a few moments later. No rhythm at all, but he made up for it with grinning enthusiasm.

A verse and a chorus in, something caught my eye on the far side of the gymnasium. "Take me over to the basketball hoop, will you, Max?"

"All righty then, Doris. Whatever you say." Step by step, we danced our way over, with Max tramping on my feet more than the floor. But that was all right with me, because by the time we made it to the foul line, there was Mrs. Coleridge, guarding the punch bowl.

Her eyes roamed the crowd generally, then—spotting a couple both in khaki, maybe?—she stared directly at me, her jaw falling slightly ajar. Hollywood couldn't have planned it any better.

And me? I lifted a hand off of Max's shoulder to wave . . . and took another whirl toward dancing the night away.

CHAPTER 3

Gordon Hooper

January 5, 1945

The smell of government-issue meatloaf could cling to a place for days. Better than the stench of the glob of canned meat we mixed up on fire drops, but still, not appealing.

So my nose got turned around when I entered the cookhouse and smelled roast chicken.

A glance at the chow line told me that it hadn't been my imagination. Mrs. Edith Morrissey, our district ranger's wife, presided over the line, nearly popping her apron strings in pride and holding her pair of tongs like a scepter.

I grabbed a tray and held it out. "Christmas come twice this year, Mrs. Edith?"

She plopped a large thigh on my plate, *plus* a drumstick—the benefits of being nice to the cook. "Didn't you hear? Roger's going to . . ." She shrugged. "Well, it's his birthday."

I glanced over at Roger Kirkwood, sitting next to Jimmy Morrissey, the only two non-CO smokejumpers, both of them fresh out of high school and sure they would live forever. "Did he petition Roosevelt to declare it a national holiday?"

Mrs. Edith picked up a spoon and waggled it at me as we moved down to the vegetables, the crow's-feet around her eyes crinkling in amusement. "Now, Gordon." A generous scoop of green beans hit my plate, along with a fist-sized baked potato. "He's not a bad young man, or I wouldn't want my Jimmy spending time with him. Just a little full of himself. He'll learn."

I scanned the cookhouse for my friends. Not that it was hard to find them: eighteen of us smokejumpers clustered into two groups, the COs and the two townies, plus the two dozen staff and rangers who worked at the park, taking up half of the tables in a cookhouse meant for one hundred boisterous Civilian Conservation Corps men back in the '30s.

Charlie Mayes spotted me from across the room and waved to an open seat across from him, next to Jack. Lloyd and Shorty were there too, but it was the ever-dour Thomas Martin that made me look for another table to join.

Only for a moment, though. *No sense in leaving Jack alone to face him.*

As I passed by the table full of rangers, I sneaked a look at Sarah Ruth Morrissey, seated amid the gruff and grizzled men in their green uniforms, like a bluebird in a pack of grouse. As usual, she preferred their company to us fellows her own age.

Her eyes met mine.

Caught.

I nodded at her, and she tilted her head in what might have been a nod, or maybe it was just a crick in her neck. That was Sarah Ruth. Pretty as a sunrise, but if I'd heard a rumor that she was raised by a pack of mountain lions in her early years, I wouldn't have been surprised. Quickly, I veered away, before I could start blushing.

Shorty Schumacher looked up at me as I set my tray down. "Say, Gordon, you've got Mrs. Edith wrapped around your finger. What's with the grub?"

"It's a miracle, I'm telling you," Charlie declared, then shot a cautious look at Thomas—the Apostle Tom, as Shorty called him. Except Lloyd, we COs were all religious, but Thomas was especially devout.

He was already frowning and opening his mouth to start a treatise on the nature of miracles when Mr. Morrissey strode to the front of the cookhouse, his gray hair glinting in the bare-bulb light.

"Attention, men," he said, as if a commanding officer addressing his troops. It ragged on us when he did things like that.

As the chatter died down, Morrissey went on. "Tomorrow, Roger Kirkwood will be presenting himself for service in the United States Navy."

Roger stood up and saluted, then smirked in our direction.

There was a murmur of approval from the table of forest rangers and a shrill whistle courtesy of Jimmy Morrissey—Earl and Edith's son and Roger's best crony. *So that's what Mrs. Edith didn't want to tell me.* Today wasn't just any birthday—it was Roger's eighteenth birthday.

"Kirkwood, we thank you for your hard work in fighting fires here at home," Morrissey continued, "and we wish you well as you serve your country in a new way. We'll pray for your safe return."

Mrs. Edith started a good-natured cheer, and I clapped politely, until I realized that the men at my table were sitting stock-still, hands frozen on their silverware or trays—in Shorty's case, with a piece of chicken halfway to his mouth.

Roger grinned like he was being photographed for the newspaper, then leered at our silent tables with a superior smirk that only a freshly minted eighteen-year-old could pull off.

Once the clapping died out, Morrissey went on. "One other announcement. As of tomorrow, we will be reinstituting the fire watch."

39

This time, even I joined in the groaning. *Not more lookout duty.*

"As some of you"—he looked directly over at Jack—"have pointed out, there have been more winter fires than usual this year. While we typically only man the tower during peak season, I've decided to make an exception. We'll be back to normal rotation: CPS men and regular forestry employees will alternate at the Flintlock Mountain lookout with shifts of one week."

Sure, for the first day, the rest from physical labor would be nice. There was even a good collection of books tucked away up in the lookout tower. But by day three, the silence would start to grate, and after a week, even the crowded bunkhouse would sound like paradise.

"I won't apologize for the inconvenience," Morrissey continued, staring down all of us in turn with pale eyes, like an osprey on the hunt. "All those assigned will do well to be vigilant. If these forests burn, the damage to our nation can't be underestimated. We don't have the manpower to fight a disaster like the Great Fire."

All the old-timers talked about that fire using the same tone of doom. It had been headline news all across the nation in 1910, the year my parents first met. Three million acres were destroyed by the end of it, gouging through Idaho, Montana, and Washington. It was our job to make sure it never happened again.

"And now, let us pray." We all bowed our heads as grace was spoken over the last cookhouse meal Roger Kirkwood might ever eat.

"Almost makes you think we oughtn't to eat the stuff," Shorty said glumly, after the amen. "On account of dinner being a war celebration."

Though none of the other boys slowed down much—Lloyd actually eyed Shorty's portion—we all glanced at Thomas, who thoughtfully tapped a fork against the corner of his mouth.

Then he nodded. "First Corinthians 8. Even food sacrificed to idols is clean for any believers who can eat it with a clear conscience."

Shorty's round face brightened, and he took another chunk out of the wing on his plate, muttering around it, "Thank God for First Corinthians."

I scooped another forkful of potatoes, trying to lose myself in the complaints over lookout duty starting up again.

Across from me, Jack stood, just like I'd known he would. It was always Jack.

He paused and looked right at me, inviting me to join, but I stared down at my canned peaches instead. When I looked up again, he was walking over to Roger's table.

Just like he walked over to them every single Friday night before our bonfire, or when asking for any concerns to bring to Morrissey at their monthly meeting, or when some of us decided to go into town for a hard-earned burger. No matter how wide the gap was between us, Jack would never stop trying to cross it.

Alone.

It seemed to take a year for Jack to cross the cookhouse with his slow, deliberate walk.

"It's nothing but pride."

Thomas's voice in my ear made me jump, quiet though it was. The others hadn't even noticed Jack, arguing with Shorty about whether he'd really been attacked by a mountain lion while on lookout duty the summer before.

I didn't turn away from Jack, who was saying something to Roger and his friends that was too quiet for me to hear. "I don't know what you mean."

"The Scriptures say we should expect to be hated in this world. But Jack wants to be loved by everyone."

I frowned, not sure how to respond. Wasn't that the goal of peace? To love and be loved by all?

Across the cookhouse, Roger's donkey-bray laugh seemed to echo against the exposed pine rafters, making even Shorty stop his latest tall tale and look over. "Yeah, right. It's too bad you're too yellow to fight alongside me," he crowed to anyone listening.

"What's the matter with him?" Shorty wondered aloud.

"Aw, the same as usual," Charlie said, waving at him to get back to the story.

While Roger jeered something I couldn't quite make out, I watched Jimmy. Lanky arms folded over his chest, thick eyebrows set, his expression unreadable, as usual.

When we'd first come to Flintlock Mountain, he'd been in his final years of high school, proud to show off what he knew about the forest to the new recruits. But then his older brother died in the war, and since then, Jimmy barely spared a moody grunt in our direction. *What are you going to do now, Jimmy, left in the forest all alone?*

Like a deer who sensed it was in a hunter's sights, Jimmy's chin snapped up. His eyes met mine, lit with a "Who do you think you're looking at?" hostility. I jerked my gaze away and pretended to be engaged in our table's conversation.

Soon, Jack slumped down next to me. "I had to try."

I nodded. Someday, even Jack would give up, and no one would walk across the gap at all. And they'd have only themselves to blame.

My supper finished, I was thinking about licking my plate when ranger Les Richardson strolled over, holding a few letters fanned above his head. "Mail call, boys!"

Shorty got a postcard from a friend at another CPS camp, and Charlie, Thomas, and I all had letters from family. Mother tried to write a few times a month—short letters mostly, asking me questions and saying hardly anything about her own "dull routines," but they were better than what Jack got, which was a card at Christmas with his parents' names and a ten-dollar bill. Dorie never signed it.

Still, Richardson paused behind Jack, holding a crisp envelope out in front of him. I glanced at the stamp in the corner. A blue victory eagle emblem. No return address.

Not again.

"Another one for you, Armitage." He grinned, exposing crooked teeth, and let the envelope fall to the table. "You got a girlfriend?"

"I'm afraid not." Jack laughed, and to anyone else, it probably sounded as carefree as a summer Saturday. But I was his best friend. I saw the slight wince around the corner of his eyes as he took the envelope.

The others had discovered both a green scarf and a picture of Charlie's fiancée, Marie, which Shorty was holding aloft, whistling like she was Miss America instead of a shyly smiling waitress while Charlie hollered at him to give it back.

I was the only one watching as Jack opened his envelope, pulled out the article, and read.

He never crumpled it up like I would have done, tossing it in the rubbish bin we filled with tinder for Friday night bonfires. Instead, he folded it neatly in half and tucked it in his shirt pocket.

None of the rest of us ever got the anonymous articles, and I'd asked Jack before who he thought was sending them, all about the latest battles and worst news of the war. His best guess was some high-school friend who'd joined the military.

I slapped him on the back. "Don't let some prankster get to you, Jack. We're doing the right thing."

"Yeah," he said, his voice charged with more uncertainty than I'd ever heard. "I hope so."

There's nothing like a crew of smokejumpers to make sure a campfire gets put out properly. By the time we were done prodding for any half alive coals, the ashes were paste, leaving me shivering down to my socks.

"It's almost curfew," Thomas reminded us, distinguishable in the sudden darkness only by his voice.

"Who made you blackout warden?" someone—Hank?—said, which is what all of us were thinking.

For once, I led the noisy charge over the dirt path from the bonfire area to the bunkhouse, half of the men behind me exhausted from a long day, the other half chattering about the weekend stretching out in front of them.

That's how we burst into the bunkhouse, with its neat row of a dozen bunk beds . . . to see Jack sprawled out on his bunk, scribbling in his journal. He barely looked up when we entered.

Something wasn't right.

The others dug around in trunks for pajamas and toothbrushes, hurrying to get ready in the few minutes we had before lights-out.

I sat down on my own lower bunk, next to Jack's. "You weren't at the bonfire tonight."

He shut the journal, gripping it tightly. "I've missed some before."

Which was a lie, and we both knew it. Jack was always at the bonfires. Tenting the wood to start it, inviting Jimmy and Roger to join—though they never did—and starting a round of stories with a hushed, "Gather round, my children, and listen to a tale that's truly true," a phrase borrowed from his father's stories.

I started to work the knots loose from my bootlaces, which were just as unyielding as Jack seemed to be. "Any particular reason you skipped tonight's?"

44

"I had some writing to do." When I didn't give up, he waved me away. "I'm fine, Gordon."

I studied him. Thumbs smeared with pencil from writing who knew how many pages in his journal. Face lined with worry. Eyes that couldn't meet mine.

That's not how I would have described "fine."

"What's the matter, Captain?" Shorty, his towering six-foot-three frame sticking awkwardly out of plaid pajamas, cut in, leaning against Jack's bunk with arms akimbo. "Too much fried chicken giving you a stomachache?"

"That's probably it." With the spotlight shifted off him, Jack knelt at the foot of his bunk and tucked the journal away in his trunk and locked it, as usual.

Whenever Shorty teased him about locking his trunk among friends, Jack made some joke about not trusting Lloyd, our resident socialist who wanted to redistribute wealth. At which point, Lloyd couldn't resist launching into a defense of how real socialism worked, and Jack escaped without further questions.

Once Thomas had enforced lights-out, I could hear Jack's bed frame creaking as he got settled.

"So where were you really?" For a while, our voices would be covered with the grumbles of men finishing the process of getting ready for bed as they stumbled around in the dark.

"I told you. Writing." He must have known I wouldn't accept that for an answer, because he sighed and added, "And talking to Morrissey."

Now we were getting somewhere. "This late?" Morrissey's family lived on national forest property on the other side of the clearing from our bunkhouse. "About what?"

For a minute, silence stretched so long I thought Jack was pretending to be asleep to avoid telling me.

"I volunteered for lookout duty."

"Are you crazy?" I whispered, loud enough to earn a shush from Charlie on the bunk above me. "Why?"

"I need some time alone, that's all. To think." He sighed. "Listen, Gordon, don't tell anyone."

I snorted. "They'll be glad it's you and not them. I hear Shorty set up a chess game last time, playing against himself. He still lost."

Jack's laugh was muffled, like he'd turned his face to his pillow to keep from busting up, just like old times back in college, when we'd had no worries about the draft or the war.

"Your secret's safe with me," I promised. If he wanted a week of boredom, he was welcome to it.

"Thanks, Gordon." He sounded relieved, the gloomy tone—so unlike him—gone again. "You're a good friend."

It was enough to make me roll over and close my eyes. Jack was stressed by another anonymous letter, that was all. Everything would be all right in the morning.

CHAPTER 4

Dorie Armitage

January 9, 1945

The real trouble with working in the Transportation Corps wasn't the busted distributors or the infernally complicated army truck engines, but instead getting oil out from underneath one's fingernails before a date.

I tossed the nail file on the dresser in surrender, my attempt at good grooming only half complete. The fellow I'd met at the New Year's dance would just have to face the fact that he was stepping out with a Fort Lawton garage girl. Arthur? Arnold? No, Archie, that was it. It was so hard to keep track of names after a party.

After changing into my favorite civvies—a green dress with white polka dots—I started in on my bird's nest of hair. The difference between glamorous curls and overgrown shrubbery from the set of a Gothic horror film is hours of care, not something you can pour out of a bottle and apply in three minutes. I set to work determinedly with my brush and curling iron.

Having a mirror and nightstand was an unheard-of luxury. The WAC barracks had been inside the fort for a while, but they soon needed the space and exiled us to an old hotel in town. Even though we'd lost the view of the bay out our windows and they'd gutted

47

the hotel beds and put in regulation cots, none of us girls gave a squeak of protest.

Back in my early enlistment days, I'd been dying to be sent overseas. Pounding away on a typewriter in North Africa or sorting mail in the Pacific sounded hopelessly romantic, not to mention possibly riding in an airplane—a childhood dream that both Jack and I shared. But when I first saw the brass fixtures of the private baths in every Stratford Hotel room, all my jealousies of the girls "over there" went right out the window.

As I jabbed pins into my dark locks, I hummed the Paramount Studio theme. There was something thrilling about the theater—especially the dazzling blink of the marquee, once blacked out after sunset but blazing again in full glory now that reports of Pacific victories put to rest fears of nighttime bombing raids. While I watched those beautiful people flickering up on the screen, I could forget about the latest recruitment numbers, the riot between American soldiers and POWs, the casualty reports . . .

"Doris."

I glanced up to see my roommate, fellow Private First Class Phyllis Stanley, stationed in the doorway, galoshes in hand because she always remembered to take them off at the front door.

"Margaret told me a young man's here to see you," she continued, disapproval dripping from her voice into the puddles I'd created with my own galoshes, still on my feet.

"Really?" I started and glanced at the clock. A full half hour early? Funny, Archie hadn't struck me as the punctual sort. "I'll be right down."

"Are you sure you should—?" Phyllis began, but I wasn't going to tune in to Radio Sour Stanley anymore, where the number one single week after week was "Disapproval of Dorie's Choices."

"Now, there's no use scolding," I said, jamming on my black

pillbox hat to cover my unfinished hair. "As long as I'm back in time for curfew, a night out is squarely within the rules."

"But he's a—"

"—perfect gentleman," I finished for her, applying a touch of Headline Red lipstick and blotting it with a hanky. "Look at him, arriving early. It's positively chivalrous." I didn't mention the way Archie had ogled me after monopolizing me on the dance floor. Agreeing to a date was the only way I could get him to leave me alone.

I tucked my coat in the crook of my arm, dashing down the stairs to the second-floor landing. Then, with a look over my shoulder to make sure no one was watching, I sat on the bannister. A girl has to make an entrance, and I'd tried it while dusting for Saturday morning inspection. Archie would love it; men always did go for girls who could make them laugh.

The familiar rush fanned through me as I let go and slid down, a few seconds of controlled falling.

Is this what it would be like to fly?

I could see a pair of dull boots and army khakis by the front door as I descended, and had just enough time to wonder why Archie hadn't changed into his civvies for the date before the rest of the soldier came into view.

Not slicked-back Private Archie What's-His-Name.

But the lieutenant from the dance, the one who'd been turned away and directed to the colored USO, staring at me like I'd just fallen through a hole in the ceiling.

Or, well, like I'd just slid down a bannister toward him, giggling like a fool.

Which, unfortunately, I had.

I ground to a halt on the second-to-last stair, gripping the balustrade to keep from toppling over at his feet.

49

"Good evening, PFC Armitage," he said formally, taking off his hat.

"Lieutenant Leland," I managed, tottering off the railing. Heels on the stairs again, I tried to sound professional. "I'm surprised to see you here."

Maybe Archie was in the dayroom, or to the left toward the reception desk. Oh, how was I going to get past the lieutenant without making things any more awkward?

"Yes, well . . ." He seemed at least half as flustered as I was, so that was something. "Do you have a moment? I have a few questions to ask you."

"Me?"

He nodded, and I used the pause to duck past him and through the archway. "Normally, I'd be happy to, but I have to meet with . . ."

I stopped. No sign of Archie in the hallway or the dayroom, and with the Christmas tree that had once stood between the tall windows hauled out, there wasn't anywhere for him to hide.

Suddenly the half hour early and Phyllis's particular disapproval made sense. I turned and looked at Leland. "*You're* the one who came to see me?"

His face had "Didn't I just say that?" scrawled over it.

"If you'll allow me to explain," he said, and again I was struck with the unexpectedness of him, the paratrooper emblem beside his silver officer bar, the crisply enunciated words that sounded so at home coming out of his mouth. "I'm in Seattle on a special assignment."

"So you mentioned."

"Which involves your brother."

Of all the ways I thought he might finish that statement, dragging Jack into it had never occurred to me.

I could tell he was watching me for a reaction, and I really tried not to give it to him. But it was no use. I could feel my joints stiffening up with tension, like Oz's Tin Man.

"You want to talk about *Jack*?"

"Yes, ma'am. Major Hastings told me one of the WACs here was the sister of a conscientious objector—apparently it came up in your records."

By the time you were done with the interview process, the army knew practically everything about you, from your birthday to your preferred brand and style of garters. I'd told them about Jack straight off rather than risk them finding out later.

"When we met the other night," Leland continued, "I recognized your last name, and when I checked my records, I found a Jack Armitage listed as a conscientious objector at one of the camps in this region I'm planning to . . ." He coughed. "Well, I recognized it, that's all."

"But there must be hundreds of Armitages in the country."

He shrugged. "I wrote about nine miles of academic papers while getting my degree from Howard University. I'm good at research. Now, PFC Armitage, do you have a minute?"

I glanced at the mantel clock. Assuming Archie was on time, I had twenty-six, but I wasn't sure I wanted to donate a single one of them to the topic of Jack. "Listen, I'm nothing like my brother."

"Yes, the uniform was my first clue."

Was that a joke? I studied him closely and noted the corner of his mouth turning up. Aha! The man *did* have a sense of humor. That could be useful.

Before I could comment, a familiar voice filled the hall. ". . . and I hear you've conspired to host a variety revue for Valentine's Day."

Sergeant Helena Bloom was the dread of all of us, finding dust and fault where no one else could and filing frequent reports with Captain Petmencky.

I wouldn't say I squeaked exactly, but a surprised sound did leak out. "Come on," I said, yanking Leland into the dayroom and toward the mantel, still decorated with wilting holly boughs from the holidays. There, no one could see us from the hallway.

He opened his mouth like he was about to ask what I was doing, so I placed a finger over my lips and jerked my head toward the doorway.

The footsteps became louder, and the sergeant's voice with it. "I would like to attend the dress rehearsal."

"Oh, but it's all informal." The second voice belonged to Clarice, a chum of mine and our social coordinator. "We're not even sure there will *be* a dress rehearsal."

Her voice became dim as she trooped down to the gig list, likely to make sure the correct girls were serving out their penalties on KP duty. "There will be now. We don't want anything veering toward the burlesque."

Once I couldn't hear Clarice's protest, I breathed again. "Close call, Lieutenant. At ease."

Judging from his tin soldier–straight posture, ease was the last thing he had planned. "This is official army business, PFC Armitage." The chill was back in his voice, like a spring Seattle day turned suddenly rainy. "I'm not here for a social call."

"I know that," I explained patiently, still eyeing the hallway, "but most men who stop by here to visit are."

"Aren't WACs allowed free time?"

"Officially, yes, as long as we behave ourselves. And we can invite guests to dinner if we reserve a place for them in advance. But my superiors don't approve of frequent gentlemen callers. All the same, a girl's got to have a little fun every now and again. How else am I going to see all the latest movies on a WAC salary?"

I waited for a chuckle, or at least a smile. None came. In fact,

52

he seemed to have a gift for making his face a perfect blank slate, eyes aimed slightly downward. I'd met men difficult to read, like a book in another language, but Leland seemed to have the magical ability to make the pages perfectly blank when he wanted to.

I found myself—of all things—*blushing*, like Violet whenever she talked to anyone of the male species.

He must think I'm a featherbrained little opportunist. Which of course wasn't fair at all.

"Anyway, we should be safe for now. Clarice and the gig list will occupy her for a while." I plopped down in the settee we'd recently re-covered to spare it from its previous frayed floral upholstery. "You were saying?"

Leland nodded and remained standing. "How often do you contact your brother?"

"Never."

His expression barely flickered. "Ah."

I rolled my eyes. "Do you know, Lieutenant Leland, you can fit more judgment into one word than most people can cram into a full speech? Do they teach that to paratrooper units? How *did* you end up in a paratrooper unit anyway?"

"It wasn't judgment," he said, and for the first time, there was a hint of fluster in his voice, which made me unreasonably proud. "It's just . . . I shouldn't have assumed." My second question, if he heard it at all, he ignored.

Then, so suddenly I blinked in surprise, he backed toward the door a few steps. "Thank you for your time, PFC Armitage. But I think my commanding officer was right."

Something here was fishier than a Friday lunch special during Lent. I stood, motioning for him to stay. "Hold on. Right about what?"

"I was told," he said, "that it wouldn't be worth my time to talk to you. And now I see why. Anything I say might upset you more."

Sending Leland away myself was one thing. Hearing him say he was worried about upsetting me, like I was a Victorian damsel who kept smelling salts tucked in her corset, was quite another. "Why don't you ask your questions and let me decide if I want to be upset?"

He seemed to weigh that and finally nodded, stepping back to his place in front of the mantel. "All right. Since your brother is one of them, what do you think about the COs' character?"

"Don't you listen to the news? They're cowards. It's as simple as that."

A pause, a long one this time. "Do you always treat conversations like you're neutralizing an enemy position, or is this a special exception?"

It was an exception, I realized. Normally, I was all charm. But he'd taken me off guard, and questions about Jack . . . well, they were another matter.

"You asked for the truth. I'm giving it to you."

"Maybe you should take a second look. People are never simple. Once you see past old prejudices and first impressions, you'll see that the most overlooked ones can be . . . useful."

"Am I one of those overlooked people who might be useful?"

"That depends on whether you're going to tell me what you think of the COs' character."

Just like the army band that had played at a Seattle parade on election day, he didn't miss a beat. I got the sense he was secretly the conductor.

"I can't tell you much about their character in general, Lieutenant, just what I saw. Jack let his starry-eyed roommate turn his head with thoughts about peace."

I'd overheard Jack and Gordon arguing with Daddy late into the night just before Thanksgiving, but once I'd realized they were going on about politics, I'd left them alone, sure it wasn't serious.

"There was nothing I could say to change his mind. Not when the war started, not a year later when he and Gordon were drafted. He chose Gordon over me. Over all of us."

I knew I was getting emotional, because Leland coughed to fill the awkward silence before changing the subject. "I'm sure it felt that way, but what I want to know is: Can the COs be trusted? Are they loyal to their country?"

"I can't see how, if they weren't even willing to fight for America."

Nothing in his face changed that I could point to, but I could tell he wasn't satisfied with that answer, which put a bee in my bonnet, all right. There was no point in even asking me if he thought he already knew.

"Thank you for your help, PFC Armitage," Leland said with a nod. "If you'll excuse me—"

Oh no, he wasn't about to get away that easily. I stood and ducked behind the settee, blocking his path to the door. "Why do you need to know, anyway?"

He gave me a lukewarm smile. "I'm not allowed to say. And please don't speak to your fellow WACs about this conversation. It's classified."

"Classified, eh?" This was serious, whatever it was about. "But why you? I mean . . . a black paratrooper from Georgia?"

"Stationed in Georgia," he corrected. "I'm from Detroit, born and raised."

That would explain the lack of Southern accent. I glanced at the clock. Twelve minutes. Hopefully Archie wouldn't be early. I couldn't imagine him taking a polite interest if he stumbled into this conversation.

"But how did you do it?" I pressed. "If you don't mind my saying so, I've never seen a black officer before."

He nodded as if he'd expected the question. "I grew a moustache."

My eyes darted involuntarily to his lips. "I beg your pardon?"

"All my life, I've been told how young looking I am. No one's going to take orders from a baby-faced fellow. So, I grew this." He stroked the neat moustache—which was, I had to admit, quite dashing. Like Clark Gable's in *Test Pilot*. "Facial hair. The secret to command."

Even though a half smile hadn't appeared, I could hear it in his voice, and I crossed my arms. "You're patronizing me."

"And you were doing what exactly by assuming a black man couldn't work through Officer Training School like anyone else?"

That made me pause a moment. Had I been patronizing too?

Of course not. That was silly. I was just asking an innocent question.

The insistent ticking of the clock filled the silence, each one a warning gunshot. Nine minutes. *Time to say good-bye, Dorie.*

"Well then," I said, stepping out of his way, "I promise I won't tell anyone about your questions about Jack." Once army men started throwing around words like "classified," things got touchy fast.

"Thank you." Leland got most of the way into the hall, then stopped. "You don't know what your brother is doing there, do you?"

I shrugged. "It's middle-of-nowhere Oregon." Mother had given me his address, so I knew at least that much. "National park tasks, I guess. Something safe the CPS could spin into being 'work of national importance.'"

He didn't contradict me, but from his expression, I could tell I'd guessed wrong. "I don't think 'safe' is the right word. Do you ever pray for your brother, PFC Armitage?"

I felt a half second of shame. "No."

He buttoned up his coat and looked soberly at me. "I think you might want to start."

FROM DORIE TO HER PARENTS

January 10, 1945

Dear Mother and Daddy,

It's pouring buckets of rain here, and we're all tucked inside the Stratford for a cozy night in. Now that I've jotted a few lines to some of the hometown fellows stationed overseas, I thought to sit down and write to you. Honestly, while I miss both of you to pieces, when writing a bona fide update, there's not much to say.

I've gotten a few motorpool requests that pulled me away from the garage, I'm to be the Master of Ceremonies for the Valentine's Day Revue (since I haven't a single real talent beyond fixing cars), and I watched a new movie last night (Laura, a thrilling mystery—I simply must have a clock with a secret compartment now). Oh, and I'm memorizing a speech for a WAC recruitment tour of women's clubs and high schools around Seattle. That's about all the news that's fit to print.

Also, I was wondering if you happened to know how Jack was doing. I know I've never asked about him, but . . . he was on my mind, that's all.

Maybe it's the dreary weather, but I'm feeling the tiniest smidge of homesickness. Wouldn't it be glorious if we could go back to the time Before? I'm happy to be seeing a new part of the country and doing my patriotic duty, but I can't help but think of snowbound January nights back home, stirring hot chocolate with a peppermint stick, Jack slumping asleep against my shoulder before Daddy could finish his latest tale. No worries or news of war or blackout drills. Everything safe and warm and peaceful.

Ah well. Time enough for nostalgia after the war is won.

Hope everything's well with you, and do give Shep an extra treat for me tonight, will you?

> *All my love,*
> *Dorie*

FROM GORDON TO HIS MOTHER

January 10, 1945

Dear Mother,

Greetings from Oregon. I hope you're staying healthy. Aunt Harriet wrote and said she visited you last week and you didn't seem to be in your usual spirits. Is everything all right? Or was Harriet just in one of her overly critical moods and spent the whole visit griping? (That's what she did in her letter to me anyway—Roosevelt is a communist, her next-door neighbor might be stealing their mail, and her ancient cat is afflicted with acute gout.)

As for me, I'm well enough. The other fellows have been on edge this week, and we all know why: Jack is gone to lookout duty. He's been our crossbeam for so long that it's a wonder we haven't all collapsed without him. Silly things, fights over someone using too much hot water at the shower house, accusations of laziness on dishwashing duty, old grudges dragged out. Nothing serious, but we'll be grateful to have him back this Friday night, that's for sure.

Did you happen to read the copy of Walden *I sent to you? I'm glad at least that you've had more time to read these past few years. That's all I enjoy about fire duty—the books and, I suppose, the quiet. Right now, I'm writing this while hearing, in one ear, a debate about whether competition in sporting events is inherently anti-Christian, and in the other, a discourse on how many days one can reasonably go without a shower. We're a sophisticated lot here.*

Almost lights-out, so I'll sign off.

Gordon

CHAPTER 5

Gordon Hooper

January 12, 1945

"Remind me again why we're taking pictures of dead birds?" Charlie asked as he knelt on the weathered boards of the ranger station. He took his camera out of its leather case and cradled it like a baby.

"So I can sketch all the details later." I passed my handkerchief over the extended wing of a golden eagle, coming away with a spotty layer of grime and dust. "Sarah Ruth, don't you ever clean these?"

She harrumphed from behind the secretary's desk where she surveyed our work, dressed in her usual blouse and trousers, her Forest Service jacket draped over her chair. "Of course not. I've got *real* work to do. Memos to type, grazing petitions to approve, timber company negotiations to pass on to Father."

"Sounds fascinating," Charlie quipped, his grin a quick flash of white against his dark skin.

"And no time for *housework*," she finished, wrinkling her nose. "It took me nearly an hour to unscrew all of those birds from the wall where they belong."

"Which we appreciate," I said, trying to mollify her. She grunted and went back to her typewriter, fingers tapping out a rhythm on the keys.

But secretly, I knew Sarah Ruth was wrong. Birds didn't belong stuffed and mounted on a wall or over the wide stone hearth, on display in death. They were meant to fly. And I was determined to make that happen, even if it was only in sketch form.

James Audubon had done the same in the 1830s. Back then, his detailed full-color plates showing birds in their natural environment had awed both the art and naturalist world. My task was no *Birds of America*, but I meant to make the trail guide brochure Morrissey had commissioned from me as professional as possible.

"There's no challenge to this." Charlie knelt and clicked his camera, capturing the eagle's tail feathers. "What's next? Gonna yank some trout fillets out of the icebox, toss them in a pot of water, and call it fishing?"

I gave him a flat look to prove he wasn't funny. "Just take those pictures, Charlie."

He'd do a good job of it too. Before he'd joined the CPS, he was making a decent salary at a black-owned radio repair shop in Pittsburgh and saved enough for a camera—a Leica model. I knew because he'd snapped at me once for calling it a Kodak, though unlike Shorty, I hadn't borne his wrath by labeling his photos "snapshots."

Morrissey started covering the costs once he realized that postcard pictures of the Flintlock Mountain trails would be good for tourism. He took the film with him whenever he went out of town to someplace where the drugstore was sophisticated enough to have a darkroom. Charlie had produced some fine images of the forest in summertime and the Flintlock Mountains viewed from the lookout, as well as my personal favorite, a fawn asleep, surrounded by curled maidenhair ferns.

But even Charlie couldn't sneak up on a western tanager snacking on insects, not close enough to get a clear image of the angle of its wings as it perched on a branch. His photos, like my ink sketches for the brochure, would have to make each species recognizable to casual birders without any color.

Not that there would be droves of them using my guide. Flint-lock Mountain, a few thousand acres carved out of a larger national forest, had no spectacular waterfalls or geysers, just trails, a gently sloping mountain, and plenty of wildlife. With the war on and gas hard to come by, even the summer and autumn had been, according to Sarah Ruth, "lean" compared to the late '30s.

Satisfied that Charlie had the golden eagle well under control, I moved on to the barred owl that used to lurk in the corner by the fire poker, clearing off a few cobwebs. Then, making sure my body was between the bird and Sarah Ruth, I lifted the brittle wing an inch, shifting it to better show the distinct variegated pattern of the underbelly.

The clack of typewriter keys paused. "Gordon Hooper, you better not be touching those birds after I *specifically* told you not to."

How did she *do* that?

I let the wing go, and it stiffly slid back into place. "Don't worry," I managed, "all's well here." The barred owl stared at me accusingly with black-marble eyes.

"They're very delicate, you know," she said, repeating the lecture she'd given me when we arrived. "Most are twenty years dead, except for that one." She pointed to the pheasant, plumage splayed out wide. "That one, I shot. And my aim is still good, if you catch my drift."

I could only meet her warning glare for a second before swallowing hard. "Understood."

Charlie came up beside me, peered at the owl through his lens, then shook his head and moved the owl closer to a patch of afternoon sunlight. "Say, Jack's coming back from lookout duty tonight, isn't he?" he asked me, as if it were only natural that I'd know his whereabouts.

I counted the days in my head. All the weekdays blended together, mere scratches on the wall to mark our war-long sentence. "Should be."

It couldn't come too soon. We needed someone to remind Thomas and Lloyd there were more important things to do than argue about politics and religion, chuckle at Shorty's jokes when the rest of us were tired of them, and smooth things out with the townies.

Charlie went around to get a shot of the barred owl from the side, his face half disappearing behind the camera. "Did you hear that the Oregon Department of Forestry is so short on men, they're planning to train some local boys as lookouts for the summer season? Some women too, from what I hear."

"Interesting," I said, shooting a glance toward Morrissey's office, the door closed. He hadn't been in all morning, probably making the rounds with the other rangers.

Sarah Ruth stood with a file folder of papers and jabbed a fountain pen in our direction. "Are you saying a woman can't be just as good of a lookout as a man?"

"No, ma'am, not a chance." Charlie's disarming laugh gave me a twinge of jealousy. I'd be a sputtering mess if Sarah Ruth had leveled a line like that at me. "Anyone who's had a mother knows women could beat a man at sharp-eyed attention any day."

"Thinking about joining up, Sarah Ruth?" I asked.

She shook her head, then opened her father's office to drop the file inside. "I served my time when I was seventeen. And I don't mean to go back."

"Really?" I didn't bother concealing my surprise. Lookout duty seemed like it would be at the top of Sarah Ruth's list of leisure activities: uninterrupted time in her beloved forest. "It's got to be better than grazing petitions and timber negotiations."

All I got for that attempt at humor was a raised eyebrow. "You of all people ought to know we don't always get to pick the work we do."

"Too bad they don't let women become smokejumpers," I joked.

"Too bad," she repeated, looking out the window toward the airstrip where the Trimotors would land to heave us up into the sky. A small sigh eased out of her before she turned away again.

She really means it. It didn't make sense to me why anyone, man or woman, would want to parachute into an inferno.

"Anyway, I hope Dad trains them well, especially the teenaged boys. Come July, I don't want a bunch of loafers taking over for—"

She was cut off by the metallic clang of the dinner bell.

Once.

Twice.

I quickly thought back to the Spam sandwiches we'd wolfed down at noon. Yes, we'd eaten lunch. No, it was too early for it to be supper.

Another ring. "Oh no," I said, staring at the door, waiting for the fourth ring that broke through the air, loud and clear, the signal for any available smokejumpers at the camp to report for duty.

Someone in our region had called in a fire.

"How . . . ?" Sarah Ruth said, her eyes darting toward the phone resting snug and silent in the receiver on her desk. Fire reports always came through the ranger station.

No time to bother about that. Charlie was already halfway out the door, his camera abandoned by the hearth, and I followed him, yanking on my coat as I charged into the gray afternoon.

We gathered around the flagpole in the center of the cluster of forest property buildings, the usual meeting place for a fire signal. Behind us, the rope hanging from the bell pull swung eerily . . . but the ringer was nowhere in sight.

A sick feeling overtook me, a certainty that something was wrong, the way the forest gets quiet as a grave when a predator comes near.

"Hello, fellows!" Shorty, emerging from the cookhouse with his apron from kitchen duty still tied around his waist, jogged over to meet us. "What's going on?"

I shook my head. "I wish we knew."

Charlie nudged me. "If it's only a two-man jump, Shorty and I can take it." He'd been there the time I got caught in a tree and never once teased me about it or told any of the other fellows.

"Says who?" Shorty hollered. "Don't you go drafting me, now, Charlie—the army tried that already."

I glanced around. The others must have been too deep in the forest to come yet, assigned to trail clearing or fence building. Once we got our orders, the ones selected would change into the fire-resistant uniforms from the storage garage, grab and check our chutes, and wait near the landing strip for the plane.

"Here he comes," Shorty said, pointing.

The Forest Service pickup truck, Morrissey's pride and joy, rumbled down the trail toward us, and I felt a moment of relief. Morrissey must have rung the bell, then run to the garage to get his truck. That was all. Now that he was here to give orders, everything would be all right.

The driver's door opened, slammed shut. All joking stopped as soon as we saw Morrissey's face, taut and pale.

"How many do you need?" I called.

"All of you. Anyone we can find." His voice strained with tension. "Boys, it's here."

Charlie's voice was tentative, clearly as rattled as I was by Morrissey's change in demeanor. "Sir?"

I saw the answer in Morrissey's wild eyes, thrown out of their strict regimentation. Genuinely afraid. He pointed to the sky, and where I'd once seen only stormy clouds, I noticed a darker stain against the sky: smoke.

"The fire. It's in our forest."

You'd think you'd get used to it after a few fires, but you didn't: the way the flames raced through the underbrush, the terrible splinter of falling branches, and most of all, the heat.

Not only did you feel the heat, but you also saw it wavering in the air, heard it in the cracks and pops of sparks, smelled it thick and heavy in your lungs like a summertime fever, tasted it in ashes and sweat for hours. The fire became your entire world, taking every sense captive till you thought you'd never know anything else.

And as soon as the fire bell rang again, you remembered what that was like, no matter how hard you tried to forget.

Instead of a Travel Air or Trimotor plane, we jumped into the bed of Morrissey's truck, along with Les Richardson and a couple of the fellows working out by the woodpile. We rattled down the trails—too narrow, really, for this duty—but it was faster than hiking in.

By the time the smoke in the air made it hard to breathe, Morrissey had thrown the truck into park. "Grab the supplies," he ordered the five of us smokejumpers, slamming the door, "and start digging." Richardson followed him as if on a silent signal, and they were gone before we could ask what they were up to.

"They're inspecting the damage. Seeing if they need to radio in another crew," Charlie guessed.

"Or," Shorty theorized sourly, as I shoved him out of the truck, "they want us to do all of the digging."

John Miller—an Amish man who we called First John because we had three men by that name among us—hauled out the pack of tools from the bed of the truck, handing one to each of us. "We should pray for rain," he said, looking up at the threatening sky.

And pray I did, but as we jogged closer, a quick glance told me we wouldn't need help from Missoula. Maybe we wouldn't even need to bring in more of the men from camp. It was a small fire, but the ground was scorched and covered in burnt debris. Juniper bushes and groundcover, twisted and tangled, glowed orange with flame, and around the boulders that dotted the terrain, I couldn't see a single rabbit or squirrel. The animals always knew when to dart for cover.

The five of us stationed ourselves apart but still within line of sight, starting at our anchor point, a boulder that would block the spread of the fire. *"Always watch each other's backs,"* Morrissey often told us, and you could almost see flashbacks of the Great War in his eyes. *"Never leave a man behind."*

With a small crew, the step-up method was best, with Shorty at the head because he had the loudest voice. He'd shout out in intervals, and we'd each scrape away a layer about two feet wide before moving on to finish up what the person in front of us had started: first greenery, then roots and loam, finally exposing the mineral earth, where the fire would find nothing to burn.

As I dug, falling into the familiar monotony, I couldn't help but wonder. Why hadn't Jack, up in the fire tower, called to report the blaze before it got even this bad? I'd have thought he'd see the smoke and report it immediately, especially during stormy weather, where we'd been lectured to trace every visible lightning strike to the ground and watch for signs of fire.

That said, our blaze sure wasn't the Dante's *Inferno* I'd pictured from Morrissey's reaction. With all of us working, we'd have it contained in an hour or two, especially if it started to rain.

I'd just stopped to wipe a trail of sweat away from my face when

I heard sticks crack off to the west and caught a glimpse of—was that the outline of a man disappearing behind a rocky outcropping within the fire's border?

No. I rubbed my throbbing head and realized I hadn't grabbed a canteen from the truck to loop around my neck. Stress and dehydration were making me see things.

Could be Morrissey or Richardson.

But why would they go into the fire? Smokejumpers were drilled against that. Keep one foot in the black—the safe zone where the fire had burned away all fuel—but always stay on the perimeter. If the flames spread faster than we could dig, then we fanned out with them, looking for rivers or creeks if needed. Surrounding the fire was one thing. Running into it was quite another.

I squinted into the woods, trying to see movement past the sting of smoke.

"Get back to work!" Shorty called, using his Pulaski to cut a groove in the earth. So I did, forgetting everything but the fire line in front of me.

Without so much as a drop of rain to help us, we pounded the ground with the Pulaskis, furrowing a trench like the devil himself had started the fire and meant to spread it across the whole state of Oregon. Morrissey and Richardson had to be watching from somewhere.

Why aren't they digging with us? Sure, Morrissey was in his early fifties, but he was fit, which we learned the day we challenged him to join our game of basketball and he dribbled circles around us. It couldn't have taken them this long to patrol the perimeter of the fire and radio for backup.

I paused and looked around again, pretending it was to stretch my sore shoulder muscles. No shadowy figure inside the wavering heat of the fire. Had I imagined it?

Soon, I could feel the heat inside me from the physical exertion and the heat in the air as the fire licked closer to us. When I glanced behind me, I could see a trail of flames racing down a patch of dead moss . . . and then fizzling out along the frayed, exposed roots and dirt heaps of the fire line I'd just dug.

That'll teach you to try to burn down a forest filled with CPS smokejumpers.

"Hey!" Shorty cried, and when I followed his pointing finger, I saw Morrissey and Richardson emerging from the smoke behind me, lugging something wrapped in one of the tarps we used to haul equipment. They were headed for the truck.

"Need help?" I called, setting down my Pulaski. The others had it under control by now. The fire line almost circled the charred patch of forest, and I'd felt the first few sprinkles of rain, a welcome relief.

"No," Morrissey snapped, but I watched Richardson stumble under the weight, coughing roughly.

I stared closer at the bundle they carried. *Wait.* It couldn't be . . .

I lurched forward, boots kicking up ash, toward the men and the burden in their arms.

"Get back to the fire, Hooper." Morrissey's voice cut through the choking smoke, loud and clear. "That's an order!"

But I didn't, couldn't. Something about the limp but solid form of that canvas-covered bundle, the way it took two grown men to carry . . .

I ran straight up to them, ignoring Morrissey's shouts, and pulled the corner of the canvas away.

It was hard to tell at first, the burns were so bad. But I knew.

The rangers were carrying a body.

Jack's body.

CHAPTER 6

Gordon Hooper

January 12, 1945

Nobody had to tell us to gather around the rusty metal barrel of a fire pit by the cookhouse that night. Instead of joking and making plans for our day off, we sat on the damp log benches in silence, staring down the path toward the ranger station.

He's not dead, I reminded myself. It was the only coherent thought I could muster, so I repeated it. *He's not dead.*

Not yet.

The other fellows told me a plane had landed on the airstrip on the other side of camp a half hour earlier, while I'd been out in the rain finishing up the fire. As usual, Jack went into the plane first. But this time, he wasn't hustling the rest of us over, telling us we'd already checked our parachute packs eleven times, so why make it a dozen? This time, they'd carried him inside to the metal bench against the fuselage and strapped him down, limp and smelling like ash and smoke. Just another cargo load going up into the sky.

Will he ever come down?

I blinked. Sweat or tears—something salty—dripped into the corner of my mouth as I stared at the ranger station door. Waiting for word of what had happened to Jack.

When Morrissey finally came out, his posture was military-manual erect, as always, but as he approached the ash-filled pit, I could see dread in his face, aging him a decade with each step.

Please tell us something hopeful.

Please.

Morrissey stopped dead center in front of us, and the other COs and I waited, wanting news and fearing it at the same time.

"As some of you have likely already heard, Jack Armitage didn't walk away from this afternoon's fire."

"But . . . but he's all right now, isn't he?" Shorty asked, worry shading his usually confident voice.

"He's critically burned, Schumacher. Unresponsive." Morrissey frowned even deeper, then pushed on. "There's no easy way to say it. Armitage is still unconscious, and he might never wake up."

Shorty tightly shut his gaping mouth, Thomas looked unusually grim, even for him, and the rest of us just stood in silence.

"Never wake up." What a terrible way to think about dying. But that was Morrissey for you, not one to mince words. And today, of all days, I didn't want him to.

"What happened?" It wasn't until I heard the raspy tone of my own voice that I realized how dry my mouth was.

"Armitage went in too close to the fire without a team around him or the proper equipment." Morrissey delivered the facts almost mechanically, like the voices on the radio who'd been given the news report about Pearl Harbor to read and hadn't yet processed it themselves. "A snag was burnt bad enough to fall on him. It trapped him until Richardson and I pulled him free, already unconscious. A terrible accident."

An accident.

Sure, they'd told us all along, even in the application brochure, that smokejumping was dangerous and unpredictable. Your parachute cord could get tangled around your neck. You could break your leg on a landing. A conflagration could flare up unexpectedly, cutting you off from help.

An old dead tree could crush you.

But it had all sounded so abstract, like the numbered diagrams in the training manual or a problem from one of Jack's statistics classes.

If you followed all the steps, if you obeyed orders and did everything right, if you prayed every night before you went to sleep to a gracious God . . . none of that could happen.

Except I knew from looking at Morrissey's face, exhaustion scoring every line even more than the mixture of sweat and grime, that it could. It had. And to Jack.

When I closed my eyes, I could see him, the awful, burned arms and neck, the gaping mouth, the chest I didn't realize was still breathing, but only barely.

I hadn't gotten there in time.

By now, Charlie and a few others were crying openly, and Shorty looked like he was going to be sick. Only Lloyd seemed perfectly calm. "Where is he now? Can we visit him?"

"We flew him out to an army hospital. He's getting the best care they can give him." Morrissey looked right at me then, as if none of the rest of them mattered. "But, fellows . . . it doesn't look good."

I numbly raised my hand and waited to be acknowledged, like an awkward adolescent scholar. "Best case scenario, sir." Morrissey frowned, as if it were against forest ranger policy to be optimistic. "Please," I added.

The pause stretched out, and I didn't even have the strength left to hold my breath. Finally Morrissey lifted his broad shoulders in a shrug. "If Armitage wakes up—a few days, a few weeks, who can say?—he'll be badly burned. Movement will be difficult, especially anything with his hands."

I thought about the late nights Jack had scribbled in his journal, the way he'd twirled the pencil like a baton between his finger in the pauses. He'd never do that again. But even that was better than the worst, most likely scenario.

God, help him pull through.

To which the heretical part of me that had grown up under my father's religious skepticism whispered, *Wasn't God the one who controlled the lightning fire in the first place?*

Please, I added.

There wasn't any answer, no burning in my stomach, no Scripture from the Apostle Tom, no Inner Light to guide me. Nothing but emptiness and the echo of the sound I'd made when I saw Jack's body being loaded into the truck and driven away. A cry that felt like it would tear me apart.

Morrissey was still talking, and I forced myself to listen to the sounds coming out of his mouth. ". . . we've notified his family, of course. I'll give you any reports I hear, but no one is leaving this camp to visit Jack. He would want you to be here."

Convenient that what Jack would want is what the Forest Service and the US government want too.

"Are all the other snags cleared away from the site?" Lloyd asked, back to the newspaper-factual report. "Or should we get to that tomorrow?"

That simple question cut through my haze. How could he talk about work assignments as if what mattered most about this situation was a protocol check?

At least Morrissey shook his head. "The fire is completely out. No one needs to go back to the site."

"Good," Lloyd said, nodding curtly, and the word blew the embers of my anger into a flame. As if anything about this situation was good.

"Count slowly, Gordon. Think of hopeful things. Count them, and let the angry thoughts slip away." My mother's soothing advice, which I'd heard so often in my childhood, came back to me now.

One. Jack was still alive.

But he might die any second now, somewhere far away.

Two. I'd found an old towhee nest tucked in the bushes near the cookhouse, waiting for spring.

I didn't make it to him in time.

Three. The sun kept rising and setting over the mountains, ignoring our small human tragedies.

There was nothing I could do.

"It's no use, Mama. It's not working. I'm still angry." How many times had I said that, given up?

"Any man who would like to take the day off may do so. However, from my personal experience—" Morrissey's voice caught, as if even saying the word "personal" was too much for him—"hard work is your best friend in times like these."

We all remembered the way he'd thrown himself feverishly into work when the telegram announcing his son William's death had arrived. Morrissey seemed to walk a bit heavier after that, shut himself away in his office more often instead of walking among us.

Without so much as a word of condolence or a prayer, he bolted briskly for the ranger station.

I jogged after him. "Mr. Morrissey, sir."

He turned slowly, his expression empty and composed. "Yes, Hooper?"

"I think . . ." I paused, knowing what I was about to say would sound crazy. "I think there was somebody there. During the fire. I saw a person—a man, I think—duck out of sight inside the debris."

74

"Hmm," he said, and with his impassive face you couldn't tell if he was surprised or skeptical or angry. "Did you see who it was?"

Even when I closed my eyes, the image didn't come back to me clearly. "No. It was just a blur, really, with all the smoke. Movement, the shape of someone's back. Did you see anything?"

Morrissey shook his head. "Hooper, weren't you the one who about wet himself the first time you heard a cougar growling up in the hills?"

Somehow, in the middle of the wasp's nest of emotions I was feeling, that comment found an empty spot to sting, and I felt my face reddening to its usual hated blush. Fine, so I'd arrived at the forest a city boy down to the squeaky heels of my wing-tip shoes, but that didn't mean I was blind. "This is different. I saw a human being, I'm sure of it."

"I'm not saying you didn't see anything, Hooper. Just that you might not have seen what you thought you did."

Could he be right? In the stress of the fire, could I have caught a glimpse of a deer bounding away from the heat and thought it was a person? Just a trick of the light and smoke?

Honestly, I wasn't sure. Right then, I felt like my two-year-old, government-issued bootlaces: frayed around the edges and one good yank away from snapping.

"I just thought . . . I thought whoever it was might have started the fire."

Morrissey grunted. "You saw the storm. It was another lightning strike, just like the last one."

"Then why didn't Jack report it from the lookout?" Morrissey watched me like a hawk sizing up his prey, but I wasn't about to back down. "Or did he?"

"Are you accusing me of ignoring a distress report for my own forest?"

I didn't answer.

"I can't tell you why Mr. Armitage didn't call in the fire as soon as he saw it instead of trying to go down there himself. But that's obviously what happened." He took in a deep breath, grip tightening on the high-crowned hat he'd yanked off his head.

Well, what do you know? Earl Morrissey was *angry*. He was better at controlling it than most. But I saw it, just beneath the surface, and it made me strangely glad.

Someone cared. Someone was at least half as upset as I was.

"Is that all?" he asked, placing his hat back on, the professional image back in place with it.

"What kind of tree was it?" I blurted. The blank look didn't so much as budge, so I added, "The snag that fell on Jack. The one you found him caught under."

"Hooper, if I tell you that, you'll run through my forest and chop down every single one of that variety you can get your hands on. And I wouldn't trust you with an axe right now."

"I'm a pacifist, remember?"

"Sure. A pacifist with a temper." He squinted at me like when I studied birds through the binoculars, looking for their distinct markings. "I've watched you, Hooper. Don't think I don't notice."

I inventoried my twenty months at the park. Had he seen me excuse myself from dinner to kick the metal garbage can over when Shorty had asked why my father never wrote? Did he notice the way I clenched my fists whenever Jimmy or Roger made one of their stupid comments about conchies? Or see how much effort it took not to lash out when someone at the local church slighted us, when all I wanted was a place to worship on Sundays?

Or maybe he was so used to spotting hidden embers that he could just feel anger seething inside of me, ready to burst into flame.

I took a deep, steadying breath, the way Jack had taught me to.

Sometimes it worked better than counting. "Never mind that. I just want to know. What tree?"

The pause stretched out a few seconds before he replied. "Larch. An old, rotting larch."

Maybe it was the glance to the side, but something about the way he said it reminded me of my mother when she had dodged the truth to keep Nelson, my father, happy. Not mentioning the ice cream we'd bought at the drugstore, or smoothing things over by saying whatever half lie came to mind, or pretending she'd made the sketches in my notebooks since Nelson thought art wasn't "masculine."

Or was it just my imagination—again?

I watched Morrissey carefully, trying to keep my voice neutral. "Awful bad luck for Jack to be standing next to the only tree in the forest ready to fall like that."

He stared back, and I might as well have been standing on train tracks as an engine came careening toward me. "Listen, Hooper, I've only ever lost two men to fires in all my thirty years as a ranger. And I don't mean to lose another one, so you listen to me: Be careful."

CHAPTER 7

Dorie Armitage

January 12, 1945

The sunny yellow façade and gables of the administration building usually brought a vaguely out-of-place cheer to Fort Lawton, but today I stared up at it grimly.

Don't be silly. There's nothing to be worried about. Just a meeting with Captain Petmencky. One that you *set up.* I tugged on the chain around my neck, and my dog tags jingled, stamped with my name and serial number just the same as the battle-bound boys leaving our harbor in a spanking-new destroyer. *You're a soldier now, Dorie.*

With that fortifying thought, I charged up the steps and inside, past the *tat-ta-tap* of typewriters and warm, feminine voices answering the telephones for the higher-ups behind oak office doors. The administrative WACs—with their hair perfectly in place and not a spot of motor oil on them—nodded at me as I walked by.

Secretly, with all their talk of independence and equality, this was where the army wanted their women. When we'd first arrived at Fort Lawton, my own platoon, trained as drivers and mechanics, was told to fill desk jobs in the port engineers department. I led the girls in a strike, where we simply refused to leave the barracks until we were allowed to do the work we'd been trained for.

Lieutenant Ida Stoller, our commanding officer at the time, had defended us stoutly and wheedled a reluctant "trial period" from a grim-faced officer.

When the trial ended, Max and his buddies practically begged the officer to let us stay on, and so the grease monkeys of Fort Lawton became a co-educational lot.

But now Lieutenant Stoller was gone, and there was a new commander in charge. And today, I had to face her.

"I was starting to think you weren't coming." Bea, stationed outside the office as Captain Petmencky's personal assistant and secretary, gave me an encouraging smile. I'd told her about my mission the night before. She stood, rising above the towering stacks of national newspapers that the captain read first thing every morning so she could be informed of world events. "You'll do fine, Dorie."

Drat. She could tell I was nervous. "Thanks, Bea. You're a pal."

With one last fortifying breath of air from outside Captain Petmencky's office, I did an about-face toward it and knocked.

I'd been inside once. Before Christmas, Captain Petmencky had presented me with my speech to memorize for the rallies and women's luncheons several of us had been selected to attend for the spring recruitment tour. An upbeat, "proud-to-serve-the-boys" ditty, as impersonal as the overcoats they'd handed to us our first year, all the same formless size, no matter our heights.

"Come in," the voice behind the door said.

This was it. *Stand tall. Walk with confidence.*

I strutted into Petmencky's office, my leather portfolio tucked under my arm like I was a movie star disembarking the Hollywood Victory Caravan to the cheers of adoring fans.

The captain sat barricaded behind her bulwark of an oak desk. "You asked to see me, PFC Armitage," she said in a voice that indicated the documents before her were Very Important Business and I was only a distraction.

Gathering my courage, I took a step forward instead of retreating. "Yes, ma'am. It's about the recruitment tour."

She raised an eyebrow. "Don't tell me you've misplaced the speech I gave you."

"Of course not." I had it all but memorized already, coaxing one of my fellow WACs to drill me on it at least once a week until they were all bored to tears. "I actually have a few ideas for the program." I took a deep breath and clutched my portfolio. "Literature to hand out, slogans for the banners, that sort of thing."

She barely looked up, yet her expression looked as though I'd suggested we all eat herring and cabbage for breakfast. "We have a team in the Signal Corps who prepared materials for the tour months ago."

"Yes, I read them." Before I could stop myself, I rushed forward. "And, if you don't mind me saying so, they were dreadfully dull." *A Book of Facts about the WAC*, their main pamphlet was called. If they thought it was a clever rhyme . . . it wasn't.

"I suppose you'd want to turn it into something churned out by Action Comics? Or a script that could star Ingrid Bergman?" The captain's voice had gone from "dry as toast" to "dry as the Sahara in August."

"Of course not." I'd cast Olivia de Havilland in a WAC promotional film before Bergman any day, but that was a point for a different conversation. "But there's no harm in telling a few stories instead of citing statistics. Maybe adding some sketches."

This garnered one of the captain's famous raised eyebrows, arched in such disapproval that an inexperienced cadet might limp away in shame. "Artwork is expensive. We've spent enough on posters."

Just go before you embarrass yourself, part of me said.

But another part of me spoke louder. *No. Stay and fight.*

I fumbled with the clasp on the satchel. Why did my hands have to shake *now*? "If you'd just look at my mockups—"

She waved me to stop, her voice all business. "Doris, you're a garage girl. And a fine one, from what I hear. Aren't you happy there?"

Since Captain Petmencky treated compliments like they were regulated by the ration board, I should have been flattered, but instead I somehow felt smaller. "Well yes, it's just that—"

"We all have our skills, and the army is built on the principle that all of us follow that specialization, that chain of command."

Papers still in hand, I tried again. "But this *is* one of my skills. If you'd only listen—"

"Miss Armitage," the captain interrupted, "I've heard all about your 'skills.' Talking your way out of punishment when you arrive after curfew *again* is hardly evidence of the sort of persuasive ability we need."

I thought better of pointing out that it clearly hadn't worked, since Sergeant Bloom had reported me anyway.

"Neither does a full month of convincing your poor cook that someone smuggled a cat into the barracks by leaving out saucers of cream prove you have the right sort of creativity."

Well, there *had* been that time, but it wasn't entirely my idea. . . .

"And the fight that broke out over you between two men at the WAC summer fete does not give me confidence in your ability to inspire loyalty."

"I think I understand your point, Captain," I interrupted, backing toward the door before she could pull out my full two-year record.

I was the flirtatious garage girl. Pretty, perky, and perfect for shoving into the spotlight to deliver a patriotic speech written by someone else.

Once I hotfooted it out of there and calmed down—which I'm sorry to say involved a good deal of uselessly banging wrenches about while pretending to work at the garage—I realized it was my own fault. The cost of getting into minor trouble, wearing too much lipstick, and having a sense of humor was that I couldn't be trusted with serious work.

You'd have gotten bored with it anyway. Nothing nearly as satisfying as fixing an engine. Just paperwork and propaganda.

"Doris Armitage?" a voice called from the garage door.

I paused, looked up . . . and nearly dropped my toolbox. *Oh no.*

It was Freddie Wiley from the base post office. I'd gone bowling with him three Friday nights in a row until he *proposed* to me, of all things. He'd followed me around like a lost puppy even after I turned him down. But that was five months ago.

The quick, panicked thought, *What is he doing here?* was quickly followed by *Can I hide inside one of the staff cars until he goes away?*

Clearly, he'd already spotted me, since he was shuffling his way over. "Hello, Doris."

Time to be gracious but firm and get ready to holler for Max if I needed him. "Freddie, I know you admire me, but I thought we'd decided—"

His face was stony as he extended a paper. "I'm here on post-office duty, Miss Armitage. It's a telegram for you. They said it was urgent and to bring it to you here."

"Oh," I said. The gap left by my relief was filled up with foolishness. "I'm sorry, Freddie, I shouldn't have—"

"Just take it," he snapped, which I probably deserved.

I snatched it from him, scanning the names. From Daddy and Mother.

Only a few lines, and even that surprised me, given the cost of sending a telegram—no matter what Roosevelt declared, Daddy was still sure we were in the middle of the Depression and grumbled about tipping the milkman a dime at Christmas.

I gathered myself enough to read the actual words, then wished I hadn't.

```
JACK BADLY INJURED. NOW AT ARMY HOSPITAL.
CALL WHEN ABLE.
```

CHAPTER 8

Gordon Hooper

January 14, 1945

Mr. Wainwright, a deacon in a tweed suit a few inches too short for his arms, held the communion tray like it was the Ark of the Covenant and he might get stoned if he passed it the wrong way.

Which meant, as always, that he moved past our row without stopping. No one else ever sat with us on Sundays, not even the Morrisseys, so it was just a dozen COs in the back, where respectable churchgoers could keep their distance.

Not all of us, though. Lloyd, being an atheist, didn't put any stock in church, and Charlie didn't think he'd be welcome—he was the only black man in town, as far as I could tell. The CPS, filled with Mennonites and Quakers and other groups with an abolitionist history, believed in integration, and the Forest Service allowed it, but Charlie decided it was "best not to push things" where the rest of the country was concerned.

Jack had talked to the preacher once about why we were passed by for communion after the service. "Denominational differences" was the only reason he cited, though anyone with a pair of eyes and good sense could see the conversation had gone on far longer than that.

To me, it made no difference. Quakers didn't observe the Lord's Supper formally, choosing to celebrate Jesus in every meal with fellow believers. As I looked down the pew at the others, though, I could see the disappointment on the faces of some of my friends when "This do in remembrance of me" didn't include them—again.

Down the well-trodden aisle to the altar at the front, the Reverend Chester W. Jamison intoned, "Let us pray," after leading his flock in the taking of the blood and body of Christ.

I had half a mind to think that the reason the congregation of the only church in Clayton bowed their heads and closed their eyes during prayer was because they were bracing themselves in case of falling brimstone.

Reverend Jamison's services were nothing like an assembly of Friends, where we sat in silence until someone had a message to share with the group, laid on their heart by God. No, if God spoke with a still, small voice, it seemed Jamison was trying to distinguish himself by employing a loud, large voice, competing with his tent-revival brethren for volume and vividness.

Today, as ever, the reverend prayed for the troops and the war in great detail, his voice aimed at our row like a weapon. ". . . and make us, your people here on free soil, able to do our duty to resist evil wherever we find it," he finished over the sounds of the matron coaxing the strains of a familiar closing hymn out of the slightly flat piano.

I glanced over at Thomas, on one side of me, his face hard as flint. Shorty, on the other, flipped through the hymnal until his eyes landed on the lyrics, finger tracing the words to "The Battle Hymn of the Republic."

We stood respectfully but didn't trill out the "Glory, glory, hallelujahs" to the hymn along with the rest of the congregation. The way I saw it, you should only sing a song if you meant every word, not pick through it like an army censor and keep the bits you liked. And this one, written during the Civil War, glorified marching into battle.

I thought of my great-great-grandmother Clara, driving a false-bottomed wagon through the night to smuggle slaves to freedom. "We believe there is a better way," she would have said in her gentle voice, even after the Confederacy declared their independence. "The Lord's way. 'For all they that take the sword shall perish with the sword.'"

I caught a glare from an older woman trussed up in a ruffled blue dress, standing across the aisle from us. She whispered something to her husband that I couldn't hear, but knew the gist all the same. *"Look at those boys. So haughty. And they wonder why they don't belong here."*

But it was all right. I could weather any judgment, knowing that Great-Great-Grandmother Clara would be standing silently by my side.

We endured all five verses before the words of benediction ended the awkwardness. Shorty sprang up, practically shoving the other COs in the row ahead of him to make it to the aisle. "Coming, Gordon?"

"You go on," I said, waving him ahead. "I'll catch up." He didn't spare a glance back for me, eager to get out into the churchyard, the better to view the young ladies of the congregation before we piled back into the bed of Morrissey's truck.

As for me, I didn't care to wait in the cold for Mrs. Edith to finish chatting with her friends. All I wanted was Quaker-meeting silence, somewhere I could hear my own soul.

So I sat, ducked low in the last pew, where I could only faintly hear the murmurs of subdued appreciation the members offered to Reverend Jamison on their way out.

Once the last congregant had passed through the doors, I was finally alone in the quiet. It settled around me like mist on a dewy spring morning. Reassuring, enveloping, complete. Here, I could breathe in my prayers and worries and questions and breathe out calm.

Beside me, the wooden double doors of the church creaked open, and even though I wasn't doing anything wrong, I froze. Soft footsteps padded down the aisle, and when I looked up, I saw the person belonging to them: Sarah Ruth Morrissey.

Looking over her shoulder once, as if someone were following her, she slipped up to the front of the church, her oxfords hitting a creaky board only once. When she reached the altar, she extended her hand toward the cross there, rubbing it on the side.

And it looked like she bent her head and . . . whispered to it.

What in the world?

I must have leaned too far forward, because the pew creaked underneath me, and Sarah Ruth jerked her hand away and spun around like she'd been caught dipping into a collection plate, the hem of her dull brown skirt swirling around her knees.

I stood up so she'd know it was just me. "Hello, Sarah Ruth."

"Gordon," she said coolly.

"You look lovely today."

Which was true, but I should've known better than to actually say it. Sarah Ruth treated every compliment like an insult in disguise. Nobody in Clayton had fancy city clothes, but Sarah Ruth's Sunday best always looked especially dressy—probably because I mostly saw her in the square-shouldered lines of the Forest Service uniform.

"You weren't singing the last song." Sarah Ruth made the statement calmly, like it was a perfectly natural response to what I'd said instead of a complete evasion. "Why not?"

87

Well, she *had* asked. No reason why I shouldn't answer. "Because I don't see God in the watch fires of a hundred circling war camps. There, I only see violence."

She tilted her head, the auburn strands catching the early afternoon light pouring in through the sanctuary windows. "Where do you see him, then?"

A good question. Ever since the fire, it had been hard to see or hear from him at all, so I tried to remember what it had been like when God felt near. "Well . . . in the beauty of sunset over the mountains. Or the trilling of a waxwing. Or even something as simple as the warmth of a blanket and good conversation on a cold evening."

I stopped. There I went, rambling again. *"Never bore a lady with philosophy, Gordon."* Dorie had told me that once, long ago, laughing prettily and touching my arm.

But Sarah Ruth only shrugged, stepping away from the cross and moving toward the first row of pews. "Sure, God is there. That's why I love the woods and the mountains. But he might be in the fires too."

Before I could respond, she tilted her head at me and lowered her voice. "Want to know a secret?" I nodded, because what else could I say? "Dad wonders if all forest fires are bad."

"Excuse me?" The first subject change—away from a compliment—had been expected. This one came out of nowhere.

She nodded sagely. "Think about it, Gordon. Before 1905 and the founding of the Forest Service, fires burned through these mountains every year with no one to stop them. And what harm did that do?"

I felt myself shifting back into my university debate club days. "We also didn't have people cutting down thousands of acres to build highways and department stores back then."

Her smile, slight as it was, felt like a triumph. "Granted. But live in a forest long enough, and you'll realize everything is connected. Without the occasional wildfire, streams can get crowded out by too much vegetation. Ground cover like juniper can take over grazing land. New meadows won't form, and the predators that depend on them will go hungry. Not now, sure, but after decades of flying in with our planes and shovels, what's going to happen to that balance?"

There was a strength to her words that took me aback, a hornet hum of certainty, the kind I felt when I read Thoreau's passionate essays about nature in *Walden*. "I never thought about it."

"Dad has," she said simply. "Oh, there's nothing he can do about it—if he said something like, 'Maybe we should allow some fires,' he'd get laughed straight out of a job. But he wonders, and just because some higher-up decided on a strategy of total suppression doesn't mean he blindly accepts it. You wouldn't guess just looking at him, but Dad's a rebel."

"So that's where you get it."

She leaned against the nearby pew and grinned. "You could say that."

I felt a surge of victory. It wasn't quite a compliment, and she hadn't quite accepted it, but it was close, wasn't it?

"So, Gordon: What if war is like a wildfire?"

It appeared she hadn't been changing the subject after all. "I don't understand."

"Maybe sometimes you have to use fire to burn away the old, twisted ground cover to make room for new life."

Ah. A metaphor. That I could work with. "War can't burn away human sin."

"No. But we all have to do our part to resist it. Men like my brother William are called to raise barricade lines to keep the fire of evil from spreading and destroying."

"And men like me?" I knew the names the others called us, both to our faces and behind our backs. But I'd never heard Sarah Ruth voice an opinion, either for or against us.

Her measuring eyes took me in, and this time, she didn't look away. "There's a season to everything. Maybe you're meant to come back to the scorched earth and help something grow again."

Beautiful words. But were they true?

I shook my head. "I don't know if I can accept that. The reason Jack and I came here in the first place, when everyone we knew mocked or hated us for it, was because we believe it's always wrong to fight and kill."

She took a step closer, and I could see her inhale deeply. "Gordon, about Jack . . ."

The fear and loss came back in a rush. Jack. In a hospital somewhere, alone. "What about him?"

"Just . . . don't be too sure you're right. That's all." She shrugged and couldn't keep meeting my eyes. "Especially about something as complicated as war and peace." With that, she turned on her heel, striding down the aisle like a mountain-bound ranger with a mission.

I had to ask, before she left for good. "Why were you whispering to the cross?"

She stopped. Turned. And I'd never seen her eyes like that before, so serious and sad. "Dad used to pray that way sometimes. Before Willie died."

That didn't answer my question—not really. "Were you praying too?"

As she angled toward me, one hand on the door, the light from the lone stained-glass window at the back of the church gave her a halo of gold and red and green. "Just burning out some old, twisted ground cover." Her voice was almost a whisper again.

"Sarah Ruth!" The holler cut through the quiet so abruptly that we both flinched. Jimmy's head poked into the sanctuary. "C'mon, before Mom gets hung up again with—"

That's when he noticed me, and his general teenage impatience to get to lunch was replaced with unmistakable suspicion. "What're you doing with *him*?"

"It's called conversation, little brother. You should try it sometime." Sarah Ruth's voice had lost all of its wistfulness, snapping back to her usual smirk. "Most people enjoy it, I'm told."

"Aw, come off it." Was it intentional, the way he placed himself in the gap between the two of us?

Sarah Ruth angled herself around him as she walked toward the door. "It was good to talk to you, Gordon." As if we'd been discussing the weather or the latest radio show instead of grief and prayer and the burden of peace.

"You too," I blurted, pretending not to notice the warning glare Jimmy gave me before the doors closed, the silence no longer comforting.

So Sarah Ruth didn't think we were cowards. That was good. But what had she been about to say about Jack? And she couldn't be right about some men being called to fight and others to make peace . . . could she?

I should have hurried to catch up with Sarah Ruth and Jimmy, back to the truck and the national forest. But there was one more thing I wanted to know.

Sure enough, I leaned over the altar and saw that the place where Sarah Ruth's hand had rested on the wooden cross had been rubbed smooth.

A few hours later, I found myself kneeling beside Jack's empty bed with a cardboard box and too much on my mind.

Morrissey's instructions had been clear. While the other men had their usual free Sunday afternoon to use at their leisure, I was assigned to sort through Jack's things. Anything government issued stayed. The rest would be sent to his family.

Still no word on Jack's condition. Something about entering the bunkhouse, empty and cold, and seeing his perfectly made bed caught me in the gut.

I clutched the box tighter. *He's not dead.*

But either way, it was clear that even if Jack woke up, he wasn't coming back to Flintlock Mountain.

A pile of belongings rested at the foot of the bed—someone had clearly retrieved them from the lookout. A shaving kit, a toothbrush, two changes of clothes, a blue towel frayed at the edges, the necessities of daily life. I sorted through them, trying to remember what we'd been given two years ago when we joined up and what Jack had brought from home.

That task done, there was only one left. I knelt beside the trunk at the foot of Jack's bed and tested the lid.

Locked, as always.

Thankfully, one of the privileges of being Jack's best friend was knowing he kept the key inside the Bible on the small bedside table. I turned the key, opened the lid, and started sorting.

When it came to what the government allotted us, the pile was small. Boots. The canvas coveralls we used on jumps. The blanket folded neatly at the foot of the cot.

All that remained was a box of tacks, a set of pencils in various stages of nub, and a Sunday dress outfit, complete with a tin of shoeshine and a polishing rag that I borrowed for church days.

Then, a surprise: not one journal but four, arranged in a small stack.

I allowed myself a smile. *He really did write down everything, didn't he?* The journals were all exactly alike—plain black-and-white composition books—so I'd never noticed when he'd filled one and started another.

Lifting the stack revealed one more item at the bottom: a snapshot of the Armitage family at what looked like a picnic, his parents framing their two children. A younger Jack aimed his usual Hollywood-charm smile at the camera, but Dorie tilted her head, smirking more than smiling, about thirteen years old but displaying not a hint of awkwardness.

I shook my head. He hadn't kept it tacked to the wall or out in a frame. But his family was still with him, whether they wanted to be or not.

Taped to the back was a paper in Jack's hand, reading, *Dorie's new address.*

I glanced at it.

What was she doing at a hotel in Seattle? That was a long way from small-town Pennsylvania.

Even as I asked the question, I wondered if I knew. She'd married a military man, hadn't she? Gone across the country to follow him, maybe an officer who got a cushy stateside job at one of the ports in Washington.

It's her choice if she did, Gordon. Whatever she did, it wasn't just to spite you. I knew that, just as I knew, deep in my heart, that, war or no, the sharp differences between us would have made us the kind of cat-and-dog couple my parents had been. Still, it stung, picturing her sauntering through the streets of Seattle on the arm of an officer in a spiffy dress uniform.

Had Jack ever written her? I didn't think I'd ever seen him at it, although it was hard to tell, given all the scribbling he did in his notebook.

I decided to put the journals on top of the box, for Jack's parents to see first. Let them remember who Jack was, not the conscientious objector, but the man.

My hands moved to fold the flaps of the box inward, and then I paused.

That one second was all my curiosity needed.

Jack had never let us touch his journal, had shielded it even from me when I tried to lean over and read a line.

To know what he was thinking just before he died . . . well, it might help me find closure. There were so many questions I couldn't ask him now. Surely he wouldn't mind if his best friend took a short glance.

I opened the first one, with *October 1942* emblazoned on the front, and started reading.

It wasn't a journal.

That was clear by the bold heading: *Danger on Planet Xylon. By Jack T. Armitage.*

I couldn't help smiling, then laughing when I read the first few pages. It was a radio play, of all things. Not a factual account of CPS service for future generations like we'd all thought. A science-fiction drama about a space explorer named Captain Jackson Andromeda, clearly autobiographical.

Some of my laughter was at the comedic bits. Some . . . well, let's just say it was clear Jack was a beginner. Not that I could have done better, but I imagined some of the lines would be absurd spoken out loud, especially once the aliens joined the program.

Behind the notebook, held together with a paper clip, was clearly the rough draft, pages of smudgy lined paper with pencil scratch-outs as well as arrows that made the whole thing look like the most complicated football playbook known to man.

"We're going to have fun talking about this when you wake up, Jack," I said. No one answered, and the silence felt heavy.

I paged through a few of the other notebooks—late 1943 was Jack's hackneyed Western period until he shifted to exaggerated film noir in early 1944—before placing them back in the trunk, when I noticed a loose sheet had fluttered to the ground. It was a notebook page with a torn edge, folded in half. Another rough draft.

And as I read all the way through it, I thought again of Dorie Armitage. Whoever she'd become, whatever she was doing, Jack had written this scene for her.

CHAPTER 9

Dorie Armitage

January 17, 1945

The freshly painted boards of the enclosed porch of the base hospital creaked as I wheeled Staff Sergeant Howard Mitchell out of the convalescent wing. Even in January, he insisted on getting an hour of fresh air from the cracked-open windows. "Good for the constitution," he always said. "And Lord knows mine needs amending." He chuckled, then inhaled deeply, as if the bracing wind off Puget Sound might regrow his left leg, amputated at the knee.

I situated him in front of the window that offered the best view of the parade grounds.

"Good thing you came to visit today, Miss Doris. I'd just gathered up enough news for a letter."

"Howie, you *always* have something to say," I teased, tilting another of the porch's chairs toward him and setting my portable writing case on my lap.

He threw his whiskered head back and laughed, drawing attention from a few of the other fellows staring blankly at the dismal sky. "Fellow's got to keep the folks back home entertained."

I knew the rough outline of Howie's story: He'd been ambushed by guerilla warriors in Guam and was now settled in for recovery at the port of embarkation. But Dr. Pemberton had warned me from the first that I shouldn't ask too many questions related to the men's combat experiences when I visited the base hospital on Wednesday evenings. "Just be a friendly face," he'd advised.

My eyes wandered down to the blanket around Howie's thigh, dropped flat where it ought to have surrounded a healthy lower leg. It was the least I could do, with all they'd sacrificed.

He cleared his throat. "I know I'm a real fine specimen, Miss Doris, but you'd best keep your eyes on my face."

I flushed the way I always did when caught staring. "Gosh, I didn't mean—"

His hand batted my apology away. "Better settle in now, because I plan to run that fountain pen dry."

I obliged, scratching out Howie's words to his darling wife, Christine. There was no way to include his gestures or the affectionate look in his eye when he reached, "All my love, Howie," but I did my best.

Then, on went the eagle stamps we could purchase at the PX, and soon the letter would be winging its way home to Olathe, Kansas. "Good," Howie declared, after checking over the address. "Man ought to look after his family. I don't stand by the boys who barely give their folks word."

My hand stilled on the paper for a moment, and then I focused on folding the letter into perfect thirds. If he knew I'd never once written a personal letter to Jack after he left home . . .

And now it was too late.

For five days, I'd dealt with the news about Jack by filling my days as full as possible—work and outings with the girls and even a second date with Archie. But as soon as bed check came every night, I found myself staring at the cracked plaster of the ceiling, remembering.

Not the Jack who folded his arms and set his jaw against my pleas not to join the CPS. The Jack who saved his paper-route money to give me a satin-lined doll buggy for my eighth birthday, who defended skinny Davy McIntire against the school bullies, who always had me gut the fish after an outing on the lake because he couldn't stand to look at their sightless eyes.

And now he was injured—maybe fatally—somewhere far away.

After Freddie had given me the telegram in the garage, I'd hurried back to the hotel to call home. There had been a fire, a terrible accident, and the army was now keeping Jack for treatment but wouldn't release his location. Nor could they say what his chances were of getting well, only that he was in "critical condition."

He was a smokejumper, I found out. Somehow, even without a uniform, my brother had been the first to ride in a plane after all.

"You all right, sweetheart?" Daddy had asked after giving the details. He hadn't called me that since before high school.

I asked where Jack was being treated, but they didn't know. Even if they'd been able to pay for a train trip all the way out west—they certainly didn't have the gas rations to drive—the army insisted he was in too critical a condition for visitors. They hadn't pressed any further. Too distraught, I suppose, to squabble with regulations.

Now, without any updates, the omission bothered me. Like a few lines had been censored out of a report. And why had they taken Jack to an army hospital instead of a local one? How could he have been hurt so badly? Was it really the accident they claimed?

"You all right, Miss Doris?" When I looked up, Howie's eyebrows were knitted together, the crinkles from beside his eyes gone.

I cleared my throat. "Just homesick, I suppose."

"Reckon we all are."

I tucked the letter into the envelope and sealed it. "Was there anyone you didn't get to say good-bye to, Howie? Properly, I mean." The words came almost on their own.

"Well . . ." He shifted in the wheelchair, fiddling with a frayed corner of the seat. "My daughter, I guess."

Even with effort, I couldn't keep my eyes from widening. "You have a daughter?" That hadn't come up in any of the letters, unless she was one of the names he greeted at the end.

He took out a picture, not the wedding photo he'd shown me before, but a snapshot of curly-haired Christine smiling down at a squinting infant, a frilly bonnet tied under her chubby chin.

"She's beautiful." All babies were, wrinkles and matted hair and all. "I'm surprised you aren't crowing about her to the rafters."

"We didn't mean to . . . well, we got married so sudden, to have some time together before I joined up, and . . . Emily was a bit of a surprise, let's say. I met her once, just after she was born, when I was on leave." His usually cheery face fell into a frown. "Wouldn't you know, she screwed up her pretty little face and bawled her eyes out every time I tried to hold her."

"Babies are like that."

"So I'm told. Truth is, I don't know squat about being a father. Or a husband either, really." He took the envelope from me, turned it over in his hands like he was thinking of tearing it up, his eyes as distant as his more shell-shocked companions. "You've just got to wonder . . . what'll it be like when I go back?"

"You'll be there for them, Howie," I said firmly, putting a hand on his shoulder. "That's what. And I bet that's all they want. Just a husband and father who's willing to give it his all, even if you make some mistakes along the way."

He scratched his whiskered chin thoughtfully and looked at me. "Well, I hope that's so."

"I know it is."

He seemed to roll that around, not quite convinced, but not quite as scared looking as before. "And what about you?" I opened my mouth to dodge the question, before he added, "Nobody asks something like that unless they were thinking of their own situation first."

He had me there. I decided a partial truth was all that was needed. "My . . . my brother was drafted two years ago. We don't talk much now."

Howie nodded to the stamps tucked under the ink blotter. "You can change that, you know."

No, I can't. He's far away, maybe dying, and I never got a chance to make things right between us.

But I couldn't say that. I hadn't told anyone, not even Bea or Violet, the news. It would hurt too much, I reasoned, to even say the words out loud.

No. The only way to move on was by forging ahead. After wheeling Howie inside and making my rounds—I took dictation on another letter, read a chapter of a Zane Grey Western, and played two games of hearts and one of gin rummy—it was time to hoof it back to the Stratford. Even in our refurbished hotel barracks, curfew was taken seriously.

Just past the doors, Violet was stationed behind the stained-oak registration desk, in charge of quarters duty. "Two letters for you today, Dorie." She pushed them across the desk at me as I signed back in on the register.

"A bonanza. Thanks." Occasionally, one of the men I'd gone on a date with sent me a postcard or a letter. *Who will it be today?* Bert, the dashing corporal running missions up in the snow-covered Aleutian Islands? Wade, a Montana cowboy who hoped for the

Pacific theater because he'd always wanted to see a real palm tree?

As soon as I was up a flight and out of sight, I took out the two envelopes . . . and frowned.

Of all the men I'd been expecting to hear from tonight—or ever again—Gordon Hooper and Lieutenant Vincent Leland were not among them.

FROM VINCENT LELAND TO DORIE ARMITAGE

To PFC Armitage,

I hope this message finds you well. I tried to call but was told you were unavailable, so I decided to hand deliver this note myself.

I've heard the news about your brother, and I want to tell you how sorry I am. War is terrible, and I hate every injury and lost life it causes.

My superior believes you'd be granted an early furlough if you explain the circumstances, a week or two to visit your family in this difficult time.

Now, if you're thinking, "I can't desert my post. What will people say?" I'll tell you something I've learned the hard way: Don't you ever let others' expectations keep you from doing the right thing.

Which, in this case, is going home. They need you, even if you don't think you need them, especially if Jack doesn't pull out of this.

Think about it, that's all I'm asking.

I'll be leaving Fort Lawton as soon as the army finishes some negotiations I'm involved with, but if there's anything I can do, let me know. I'm stationed temporarily near Major Hastings's office. You might mention his name if you need some authority to back your furlough request.

And listen, those questions I asked you last week: I'm sorry for pushing you. If I'd known what was going to happen, I wouldn't have, especially asking about whether you pray for your brother. That didn't cause what happened to Jack, so don't let yourself think it for a moment.

Lieutenant Vincent Leland

FROM GORDON TO DORIE

January 14, 1945

Dear Dorie,

It's been over three years since I last wrote you, and I don't know if you want to hear from me now. But since they won't let me visit Jack at the hospital—I begged our district ranger twice already, but "the CPS has rules"—I had to tell you how sorry I am.

I'm sorry Jack was hurt so badly. Sorry he was so far away from your family when it happened. Sorry I wasn't there to help him.

It doesn't feel like nearly enough.

They won't tell us much about how he's doing, or even where they're treating him, but we know he hasn't woken up yet and that he might not. I can't imagine how awful it must be for you.

I know you didn't want Jack to join the CPS with me, but

102

you should know that he was brave, selfless, and everything a good soldier should be. Even to the last. Our district ranger, Earl Morrissey, thinks he rushed to the fire as soon as he saw it, trying to put it out himself without any equipment. Always looking after others. Still, I wish he would have called it in like he was supposed to. It's awful, isn't it? The one time in his life Jack broke the rules, and this is what happened.

If you were here, maybe Morrissey would tell us where they're keeping him, being family and all. It's enough to make a fellow worried, the way they won't tell us much of anything. But I know it may just be the stress of it all wearing on me. On all of us.

Another reason I wanted to write was that I found the enclosed page in Jack's things, along with your address. It's part of a radio drama he was working on, written the night before he left for lookout duty.

I don't want to meddle, and I'm sorry if it brings up unwanted memories, but I felt like I had to send it to you for any comfort it might give. I'm sure you and your parents are taking this hard. I pray for all of you often in this difficult time. Maybe God can find us in the fog. He has to be there, just out of reach. Doesn't he?

Gordon Hooper

FROM JACK ARMITAGE'S NOTEBOOK

Raymond Steele, Private Eye
Act One, Scene One

[SFX: feet on creaking boards, office door shutting]

JACKSON: Mr. Steele?

STEELE: That's my name—don't wear it out.

JACKSON: Say . . . I-I've got something I could use your help with.

STEELE: Doesn't everyone? It's about a dame, isn't it?

JACKSON: Jiminy! How'd you know?

STEELE: It's always about a dame. Did she, what, run off with your best friend? Walk away with all your dough? Drop out of your life?

JACKSON: That one.

STEELE: Shoulda guessed that first. Listen, pal, I'm a private eye, not chairman of the local Lonely Hearts Club. Now scram.

JACKSON: It's not like you think. She . . . she's my sister.

STEELE: Go on.

JACKSON: I can't find any trace of her, no matter how hard I look. It's like . . . she disappeared.

STEELE: Just the facts, now. I'm on a tight schedule.

JACKSON: Nora and I haven't talked in over a year, but we recently came into some inheritance money, and the family lawyer asked me to reconnect. After she didn't return my calls, I tracked down the dump where she'd been living. Her landlord told me she

stiffed him on the rent and ran off with some citified card shark.

STEELE: Think she'd do that?

JACKSON: I dunno. Guess I didn't know her as well as I
thought. But it didn't sit well, you know? Like something bad had happened to her. Maybe even . . . foul
play.

[SFX: dramatic chord]

STEELE: Listen, pal, there's not a day that goes by
without some upstanding girl getting dragged down
into the muck of the wrong part of town. Not organized crime—the disorganized sort. Broken promises
and empty stomachs, doing what you got to do to
make it. Just how it goes.

JACKSON: Look, I know what you're thinking, but I'm
not gonna give up on her. Not that easy. Not until I
make sure she's all right. We've got to find my sister.
Whatever it takes.

STEELE: Whatever it takes is letting me do my job,
buddy. I'm the gumshoe here. You're just a pair of
old work boots slowing me down.

JACKSON: Does that mean you'll take the case?

STEELE: Against my better judgment, sure. The Mystery
of the Missing Sister. It's got a ring to it. Time to hit
the streets. No case is so cold that Raymond Steele
can't be hot on its trail.

FROM GORDON'S MOTHER, JANE MCCARDELL, TO GORDON

January 15, 1945

Dear Son,

I got your second letter in as many days. I'm so sorry to hear about Jack's injury. Your letter made it sound quite serious. He'll be all right, won't he? It's dreadful for a mother to think about things like that. Are you sure you can't transfer to another branch of the CPS? I hear several are working at homes for the elderly or asylums, which can't be so bad as fighting fires.

My routine remains unchanged and unremarkable. Probably why I seemed to be low in spirits. There's something just so . . . daily about days here. It's been a long time. And I miss you, son.

I did read Walden, *but I'm sorry to admit that I didn't care for it. It's hard to appreciate Thoreau's musings about the beauty of lakes and the feeling of grass under one's feet and seizing destiny in my current circumstances.*

Also, you shouldn't be cruel to your aunt. You know your uncle is losing his hearing and probably doesn't respond with nearly as much sympathy as she would like.

I look forward to the time when this awful war is over again and you can visit me. I hope and pray that day will come soon.

Your mother

FROM DORIE TO HER PARENTS

January 17, 1945

Dear Mother and Daddy,
   Well, wouldn't you know, after a year and a half in the

motorpool here, I've been reassigned. For the next two weeks, I'll be the aide for a special mission. Can't say more about it than that, other than that it's still in the Pacific Northwest. (Nothing dangerous, Mama. Don't fret.)

So don't write to me at Fort Lawton anymore, as it would waste a stamp. I can't give you a new address at the moment, but I'll do my best to call once or twice to hear if you have updates on Jack.

He'll recover, I'm sure of it. We just have to keep our chins up. And you'll be glad to know I'm even doing some praying. (It's been a while. I'm not convinced God is listening, but it can't hurt to try.)

I love you both. And miss you.

Your daughter,
Dorie

FROM DORIE TO VINCENT LELAND

January 18, 1945

Lieutenant Leland,

Well, I'd say you've got a record better than Joe Lewis in the ring. You were right. My very first thought was that the WACs couldn't carry on without me for two whole weeks, and what a disappointment I'd be if I took a break.

My second thought was how deliciously just it would be to stick Sergeant Bloom with my absence after she'd punished me with a week of KP duty for being out after curfew.

But my third thought was that you might be right after all, and that, at least, is more noble.

So I marched down to Petmencky's office first thing this morning to plead my case, which involved dropping names and working up some crocodile tears. Now the paperwork's all signed. I'm out on the 5 PM train for twelve days of furlough.

I hadn't thought to worry about whether my lack of piety was to blame for Jack's injury until you brought it up. I hadn't thought much about Jack at all, actually. You can crowd out even the worst of news if you fill your days with other noises, I've learned. But still, I appreciate you trying to reassure me.

It's ironic, isn't it? Here at the fort, I'm surrounded by men— coworkers at the garage, dates to the movies anytime I want them, pen pals stationed overseas—but Jack is the one man who's always been there for me. Even when I wasn't there for him.

Maybe I can be now.

Since I'm in a hurry, chances are good I might not see you before I go. If that's the case, thanks for everything. I mean it. Like you said, my family needs me, and I intend to be as helpful to them as I possibly can be, no matter what it takes.

Sincerely,
~~PFC Doris Armitage~~
Dorie

CHAPTER 10

Gordon Hooper

January 19, 1945

"All right, boys," Mrs. Edith said, straining to plop down two gunny-sacks of potatoes between us on the dish-room counter. "How about hobo packets for dinner tonight?"

"Why, Mrs. E," Shorty said sweetly, batting his eyelashes at her, "I'd just lick the plate for anything you made."

Her eyes lit with amusement at his blatant flattery, and I started to laugh, then remembered again.

Jack hadn't woken up yet.

That's how it was these days. Moments when life was almost back to normal . . . and then I'd remember my daily trek to Mor-rissey's office. Today's answer was the same as the past six: Jack was still alive, with no change to his condition. The doctors were worried. We should all pray . . . and wait.

"Why do you call them hobo packets?" I asked, taking the po-tatoes over to the sink to scrub them and trying to force my mind out of that rut.

"Hmm? Oh, one of the CCC men used to call them that. It must be a decade ago now." Mrs. Edith shook her head, smiling. "Roy Someone or other. He was a roguish fellow—might've been a drifter himself once. Charming, though. Sarah Ruth thought so, anyway."

"Oho," Shorty crowed, the dishcloth he'd been about to whip against me as I passed by going limp as he focused on Mrs. Edith instead. "Is that so? Paulette Bunyan had a sweetheart?"

Mrs. Edith chuckled at Shorty's now-familiar nickname. His fictional tall tales of Sarah Ruth's heroic exploits in the wilderness were bonfire-night favorites. "Yes, it's true."

I tried to picture tough, independent Sarah Ruth as she was in the mid-'30s—sixteen, maybe?—sighing wistfully after one of the Civilian Conservation Corps workers assigned to the forest for the summer, the object of her girlish crush . . . and failed.

"Whatever happened to him?" I couldn't help asking.

Mrs. Edith shrugged. "Why, he left after the job was done, I suppose. They did good work—many of our buildings and trails are thanks to them. But we never heard from Roy after that summer."

"Good," Shorty declared. "Might give another fellow a chance, eh, Gordon?"

My face flushed at the implication in Shorty's voice. This was Sarah Ruth's *mother* he was joking with, for pity's sake.

Mrs. Edith waggled a knife in Shorty's direction before handing it to him properly, handle first. "Now get to work, you two. I don't want you spending all your time jawing."

As I peeled, I tried to imagine the final product: a tinfoil mass of salt, pepper, bits of leftover bacon, and creamy goodness. There was something romantic about Roy-the-CCC-man's name for them if you imagined them cooked over a fire by a train hopper wearing fingerless gloves rather than cooked in an oven by a beaming woman who sang an off-key version of "Oh My Darling Clementine" as she worked.

"The trouble with potatoes is," Shorty philosophized, once Mrs.

Edith had gone inside the kitchen, leaving us to the dish room, "they just aren't easy enough." He held up his latest tuber, where he had carved a frowning face, with a rotten spot as a nose. Then his own face sobered. "Say, are we . . . do you think we should have a bonfire tonight?"

Oh. It was Friday.

"Why are you asking me?" I tossed a potato in the pot Mrs. Edith had set out.

"You just . . . Jack always . . . and you're his best friend." He toed the floor awkwardly and nodded out the window toward the fire pit. "I thought you and me could help set things up."

It might be good to have a little normalcy. Have something to do besides mope and wait. "Sure, why not? We'd just need to get a stack of old newspapers from Morrissey for tinder."

Wait. Newspapers.

My knife clattered against the counter. "I'll be back," I said to a confused-looking Shorty, running out the back door toward the bunkhouse. Hopefully he'd think I had an emergency urge to use the latrine.

Right before Jack's week at the lookout, he'd gotten another newspaper article, but I hadn't seen any of them in his things when I searched. *Maybe he threw them away.*

But no. That didn't seem like Jack. He'd always said, "Even if we don't agree with the war, that doesn't mean we should pretend it doesn't exist."

Inside the bunkhouse, I searched under his bed and mattress and pushed the nightstand away from the wall to see if something was trapped behind it, finding lint and a gum wrapper but nothing more.

I flopped down on Jack's bunk, springs groaning, closing my eyes. Had I ever seen him tuck the anonymous letters away somewhere other than his pocket? No memory surfaced. I sighed and opened my eyes.

Only to look up at the wooden frame that formed the top bunk . . . where nearly two dozen newspaper articles faced me, some faded to a mild yellow, each secured in the corner with silver tacks, matching the box I'd found in Jack's trunk.

Well done, Jack. It was a good hiding place . . . except that it meant Jack was forced to stare up at the depressing headlines every night and see them first thing when he woke in the mornings.

Based on the progression of dates and coloration, the newest was at the end closest to the foot. I carefully removed the tacks and took it down. The headline was even grimmer than usual: *Thousands Liberated from "Murder Factory."*

I scanned the newsprint underneath. The Russian Army had broken through to some kind of Nazi prison camp in Poland, where the Germans brought trainloads of dissidents to work. By the time the Red Army came, there were only starving, emaciated men, women, and children left. 150,000 estimated killed.

It was a short article, just a few lines and with no pictures, but it chilled me in a way that some of the others Jack had let me see, about various battles or maneuvers, had not.

Children?

Something caught my eye, a smudged line in pencil underneath the article, crammed into the margin. *This is what happens when a good man does nothing.*

I searched the other articles. No pencil messages scrawled there. Whoever had sent this was increasing the pressure. But why? What possible motive did he have?

I tried to imagine I were Jack, a leader with a strong sense of responsibility, already feeling uncertain about his choices, without any support from his family or church. How would he feel, reading this article and all the rest?

No. He would understand he's acting out of conviction, not fear.

That was how the Jack right after Pearl Harbor would respond, or the Jack who first told me about the CPS smokejumper program.

But the Jack of three years into the war, during a long winter of inactivity, after reading about women and children murdered by the Axis powers?

"He'd be feeling low."

I'd said it out loud, quietly, and putting it to words made it feel more real.

A second thought came, as logical as one of Jack's algorithms.

What if the reason he rushed into the fire alone, despite all safety training warning against it, was because he didn't care if he made it out or not?

"You all right, Gordon?" It was Shorty's voice, uncharacteristically hesitant, coming from the doorway, but I didn't turn around, tucking the newspaper article into my pocket much like Jack always had.

"I was just . . . thinking." I couldn't lie, even if I didn't want to tell him the full reason. "It doesn't make sense, what happened to Jack. It was so . . . sudden."

"Fire often comes down from heaven with no warning."

I groaned at the deep, authoritative voice. If I'd have known *he'd* come in with Shorty, I'd have kept my mouth shut. But there he was, the Apostle Tom himself, leaning in the bunkhouse doorway and looking somberly at me as I rolled off the bunk and turned to face them.

Shorty's laugh had a nervous tinge to it. "Come on, this isn't the Old Testament."

But I wasn't ready to pass it off as a joke, not when Thomas's deep-set eyes were so serious. "What are you saying, Thomas?"

And then he began to sing in a mellow bass the words to Sunday's hymn as he walked toward me. "'He hath loosed the fateful lightning of his terrible swift sword.'"

Lightning. He couldn't mean . . .

"What are you saying?" I repeated, this time through gritted teeth.

Thomas was unruffled, looking directly at me with cool blue eyes. "You're a man of faith too, Gordon. You have to admit it's possible."

I realized he was going to force me to say it, that he wasn't brave enough to make the accusation outright. "You think . . . *God* set that fire?"

"'The Lord knoweth how to deliver the godly out of temptations, and to reserve the unjust unto the day of judgment—'" he paused and looked significantly at me—"'to be punished.'"

I couldn't explain it or justify it, but something in me snapped. Or maybe that was just the sound my fist made when it cracked Thomas right in the jaw.

He curled his arms protectively around himself but didn't resist when I shoved him, knocking him to the floor.

I felt Shorty's arms around me, pulling me back.

"How dare you!" I shouted, lunging for Thomas again, twisting out of Shorty's grasp. "You've got no right."

He didn't fight back. Maybe it was self-righteousness, or maybe he was afraid of being struck with another judgment from God, but the fact was that Thomas Martin turned the other cheek and let me hit him again, which I did.

And regretted it, as always, just a few seconds too late.

"I'm sorry," I mumbled, the words feeling thick and insincere on my tongue. "I . . . I didn't . . ."

Shorty was staring at me like you would at a rabid animal a

distance away, and Thomas lay on the floor of the bunkhouse, breathing heavily.

Now they'd all know the real reason I'd become a Quaker, why I held so tightly to nonviolence. I'd always hoped if I really believed it sincerely enough, maybe it would change me for good. Maybe I wouldn't end up like my father and his father, with their half-drunk tirades and shouts of rage.

And yet, here I was.

With effort, Thomas hauled himself up, wiping his bleeding nose on his sleeve. Then he looked right at me. "'For it had been better for them not to have known the way of righteousness, than, after they have known it, to turn from the holy commandment delivered unto them.'"

My hand fell to my side, knuckles throbbing from where they'd connected with cartilage and bone. Whatever wrong ideas he had about Jack, he was right about me.

I might be angry at God and everyone else for what happened to Jack, but God was angry with me too. And he had a right to be.

I let the door slam as I ran, Shorty calling after me. Not into the woods, just out to the worn track around the landing strip. A dozen laps wouldn't clear my mind, but maybe they would help somehow.

Blessed are the peacemakers: for they shall be called the children of God. The Scripture came back to taunt me now, yanking my guilty conscience down even farther with shame.

I'd really done it now. There went the only blessing I had left.

I was a child of my father, all right. But this time, it was only my earthly one, whom Mother and I had tried so hard to bury.

Once I'd finished running, sweaty and spent, there was only one option. Turn myself in to Morrissey.

115

Please don't let her be here, I prayed as I pushed open the heavy door. Sometimes, during work hours, she was at the cookhouse, or checking inventory, or loading in a delivery.

But no. Sarah Ruth Morrissey was stationed at the secretarial desk in the ranger station's entryway underneath a large trail map and illustrated posters of the flora and fauna of Oregon. She looked up when I entered and studied me, breathing hard from the run, my coat stripped off in my arms. "You don't look so great, Gordon."

Thanks a lot. "I need to speak to your father," I mumbled, looking at the scarred wood floor, the cheerful fireplace, the taxidermy birds nailed back on the wall—anywhere but her searching face.

"Sorry," she said, nodding toward the carved wooden bench beside the door, "you'll have to wait. He's . . . busy."

In the quiet that followed, I could hear muted voices, and while I couldn't understand all the words, I had a good idea of who was saying them.

Thomas had made it here before me.

And Sarah Ruth's desk was right beside the office door.

Combine that with the sympathetic look she'd aimed my way, and it didn't take Raymond Steele, private eye, to figure out that she knew more than she was letting on.

I sat, the tight muscles in my legs easing, and thought about reaching for the battered guide to North American trees, anything to put a barrier between the two of us in the awkward silence.

"You know," Sarah Ruth said, pushing her chair away from the desk to prop her boots up alongside the half-finished letter that poked out of her typewriter, "I've known some fellows who have a moral code, and some whose moral code has them . . . throttled around the throat. There's a difference."

I struggled to find a response and came up empty. "That's certainly . . . vivid."

She opened her mouth to say more, but the office door creaked open, and Thomas stepped out—not smug, just sober, though the effect was lessened by the handkerchief dangling from his swollen nostril.

When his eyes met mine, it felt like staring into the face of an Old Testament prophet. Daniel, maybe, coming unscathed out of the lion's den, only to watch the pagan king throw his enemies into it in his place.

There was nothing I could say in my defense. His very presence, the shadow of a coming bruise darkening on his cheekbone, condemned me, the violent pacifist.

"Hooper," he said, nodding at me as he strode toward the door.

"Have a nice day," Sarah Ruth called pleasantly after him, which almost made me smile. I'd noticed that Sarah Ruth never used that sticky-sweet voice unless she really disliked someone.

The door shut. "What did he say, anyway?" Sarah Ruth asked as I stood. I must have let my surprise show, because she rolled her eyes. "Come on, Gordon. I know you wouldn't go around throwing punches for no reason."

That comment, even delivered with her usual gruff air, gave me confidence enough to tell the truth. "He told me that maybe . . . maybe what happened to Jack was God's judgment."

"Well, if that's not a bunch of tin-can Spam," she said, scowling. "I would have punched him too."

The image of tiny Sarah Ruth swaggering up to Thomas and clocking him a good one was almost amusing . . . except looking at her, narrow eyed and tense, I could believe she'd do it.

"There's a lot of judgment in the Bible."

"And a lot of grace." Then she looked away, taking a wavering breath before looking up again, trying to smile. "When I learn how to find the balance, I'll let you know."

In characteristic Sarah Ruth style, she didn't finish the conversation but knocked on her father's office door. After poking her head in and presumably tapping out some sort of silent Morrissey code to ask if he was free, she gestured me forward.

I came, trying not to feel like a blindfolded man led in front of a firing squad.

She must have noticed, because when I passed close enough, she put a hand on my arm—not a delicate pat, but a bracing grip, like she was hauling me up out of a deep, dark pit.

"Thanks," I managed.

All she did was nod, her wide hazel eyes serious without a sign of a forced smile in sight, before letting go.

She'd heard what I'd done. But she also knew what it was like to have regrets. Whether they were old and scarred or fresh and lingering, she knew. And that helped.

Inside the office, Morrissey rubbed his temples with work-calloused hands, a study in disapproval against a background of filing cabinets and bookshelves. "Hooper," he grunted, indicating the cracked green leather chair opposite his desk. "Sit."

There was none of his daughter's sympathy in his tone. Then again, I didn't really deserve it. "I came to tell you—"

"Save your breath. I already know." I wondered exactly what version Thomas had given him, but I didn't try to protest. He sighed, long and loud. "Between this and the army inspection, it's been a long day."

Curiosity cut through my guilt. "An inspection, sir?"

His hand waved vaguely at a stack of paperwork. "I got the telegram yesterday. Something about the Red Cross and the YMCA and some negative press reports about Civilian Public Service camps. How they chose this spike camp to send someone out to, I'll never know."

That kicked awake a sleeping corner of suspicion. "Does it have anything to do with Jack's injury?"

"Doubt it," Morrissey grumbled. "For one thing, the army doesn't make decisions fast enough." He squinted at me. "But don't change the subject, Hooper. Martin told me about the incident."

I looked down at my hands, so different from the tight fists they'd been less than an hour before. "Yes, sir."

He sighed heavily. "When we agreed to work with the army to let you fellows help out the forestry department, one of my rangers joked, 'At least we won't have fights breaking out like in the Civilian Conservation Corps days.'" Morrissey ran his hands through his hair, like I was personally responsible for some of the new gray growth. "Well, here we are."

"I'm sorry, sir." What else was there to say? "It was wrong of me."

"You better be careful, son. That temper of yours is going to get you in real trouble someday."

As if it hadn't already.

"I know." But knowing didn't seem to help. Every time I thought I'd beaten my anger down, it found a way to pop back up again for another round, looking, sounding, feeling just like my father. I hated that, just the way I'd hated him.

After some hemming and hawing, Morrissey decided to take me off KP duty for the day and sentence me to fix the latrine roof. By the time the supper bell rang and I came down, that latrine had old slate shingles yanked off and new asphalt ones slapped on. I'd spent so long smelling the contents of the latrine that I couldn't tell if I smelled any better myself. My fingers felt cold enough to fall off, and besides that, I'd skipped lunch, too embarrassed to face the other fellows.

My stomach growled and so did the rest of me, especially when I saw Thomas leaning against the bell tower between the ranger station and the cookhouse.

I kept my steps even and my eyes just slightly down. *Don't look at him. Don't think about what he said.*

Eventually, I'd find the courage to apologize. When I could say I was sorry and mean it, when it wouldn't feel like a betrayal to Jack. But not today.

Then I frowned, noticing that, instead of the usual line outside the cookhouse before Mrs. Edith let us all in, there was a crowd around the ranger station, rangers and smokejumpers talking among themselves.

"What's going on, fellows?" I asked, joining them. They parted to let me in, and I realized that it was a miracle, something newsworthy happening just now. Maybe everyone would forget about my punching Thomas.

"The army sent a WAC," Jimmy said, his voice near awed, "and a pretty one, too."

I frowned. "A WAC?" Was that some kind of weapon?

"You know, a woman soldier. Except I don't think they do any fighting," Shorty added hurriedly, probably noticing my frown. "Mostly support."

I was halfway through wondering what kind of woman would don a man's uniform to go to war when the station door opened.

Now I was staring too . . . but not for the same reason as the other men. Because when I finally met the gaze of the uniformed army agent sent to report back on our spike camp, I saw the same bright eyes and enthusiastic smile that had fascinated me three years earlier.

It was Dorie Armitage.

CHAPTER II

Dorie Armitage

January 19, 1945

There's nothing like seeing the man who broke your heart and broke up your family shocked speechless.

I'd wondered if Gordon had requested the same CPS camp as Jack. And there he was, looking like a trout on a bank, flopping with his mouth gaping open.

Good to see you too, Gordon.

I smiled just the slightest bit, and he slammed his mouth shut, face pale. He was still handsome in a boy-next-door sort of way, but not at his best today, wearing grimy clothes, his blond hair matted to his head with sweat.

Morrissey cleared his throat behind me, and I stepped aside to make room for him. In his hands, he clutched the letter of recommendation—forged by Bea's secretarial skills—from Captain Petmencky and Major Hastings, explaining my purpose here, and he stood straight as the evergreens that fringed the clearing. "Men, this is Private First Class Nora Hightower. She's been sent by the army to evaluate our camp. She'll be here for—"

Here he turned to me, clearly realizing I hadn't yet supplied that detail. I smiled brightly. "Until I have enough information to satisfy

THE LINES BETWEEN US

the War Department." Though if I didn't return to Fort Lawton by January thirtieth, when my furlough was up, I'd have to come up with an explanation that didn't involve desertion.

"She will be scheduling times to interview you about your experience here," Morrissey continued. "I would ask you to cooperate fully with her, since, as you know, this camp is funded by the army."

Some of the younger men, the ones not wearing Forest Service uniforms, flinched at that. My, the COs didn't care to be under War Department control, did they?

"But, sir, that's . . . she's—" It was Gordon, who clamped his mouth shut almost as soon as the words left his mouth, the half-stricken look still plain as day on his face.

"Do you have something to say, Hooper?" Morrissey asked. Whatever he saw in Gordon's absurdly transparent expression prompted his next question: "Is PFC Hightower a friend of yours?"

My breath hitched.

Don't. You. Dare.

Instead of shaking his head, Gordon paused, and every nerve in my body tensed, because I knew.

He was going to announce I was Jack's sister, right there and then, in front of everyone.

It came back in a flash, a memory from three years ago. Gordon, sitting across the hearth from me, orange-gold in the light, telling a story about how he'd once been tricked into buying rocks from an eight-year-old swindler. I could barely breathe, I was laughing so hard. "Gordon Hooper, you're telling me a fib," I'd managed, gathering in a deep breath.

It was like someone had doused him with a bucket of water, the way all the laughter went out of his eyes. "I don't lie, Dorie," he'd said, adorably earnest. "I've known a liar, and I will not be like him. Not ever."

"What was your name again?"

I blinked at Gordon's question, yanked forward three years and a few heartbreaks, away from the golden glow and into the bright January sunshine. The way he looked at me, I could see the struggle inside, like our old connection and his conscience were arm wrestling to see who'd win out.

"Nora," I said without a single stammer or stutter. "PFC Nora Hightower." And I stared right back, trying to twist that arm down.

The half second he took to turn back to Mr. Morrissey felt like enough time for me to get my first gray hair. "I don't have any friends in the military, sir. And I've never met a Nora Hightower."

I gave him a generic smile, but inside, I was ticking off his statements. Not a one of them a lie, if not fully true either.

How did he do that?

And why did he feel he had to?

The rangers and COs were still staring at me, and I realized that was my cue. I gave a slight bow in their direction. "Thank you for your gracious welcome. I look forward to speaking with each of you."

A young man who somehow managed to keep up his tanned good looks even in the dead of winter shot his hand into the air.

"Yes, Schumacher, what is it?" Morrissey said it wearily.

Instead of answering, the young man turned to me, indicating my barracks bag, abandoned outside of the ranger station. "Do you need help hauling your luggage, ma'am? Because I'm the strongest one at this camp, no question about that." A bearded fellow behind him snorted in disapproval.

It seemed, in uniform or out, there was always a flirt among the bunch. "What's your name?"

He beamed. "Shorty Schumacher, ma'am, from Wooster, Ohio."

Which made me laugh, given that the man in question was

head-and-shoulders taller than me, and they'd had to let out the hem of my uniform skirt to get the right size. "Well, Shorty, as for your offer, I've been in the WAC for over two years now. And if there's one thing that's taught me, it's to never accept help from the most eager male volunteer." I strutted down the three stairs to the level of the men and made a show of scanning the crowd, then pointed straight at Gordon. "You!"

The gaping-trout look made a reprise. "Me?"

"Yes. Would you help carry my things? It looks like you're already"—I sniffed deliberately, as if I'd caught a whiff of him on the breeze—"*fragrant* from hard work. So this won't change much."

Shorty hooted and swatted Gordon on the back. He blushed, poor thing. I'd forgotten how easily he did that. "Where to?"

"The Morrisseys have been kind enough to let me stay with them for the rest of my visit."

Which wasn't the full story, of course. Earl Morrissey had been careful to introduce me to his daughter and secretary, Sarah Ruth, a petite, trouser-wearing woman whose handshake felt like a test of character. I'd returned it with an equally firm grip.

When she heard I'd planned to stay at the motel in town and have a ranger drive me in each day, she wouldn't hear of it. "It's not safe, a woman alone in a dump like that. Besides, Dad, you know I'll be gone this next week. She can have my room."

She hadn't said where she'd be off to, and I hadn't felt like pressing, since I was busy weighing the pros and cons of staying with the Morrisseys. I'd be closer to the men, able to get answers more quickly. But keeping up my charade directly under the district ranger's nose could get complicated.

Thankfully, I enjoyed complications.

Once we were away from the rest of the lot, all dismissed to supper, I took a longer look at Gordon. He'd filled out since the last time we'd met—hefted my bulging canvas barracks bag like it was a petite valise—but what caught me most was the fact that he refused to meet my eyes.

Embarrassed to see me, Gordon?

Or embarrassed by me?

"Well, well, well." I spoke after checking over my shoulder to make sure we didn't have any eavesdroppers lurking beside the national forest buildings on either side of the path. "Sure are a long way from New York, aren't you, Gordon?"

He had been the first city boy to be sweet on me. Unlike the farmers' sons with their dirty fingernails and stumbling speech, Gordon wore a faded but store-bought suit, dreamed of travel, even quoted philosophers and poets. Too often, in my opinion, but still, there was something polished about Gordon Hooper that couldn't help catching a girl's eye.

Now, wearing muddy boots and a sweat-stained shirt under a tattered coat, he could be any old corn-fed day laborer. *How far the mighty have fallen.*

His head flicked in my general direction, if only for a moment. "What are you doing here, Dorie?"

I planted my hands on my hips. "What do you mean? You practically summoned me."

His mouth worked to form words, and only puffs of white came out in the cold air. I'd never seen debate champion Gordon Hooper at such a loss. Then again, I'd only really seen him for five days at Thanksgiving three years earlier, palling around with Jack. Could I really be surprised that I'd made him into a more impressive figure than he really was?

"Dorie, I didn't . . . You weren't supposed to . . ." He seemed to give up on both of those options and landed on something more straightforward. "Are you actually in the Women's Army Corps?"

Hadn't I thought from time to time that Gordon Hooper would have a conniption if he knew I'd spent the war in uniform? This was even better than I'd planned.

"I've been a WAC for over two years now," I said with dignity, "which you'd know if you weren't hiding away in some forest, waiting for the war to end."

He didn't take the bait. "Did you . . . are you fighting, then?"

I was tempted to make up some nonsense about my prowess with a machine gun but decided against it. "Our weapons are switchboards, air-traffic control headsets, and, in my case, a ratchet and the occasional blowtorch, but I'm as military as any South Pacific–bound GI, thank you very much. Now if you'd listen—"

"But you're not really here to conduct a report for the army, are you?"

I took a deep breath. "Gordon, I know you're very smart, and it's difficult for you, but will you shut up for just one second and let me talk?"

Which he did, worry still etched in lines across his face, making him look older than his—what was it?—twenty-five years.

I took advantage of the silence to drop my next line, one that had echoed in my mind all throughout the bone-rattling train ride here: "What if what happened to Jack wasn't an accident?"

He must have expected it, because he only paused a moment before countering, "Anything can go wrong with fires, Dorie. It's awful, but it happens."

The soothing way he talked, the outright pity in his eyes, made me place my hands firmly on my hips and scowl. "You're the one who said you were worried because no one would answer your questions. And now you're backing down?"

"Listen, Dorie, I've been thinking about this for days." He set the barracks bag down on the well-worn dirt path, jamming his hands into his pocket. "Say Jack snooped into something he shouldn't have, or made someone angry, or got into trouble."

I'd thought about all those scenarios, wondered who on earth would be enemies with Jack.

"Imagine someone . . . attacked him out there in the woods," Gordon went on, his Adam's apple bobbing as if that were hard to say aloud. "Then, what, did they start a fire to cover up the evidence? That's ridiculous."

I frowned. Was he right? If this were a detective novel, I was stuck in the first-chapter suspicion of foul play, while Gordon had flipped to the accusation at the ending. It was a bit farfetched when you looked at it that way.

Still, as with any story, there was a lot of missing information in between.

"I don't know what the connection could be, but I'm going to find out. Unlike you, I don't abandon questions when there is no easy answer."

"That isn't fair."

I shrugged. "The way I see it, all's fair in love and war, and we're dealing with both."

"You don't love Jack. If you did, you wouldn't have abandoned him."

I took the breath that had caught at the accusation and pushed it out into a sharp reply. "Who did the abandoning, Gordon? Was it me . . . or the two of you? Abandoning your families and your duty to your country?"

There. His jaw tightened, like he was holding something back. I'd finally scraped something under the calluses of his rational philosopher self, and he didn't have an answer. "Now, are you going to help me or not?"

Confusion replaced anger in the space of a second. "Help you?"

"That's what I said." It wasn't how I'd meant to make my request, but there was no going back now. "I'm an outsider asking questions, trying to get some idea of what happened, but you know these men. Surely if someone suspected anything was afoot, they'd tell you."

"What if nothing is—" he grimaced as if it pained him to say the word—"*afoot*?"

I'd wondered that myself on the trip from Seattle, so I told him the only answer that satisfied me. "Then at least we'll know." My voice dropped lower. "I read that radio scene you sent, where 'Mr. Jackson' said he'd do anything to find out what happened to his sister. Well . . . maybe it's my turn."

It was like I was looking at the old Gordon, the one from my memories, flushed with firelight reflecting from the hearth, ready to listen to all of my ideas and dreams.

And so I aimed with the only line I was sure would reach the man I hoped he still was, deep down. Not the one who had made excuses about ethics to the draft board. The one who was a decent person and my brother's best friend. "Please, Gordon. For Jack."

Errol Flynn as Robin Hood couldn't have struck a blow so true.

Gordon studied me in the way that had made me blush back in the old days. Now it only made me impatient. "Would I have to lie?"

I couldn't help letting out a frustrated breath. "The whole point of this is to find out the truth." Couldn't he see that?

"But would I have to lie?" he repeated.

"Maybe not. You could just ask questions on my behalf."

"I'll think about it," he said finally, after a pause long enough that, if you asked me, he could have thought about it then and saved us the trouble. With a grunt, he hefted up my barracks bag and started down the path again.

At least it wasn't an outright no this time. "Trust me, Gordon. It's the right thing to do."

"Trust *Nora Hightower*?" The way he stressed the false name, with the slightest smirk, made me itch to fire off a comeback. But my quiver of wit was empty.

That could mean only one thing. Gordon Hooper's conscience was my mortal enemy. Again.

CHAPTER 12

Gordon Hooper

January 19, 1945

If he'd just gone home after dinner instead of hanging around, we wouldn't have had to deal with him at all. Could have lit our bonfire and gone about our business, no one bothered.

But no, there Jimmy Morrissey stood, only a dozen yards away, leaning against a fence and smoking—or holding a cigarette between his fingers anyway. I'd seen him turn as green as bread-mold once when he'd actually taken a long drag on it.

Seated on the fallen logs that surrounded the rusty bonfire barrel, we watched the pinprick marking his mouth glow red in the semi-darkness just beyond our ring of fire and warmth.

"Well, anyone gonna invite him?" Charlie said, putting into words what we were all thinking.

"Like Jack always used to" was the unspoken rest of the sentence, and also the reason everyone, from Third John balling up newspaper to the quiet Bontrager brothers to Thomas with his still-swollen nose, looked at me.

"Blessed are the peacemakers."

I'd failed at that once already today. Maybe I could make up for it now.

"I will," I forced myself to say, rising to a stand. Charlie gave me an encouraging smile, but my feet still felt heavy as I dragged myself over to the fence.

Maybe with Roger gone and after what had happened to Jack . . . maybe this time . . .

Jimmy looked up as he heard my footsteps crunching toward him on the rocky path, and the glow of the cigarette travelled toward his mouth for a quick puff, as if to prove he really was smoking. "What are *you* doing here?"

An excellent question.

"We've got popcorn," I blurted.

Good opening, Gordon. It was like I was asking a girl to the high school dance. Which, come to think of it, I never had. Maybe then I'd have more practice at awkward situations.

"If you'd like to join us, I mean," I added. "For the bonfire."

"You don't really want me there." But even as he said the words, the way he glanced over at the distant glow of the fire told me it wasn't popcorn he was hungry for.

Connection. One of humankind's basic needs, the philosophers agreed. The COs had it together. I was no socialite, but I'd never been with a group of people who understood me the way my fellow pacifists did. Did Jimmy have any friends like that, with his brother dead and Roger deployed?

We stood there for a moment, staring into the dark, each waiting for the other to speak next.

I tried my best. "Have you heard anything from Roger yet?"

He shrugged. "Nah. Said he'd write, but you know Rog."

I didn't, actually, other than the fact that Roger had a large vocabulary of insults. "Why didn't you join up with him? You're eighteen, aren't you?"

Jimmy's eyes turned to slits. "Nineteen."

We were back to one-word answers. This didn't seem like the right direction. I waited for an explanation, or at least an excuse, but none came. "Think you have a right to know all about my life, huh?"

Under his glare, I felt the same sensation as when I stepped out of the plane: like I was plummeting helplessly, with no way to stop or slow down. "I only wondered—"

"I don't want to come to your stupid bonfire, all right?" He puffed the cigarette in my face for emphasis, the effect ruined by the fact it made him hack out a smoke-ridden cough.

We were changing subjects so quickly that it almost made me dizzy. "Why not?"

"Because you . . . you think you're so much better than the rest of us." He nodded, scowling. "All of you with your fancy diplomas and vocabularies . . . it makes me sick."

For every one of us who came to our convictions in academic halls, there were three more born-and-raised Mennonite farm boys like Shorty, who'd dropped out of school at age ten to help with harvesting. We COs were the strangest family the US had known—Protestants, Catholics, Jehovah's Witnesses, atheists. Philosophers and filling station attendants, married men and confirmed bachelors, city boys like me and some who had never seen a building more than three stories tall in their lives.

I tried to think of how to say all of that, but the right words seemed to be just out of reach. "But didn't your brother go to college?"

He snorted. "Yeah, and look where that got him."

"I don't understand what you mean." What was going on here? From what I knew, everyone in the Morrissey family had loved William, but the way Jimmy was glaring at me . . .

"It's none of your business. Don't talk to me about Willie. And

132

leave me alone. I was doing just fine before you got here." He threw the cigarette on the ground and twisted it into the dirt with his foot.

Sorry, Jack. I tried.

"Hullo there, boys!" a cheerful voice sang out, and Dorie stepped from behind the ranger station, wrapped snugly in a pleated blue coat with a fur collar. Under the pale white of the camp's only streetlight, a concession that Morrissey hated because it dimmed his beloved stars, she seemed almost to glow. "I was told there was a bonfire around here. Want to point me in the right direction?"

Jimmy mutely jutted out a signpost arm, as if she could miss the only other light source among the dark-windowed national forest complex.

"Super," she enthused. "And you must be Jimmy Morrissey. You look the spitting image of your sister."

"Yeah. That's me." I recognized the half-stunned look on his face, one Dorie probably received from every male she encountered.

"Your mother sent me over to get to know you fellows before I begin the interviews tomorrow."

Interrogations, she meant. Did she really think she could disguise her questions about the fire that killed Jack as an innocuous army report?

"So, what do you say?" she asked, smiling widely enough to throw out a beam of heat. "Are you game to join us?"

"Nah," he said, backing away a step. "Can't. I've got . . . plans."

"Suit yourself," Dorie said cheerfully, ignoring the obvious excuse. "But we'll be here all night if you change your mind." And, of all things, she grabbed my arm, tucked in snugly beside me.

"Start walking," she whispered. "He'll follow eventually."

Fat chance.

I kept my voice low too. "What are you really doing here?"

"Like I said, I want to get to know the boys. Gosh, Gordon, not *everything* I say is a lie."

"Can you blame me for wondering?"

She ignored that jab. "Plus, Sarah Ruth was packing for some trip, and dear Edith was cleaning for my arrival. I didn't want to be underfoot."

Maybe she'll be a good distraction. After all, hadn't I thought how awkward it would be without Jack to keep the conversation going, draw out the shy fellows, and rattle off one of his stories or riddles?

I wasn't like that. Give me time to plan what to say and I could make a decent enough showing, but small talk was so . . . small. Anyone could see what the weather was, no one needed to rehash an entire baseball game, and what was the point of asking how people were doing when they'd just say they were fine? But it's not like you could just sit down at a dinner party and say, "What do you think are the dangers and advantages of labor unions?"

The moment we got within earshot, Shorty popped on up like Wonder Bread out of a toaster, all grins. "Well, if it isn't our favorite WAC! Come on and join us, Miss Hightower."

Others seemed wary, edging away from the log Shorty gestured to.

"Now tell me, boys, do you do this every night?" Dorie asked, settling neatly on the log, her legs crossed at the ankles.

"Just Fridays," Second John volunteered. "We have a later start before chores tomorrow morning, and then . . ." His eyes suddenly widened, and I turned. *Please don't let it be another raccoon in the cookhouse trash.*

Only to see Jimmy Morrissey shuffling over, hands jammed in his coat pockets.

When I looked at Dorie, she was smirking back, bringing out the dimple on her left cheek.

I stepped aside to widen the circle and let Jimmy in. "Welcome. We're glad to have you."

One quick glance up at my face as he passed, that was all. "Thanks." He looked at the other fellows, who were openly staring. "I heard there was popcorn."

And even I had to admit that, for all her faults, Dorie Armitage had done at least one good thing tonight.

Later, after the fire flickered to glowing embers and some of the banter had died down, Shorty made his usual request: "Who's got a story?"

It was no surprise when Dorie stood to a few hoots of appreciation for the "new girl."

But it *was* a surprise when the first words that left her mouth were, "Gather round, my children, and listen to a tale that's truly true."

I saw my frozen expression reflected in a ring around the fire.

We'd heard those words before, nearly every week. And we all knew perfectly well who usually spoke them.

In the sudden quiet, Dorie's eyebrows lurched up just a fraction. Did she realize what she'd just done?

Help her.

But what was I supposed to do?

"Say," Third John piped up, "who do you think you are? Jack?"

Only the barest second of a pause passed before she tilted her head and asked, "Who's Jack?"

I knew she was only covering for herself, but it still rankled, hearing her dismiss her own brother so easily.

"The fellow who started every story with that line," Lloyd finally answered. "He's gone now."

"Ooh," she said slowly, turning to me with a smile. "So that's why Mr. Hooper told me to say that. I thought it was just a tradition."

They relaxed, even Lloyd . . . all except me. *Ah, that makes sense,* they were thinking, accepting the quick lie because they wanted to trust the woman telling it.

The distraction dealt with, Dorie launched into a saga of the imaginary cat her fellow WACs pretended to have by setting out dishes of milk—Bogie, named after Humphrey Bogart.

But I couldn't focus, couldn't laugh along with her punchlines or the caricatured imitation of the furious cook searching for a cat who never appeared. Sure, I wasn't speaking the lies, but I sat there while Dorie did, not contradicting her, which felt just as bad. At least that's what Quaker ethics would tell me.

"To this day," Dorie said, her voice all mischief and merriment, "Cook still inspects us for cat hair when we come on KP duty, and she swears she's heard a cat in the hall. Just like this." Her voice changed to an inquisitive meow, then a rumble of a surprisingly realistic purr.

This drew appreciative applause, and Dorie threw herself into a bow.

I busied myself with adding another log to the fire as the others debated who would have to follow that act. Shorty, not taking the hint that I wasn't volunteering, piped up. "How about you, Gordon?"

I fell back on the line my own mother had used a hundred times: "Nothing dramatic has ever happened to me."

As I said it, I relived it all again in my mind: the limp hand sticking out just past the back tire, the choking fumes, the sirens, too late to do any good.

Hadn't I said I never lied?

*That's personal. A family matter. They don't need to know about
that.*

"Why don't you tell them about Clara?" Dorie suggested.

I stiffened. Nora Hightower wouldn't know about Clara Hooper,
not if we'd just met.

But I didn't say that, of course. If they questioned her, Dorie
would throw out another lie, and they'd all believe her. Again.

And I would say nothing. Again.

"Oooh, Claaara," Shorty singsonged, batting his eyelashes furi-
ously, the way he always did when the conversation turned to girls
back home. "Who's that?"

I raised a brow. "She was my great-great-grandmother."

"Oh." Shorty deflated, but only temporarily, having a large backup
stash of hot air to refill with. "Well, go on. What was so special
about her?"

"I don't tell stories." Not like Jack.

Dorie clicked her tongue. "Oh pish. That's no excuse. We want
to hear about her, don't we, boys?" There was a general chorus of
agreement.

I glared at her. She smiled warmly. And all the others waited.

There was nothing to do but to launch in. "My Quaker ancestor
Clara Hooper was born all the way back in 1821. Nearly every slave
who passed through her doors made it all the way to freedom in
Canada."

I told them what I knew, the stories my mother had passed
on about a relative with real courage and conviction. About the
false-bottomed wagon she used to deliver her husband's carpentry
work—along with extra cargo. About the hidden root cellar dug
deep and wide and filled with blankets and provisions. About one
man who'd come all the way from Louisiana, nearly mad from
being bit by a rabid animal, and how she had nursed him back to

health without getting caught by Hiram Bates, the shifty local sheriff.

"Seems too crazy to believe," Shorty said, shaking his head. "You're not making this up, are you?"

I shook my head. "My mother found and transcribed Clara's diary, recording the names of the freedmen and women she helped, along with stories of their escape."

Lloyd stood and stirred the fire, casting a long and eerie shadow. "What happened to the ones who didn't make it?"

I frowned. "What do you mean?"

"You said that 'nearly' all of the slaves escaped. That implies that some did not. What about them?"

Leave it to aspiring lawyer Lloyd to notice a detail like that. I searched my memory through all of the tales Mother had told about Clara as she referred to her diary with its spindle-thin handwriting. I couldn't think of an answer.

"Guess I never asked. I'm sure they were caught somewhere along the way and sent back. Mother always did like stories with happy endings." Probably because her own life didn't have enough of them.

"I know all about that," Dorie chimed in. "I about threw my umbrella at the screen when the credits rolled on *Casablanca*. What's the point of crying when you can laugh?"

"And that," Shorty broke in, tossing a candy bar wrapper into the fire so it flared up, "is why I ought to get to go next."

Despite groans, Shorty insisted that Miss Hightower, at least, hadn't heard this one, and regaled us all with the time Sarah Ruth Morrissey, in her lumberjack alter ego as Paulette Bunyan, tamed and rode an elk through the Cascade Mountains to deliver an urgent message to the national park there.

All of it nonsense, but Shorty told it with a perfectly straight face, and it was nice to hear a woman's laughter weaving in with ours.

By the time curfew approached and we'd doused the fire—checked and double-checked for any embers—I'd almost forgotten some of my worries about Jack, about the future, about what Dorie was doing here.

Almost. But it never quite left me, the feeling that things weren't what they should be.

Don't worry. He'll recover and be back here in no time. That's what Dorie would assure me, and that night, I chose to believe it, because I didn't want to think about the alternative.

CHAPTER 13

Dorie Armitage

January 20, 1945

Typically, a detective's initial investigation produces a long list of the victim's enemies, indiscretions, and clandestine activities. Jilted lovers, mobster cousins, gambling debts, embezzlement, blackmail, that sort of thing.

But my interview with First and Third John as they swept the mess hall hadn't produced a speck of dust on Jack. Oh, we'd gotten around to the subject of the fire. An enthusiastic description of the thrill of smokejumping had turned suddenly sober when I asked if anyone ever got hurt. But they'd passed along the party line: One of their men was injured in an accident a week before. He'd been well liked, responsible, and hardworking.

The only fragment of information I'd gained was simple but possibly useful: Thomas Martin hadn't gotten along with Jack.

"He doesn't get along with most people, though," Third John added, ducking his head at a reproachful look from First John. "Anyway, I heard them fighting not too long before . . . you know. The accident."

I was fairly sure I remembered a Thomas from the bonfire the night before, the dour-looking fellow with a short, dark beard and

140

an ugly bruise under his eye. His glare had fallen often enough in my direction that I suspected my military credentials didn't impress him. "Do you know where Mr. Martin might be now?"

"Behind the ranger station. He got sent to chop wood with Jimmy Morrissey."

To keep my cover of an official report, I asked them a few meaningless questions about the food quality and medical care, taking notes as if all of it mattered. By the time I'd broken away, Jimmy was alone, leaning against a stack of newly cut wood with his nose in a comic book, which he tried to hide behind his back when he saw me.

"You just missed him," he said when I asked after Thomas. "Started the walk into town only ten minutes ago to go to the hardware store. Why d'you want to talk to *him*?"

"Nothing much. I just hear he's the one to go to for lighthearted conversation."

Jimmy frowned and cocked his head, like he was wondering why the War Department would need that. Then his face brightened. "Say, I was thinking of going into town today. If you want someone to walk you there."

That was a thought. Sure, I could wait until Thomas came back, but this could be a good chance to get him alone—and to ask Jimmy Morrissey a few pointed questions along the way.

So that's how I ended up jaunting down a dirt road toward civilization, enjoying the warmth of the sun on my face and listening to Jimmy recall the entire plot of the latest Superman comic to me after I foolishly feigned interest. It took me the whole trip to find a gap to transition the conversation to what I really wanted to discuss.

"Did Superman ever rescue anyone from a fire, Jimmy?"

You could see him mentally flipping through a dusty archive

of hundreds of dogeared comic books before blurting, "Sure! The one about the circus. They made a Technicolor cartoon of it. Lois Lane was cornered by a giant gorilla, see—"

"Oh my," I said, trying to head this one off, "but what about—"

"—and Superman tried to rescue her, only he wrestled the gorilla right into the power lines and set the tent on fire." Jimmy gestured to an imaginary canvas stretching up above him. "Then he saved the day by snatching Lois out of the flames just in time."

"Fascinating." By now, we'd made it from the dirt road to the paved main street of Clayton, two miles from the national forest's entrance. It reminded me of my own hometown: the storefronts faded but neat, inviting displays in their windows, and folks who nodded at you as you passed by.

I tried again to gain control of the situation before I heard a summary of every Technicolor superhero cartoon ever made. "Wouldn't it be nice if all fires were that easy to deal with? No one getting hurt?"

If he caught my implication, he sure didn't show it as he nodded eagerly. "I'd take Superman over our crew any day. Wouldn't that make digging the fire line easy!"

I sighed. Apparently, subtlety wasn't the right approach. Time for another attempt. "Speaking of which, I heard about an awful fire just last week. Were you there, Jimmy?"

Almost instantly, the excitement faded from his eyes. "No."

"But a man was injured fighting it."

"Yeah," he said, staring down at the sidewalk.

We'd gone from full soliloquies to one-word answers in the space of a single question. Normally, that would look suspicious, but Jimmy looked more afraid than guilty. He was, after all, just a kid, and I imagined Jack's burns had been terrible to look at.

"Do accidents like that happen often?"

He shook his head. "Hardly ever, especially with a fire that small. That's what I tried to tell Ma." His voice rose defensively. "She wants me to quit smokejumping now."

"Ah. I see." That explained his sudden sour mood.

"It's not fair."

"Very little in life is." I instantly hated myself for quoting Sergeant Bloom's favorite line.

"Well, we've made it." Jimmy pointed down the road a piece to a storefront so crowded with signs—*Varnish and Paint*, *We Have Batteries*, *Plumbing and Electrical Sale*—that there was no room for the goods they claimed to stock. "And there's Thomas."

Ahead of us, I recognized the bearded man in a dark coat on his way out of the hardware store.

Excellent.

Now, how to get rid of Jimmy?

I quickly scanned the signs until I saw one I could use. "Would you mind leaving me here and catching up with me later?" I asked innocently. "After I speak to Thomas, I have to stop by the drugstore to pick up some . . . lady things."

Sure enough, I saw heat creep up the back of Jimmy's neck toward his face to match his nose, red from cold. "Is twenty minutes long enough?" From the panic in his expression, he clearly had no idea how long it took to purchase "lady things" and wasn't about to ask for details.

I tried desperately to contain a laugh. "That would be plenty."

"Okay. I'll be . . ." Whatever reason, real or invented, he'd originally had for coming to town had apparently fled his mind. "Going to Casey's. Sure. You want a soda, Miss Hightower?"

Excellent. An interrogation followed by a personal beverage delivery. "I'd love that," I said, adding extra charm to my smile. "If they have any Grapette, I'll take one."

Two swaggering teenagers crossed the road in front of us, the sort who probably got detention at least once a week.

One of them jerked a nod at Jimmy as he passed, and he barely raised his hand in response. In fact, I thought I'd imagined it, until I stepped off the sidewalk and Jimmy said, real quiet, "Hey, Miss Armitage? Stay away from those fellows, all right?"

I played innocent. "Friends of yours?"

He muttered something I couldn't quite make out, then hurried away in the other direction, on a quest for Grapette.

Of course, there was almost no chance I'd be avoiding his cronies, because they were headed directly for Thomas Martin, who clutched a small brown paper bag.

It wasn't hard to figure out what was going to happen next. Jimmy's friends had voices that carried to me as I crossed the street, raised several notches by bluster and bravado.

"Aren't you gonna answer me, conchie?" The fellow with curly dark hair tore the bag from Thomas's hand, and as the paper fell away, it unleashed a rain of small, dark pebbles that scattered across the sidewalk and into the gutter.

No, not pebbles. Sunflower seeds.

"Nah, I bet he hasn't got a tongue *or* a spine." The blond one shoved Thomas square in the middle of his chest, and he stumbled off the curb, falling to the pavement.

Blondie was raising his boot-clad foot to kick Thomas while he was down when I brought out my best sergeant snarl. "What's going on here?"

And didn't they jump like the schoolboys they were, turning to face the wrath of the teacher. Dunce caps for both of them.

They relaxed a bit once they realized I was a stranger, not one of their mothers or the preacher's wife or any other female with real authority in their lives.

144

"He's a yellow-bellied conchie, lady," Blondie said, clearly expecting that to be enough of an answer. Thomas struggled to his feet, slightly favoring his right leg.

I smirked, keeping their attention squarely on me. "Oh, I'm seeing a display of cowardice, all right, but it's not from him."

The leader's attitude changed almost instantly from bravado to hostility. "This is none of your business." He grabbed my arm, as if to yank me away.

In a flash, I flexed my arm against his, tightening my grip before twisting loose like we'd learned in training. He rubbed his arm where I'd broken free. "Say, what's your problem?"

That does it. I took off my coat, yanking my arms out one at a time, and the brown-haired stooge hooted, "She's gonna fight you, Elmer!"

Elmer's bravado and shoulders drooped, as if he was contemplating whether he should hit a girl, until he noticed the uniform I'd revealed. "Y-you're a soldier?"

"That's right. A bona fide GI Jane. And I'd like to order a retreat." When they didn't move, I added, "Yours. Now."

And didn't they just scatter like dandelions in the wind.

I chuckled to myself. By this time tomorrow, the whole town would know a WAC had arrived in Flintlock Mountain District.

Thomas was trying to brush the dirt from his pants where he'd hit the ground. He looked up only briefly, and I noticed bruising around his right eye. From the bullies? No, it had been there before, at the bonfire. "You shouldn't have done that. 'Vengeance is mine; I will repay, saith the Lord.'"

I smiled jauntily. "Well, what do you know? God decided to repay by sending me to shout some sense into two knuckle-headed bullies."

When he bent down to scoop up some of the scattered birdseed, I joined him. He shoveled a few handfuls into his pocket, but much of it had gotten into the gutter or was scattered in the slush-ridden dents and dimples of the street. "Are you going back to buy more?"

He shook his head. "Can't. We only get paid a few dollars per month."

Was he exaggerating? That was practically slavery. "Why do you spend some of it on birdseed, then?"

"We've got a feeder near the bunkhouse. I like to have something cheerful to look at in the winter."

"Oh." I'd been expecting something a bit more high-minded.

"Also, as the Scriptures say, 'Behold the fowls of the air: for they sow not, neither do they reap, nor gather into barns; yet your heavenly Father feedeth them.'"

There it was. "Your heavenly Father picks up the hardware store tab, eh?" I dropped the seed I'd collected into his cupped palms, then thrust my hands back into my pockets to get some warmth.

"No. But I'm the son of my Father, and I do my best to keep up the family resemblance." He nodded his thanks, but I could see disdain under the polite veneer. "Thank you for your help. If that's all, I'd like to get back."

I couldn't let him leave before I'd asked him anything. "Actually, would you mind escorting me to . . ." Where was it Jimmy had said? "Casey's. Jimmy Morrissey is meeting me there."

The conflict between what Thomas wanted to do and what he knew he ought to do was clear on his face. "All right," he finally said, duty winning the round.

I got the feeling that with Thomas Martin, duty won every round.

He beelined down the street, clearly in no mood for light conversation, but I dogged his steps, grateful for those physical training drills at boot camp. "I've been talking to some of the other men for my report. Jack Armitage and his terrible accident keep coming up."

"I'm sure."

Once again, the conversation took a verbal bullet to the heart and died without another sound.

Maybe with Thomas, the key was to be direct. He seemed to share Gordon's aversion to deception in all forms. "Some of the fellows said you quarreled with Jack before he left for the lookout. Is that true?"

For a moment, there was no sound except our footsteps scuffing the sidewalk and the occasional car rumbling by on the street. "You could say that."

"That's a shame. If he doesn't make it, those will be the last words he heard from you. It's a weighty thing to have regrets."

That, at least, was true. Uncomfortably true.

Thomas stopped so suddenly that I nearly tripped over him. "I don't regret anything I said to Jack." His eyes were burning, and I felt we were on the edge of a discovery. "You see . . . I warned him."

Another long pause. Although I had a suspicion Thomas had hated every Hollywood movie since talkies were introduced, he sure seemed to borrow his sense of drama from them. "Warned him about what?"

"That I'd found this underneath his mattress." He reached into the pocket of his coat and drew out a tri-fold brochure. I took it between two fingers, half expecting to see a pinup girl, but no smoky-eyed dame smoldered out from the top page of the glossy paper. No, it was a sharp-eyed eagle under a banner for the United States Army.

Your Country Needs You, the headline read. A recruitment brochure.

There had to be some mistake. Probably someone had left it in Jack's things as a prank. "Are you sure it was Jack's?"

"I thought of that. But when I confronted him, he admitted to it. Said as he learned more about what the Axis powers were really up to, he wasn't sure what was right anymore." Thomas's voice was equal parts scorn and bewilderment, as if he still couldn't believe Jack had said something like that.

I tried to process it. After all those late-night arguments from his moral high ground, Jack had been at least considering joining the military.

Gordon didn't know, did he? No, surely he would have said something to me.

"I-I suppose that must have been a shock to you."

"I told Jack he was betraying his conscience, if that's what you mean." Thomas shook his head in disgust, too absorbed in his story to notice my surprise. "My father refused to fight in the Great War. He was court-martialed and thrown in prison for nearly three years, where the guards beat him for sport."

It sounded like the plot of a movie—one set in a country other than America. "Couldn't he have been a medic or an ambulance driver?" I had researched that option, tried to persuade Jack a 1-A-O classification was the perfect compromise. "Some kind of support staff, I mean."

"If he had, what would he have been supporting?"

The answer hung between us. War. Violence. Endless trench warfare. I'd heard from enough graying veterans to know they'd hoped brutality like that would never again call the world back to war. But it had, only twenty years later.

"I was five years old, my oldest sister seven, when Father was taken to prison," Thomas went on. The story seemed to come out of him now on its own, with no more dramatic pauses. "We did all we could to help with chores, but my father's pitchfork was twice my height. Our brethren at the church tried to make up the difference, but after one year stretched into two and it was clear no pardon was coming, we had to sell the farm. The land that had been in my family for five generations, that was supposed to be my inheritance . . . gone."

I pictured all the strong, suntanned farmer boys I'd known growing up, the proud way they bragged about the latest harvest. "That must have been very hard for you."

Thomas stopped, frowned. "I didn't say . . . that wasn't the point. But yes. It was hard." And his gaze seemed to be somewhere else for a moment. Where, I couldn't say for sure. Maybe in the schoolyard, standing up to bullies taunting him for his jailbird father. Maybe back on his favorite spot on the farm, breathing in the smell of freshly plowed dirt. Maybe on the front porch when his father came back a different man.

He's a CO, Dorie. He doesn't deserve your sympathy.

But that was silly. COs were people too, whether I disagreed with them or not. And they had their own wounds, just like Howie and the others at the base hospital.

Thomas blinked, and wherever he had been, now he was back on the slush-covered Oregon street next to me and clearly unhappy about it. "After all my family suffered, I couldn't believe Jack would just . . . abandon his beliefs like they were nothing. I was furious."

It still barely made sense. Jack, a soldier? The last time I'd spoken to him, he'd been so infuriatingly sure of himself, full of arguments and justifications.

But if Thomas was telling the truth, if he really had been furious at Jack for going against his beliefs and possibly leading others astray . . .

It was time to press. "Mad enough to hurt him?" I eyed the

bruise on his face, a blotch of variegated navy and plum. "I see he put up a fight."

"That?" His laugh was sudden and sharp. "No, Jack didn't give me that bruise. You find Gordon Hooper and ask him whether I would hurt anyone. Then you'll get your answer."

Gordon? No, he couldn't have.

But then again, what did I really know about him, other than what he claimed to believe?

I tucked the brochure away in my pocket as evidence without asking if I could keep it. "You're sure you didn't feel like the Lord needed some help revealing the truth about Jack?"

He stepped to the side to look at me, and I felt the cold of the wind for the first time, as cutting as his stare. "You really don't understand what we believe, do you? What it means to leave justice and vengeance to God?"

"Maybe I don't," I said slowly, watching him for any tell-tale sign of lying. Broken gaze. Nervous twitch. Carefully rehearsed justifications.

But Thomas just looked directly at me, as if he was suddenly the one interrogating. "As an outsider, you'll never be able to understand. But I know what I said was right."

The self-righteous air of his words grated on me, and even though I knew I should let it alone to focus on my questions, I couldn't resist. "It doesn't sound like you were especially kind."

"Kind?" His brow furrowed as if he couldn't remember the meaning of the word.

"There's more to loving your neighbors—or your enemies, for that matter—than just not killing them, you know."

He jerked his head toward me, surprise on his face for a moment. But only a moment. "Yes. Sometimes it means warning them. Like a watchman has a responsibility to raise the alarm if he sees a distant danger coming. 'Whosoever heareth the sound of the trumpet, and taketh not warning; if the sword come, and take him away, his blood shall be upon his own head.' I did my part."

Then he pointed across the street, past a filling station, to a soda fountain with *Casey's* written in punched-out metal letters over a striped awning, and turned to leave, satisfied that he'd had the final word.

Well, I couldn't let that happen. "It's not that black-and-white. About violence and all."

Thomas shook his head. "Not black-and-white. Just good and evil and the war in between."

CHAPTER 14

Gordon Hooper

January 20, 1945

Anyone who watched me slam the ranger station door knew what answer Morrissey had given me to my daily question: No, there hadn't been any change in Jack's status.

"I wouldn't get your hopes up," he'd said, sounding haggard as a hotshot after a three-day fire. "That's what happens in war, son. Not everyone makes it home."

I'd done my best to push down my frustration. "With all due respect, it's not the same thing. This isn't a battlefield."

"Might as well be." Then he practically shoved me out the door, muttering about mealtime and getting to Saturday chores.

Despite my reassurances to Dorie the night before, I couldn't help wondering whether Morrissey actually checked in with the hospital every day. Was he just trying to get rid of me?

It's just his way, being gruff like that, I told myself as Mrs. Edith heaped fried potatoes onto my plate. I couldn't let Dorie's dime-novel conspiracies get to my head.

Once I'd settled at a table in the corner, Charlie sat next to me, his coffee sloshing slightly onto his tray. "Hi, Gordon."

I forced out an unconvincing greeting in response, which he

must have noticed, because he hesitated. Then he tugged an envelope out from under his tray. "Hey, I got in my last set of pictures, including those dead birds of yours, if you want to see them."

Normally, I would have studied the stack eagerly, admiring the angles Charlie had captured and envisioning the way I'd arrange the composition of my sketches from them. Today, though, I only riffled through them, managing a few hums of approval.

Then I got to the last picture in the stack.

"I thought you might want that one too," Charlie said tentatively.

It was Jack and me, dressed in our work jeans and T-shirts, our coats flung to the side, a jagged bandsaw between us, cutting down the Christmas tree we'd put up in the cookhouse the month before. An ache cinched around my middle, seeing him with that carefree Armitage grin, waving at Charlie and the camera. While I, fresh from the hard work of sawing a massive pine, just looked tired, my halfhearted smile weary around the edges.

Still, I knew I'd keep it somewhere safe, maybe bring it out again in December, just to remember better times. "Thanks, Charlie."

"Don't mention it." He took a sip of coffee, then wrapped his hands around the mug, letting steam bloom up before he looked back at me, his dark eyes full of compassion. "We all want him back."

I glanced over at Thomas, cutting into his potatoes with perfect precision a few tables away. "You sure about that?"

He followed where I was looking. "You know ol' Thomas likes to be the one in charge. I figured he'd try to get in some kind of an insult about Jack. He doesn't mean anything by it."

I straightened the photos, keeping Jack's on top. "Could've fooled me."

"You gonna apologize to him? You know, after you . . ." He

shrugged and cleared his throat. Rumors spread quickly at Flintlock Mountain. I was sure Shorty had given an account of our fight like he was the radio announcer for a champion wrestling tournament.

"We'll see." It was a safer answer than "no" and basically amounted to "none of your business," which I couldn't outright say to Charlie, of all people, so kindhearted that he didn't like swatting spiders. "Say, what chore did you draw today?"

Not much for a change of subject, but Charlie lit into it, probably glad as I was for an escape from the awkwardness. "Cabin cleaning with Mr. Richardson. You?"

"Laundry duty." An easy job, but also one with plenty of time to stew over my worries.

I glanced down at the picture again, at Jack's straight posture, the strong arms that had torn sawdust from the massive tree behind us. So alive, especially compared to the last time I'd seen him, his body limp and scarred, carried between Morrissey and Richardson.

Now, there's an idea.

What could it hurt, really? Just so I could rest easier at night.

"Charlie," I said, trying to smile like Jack and Dorie did when they wanted to persuade someone, "I've got a favor to ask of you."

An hour later, instead of a plum job ironing shirts in the warm indoors, I found myself hacking my lungs out as I tried to sweep a chimney clean with a straw broom, bringing a swarm of coal dust into the cabin.

This is all Dorie's fault.

"Ought've brought a kerchief," Les Richardson observed, his own bearded face covered with one. Combined with the high-crowned ranger hat, he looked ready to lasso a cow or conduct a stagecoach robbery. He yanked a desiccated mouse skeleton out of a trap beside one of the bunks and flung it out the propped-open door.

Les Richardson was of the classic logger-and-cowhand ilk that used to comprise the whole Oregon Department of Forestry, the kind who didn't answer many questions and asked even fewer. He had also found Jack's body at the fire, so I'd swapped Charlie for cabin duty in hopes of learning more.

Five years ago, the department had completed a string of cabins down Antlers Trail on level ground before the terrain became steeper, leading up to the lookout. They were Morrissey's pride and joy. Only a few were occupied on weekends over the winter, but come the spring thaw, they'd be rented most every night. Until then, the only upkeep was a monthly visit to knock off any ice dams, clear out the chimneys, and check for critters.

Once I'd made another shove with the broom and held my breath to shield my lungs from the stirred-up debris, I made my opening move. "Mr. Richardson? I wondered if I could talk to you."

"Eh?" He turned a grizzled face toward me. "Nothing's stopping you. So long as you can do it while cleaning that mess."

I applied the broom to scraping the coal dust toward the door, glad that I wouldn't have to look directly at him. "Did you see anything in the fire? The one that injured Jack?"

He nodded. "Sure. Burnin' trees. And brush too." There was no sarcasm in Mr. Richardson's voice, as if he actually thought he was being helpful.

"I meant . . . a person. I thought I saw someone."

As always, it sounded crazy, like I believed in the ghost stories the rangers sometimes told us when they were feeling particularly social.

Mr. Richardson grunted and yanked his handkerchief away from his face. "I reckon you saw one of us, Hooper. Me or Morris. We was weaving in and out of the fire, looking."

I gripped my broom tighter. "Looking for what?"

For a minute, it seemed like Mr. Richardson would go back to his guarded silence, but maybe something in my expression was just desperate enough. "He had a bad feeling, Morris told me. On account of the boy didn't call in the fire."

"You were looking for Jack?" It would make sense. If Morrissey suspected something had gone wrong, that would explain why he and Richardson had taken so long circling the burn area.

"More or less." He shifted a bit. "Are you sure it's good for you to be thinking 'bout all this? Can't change the past, you know."

I wasn't about to let him off the hook that easily. "Where did you find him?"

"Near the middle. Like he'd gone charging into the center of things."

I winced and covered it by pretending to cough on the coal dust. That image of Jack as a hero, striding into the flames . . .

When I looked back up, Richardson was staring somberly at me. "Listen, Hooper. I know you were asking Morris about all this before. And he's awful cagey, 'specially when he feels it's his fault."

What was that supposed to mean? "If you and Mr. Morrissey hadn't found him as quickly as you did, he'd have died for sure." I returned to the hearth, beating the dust onto the floor to be swept cleanly away.

"I know that, and you know that, but Morris . . . he ain't sure." Mr. Richardson stood, shrugging his wide lumberjack shoulders. "Reckon it sends him back to his war days, seeing a man down like that."

I'd known that Morrissey had served in the Great War, and I'd heard stories from Shorty about shell-shocked veterans at the asylum he'd worked at before coming here. "Not all of them came back whole," he'd said, his voice unusually serious. "The kind of things they shouted . . . well, if I hadn't been against war before that, I would've been after, let me tell you."

That triggered a memory. "Morrissey told me he'd lost two men to fires. Who was the other one?"

If possible, Richardson grew even more somber. "The Basin Fire. Summer of '37. Had to call in some men from other districts, some of them not trained near well enough. One fellow got pinned in by the blaze when he should've pulled out hours before. Wasn't Morris's fault either, if you ask me, but he felt responsible, what with him assigning the lookouts and all."

Was there anything that went on at Flintlock Mountain that Morrissey didn't feel personally responsible for?

Mr. Richardson nodded and scratched at his beard. "He's a good 'un, Morris. You ever wonder why no one here's ever given you a hard time?"

I blinked at the abrupt change of subject. "I don't know what you're talking about."

"Day before you came, he gathered us all in the cookhouse. Told us we'd got some conchies coming in to fill smokejumper slots. Now, some of the rangers—I won't say who—had a problem with that. Before they'd met you and all. But Morris, he shut 'em all up. 'Every fire they put out, they'll be protecting our country just as much as the boys over there. I wouldn't wish the front line on my worst enemy.'"

He wiped sweat off his forehead with the handkerchief, as if such a long speech had taken great effort.

"He said that?"

"The very words. And the rest of us all knew his son was serving. So he had a right to say it. No one ever complained again."

Most larger CPS camps had a director and a few other staff

members from one of the peace churches or another anti-war organization who shared their values. With only a handful of men at our spike camp, we couldn't have that luxury. But even though every now and then we caught a sour look or a snide comment from the townie smokejumpers like Roger and Jimmy, the rangers had always held their peace.

And now I knew why.

The plot points were coming together, but they weren't forming the crime scene Dorie seemed to want.

I had gotten my answers. The shadowed figure I'd seen had been Morrissey or Richardson searching the area for Jack's body. Morrissey's defensiveness when I asked questions was because he was reliving the loss of his wartime buddies. The only suspicious thing about it was why Jack didn't call the fire in from the tower like he was supposed to instead of playing the hero.

And unless Jack woke up and remembered what happened, that might be a mystery we could never solve.

FROM GORDON TO HIS MOTHER

January 20, 1945

Dear Mother,

Thank you for your letter. I do think you're wrong about Walden; however, the ideal location for reading it is surrounded by the sound of running water and the smell of pines. At least I've found that to be true. Someday, maybe you'll give it another chance.

Given what happened to Jack, I understand your worry, but I can't leave. Not right now. Maybe I'll consider requesting a transfer come summer. I admit that the idea of jumping into wildfires doesn't hold even the limited appeal it did when I knew Jack would be at my side.

But for now, I want to stay at Flintlock Mountain. I need the fellows here, my CPS brothers. And perhaps, in some small way, they need me too.

Before I sign off, I have a question. It's about Great-Great Grandmother Clara's diary. Were there any escaping slaves who didn't make it North after passing through her home? I'm sure it's nothing, but you've always said "nearly," so I felt I needed to ask. You took such care in copying those stories that I don't want to get any details wrong.

It's one of my favorite memories of you, you know. Coming out late at night to get a drink of water and seeing you at the kitchen table, wrapped in your old yellow robe, painstakingly copying words from that diary. When you saw me, instead of ordering me back to bed, you invited me over, showing me how to tell the difference between a cursive e and an o in Clara's hurried handwriting, pointing out the dates in the top right corner of every new entry, telling me the diary had been hidden for years in your great-uncle's attic before being passed on to you.

"Stories have power, son," you told me. I'm not sure if I understood at the time, but I know now. I joined the CPS because of the beliefs of my church, but hearing Clara's stories made me brave enough to do it.

And it's what's left of that courage, passed down through the generations, that's keeping me here.

Your son,
Gordon

INTERVIEW WITH LLOYD ABERNATHY

January 20, 1945

Notes: Completed while hauling and stacking wood. Awfully sore. Couldn't ask much about Jack—as you can see, he was already hostile and suspicious. Didn't want to make things worse.

Me: They certainly work you hard enough here, don't they?

Lloyd: None of us are afraid of hard work, Miss Hightower.

Me: I'm glad to hear it. When it comes to your personal well-being, do you ever feel unsafe for any reason?

Lloyd: Sometimes. When I feel my rights are being violated by the government keeping us here in a condition barely over slavery. Or when military personnel interrogate us when we were promised the military would be removed from our daily lives.

Me: Do you really find me threatening, Mr. Abernathy? I'm only here to ask a few simple questions.

Lloyd: I find what you represent threatening. And it makes me wonder: Why are y'all interested in us now, three years in? We'd gotten the idea you were content to let us live out the rest of the war in peace, as long as we didn't bother you.

Me: That is a question better addressed to my superiors. I'm only here on assignment, and I do what I'm told. That's the army way, you know.

Lloyd: And that's why I'd never be in the army, even if I didn't have a philosophical opposition to it. Free societies can only exist when citizens are willing to question authority at every level, to challenge the power structure—

Me: I'll thank you for not trying to convert me, Mr. Abernathy. I've had two of your kind make an effort already, and as you can see by my uniform, it didn't work.

Lloyd: All right, then. Have it your way, but just know that some of us aren't the sheep you think we are. We see more than you know. And that's all I have to say about that.

CHAPTER 15

Dorie Armitage

January 21, 1945

It took me only two days of investigating to discover that the Morrissey family was essentially the forestry equivalent of a mobster clan.

Earl was the head ranger and godfather; Edith the motherly cook; Sarah Ruth the secretary and chief gun moll, if Edith's stories of her daughter's hunting prowess were half true; and Jimmy the grunt doing all the work of chores and smokejumping.

Granted, the Morrisseys were more upstanding than the average gang, but all of the functions and information of their national forest district went through them. If I was going to find out what happened to Jack, I'd have to talk to one of them.

That was the only reason capable of bundling me out of bed at 5:30 in the morning on a Sunday to help in the kitchen, of all places.

"Sunday morning's a big meal," Edith explained, gesturing to the rashers of bacon, stacks of egg cartons, and loaves of bread arranged on the counter of the cookhouse kitchen, "because for Sunday lunch, the men are on their own with sandwich fixings and the like. A day of rest, you know."

This doesn't feel restful.

My brain, still half asleep, wasn't quite up to its usual sharpness. How could I start without sounding suspicious? "I suppose it's odd, working with all of these conscientious objectors."

"Not really." She handed me a whisk and a bowl filled with eggs bobbing around like two dozen gelatinous sunrises. "Most of them are as good as gold."

I made a face at the eggs as I sloshed in a drizzle of milk. They winked back at me, so I started whipping them up to keep them from mocking me.

"So there isn't any tension between the rangers and the COs?" I pressed.

She took my bowl of thoroughly beaten eggs and tipped it into the butter sizzling in a massive cast-iron skillet. "Oh, every now and then, there's a spat. Some of the town boys calling names, a ranger who doesn't like to see the COs at the movie palace, a quarrel about whether to use military-sounding terms around the camp. Those were mostly handled by their leader, though, Jack." Her shoulders sagged like the Stars and Stripes on a line that hadn't been pulled taut. "And he . . . he's gone now."

There. She'd handled the transition for me. "That's the young man who was badly burned recently, isn't it?" It was easy—too easy, maybe—to keep my voice steady, but I welcomed it. Nora Hightower would be sympathetic but not sad.

"It's dangerous work, smokejumping." Mrs. Edith's motions with the spatula intensified, decimating the eggs more than scrambling them. "I didn't want my Jimmy to do it, but he and Earl insisted, so . . ." She threw up her hands, as if there was nothing more she could do.

Back to the subject at hand. "How did this Jack fellow come to be out at the site of the fire alone?"

"I'm not sure. Earl didn't tell me." Her eyes widened in alarm, as if remembering she was talking to an army investigator. "But it wasn't my husband's fault, none of it, you understand. The boy was just in the wrong place at the wrong time."

"I'm told he's in a hospital, getting treatment. Do you happen to know which one?" I tried not to make it sound like I was too invested in the answer. But if I could find out where they were keeping Jack, if I could see him again, maybe . . .

Edith frowned. "I assume it's the post hospital at Fort Missoula, since the central branch of smokejumpers is there, but I can't say I've thought to ask. I know they'll do the best they can. But Earl doesn't think . . ." She set the spatula down and brought up the corner of her apron to wipe her eyes. "My, I haven't seen him so broken up since—"

Every detective knows to always press for more when someone trails off. Often, those are the most important leads to follow. "Since when?"

"Since our son William died in the war. That was . . ." She frowned as she seemed to flip invisible calendar pages. "Sixteen months ago next week."

"I'm so sorry," I said in the same way I did if a fellow on the base drifted into a blue mood and talked about the buddies he'd lost. It was impossible to say much more.

She peeled off the first strips of bacon from a thick rasher and slapped them into the pan. "Thank you, dear."

Funny, I hadn't seen a Gold Star Service Flag displayed around the Morrissey home, usually a bloodred-bordered banner of sorrowful pride for war widows and grieving mothers. Then again, tucked into the forest like they were, I suppose they might have felt it wasn't worth displaying, since no one would see it.

Edith's hand stilled on the skillet. "It wasn't so terrible the day we got the news." Her eyes looked somewhere far away. "It was the day after. I could hardly get out of bed."

164

I thought about Phyllis hauling me out in time for roll call the morning after I'd heard about Jack's accident. "I can understand that."

"One of the COs came by and offered to make breakfast so Sarah Ruth and I wouldn't have to."

"Word spreads quickly around here, I'm sure." I tried to picture it—the conscientious objectors murmuring the news that the boss's son had died in the war they'd refused to join. Did they feel ashamed? Relieved that it wasn't them? Renewed in their conviction that fighting in a war was evil?

She nodded. "The biscuits that poor fellow made were absolutely inedible." The sad lines on her face lifted in an abrupt chuckle. "Like lumps of coal, better to burn than to eat. But I'm told the sausage turned out all right. I wouldn't know. I couldn't eat a thing all that day, or the next."

I looked around for a way to make myself useful and settled on stooping over the wooden cutting board dominating the counter, slicing bread—unevenly, but still sliced. "Where was your son serving?"

Her answer came quick and bitter. "We don't know. It was classified."

I frowned. Yes, the army was cagey with details before operations were carried out—that was the whole point of censoring mail and news reports—but afterward, grieving families were given the respect of knowing how their loved ones had served their country. "Surely they at least told you where he was buried?"

"Don't you think if they had, I'd know? His own mother?" Edith slapped the uncooked side of the bacon strips down, spattering me with stinging droplets of grease. If she noticed my sharp intake of breath, she didn't apologize.

"I'm sure the army had their reasons." But it made me wonder:

THE LINES BETWEEN US

What kind of work had William Morrissey been involved with before his death?

"That's what Earl said too. At first anyway."

Outside, the now-familiar bell rang, bright and cheery as Christmas morning. Edith gasped and looked out the door toward the benches of the cookhouse. "Here come the teeming masses. Oh, and we haven't even started the toast!"

Since that seemed about my ability level, I took on the duty myself. Not using one of the shiny models lined up at the Sears store back in Seattle, just a grill to place a half dozen slices out on at once.

As I dutifully flipped the bread every minute on cue before setting out the slices to be coated in jam and devoured by the men in the hall—smokejumpers only, the rangers were off on Sundays—I tried to think about what I'd learned, like Philip Marlowe or Hercule Poirot would. Use those "little gray cells," as the famous detective liked to say.

I had to get to the scene of the crime, but to do that, I needed both means and motive. No one I'd talked to had described the fire's location, even when I'd dropped hints. As for motive . . . what line could I use to explain why I wanted to investigate the fire?

You could ask Gordon. Then you wouldn't need to give an excuse.

Annoying how the simplest answer was also the most complicated. Because Gordon Hooper had made it clear that he wanted nothing to do with me, and I was more than happy to oblige. If he wanted to pretend the fire was an accident, well . . .

Fire. I sniffed, then flicked the spatula under one of the pieces of bread, revealing the black underside, just like the biscuits in Edith's story.

I glanced around the corner to the dining hall, where several of the men stood, as if ready to don canvas coveralls and form a bucket brigade, or however they put out wildfires.

Lesson learned. If you want to avoid drawing attention to yourself, never burn something in a room full of smokejumpers.

"Everything all right?" one of them asked.

"Oh my." Edith nudged me to the side and used her own spatula to assembly-line flip the burnt toast over to the waiting plate with enviable efficiency. "We're fine, just fine!" she trilled. Then, to me, "I'd better take over, dear."

I thought about giving the burnt pieces to Thomas to feed to the birds he loved watching.

No. Even they probably won't want them.

"But I should—"

She *tsk*ed, cutting off my protest. "Now, now. You go along and grab your grub before the boys get seconds. I've seen Dust Bowl locusts that haven't cleaned out a place as well as those fellows."

My empty stomach wasn't about to offer a counterargument, so I hung up my apron, loaded a plate from the chow line, and surveyed the cookhouse for a likely table.

There. Charlie, who from what I'd observed seemed like the friendliest of the COs, sat with three other men, chatting quietly, not in a sleepy stupor like some of the fellows.

It was interesting, the way the COs were so casual about their bold integration. Coming from the army, with separate facilities based on skin color, it had taken me by surprise at first, Charlie eating and sleeping alongside all the rest, but already it had gotten so I hardly noticed.

"I've been exiled, boys," I said, plunking my tray down beside them and dazzling the table with a smile that took a bit more effort after an earlier morning than normal.

It was clear they didn't mind my ratty old sweater or unbrushed hair from stumbling out of bed before dawn, each greeting me pleasantly.

"Do any of you gentlemen go to church?" I asked, even though I knew the answer. Most COs were as religious as saints.

"Mr. Morrissey and Mr. Boyd, one of the other rangers, take us in an hour or so," one of the Johns said. Was it First, Second, or Third? I couldn't keep the nicknames straight. "We all pile into the bed of their trucks."

"Will you be coming with us?" Hank, the round-faced fellow with a hook nose who looked like the Quaker Oats man without the white wig, looked hopeful.

"Sorry, no." I hated to disappoint him, but then again, I'd already disappointed Edith this morning when I said I'd rather not go. Church was all well and good, but remaining behind would give me several precious hours of solitude to go over notes from my investigation.

Before I could ask them about their church experiences, the cookhouse door flung open, and Morrissey stepped in. He stood resolute, like a man with something to say, but instead of demanding attention, he waited as table after table noticed him, their conversation slowing.

I shushed First John, who turned to see what the rest of us were staring at. Finally, Morrissey spoke. "This morning, I received a call at my office."

It was how he said it, more than the words itself, that seemed to fall over the room. And I knew what he was going to say, so that when he did, I almost wondered if it had been out loud or in my own slowed-time imagination.

"Jack Armitage is dead."

CHAPTER 16

Gordon Hooper

January 21, 1945

No. Every part of me throbbed at that one word. My tray fell to the table, knocking over a glass of milk, and I couldn't bring myself to care.

"... complications of his accident," Morrissey was saying. "He was not, as far as anyone could tell, in any pain." He looked at me, when all I wanted in the world was for him to look anywhere else. "The doctors did all they could, but he died sometime between 3 and 4 AM."

The world was frozen silent as the news hit us like an unexpected blizzard.

Dorie. Where's Dorie? I found her two tables over, her face placid as a summertime meadow. Almost blank.

That cut through the ache. Jack's own sister didn't care that he was dead.

Dead. As surely as if I'd traced his name in the newspaper listing of the missing and fallen on the battlefields of France or North Africa or the Philippines.

The anger in me found a target, and I narrowed in on Dorie, daring her to look my way, willing her to show any emotion.

Stop it. It won't help. There's nothing you can do.

The others were staring at me, I realized now, the ones who weren't staring at the floor or wiping away tears. No one unaffected, no one able to offer comfort or feel pity. I tried to find Sarah Ruth at her usual table. Some instinct hinted a sympathetic look from her might calm me down. But she wasn't anywhere to be found.

Do not look at Thomas. But out of the corner of my eye, I could see him standing, his face still bruised, like he was going to make a pronouncement about God's will being done.

Blessed are the peacemakers, blessed are the peacemakers, blessed . . .

And I ran. This time, instead of shouting or throwing a punch, I let the cookhouse door slam behind me, my feet pounding off the path and onto the crunch of the frost-stiff grass.

Where I was going, I wasn't sure. Not to the woods or to the mountain, where the fire tower loomed over us like the eye of God.

Back to the bunkhouse. That was it. Where I'd last seen Jack.

And as I ran, the what-ifs came again, swarming around my thoughts just like they had when Nelson, my father, had died.

What if I'd offered to go to the lookout instead of Jack? What if we'd gotten to the fire sooner? What if we'd never applied to be smokejumpers in the first place?

It hadn't been my idea, that's for sure. Jack and I had been with over one hundred others building a dam in South Dakota when the announcement came: a flyer pinned to the bulletin board, asking for applicants "tough of body and mind" to apply for the smoke-jumper program. Beneath it, an image of a brawny man holding a shovel with a look of determination gave us a picture of what we could be if we just filled out the application.

I knew from my construction days that heights made me uneasy—even nailing shingles into a two-story roof set my head spinning—so I'd flatly refused to apply.

"Come on, Gordon," Jack had begged on the way home from

170

a trip into town. "Aren't you tired of biding your time shoveling dirt and pouring concrete? This is our chance to actually make a difference. Can't you see?"

"What I see is a lot of crazies who need to jump out of planes to feel useful." At his crestfallen look, I added, "Listen, it's all well and good for you, Jack. You're the brave one. Go on and apply without me."

He'd fallen back, toeing the ground with his boot. "Aw, Gordon, you know I wouldn't leave you behind. Not for anything."

And that's how it stood: Jack had wanted to go, and he wouldn't go without me.

So I'd filled out the form and prayed I wouldn't get in, but I answered all the questions honestly, and it turns out two and half years of construction work to raise money for college had made me strong enough and the Deerfield Dam had a surplus of men. They were fine with shipping the two of us out to Missoula, Montana, for training.

I sat down on my bed, remembering Jack's face the first time we'd gone up in a practice flight. "I feel alive, Gordon. Really, truly alive." Then he'd noticed how still I was. "Hey, are you all right?"

"Gordon." The voice was higher, more feminine, than the one in my memories, and I raised my head. Dorie stood in the bunkhouse doorway, outlined by Sunday morning daylight like she was afraid to cross the threshold. "Are you all right?"

"No," I said flatly. "I'm not. Why are you?"

"I couldn't show it, or say anything, or . . ." She took a fortifying breath. "PFC Nora Hightower isn't supposed to care."

"But does Dorie Armitage?" Had she ever really cared about either of us?

She moved toward me like a sleepwalker, her voice stripped of its usual animation. "It doesn't feel real. Not yet."

I tried to believe her. After all, it could be denial leaving her numb, like I'd felt just after the fire. It could be.

She sank onto the first bed in the row like her knees weren't enough to keep her aloft anymore. I breathed in deeply. She smelled like smoke instead of her usual floral perfume.

"That was Jack's bunk." I said the "was" deliberately. It had to hit her soon, that he was really dead, that this wasn't one of her stupid stories.

But her eyes weren't on me, so I wasn't sure if she even heard. "Oh. He kept them." The frame creaked as she reached up, and her voice grew fainter still, drained of private-detective bravado. "All of them."

I wondered for a moment what she meant, before she reached up to tug on a corner of paper I'd left loose from the frame of the bed, pulling it free. Of course. The newspaper clippings.

Wait a minute. She *knew* about them. That could only mean . . . "*You* sent those?"

"Yes." The flicker of guilt I saw on her face was quickly, and literally, shrugged away. "Our commanding officer got all the major papers. I'd snip out articles now and then to send to him."

I thought of all the times I'd cursed the anonymous sender, the frustration I felt every time Jack got a new envelope in the mail. And all along, it was *Dorie*. "But . . . why?"

Silence for a moment, and she tore the newspaper article in half, then in quarters, before looking up at me with challenge in her eyes. "Why do you think?"

Thinking, my usual area of strength, felt too hard at the moment. Breathing felt hard, for that matter. "Enough with the mysteries," I snapped. "Why can't you just say what you mean?"

"Fine," she said, her usual spark back in her voice. "When it came to arguments, I knew you, Gordon Hooper, would beat me every single time, so I didn't bother trying. But if my brother saw how awful the Axis powers were, if he understood that this war was just . . ."

As her voice wavered and her gaze dropped from mine, the anonymous mail I'd thought was only meant to mock Jack had an even more sinister purpose. "You wanted him to drop out of the CPS."

"Maybe." Her voice was defensive, without even a hint of shame.

I thought of all the times Jack had opened those letters, dread in his expression, and the way he slumped in his seat afterward.

"Did he know you were the one sending them?"

"Gosh, how should I know? Probably. He knew I was stationed in Seattle. Who else would it have been?"

"Do you realize," I said, struggling against the anger rising up in me, "what you did to him?"

Some part of me knew I should walk away, go a few rounds on the obstacle course or for a run in the woods until I'd calmed down.

But she did this. It's time for her to face the consequences.

"Jack made his own choices," she said, but her voice wavered.

Was she finally feeling something? Maybe even a faint trace of guilt? *Good.*

Even though it was too late.

I stood, trying to put my emotions into movement . . . and into my words. "No, Dorie. You didn't send those clippings because you wanted Jack to give up on pacifism. Not just that anyway. You wanted him to agree with you, plain and simple. You can't stand the thought of being wrong—"

I might as well have punched her, the way she reared back. "That's not true."

"—and if that means joining the army, condemning your brother, and blackmailing him with guilt, well, that's a small price to pay, isn't it?"

There was only a split second of silence before she stood, stepping toward me, and said, low and deadly, "Take. It. Back."

But I'd seen Dorie's stubbornness before, and she couldn't bully me. "I won't. Because we both know it's true."

We were only a couple of feet apart, and something about the stiff, straight way Dorie stood told me she almost reached up and slapped me for my audacity. But she didn't argue, because there was nothing to say in her defense.

That silence, more than anything, was what spurred me on, toward the one part of Morrissey's story that hadn't made sense—until now. "They told us that Jack charged into the center of the fire, without any gear, without calling for help. Does that sound like the brother you knew?"

Whether she understood the change of subject yet or not, she seized on it, on any chance to take the focus off what she'd done. "No, it doesn't. That's why I thought someone must be—"

"Maybe no one is lying or hiding anything. Maybe your vast conspiracy is a dud, and you came all the way out from Seattle to find out that the real reason Jack ran into that fire is because . . ."

But I stopped, like a hiker at the edge of a precipice who realized it was a long way down.

It was as if the fire went out of me and into Dorie, now standing, her hands hanging in fists at her side. "Say it," she ordered, and I hated the military precision of it, as if she expected me to salute and obey.

Fine. She wanted the truth? I would give it.

"Because he looked at all that"—I gestured to the newspaper clippings— "and was reminded time and time again of how worthless he was, how much his family disapproved of him, how little he could do from here in the woods of Oregon."

Like a wildfire with no firebreak in sight, I couldn't stop, not now. "You know what I think? I think Jack looked at that smoke and remembered your words: 'This is what happens when a good man does nothing.' And so he ran into the flames, trying to do something, not caring if he made it out."

She staggered back, thudding against the bunk's metal frame. "No. That's not true."

"You didn't kill him, Dorie, but you sure did make him want to die a hero's death. Can you blame him for taking his chance?"

When she looked up at me, hazel eyes round and scared, I thought for a horrible moment that she would burst into tears.

And the horror was mostly because I realized that's what I'd wanted all along, during my whole terrible speech. To make Doris Armitage, WAC, cry.

Instead, she ran. Out the door, down the path, as far away from me as possible.

I almost called after her, but my voice caught in my throat.

What had I done?

CHAPTER 17

Dorie Armitage

January 21, 1945

I attacked the quarter-sized crater in the logger truck's fender with a dent puller I'd found on the workbench, pitting the metal tool against whatever rock had bounced up to leave a lasting mark. Morning light streamed through the windows of the forest service's garage, too cheerful for my mood. The memories had come, even if the tears hadn't.

Jack and his friend Harry making miniature trees out of whittled wood and crepe paper to set beside Harry's electric train. Jack sitting in the front row of my school recitals, ready to mouth the words to "Paul Revere's Ride" in case I forgot. Jack helping mean old Ralph Gillespie up when a snowball with a rock packed inside had given him a bloody nose.

Harry and Ralph were, last I had heard, an army gunner and a navy midshipman, respectively. Harry had gotten a Purple Heart pinned to his puffed-out chest already during the Battle of Salerno, or so said the local paper clipping Mother had sent my way. They'd had a few choice words for Jack before he'd left for CPS work.

At the time, I'd agreed with them. Now I wasn't so sure.

The COs I'd met here were so . . . kind. Respectful. Thoughtful.

No one seemed to be looking for a cushy job until the end of the war. They just genuinely believed it was wrong to kill another person, even in combat. Just like Jack.

But Jack had second thoughts, near the end. I reached my hand in my coat pocket. The brochure Thomas had given me was still there, bold and confusing. That was another thing that didn't make sense. Why did Jack have to die right when he wanted to do the right thing and fight, or at least serve as a medic?

I hadn't told Gordon yet what Thomas had revealed to me. Stupid of me, trying to spare him when he didn't care two Fig Newtons about my feelings.

But would it change anything? Gordon was genuinely broken-up about Jack, or he wouldn't have lashed out half as badly. No sense in returning spite for spite by revealing that Jack was thinking about joining the army.

Right on cue, I heard a scraping noise, metal against concrete, and sighed.

The back door to the garage hadn't been locked when I'd found it, so I hadn't bothered to latch it either, simply pushed a paint can in front of it so I'd know if someone came in. A classic spy trick. And it didn't take Lord Peter Wimsey or Sam Spade to figure out who this was.

If I'd really wanted to get away from him, I could have gone back to the Morrisseys' house. But no. I'd come to the garage to be surrounded by wrenches and workbenches and the soothing scent of motor oil.

Just in case I was wrong, in case it was one of the Morrisseys tracking me down after I'd left the cookhouse without comment, I called out, "Who's there?"

"I wondered if you'd be here."

I closed my eyes, braced myself. It was Gordon, all right. That voice, furious and cutting only fifteen minutes ago, now hesitant and hopeful.

"Well, here I am." I ran my fingers over the dent on the fender's exterior—smaller now—and pressed the dent puller against the underside, smoothing out the metal. "You all keep a tight shop in here. The tool bench is more organized than the one at Fort Lawton." Yes. That was something I could talk about, something that didn't hurt.

"We have lots of time on our hands during the winter." His footsteps slapped against the concrete until he stopped to sit on the stool by the workbench.

I didn't make another effort at conversation, for once wanting an awkward silence. He'd sought me out; let him put in the effort.

"You say Jack knew all this time you'd joined the army?"

I nodded, staying focused on the fender and seeing Gordon only in its dull reflection.

"Whenever your name came up—in a story he was telling around the campfire, or when anyone asked about his family—he said that his sister was determined and—"

"Full of life," I finished automatically, gripping the tool until my knuckles went white.

"How did you know?"

"We had a party to celebrate my high school graduation." I tried to picture those carefree times before the war, full of lightning bugs and lemonade and laughter, and almost couldn't. "Everyone made toasts. That was his. 'To my sister, may you always be as determined and full of life as you are now.'"

How many times had I whispered that to myself? When Daddy had tried to stop me from entering the WACs. When I'd been so exhausted from basic training I wanted to collapse. When I heard another lewd joke whispered about me in the garage, out of Max's earshot.

You, Dorie, are determined and full of life. You can do this.

"He was proud of you," Gordon said, drawing me away from those thoughts. "It didn't change, after he knew about . . . you know."

I set the dent puller down and turned to face him fully. "You can say the word 'army.' It's not cussing."

I expected the blush that colored his face, but not the next words that came out of his mouth. "Listen, I'm trying to say that I'm sorry, Dorie. Sorry that I blamed you for Jack's death. He never would have wanted that."

He was sorry, he said.

Did I believe him?

Gordon doesn't lie. That, at least, I could count on.

Which told me he'd meant every one of those angry words he'd shouted at me back at the bunkhouse. Yet he meant these too.

"People are never simple."

Ever since Lieutenant Leland had said that back in the Stratford Hotel dayroom, I'd been mulling it over, and it turned out he was on to something. After all, wasn't I a talented mechanic *and* a talented dancer, wearing oil-stained coveralls while dreaming of Hollywood glitz and glamour?

Gordon wasn't the only one with a few contradictions.

I polished the fender with a rag I'd found on a hook by the workbench. Good as new, the dent completely gone. "I'll probably forgive you eventually." I inspected my sleeves for traces of rust and oil before tugging them down again. "Anyway, we've both said our share of things we regret."

He blinked, probably not sure if I was sincere or not.

Fair, since I wasn't even sure myself. Looked like we'd both have to prove ourselves.

All I knew was that Jack would want us to find out the truth. No matter what it took.

"You're going home now, aren't you? For the funeral."

I felt another wave of shame, this time that I hadn't even thought of the fact that they'd likely already told Daddy and Mother the news. "I want to. But . . . I can't. I'm in too deep. And I'm getting close to something, Gordon. I can feel it."

I expected him to get frustrated again, to tell me that there was nothing to find out. Instead, he just asked, "What have you found out?"

This was my opening. Time to spring the trap. "Not as much as I'd find if you were helping me."

Now he raised his hands in self-defense, as if I was going to yank a wrench off the workbench and start swinging it at him. "Look, Dorie, I already told you—"

"You wouldn't have to lie." That much, at least, I'd decided. "I can ask questions until I turn blue in the face, but these fellows don't trust me." I thought of the dismal interview with Lloyd, the way some of the men stiffened whenever they looked at my uniform.

He looked at the ground, then briefly at me, and I could think of a dozen excuses he might make. I didn't have the energy to respond to any of them. "Listen," I said, before he could voice any of them, "it's the least you can do after you were such a bully."

Should I have played that card, right when he was most vulnerable? Maybe not, but I'd been dealt a bad hand, and it was the only ace I had left.

When he looked up from studying the garage floor, any trace of hesitation was gone, and his voice was all resolve. "What would you want me to do?"

And that was the most enthusiastic response I was likely to get from Gordon Hooper. "Ask around. See if the other COs noticed any strange conversations Jack had before he went on lookout duty, any enemies he might have made, any reason someone might . . ." I swallowed hard. *Say it.* "Might not want him to come back."

It affected Gordon too—I could see it in the way his Adam's apple rose with a swallow. "I could do that. Anything else?"

This was the opening I'd been waiting for. "Well," I said, trying to sound confident but knowing Gordon would probably see through it anyway, "there's just one more small thing. . . ."

CHAPTER 18

Gordon Hooper

January 21, 1945

Did God have a special punishment for skipping church to investigate a murder?

That's what Dorie assured me we were doing. "It might be our only chance to visit the scene," she insisted, following me down the broad main trail into the woods, the same direction I'd rattled in Morrissey's Ford the day of the fire. "And you've got the perfect excuse to be missing. Everyone knows you're grieving too much to sit through a church service."

"Isn't church supposed to be the place you go when you're grieving?" I challenged.

That paused whatever she was going to say next. "I suppose. But isn't God here too?"

I looked around the mild, sunny day, thinking about it.

The only music came from the flutter of the hatch-patterned wings of sparrows, and the only stained glass was the design the light made through the evergreen needles on the path. Lloyd claimed "communing with nature" on his daily walk was a suitable substitute for church. That was a step too far for me, but it had always been easier for me to listen to God here in the quiet . . .

as well as easier to hear the questions I'd crowded out. Loudest of them now was *Why did Jack have to die?*

No answer, just the wind in the trees. I'd studied the philosophy and ethics behind questions like that back when I was eighteen and setting out all the religions of the world before me to select the best one to join.

I'd come out of that experiment right back where my great-great-grandmother had started: the Quaker faith, with its convictions and equality and contemplation. Everything my father wasn't. Peaceful. Self-reliant. Dignified.

But could it answer this awful question?

I glanced over at Dorie, stumbling down the path in the hunched-shoulders way of someone trying to tuck into themselves to conserve warmth, a few dark curls poking out from under the red beret jammed nearly to her eyes. No chatter or small talk today, thank goodness. *Maybe she's grieving too, in her own way.*

When we'd walked for a few miles, close enough to see the edges of the burned area, I pointed it out to Dorie.

By now, the forest felt less comforting and more like something, or someone, was watching me—but not the peace of Inner Light I felt when close to an all-seeing God. No, this was a crawling unease, like a character from Jack's noir mystery script.

Stop it. Dorie's made you paranoid.

"It's awful," Dorie whispered, and I remembered that she was seeing it for the first time.

Though the trees still stood, the smaller ones were naked of their lower branches, leaving swaths of matted gray instead of dense green. The wafting scent of stale ashes hung in the air even more than a week later. Whenever we smokejumpers trooped back over a burn site the next day to find hotspots and scatter their buried pockets of coals, it struck me like that. Not a pungent rot, but the odor of death just the same.

Dorie picked her way along the edge of the exposed earth of our fire line, staring like a medic overlooking a battlefield cluttered with wounded and dead.

It wouldn't do any good to tell her this was a small fire compared to some I'd seen, infernos that swallowed up hundreds of acres, leaving behind crumbling gray ashes as far as the eye could see. The size didn't matter to her. This fire had killed Jack.

When I looked over at her again, she had her gloves pressed to her mouth, like she was filtering the air from the ashes stirred up by her footsteps—or holding in a sob.

What could I possibly say to help?

"This is going to be a meadow someday." The way Dorie looked over at me, skeptical and sniffling, made me feel foolish, but I pressed on. "Sarah Ruth Morrissey said so. The fire cleared away the undergrowth, and we'll come back and cut down any dead trees. In a few years, it'll be pocked with burrows and lined with long grasses for birds to use in nesting. Wild flowers will grow, attracting butterflies. . . ."

I couldn't finish. In the middle of winter, it was hard to re- member what spring felt like, and from the way Dorie stared down at the cold, dead ground, I knew she couldn't picture it either.

"It doesn't seem right. Like nothing should live here again after what happened."

I knew what she meant. "Don't you think Jack would rather have a meadow than a graveyard as a memorial?"

She lifted her head, straightened her shoulders, and for a mo- ment, looked every inch a soldier. "He would, wouldn't he?"

I nodded. "Now, what are we looking for?" The sooner we got

the job done, the sooner we could leave. I didn't believe in ghosts, of course, but neither did I feel entirely comfortable here.

A small notebook with *V for Victory* in red on the cover appeared out of her coat pocket, and she took up a stub of a pencil like she was going to make an itemized list of every snapped twig. "Notice every detail. Anything might be a clue." She'd lost the dazed look, and it was replaced with the grit I'd come to expect from her.

Given the task before us, we were going to need it.

There was plenty of debris, splintered branches and charred underbrush, springy-soft layers of ash that would eventually get washed away. Lots of boot prints in the muddy ashes, too, more than I would have expected, but then again, there had been a crew of us digging that day. Douglas firs stripped bare of needles on the bottom branches, juniper bushes twisted and charred, everything colored in muted greens, grays, and black.

But as I circled the burn area, one detail didn't make sense. It wasn't a clue so much as a lack of one.

There has to be another explanation.

Think, Gordon, think.

No matter how hard I tried, though, I couldn't come up with one.

You've got to tell Dorie. Regardless of how much it played into her suspicions.

After I'd made the rounds, hopping over nearly every charred log and crumbled bit of underbrush, I spotted Dorie in bright blue on the north side of the burn, the mountains behind her, where the fire lookout's roof could be seen, barely, in the distance. I jogged over.

"Didn't you say it rained after the fire?" she asked before I could get a word in, flipping back to earlier in her notebook.

I nodded. I could almost feel it on my skin, the stinging cold of that winter rain, just barely on the up side of freezing.

"Hard enough to wash away boot prints?"

"Probably." I saw what she was driving at. Why could we clearly see disturbed ground and prints when the rain should have wiped them out . . . unless it wasn't us smokejumpers who made them. I bent down, looking at a clear print just inside the fire line. The line of the sole was pressed into mud, not ash. Mud that would have formed after the rain but not before it.

"Someone else has been here."

"Several someone elses," Dorie corrected, "and not just on the perimeter."

Right. I'd seen the prints even in the center of the burned area, but I'd attributed them to Richardson's story that he and Morrissey had walked through, searching for Jack.

"Has it rained or snowed since the day of the fire?"

I thought back, the days blurred together in my mind. "No."

"Blast," she muttered. "That might've given us a timeframe." She wrote it down anyway.

It was time. I took a breath and braced myself. "Also, I noticed . . . there aren't any fallen larches."

I'd circled the burned area twice, just to be sure, wondering if maybe I'd missed it, and come up with nothing.

Instead of jotting that down, Dorie just stared at me, and I noticed the smudges of ash on her cheeks that we'd have to clean off before going back to camp. "I don't follow."

"Morrissey told me a dead larch fell on Jack, trapping him."

"Ah." She tapped her pencil against her mouth, perfectly applied lipstick gleaming. "Could it have burned up in the fire?"

"Doubt it. It wasn't a hot enough fire to leave no trace at all."

She accepted that with a nod, probably knowing as much about forest fires as I had two years ago. "Maybe Morrissey had someone cut it apart for firewood and haul it away?"

It was a reasonable guess. We had so many stockpiles around

camp that I'd hardly notice if one suddenly grew larger. "But there's no sawdust or wood chips on the ground that I could find. Any project that large would have left debris. Besides, Morrissey told me it was a snag, mostly rotten. No good for burning."

Before I'd even finished, Dorie was writing something in her notebook. I took a step closer and saw, in all capitals, *MORRISSEY LIED*.

Even though it was the logical conclusion to what I'd said, I still hated making that jump. "It could be that a branch fell and knocked Jack unconscious, and Morrissey exaggerated."

"Maybe," Dorie said slowly. "If Jack got hit in the head and couldn't move, a branch could've done it, I suppose."

I'd seen Jack's body. He'd been injured and burned, no question about that . . . but what if it wasn't from a fallen tree?

That one question opened up a dozen I didn't want to think about. Dorie already was. I could tell from the way she was pacing the fire line, muttering to herself. I heard a few of the phrases: "cover story," "What's the motive?" "attempted murder."

It's not possible . . . is it? I tried to imagine anyone hating Jack enough to kill him and just couldn't do it. Even if it was possible, why would someone kill him here? Had they started the fire, or merely used it? And what reason could Morrissey possibly have to lie about it? None of it made any sense.

And into the doubtful quiet that followed those questions was an intuition, a snatch of remembered conversation, the first hint of the motive Dorie was muttering about.

Images and memories played through my mind.

Morrissey's guilty conscience.

The cross rubbed smooth at the front of the church.

The way the fire had grown so quickly less than three miles away without anyone noticing.

THE LINES BETWEEN US

Wild flowers.

My words came out dull and heavy. "I think I might know what happened."

That got Dorie's attention, her eyes bright and pencil poised. "Talk, Gordon."

"It's not like your spy thrillers or noir mysteries," I warned. Then again, few things were. Maybe most tragedies came from ordinary people making terrible mistakes.

"Just tell me." The words practically exploded out of her as I tried to figure out where to start.

"Sarah Ruth told me her father believes some fires could benefit a forest. He thinks our total suppression strategy isn't healthy. But of course he'd lose his job if he started advocating for controlled fires without any evidence."

Understanding slowly softened the look of concentration on Dorie's face. "Wait. You think Morrissey set the fire himself? As some kind of . . . experiment?"

"Yes." I tried to trace out the steps my mind had gone through to give her a picture of what could have happened.

Morrissey waited for a stormy day, a day he knew would provide a cover for how the fire started, then lit a dry pile of underbrush only a few miles away from the camp. He figured if the rain didn't put the blaze out, Jack, a vigilant lookout, would call it in, and with a fire squad so close, no one would be the wiser. He'd get a burnt-out clearing to study and could return for tests over the course of years.

What he didn't count on was Jack seeing the fire and hiking down to it alone, hoping to prove himself. Maybe it was a broken tree limb that injured him, maybe he just inhaled too much smoke, maybe it was something else altogether. Either way, it explained Morrissey's panic and guilt, why he seemed to feel so deeply that the fire was his fault.

Because it was.

"That's awful," Dorie breathed, and we stood in silence for a moment, looking out over the ruins.

"So . . . what do we do now?"

My question seemed to snap her out of a trance. "I'll find out where Morrissey was the day of the fire. You talk to fellows working out in the woods that day, in case they noticed anything suspicious. Especially Lloyd."

That was a surprise. Of all of us, Lloyd, with his polished prose and Southern gentlemen airs, seemed like the last one who would be in the know about something this seedy. "Why him?"

The shoulders of her coat rose in a shrug. "I don't like the look of him, that's all. He's hiding something."

It couldn't hurt to humor her. "I can do that. But, Dorie, remember: This is just a theory."

"Maybe," she said, putting her notebook away, "but I think we're closer to the truth than we've ever been."

CHAPTER 19

Dorie Armitage

January 21, 1945

"You know," I said, digging through the battered box for the missing edge piece, "I always thought jigsaw puzzles were mostly put together by bored rich people, like in *Citizen Kane*."

Edith's chuckle caused the knitted afghan around her shoulder to slide down slightly. "Goodness, no. In fact, they've gotten more popular since the war started. I adore a good puzzle."

I couldn't say the same, but it was an excellent cover for conversation—so far about the routines of the national park, area wildlife, and the best recipes for working around ration restrictions. No more mention of Willie, though. I'd surreptitiously poked around the house, seeing if I could spot a Gold Star Service Flag in his memory, but the Morrissey family clearly kept their grief private.

In the time it took me to locate one border piece, Edith had filled in a three-inch square of seascape. "I must say, it's nice having another woman about. I love our rangers, but they'd sooner use a jigsaw to cut down half the forest than put together a jigsaw puzzle. And Sarah Ruth hates being cooped up indoors."

I'd determined that much from the three simple Sunday dresses that hung in Sarah Ruth's closet alongside slacks and even a pair of muddy jeans. It was hard not to snoop, staying in her room like I was.

The screen door banged open, and I looked up to see Jimmy hovering at the threshold, cheeks chapped with red, twisting his hat around in his hand.

"Jimmy, don't stand there with the door open," Edith said in the patient, rote way of a mother who's given the same instruction a thousand and one times. "We're not paying to heat the entire national forest."

He stationed himself on the welcome mat instead, pulling the door shut behind him, but didn't move to take off his coat. "Dad wants to talk to Miss Hightower."

"Oh?" I said lightly, even as my stomach sank like a safe thrown down an elevator shaft.

Stop that. It could be something perfectly harmless. He couldn't know what Gordon and I had talked about this morning at the site of the fire.

Edith looked pointedly at her son over her spectacles, the same eyes that could spot a puzzle piece with the right amount of seafoam now focused directly on him. "And where *is* your father, Jimmy? I haven't seen him since lunch."

Jimmy shifted uncomfortably. "He's . . . in his office."

"*Working?*" She said the word as if it was as bad as carousing or bank robbery.

Jimmy's answer came out as a mutter. "Yes, ma'am."

From the way she pursed her lips, I knew Earl Morrissey was going to have some explaining to do when he got home.

"It sounded important," Jimmy added meekly, casting a look at me that practically begged me to rescue him.

"It's no bother, Edith." I pushed aside my feeling of dread along with the blissfully cozy blanket she'd smothered me in. "Now, don't put in too many pieces while I'm gone."

With that, I snatched my coat off the wooden tree by the door and lit out of there, Jimmy at my heels.

"Sorry about that," he said, ducking his head. "Ma's real big on resting on the Sabbath."

I'd gathered that much. "You should have said your father was on a walk. That's allowed, isn't it?"

He scrunched up his nose. "You mean *lie*?"

"Of course not. Just a little fib. After all, when your goal is a good one, it doesn't really matter how you get there."

From the frown on his face, it seemed like this was the first time he'd ever considered such a thing. "Do you really think so?"

"Well, not in every case—it's not like I'm a criminal." I laughed lightly. "But anything's game when the greater good is at stake."

Gordon wouldn't say so.

Well, of course he wouldn't, with his strict religious beliefs. But he hadn't gone and turned into my nagging conscience.

Jimmy kicked a rock down the path. "Superman doesn't kill anyone, even if they're criminals."

It took me a moment to figure out what this had to do with anything. "Yes, well, Superman is also broader than the average football field."

"You mean player."

"I mean field," I insisted, "and when you have the luxury of being able to fly and lift cars and turn invisible—"

"He can't turn invisible."

"—then you can cling to your ideals. But the rest of us live in the real world with no superpowers, and we have to do what's necessary to get by. We can't all be Superman or Colonel America."

"*Captain* America."

"He's only a captain?" Another nod, and I shook my head as we climbed the three steps to the ranger station porch. "Gosh, who is in charge of promotions in these comics? Saving the world should get him to major, at least."

He held the door open for me, and I rewarded him with a brilliant smile that made him actually stumble as he walked away.

Inside, natural light brought out the red hues in the boards underfoot and beams overhead. It was so quiet that, if Jimmy hadn't told me otherwise, I'd have thought the place was abandoned. I tiptoed past the secretarial desk to Morrissey's office. The door was open, so a knock wasn't required, at least by my understanding of office etiquette. I peered inside.

Mr. Morrissey, still dressed in his Sunday suit, a sharp-looking fedora perched on the desk next to him, leaned on his elbow over a document. He was the picture of focus, his mouth moving slightly over the words, although I could see in the deep lines around his face that he hadn't been sleeping well.

Did you set the fire that killed my brother?

A board creaked beneath me, and he snapped to attention as I opened the door the rest of the way, trying not to look like I had been lurking. "You asked to see me, Mr. Morrissey?"

"Thank you, Miss Hightower. Please sit down." Before I could get close enough to see what it was, he tucked the paper in the bottom file cabinet drawer, closing it and turning to me with an expression just as firm. "I'll be direct."

"I wouldn't expect anything else from you." Let him decide if that was an insult or not.

"Our lookout saw someone walking out by the scene of the fire this morning."

Oh no. Gordon had mentioned the lookout tower where Jack

193

had spent his last days, but I hadn't considered that if they could see fires, they could see us. "Maybe he was mistaken."

"She," Morrissey corrected mildly. "My daughter volunteered to take this week's shift. And she's *very* observant."

Ah. Suddenly Sarah Ruth's week-long "trip" made more sense. That closed off several potential excuses, including the fact that maybe the lookout was bored or just wanted attention.

"Well. Was it you, Miss Hightower?" It sounded more like a statement than a question.

I paused, thinking frantically. Some*one*, he'd said. That meant Sarah Ruth had only reported one person. Gordon was still in the clear.

"Yes, it was," I said coolly, trying not to make it sound like a guilty confession. "I have to say, Mr. Morrissey, that I'm quite concerned by the reports I've heard about this 'accident' of yours."

He sighed, and the lines around his face seemed to sag with it. "Believe me, Miss Hightower, so am I."

A good line, convincingly delivered. But could I really trust anything he had to say?

Only one way to know.

This hadn't been my plan—I'd decided to hint around with some of the other rangers—but a girl didn't waste an opportunity when it was right in front of her. "If you don't mind me asking, where were you the afternoon of the fire? I'm surprised it was able to get out of control so close to your district headquarters."

"Just after breakfast, I left to lead a training two districts over on identifying and uprooting invasive species." The answer came out smoothly, almost as if he'd expected my question and prepared for it. "Those, if you don't know, are ordinary-looking intruding plants that weave in among the natural ones until they take over."

Now I was the one trying to decide if I'd been dealt a subtle insult. From the glint in Morrissey's cold blue eyes, my guess was yes. "And when you got back?"

"It was around two o'clock. Richardson, Carlisle, and Yates—rangers here on staff—were with me. That's when we saw the smoke, rang the bell, and ran for the truck." He paused. "I'm sure you've heard the rest."

Witnesses. That was good. People who could confirm his story. Because if Morrissey really had been gone until early afternoon, it didn't fit with Gordon's latest theory.

Unless Morrissey had someone else light the fire for him.

But who?

Morrissey folded his hands and met my gaze squarely. "I can see you're concerned about the welfare of these men. That's all well and good. But I work for the Department of Agriculture, Miss Hightower. Not the War Department. And I don't appreciate meddlers."

"I'm not meddling. I'm overseeing."

He blew out a frustrated breath. "That's what the woman from your superior's office said when I called too. 'Our representative is merely supplying appropriate oversight' were her words, I believe."

My breath caught in my throat. He'd called Captain Petmencky and gotten Bea. And thank goodness she'd read off the response I'd jotted down for her in case anyone asked for verification of my mission here. I hid my relief and nodded politely.

"Unlike you, I live in this town, and I care about the people in it, first and foremost my staff. So if you're really here to interview the COs, you have my blessing."

The "and if not . . ." hung in the air, an unspoken threat.

He suspected something. That was easy enough to tell. But it wasn't that I was Jack's sister. Something else was going on here. I could feel the subtext bristling between us, but, like a scene in a screwball comedy of errors, we were both dancing around it.

"Well," I said, standing and smiling tightly, "then it's a good thing all I want is the truth."

CHAPTER 20

Gordon Hooper

January 22, 1945

After a long day's work, hot water pouring down your back was a welcome feeling, during January in particular. Sometimes the other COs started singing in the shower—folk tunes and praise choruses from the Mennonite songbook, and even the occasional popular song when the Apostle Tom wasn't around. One time, Shorty gargled a full verse of "Too-Ra-Loo-Ra-Loo-Ral" before he choked on a high note.

The point was, fellows let their guard and their pants down at about the same time in the shower house. That made it the perfect place for a Monday night interrogation—and better, one where Dorie couldn't possibly listen in and then tell me what I did wrong.

So when I saw Lloyd lift a stiff white towel out of the clean laundry bin an hour before curfew, I did the same, hauling along my kit with its toothbrush and government-issue soap that smelled like congealed disappointment.

"Going to wash up, boys?" Shorty barreled his way past us to the door before we could answer. "Better hurry, or I'll get all the hot water."

So much for a private conversation with Lloyd.

Not like you'll find anything out anyway. Dorie probably gave you this job because she knows you'd mess up anything serious. You're useless at this.

Stop it, I ordered myself, pulling up my coat against the cold wind. That's what my father had always said about me. Useless.

But it wasn't true. I could do this.

Once we'd taken three of the four shower stalls, I took a deep breath and started in on the interrogation as I undressed. "Awful, wasn't it? Morrissey telling us about Jack like that yesterday."

"Sure was." Shorty's voice from the stall next to me, usually animated, had tempered a bit. "Don't think it's sunk in yet." Lloyd didn't add anything, but I heard the spray of his water turning on.

"I wish I'd gotten the chance to . . . say something to him before he left for the lookout." I cleared my throat over the rising emotion. *Not now.* "Which reminds me. Did either of you notice anything . . . strange about Jack before he . . . you know, before the accident?"

"Like the fact that he ate his cornflakes dry instead of putting milk in them?"

"No, Shorty. Strange like . . . something he was worried about or someone he was upset with. You know."

I winced, grateful they couldn't see my expression. Acting casual was not my calling.

Thankfully, it didn't sound like Shorty noticed. "Nothing I can think of. Except it seemed like the Apostle Tom was extra mad at him just before he left. I said to him, 'What'd he do, Tom, freeze your long johns?'" Shorty's braying laugh was distorted by the water. "He just said something about Jack not being worthy of our respect."

True, that was a step above Thomas's general dislike. I'd noticed it too, on the day Roger joined the military. But Dorie told me she'd

198

spoken with Thomas and didn't think he had anything to do with it, whatever that meant.

I turned on the shower, stepped under the lukewarm water, and pitched my voice louder. "I can't help wondering . . . what was Jack doing down there at the fire? Instead of calling it in, I mean."

"There was a shovel up in the lookout with the rest of the emergency supplies," Shorty reasoned. "Maybe he saw the smoke and didn't want to bother us with a little blaze like that. Only when he got there, it wasn't so little anymore."

That didn't sound like Jack, but I held my peace. "Say, Lloyd, did any of you fellows working in the woods see the smoke?"

Finally Lloyd spoke up. "I was building fences with a crew a few miles east of the camp. It was business as usual the whole day. We didn't even hear the fire bell ring."

Another dead end. There was one more question, one Dorie had given to me, and then I was on my own. "Why do you think they took Jack to an army hospital? Why not a closer one?"

Shorty made a dismissive noise. "How should I know? Why don't you ask Morrissey?"

I imagined that meeting, asking questions that strongly implied I suspected Morrissey of . . . what? Murder? Some kind of cover-up?

"It's . . . I can't, that's all."

A squeak of Shorty's water shutting off told me he'd applied his trademark rinse-and-be-done method of personal hygiene. "Listen, if you're worried about looking dumb in front of the boss, I'll ask him. How about that?"

My mouth opened in surprise, letting in some suds that I immediately spat into the drain. "You'll ask Morrissey the questions I just asked you?"

"Sure, why not? I say a dozen stupid things before breakfast. Ol' Morris won't think a thing about it."

"And you'll tell me his answers." This was too good to be true.

"That's what I said, didn't I?" Shorty's footsteps stopped outside my shower curtain, the hem of his bathrobe visible. "Hey, it's gonna be all right. I know this hit you hardest of all, but Jack would want us to keep going."

I swallowed hard against the sudden wave of emotion. "Thanks, Shorty."

"Don't mention it, Wingtip. That's what I'm here for."

I was so grateful I didn't even tell him to knock it off with the nickname, given to me by the citified shoes I'd been dumb enough to bring with me from college in Philadelphia.

Once Shorty had left for the bunkhouse, it was just me and Lloyd. What else would Dorie want me to ask? I wasn't any good at this, with nothing to go on but suspicions and half-baked theories.

"You'd better be careful with those questions, Gordon."

My hands froze from scrubbing soap across my body. The way Lloyd said those words . . . "Is that a threat?"

He laughed, the polished port-and-cigars laughter of a true Southern gentleman. "Of course not. I just know how the army is. What they're willing to do to protect their secrets."

"What do you mean?"

"I didn't want to say it when Shorty was around but . . . I saw something strange. Have you wondered why the army sent a WAC to our camp right now, after the accident?"

"Hadn't thought to." Because I already knew.

I braced myself for the inevitable, tried to think of what I'd say in response. Lloyd was our chess champion who was studying law and had a private tutor growing up. Of anyone here, he was the most likely to figure out that Dorie was really Jack's sister.

"Anyone can see the army is using her to investigate the fire.

Just like the army jeeps that arrived in the middle of the night after Jack's accident."

My soap slipped out of my hand to the shower floor, skidding a smudge across the concrete. Not the words I'd expected. "The *what?*"

Lloyd's water turned off, but I kept mine going, the hot spray welcome against my back now that the other two had stopped draining the water heater's resources. "You know I wake up before calisthenics to walk in the woods most mornings."

"Sure." He treated it almost like a religious duty.

"That morning, I saw two jeeps parked outside the ranger station. By the time I came back from the woods when the rising bell rang, they were gone."

I tried to process that, to sort out how it would fit with my theory of Morrissey starting the fire. "Maybe it was just the forest supervisor paying a visit. Rangers use jeeps too." To the great disdain of old-timers like Les Richardson, who remembered when *"the true vehicle of a ranger was fueled by oats and carrots."*

"Not ones with a white star and *US Army* written on them."

No way to argue with that. "Did you tell anyone else?"

"No. I assumed they came with Morrissey's permission. Now that the WAC is here, it seems like just one more instance of government interference." The sound of metal rings scraping against the rod told me he was getting ready to leave, and I could see his feet stop in front of my stall. I shut off my water, trying to think.

"Why would the army interfere in a lightning fire accident?"

The only sound in the shower house was the *drip, drip, drip* of leaky spigots.

Then, in Lloyd's debonair, radio-worthy voice, "Maybe they don't think it's an accident."

Hearing someone else say it out loud chilled me. But how did all of this fit with the other details we knew? With our theory that Morrissey had started the fire as an experiment?

Not now. Thinking could come later. For now, I had a captive witness.

"Did you see anything else?" I pressed. "Any people near the jeeps? Flashlights? Voices?"

He paused for a moment, like he was thinking. "No, that was all."

"Come on, Lloyd. You've got to have noticed something."

"Well, for one thing, I noticed that Shorty stole your towel."

My . . .

I yelped, drawing back the curtain and feeling around on the hook for something that wasn't there.

I caught a glimpse of Lloyd, clad in his pajamas and a broad smirk. "And, it seems, your clothes as well."

His laughter echoed in the shower house.

~

I always dreaded the walk back from the shower house during the winter, but with my wet hair flopping around my ears, wearing nothing but Lloyd's damp towel draped around my waist, it was especially unpleasant.

I should have been annoyed at my clean feet getting caked in dirt or nicked by rocks as I hurried along the path to the bunkhouse, but they'd turned numb as an iceberg, so I barely felt a thing.

Should've known better than to trust Shorty to do me a favor with no strings attached. When I get a hold of him . . .

"Who's there?" a voice called out.

I stopped stock-still, my fist clutched around the towel. There was only one thing to do: dive into a nearby bush to hide as a flashlight wove its way down the path toward me. The branches scraped against my bare chest as the light bobbed closer. "I know I heard something. Speak up! This is the district ranger."

I closed my eyes. Of course it was Morrissey. He had a college-dean air about him, just the person to show up at the most inopportune moments.

But why was he out so late?

"Who's there?" he demanded, closer now.

I poked my head out of the shrubbery, squinting into the flashlight beam. "Gordon Hooper, sir."

"Hooper?" He frowned, probably noticing my dripping hair. "What're you doing there?"

There was no way around it. He was going to think I'd nicked food from the kitchen or something unless I came out and said it. "I'm naked, sir."

"Excuse me?"

"Someone"—I decided against naming names, not wanting to be like Tattletale Thomas—"absconded with my clothes. Sir."

There was a pause, and then he laughed, gruff and long, which would have felt very man-to-man except for the fact that I didn't feel particularly manly at the moment. Just cold, which was why I cut him off with a snappish, "If you're finished, I'd like to get inside."

"Good. There are women on the property, you know."

"Yes, sir." I was highly aware of that particular fact. Thank God it hadn't been Mrs. Morrissey or Sarah Ruth or—I shuddered inside—*Dorie.*

He peeled off his thick mackinaw hunting jacket, revealing the Forest Service uniform underneath, and passed it through the branches to me. "Here. You need this more than I do."

I almost refused it—it was only another fifty yards to the bunkhouse—but then I thought about it. No bushes, just open road, and what if someone else was out for a late-night stroll? Besides, I'd already lost all feeling in my arms.

I grabbed the coat, soft and smelling like cigar smoke. "Thanks."

He laughed again. "This is just what I needed, Hooper. It's been a long week."

And I almost snapped that Jack's death was more than just some inconvenience that made him work late hours and put him in a bad temper. But I stopped myself. Hadn't I said I'd try to be less angry?

Besides . . . it *had* been a long week. For all of us.

"Bring it back to the ranger station in the morning, will you?"

"Yes, sir." I shielded myself with the coat and stumbled out of the bush, the branches scraping at me.

Frozen fingers fumbling with the buttons, I tugged the coat on above my towel and brushed a few leaves off of my shoulders before making for the bunkhouse. There I was, wrapped in dun-and-red tartan like my Scottish ancestors—though I'm sure Nelson's side of the family would take issue with the figure I was cutting—waddling awkwardly over the open ground to the bunkhouse. There would be no sprinting, not with the loose knot of the towel around my waist.

There were no further hails or unexpected peeping Toms, so I covered the fifty yards to the bunkhouse without incident, bursting through the door. Heads all down the row of bunks rose, and laughter burst out, along with a few joking taunts.

"That color looks good on you, Hooper."

"The height of fashion, as usual."

I ignored them all, stomping down the aisle and gaining a bit of feeling in my feet once I passed the potbelly stove that warmed our home away from home.

Shorty was lounging on his bunk with a magazine, my clothes and towel folded neatly beside him. He kept his rapt attention on the article until I cleared my throat loud enough to be heard over the growing snickers.

He looked up, a smile spreading across his face. "Gordon! Just the fellow I wanted to see. Seems there was a mix-up, and I took both of our clothes by mistake. *Awful* sorry about that."

"Mistake, my eye," I grumbled, though I shouldn't have wasted my breath since he couldn't hear me over the other fellows laughing and cheering. I grabbed my clothes, and, turning away for as much modesty as you could have in a communal bunkhouse, dropped the towel and Morrissey's coat to yank them on again.

He nodded to the coat, now discarded on the floor like a banana peel. "Who rescued you, huh?"

"Morrissey."

"Better than I could have planned it." He grinned with such enthusiasm that I almost felt the corners of my mouth tilting up too, the traitors. That was the thing about Shorty. If you could stay mad at him for five consecutive minutes, you were a stronger man than most.

"If I get pneumonia and die, I'm blaming you." I folded the towel I'd worn to give it back to Lloyd. "One minute you're offering to do me a favor; the next you're pulling a stunt like this."

"This was your payment, that's all."

I flicked some dirt off the sleeve of the mackinaw where it had dragged on the path, then tucked it into a neat bundle. As I did, a piece of paper and a gum wrapper fell out of the pocket.

I passed the jacket to Shorty. "Here. You can give this back to Morrissey. It'll give you an excuse to stop by his office."

"What am I, the dry cleaner?" Shorty grumbled, but he took it anyway, returning to his magazine with a self-satisfied smile. He'd milk this story for the rest of his life, probably.

Before Thomas could come by and accuse me of trashing the

bunkhouse, I picked up the litter that had fallen from the pocket of Morrissey's jacket . . . and hesitated. Was that . . . ?

I unfolded the paper. Yes. Written in smudgy pencil inside the torn edges were four Japanese characters.

Dorie is going to want to hear about this.

FROM DORIE TO HER PARENTS

January 22, 1945

Dear Mother and Daddy,

The army managed to get word to me about Jack's death. I didn't believe it at first. Now I just feel numb, as if I'll go to sleep and tomorrow morning someone will tell me it was all a mistake.

But I know they won't. That's the worst part of it.

I wish I could be there with you right now. Which is why I hate to give you more bad news.

I'm sorry, but I can't come home for Jack's funeral, not right now. I know you'd want me there, but trust me that I'm on a mission of great importance and can't leave yet. If anyone in the family asks after me, I wouldn't want them to think . . . well, that I wasn't there because I was still angry. I guess you could tell them—oh, what are you supposed to say? All the neighbors, all the relatives know Jack and I quarreled before we left. I'm sure the whole town knows. It all seems so far away and pointless now.

We were hard on Jack, me most of all, but he knew we loved him. He must have. I only wish I'd said it more, near the end.

I asked a fellow here, Thomas, who knows Scripture better than me to suggest a psalm someone like Jack might like. He said the end of Psalm 85. I read it tonight, and it's lovely. All about righteousness and peace and truth and heaven. Could you read that at the funeral on my behalf? I'll make it up to you when I finally can come home, I promise.

All my love,
Dorie

INTERVIEW WITH CHARLES MAYES

January 23, 1945

Notes: Completed while unloading a delivery truck into the kitchen. How a camp of around forty people can eat so many loaves of white bread is beyond me.

Me: Tell me, Mr. Mayes, do you have any regrets about applying for conscientious objector status?

Charlie: Of course not. The army doesn't want my kind anyway.

Me: Now, that's just not true. There are plenty of black soldiers. Several of them served at Fort Lawton in Seattle where I was assigned.

Charlie: Mm-hmm. Then you'd know. Did they serve with the other troops? Eat with them? Were they treated just the same?

Me: I . . . well, no. It's not the way things are done.

Charlie: Mm-hmm. See, when Uncle Sam jabs that finger of his off a poster and says he wants "you," he means he wants the white boys. Now, I don't believe in violence, but even if I did, I wouldn't put my life on the line for a country that took every chance it could get to shove me to the side. That's just fool's talk. But here, stuck in the middle of nowhere with nobody but each other, we're brothers.

Me: I have noticed that. It's . . . different.

Charlie: There's a lot about us that's different. You be sure to put that in your report. The army could learn a thing or two. When the whole rest of the world called us "yellow," we stopped caring so much about who was black and who was white.

Me: So the COs all get along with each other, you'd say? And with the other rangers?

Charlie: Well enough. We've had some trouble with the boys from town. But it hasn't been bad.

Me: What about that fellow who was killed in the fire? Everyone seems shaken by his death.

Charlie: Sure. We all loved Jack.

Me: It seems strange that there was a fire so close to a smokejumper base. Like some safety measure wasn't being followed, maybe?

Charlie: I don't know about that, but I've never seen a man so worried about safety as Earl Morrissey. All those lectures, shouting us through drills over and over, making us repeat our instructions like they were Scripture. He was shook up by what happened to Jack.

Me: Is that so? How can you tell?

Charlie: Well, for one thing, he asked to borrow my camera so he could take some pictures of the site.

Me: A camera? What good would photographs do?

Charlie: Mr. Morrissey said maybe he'd see something that could help keep it from happening again.

Me: Was there anything in the pictures that seemed . . . helpful?

Charlie: Can't say, ma'am. Mr. Morrissey takes them to get developed, and he kept those and gave me the rest, mostly nature photos and birds. Ask me, I don't think it'll do much. You can't prevent wildfires. You can only fight them—and sometimes it's too late even to do that.

CHAPTER 21

Gordon Hooper

January 23, 1945

The woodpecker's tufted head took shape under my pencil, beak aimed at the bark to bore out the beetles huddled inside. Just a few strokes at the nape, and I was ready to complete the most important part of the illustration: the eyes. I rounded the curve, shading life into the empty spheres—

"Good afternoon, Gordon!"

My hand jerked, giving the woodpecker a droop of false eyelashes, and I looked up to see Dorie swinging open the cabin door. "You shouldn't sneak up on people like that," I snapped, hacking my eraser with a pocketknife to get the point small enough to fix the blunder.

It's not her fault. You're the one who told her to meet you here. But I couldn't admit that, couldn't apologize to Dorie again. Once had been more than enough.

Dorie didn't seem bothered by my outburst, stamping her feet on the thick mat by the door and wrinkling her cold-reddened nose in my direction. "If you didn't hear the porch creaking to kingdom come on my way in, you'll make a pretty poor detective." She shivered and inspected the fireplace, standing empty against the wall. "Guess I won't be taking my coat off. Aren't you going to light that thing? It's freezing in here."

"I hadn't noticed." The chill focused my mind, and the birds that chattered in the trees just outside the cabin window helped set the mood. Those, at least, were the excuses I'd tried on Morrissey to get permission to use one of the empty tourist cabins by Antlers Trail to work on my sketches, since I couldn't tell him I needed a place away from the other boys for a meeting with Dorie.

"I have news." She turned the unoccupied wooden chair backward and sat with her legs sidesaddle, her wool beret askew and eyes bright. That was the thing about her that had caught my attention three years ago: Dorie crackled with energy. Every ordinary conversation with her turned into a Hollywood scene. "We might've finally caught a break."

I forced myself to turn my attention back to the sketch in front of me, feathering out the woodpecker's downy body. "Tell me it's better than your news from breakfast."

After I'd surreptitiously slipped her the paper with the Japanese characters wrapped inside a napkin, feeling for all the world like a criminal, we'd had a stilted conversation by the coffeepot, pausing when anyone came close enough to overhear. Eventually, I found out that Morrissey had been at a training for six hours before the fire—a story she'd verified with several witnesses.

Which meant Morrissey couldn't have set the fire himself for a controlled burn experiment. That theory, logical as it had seemed at the time, also didn't fit with the army jeeps Lloyd reported, which I'd also told Dorie about. So we were back to the drawing board, so to speak.

"Nice illustration. I bet Charlie took those, didn't he?" Dorie said, nodding at the photographs I'd spread out on the small pine table in front of me. I'd brought only the woodpecker and golden eagle, each shot from a few different angles.

"How'd you know?" I said, trying to shield my drawing from her. Suddenly, all I could see was what was wrong with it: the too-straight edges, the uneven shading on the wings, the roughed-in bark that looked like a child's scribble.

Dorie, though, didn't seem to be in the mindset of an art critic. "I interviewed Charlie after breakfast. And, Gordon, you'll never guess—he told me Mr. Morrissey borrowed his camera to take pictures near the fire."

"You didn't give me much time to guess." I gave a final pass over the bird's neck before moving on to texture the branch it perched on. Get the major things in place first, then fill in the details—that was how my artistic process worked.

There was a beat of quiet, enough to make me look up and see Dorie tilting her head severely at me. "I don't think you understand. There are *pictures*, Gordon. Actual photographic evidence of—" she flailed her hand in the air—"well, something. And Morrissey has them tucked away somewhere."

"Which means we'll never get our hands on them."

"Oh ye of little faith."

I knew Thomas would say that wasn't the proper biblical context for that particular expression.

"What about the jeeps Lloyd told me about? How is the army involved?" I hadn't had time to ask that at breakfast, even after Dorie "accidentally" spilled coffee on her sleeve and borrowed my handkerchief to blot it out.

Dorie licked a red-polished finger and paged through her note-book, as if the answer might be in there somewhere. "No idea. But it's always this way in the best mysteries. Just when the detectives feel most confused, they find the clue that makes everything fit together."

I barely kept from rolling my eyes, focusing on the drawing instead. "How many mystery novels or movies involve mysterious fires?"

"Plenty." She sputtered for a moment. "Like in *Jane Eyre*, when Rochester's house gets burned down. But that doesn't help us, since we don't have any delirious mad women wandering around."

It was finally my chance to smirk. "Oh, I think we've got at least one."

She shook her head sanctimoniously at me. "Why, Gordon, Edith Morrissey is the dearest person in the world, and you're a brute for talking about her like that."

"Very funny." How did she do that? Always ready with a witty reply, when I only thought of good comebacks days afterward.

"Then there's Dashiell Hammett—he's the best living writer of hard-boiled detectives. He wrote a story called 'Arson Plus' in *Black Mask* magazine. It's about a quirky inventor whose house burns down, killing him. The detectives think the servants murdered him, but something doesn't quite fit."

"So . . . how does it end?" I prompted.

"I don't want to spoil it for you."

"I am *never* going to read 'Arson Plus.' Or anything in *Black Mask*, for that matter."

I glanced up from my sketch long enough to see a flash of pink as she stuck her tongue out at me. "Snob. It *was* the servants who set the fire, but the inventor is actually still alive. He planned the whole thing for life insurance money." She twiddled her pencil against her cheek. "Say, do you know if Jack wrote you into his will?"

"Dorie!" That was going too far, even for her.

"Fine, fine." She snapped her fingers. "I know! In Hitchcock's *Saboteur*, an aircraft factory goes up in flames, and the hero runs to the rescue. A mysterious man hands him a fire extinguisher, but it turns out to be filled with . . ." She paused, slanting a dramatic look at me out of the corner of her eyes. "What do you guess?"

"Banana pudding," I tried, mostly just to see the annoyed look that sprang onto her face, right on cue.

"It was filled with gasoline."

"How is that even possible? For it to be correctly pressurized—"

"Oh, *don't* ruin it, Gordon," she interjected before I could finish, tossing her pencil at my head. It bounced off my shoulder and rolled across the oak drop-leaf table between us. "You have no imagination."

This wasn't helping us, only distracting me from my work. "Do you watch any movies that actually have artistic merit?"

Her eyes flicked to the window, widening slightly. Then, the next moment, her voice dropped into a husky register. "Well . . . I *do* like a good romance."

What was going on? *You're imagining things.*

"I don't know how that relates—" I began.

She pursed her lips in a mock pout, leaning dramatically against the table. "Don't be coy, Mr. Hooper. Do you mean to tell me romance wasn't on your mind when you invited me to meet you here?"

Even as she said the words, she motioned for me to pass her my pencil.

I did, and she wrote *person by window* on the corner of my sketch.

Sure enough, I saw a shadow through the calico curtain, blocking the incoming light.

Someone was watching us.

"N-no," I stammered, not sure what I was supposed to say but realizing I had to fill the air with something. "I thought you'd like to see my bird sketches, that's all."

214

Her laugh was like music. Like sleigh bells, I think I'd said once. She came up behind me and tugged on my chair, so I took the hint and stood. "Well, whatever you call it, I'd say this is a date. And whenever I go on a date with a soldier, I promise him one kiss before he ships out."

Where was this headed?

She began edging closer, dancing around me so I had to turn my back to the door to see her. "No one's ever managed to win my heart. Will you be the one, Mr. Hooper?"

And right there, with Dorie close enough for me to smell her floral perfume as she looked up at me under fluttering lashes, I knew.

It never would have worked.

Sometimes, in my weaker moments, I'd imagined what it would be like if Dorie changed her mind, wrote me a long letter saying that love could conquer any differences in disposition or beliefs.

And now here she was in front of me, all rashness and red lipstick, and it was easy to see that what we'd had together was as different from true love as a candle is from a wildfire.

"But what's this? No uniform?" She made a *tsk*ing sound that brought me forward three years to the present, holding me at arm's length for inspection. "It looks like you haven't earned your kiss."

"If that's what I have to do to win your favor, I never will."

For a moment, I saw her façade flicker. *You know I mean it, don't you, Dorie?*

"At least you're honest." She smirked, knowing the listener wouldn't realize the backward insult she'd delivered. "Well, I'd better get back to the camp. Wouldn't want any rumors to get started." She made for the door, hurrying the last several steps. "So long, Mr. Hooper. Best of luck with those birds."

This time even I heard it, the squeaking groan of wood, pounding footsteps on the porch as whoever had been listening leapt the railing and ran. Dorie, craning her neck out the door, shoved it back inside. "Well?" she said, cold air whipping through the open door. "Don't just stand there. Follow him!"

What good she thought it would do, I didn't have time to ask. I just obeyed that command and ran after our silent eavesdropper, already with a good lead on me.

Whoever it was, he was jackrabbit fast. Branches trembled ahead of me from where the intruder had passed through, so the trail was easy to follow, but I couldn't catch up.

My heart pounded with exertion—and questions. What had he seen? What had he heard? And why was he there in the first place?

Once, I spotted a glimpse of a dark coat disappearing into a stand of trees several dozen yards away. By then, my sides were heaving. Morning calisthenics or no, I wasn't used to sprinting long distances. At least digging a fire line was slow and steady work.

When it was obvious I'd fallen too far behind, I circled back to the cabin. Dorie was waiting, pacing the cabin's porch like she might wear a hole clean through it. "Well? Did you see who it was?" she called as I approached.

"No. You?"

She shook her head. "He vaulted off the porch straight into the trees before I could catch a look at his face. Even had a hat on, so I couldn't get a hair color."

"Do you think he heard anything?"

She shook her head. "I heard the floorboards creak right at the end, right before I . . . changed the mood." She smirked, which meant I was blushing again. "Even if he did hear anything, it was only a list of mysteries."

Innocent enough conversation, I supposed. Lucky for us.

"Either way, you might come back to a rumor or two." She

winked in a crinkle of smile lines. "Want me to smudge lipstick on your collar to give you a stronger alibi?"

"No thanks." I took an involuntary step backward, and when she laughed, it sounded so much like Jack's carefree laugh that I flinched.

"I'm glad you've learned your lesson from last time. I don't want to break your heart twice." She looked down at the ground for a moment, and when she turned back to me, her voice was softer. "I didn't want to break it in the first place."

It was so unexpected, so real, that I couldn't help saying, "And I didn't want to divide your family."

"No. I'm sure you didn't."

The truth lay unspoken between us: Despite our good intentions, we had each hurt the other anyway. Still, it felt good to say the words, like the first step toward not just being sorry but being forgiven.

CHAPTER 22

Dorie Armitage

January 23, 1945

The army had investigated the fire.

That was the part that didn't make sense to me, like someone had taken a piece from Edith's seaside puzzle and tossed it into a landscape of autumn leaves.

I tried to figure out where it might fit as Gordon and I walked back from the cabins. According to Lloyd, the army had come and gone in the dead of night. Why? Illegal activity was investigated by local police, so even if there had been foul play, it didn't make sense for the army to arrive, especially when the nearest military base was at least a day's ride away by train.

What had they been doing here?

That bothered me more than some curious eavesdropper—likely another CO who saw me hurrying into the woods in my bright blue coat and wondered where I was headed. Not exactly blending into my environment, was I?

"Hidey ho, friends!" The cheerful greeting split the quiet, and I looked over to see Shorty Schumacher striding down the path toward the bunkhouse, strutting like he'd just been given every ribbon at the county fair.

He flailed an arm at us in a wave. "So long, Wingtip! I'll be back in time for fire season."

Gordon stopped short. "What do you mean? Where are you going?"

"Wyeth, Oregon! CPS Camp #21 requested more men, and Morrissey said he could spare me till May at least. I jumped at the chance." Shorty grinned from under his shaggy bangs. "No offense, but in Wyeth, they've got almost two hundred COs, plus a camp store, a library, a theater, and two basketball teams. Think about *that*."

Before he could list more of the glories of Camp #21, Gordon interrupted. "Did you get a chance to talk to Morrissey? About you know what?" He leaned on the words meaningfully while giving a glance over his shoulder.

Subtle, Hooper. Real subtle.

"Oh," he said, scratching his head like he'd all but forgotten. "Sure. Gave him back that coat of his too. Never have seen anyone laugh so hard. 'Naked as Adam hiding in the bushes of Eden,' he said, and that's a quote."

I cocked my head curiously. "What's that supposed to mean?"

"Never mind," Gordon said quickly. "What did he say about those questions?"

"Oh, nothing much." Shorty scratched his back absently, oblivious to the fact that we were treating his every word like it was of life-or-death importance. "Jack never called in the fire. Richardson spotted the smoke above the trees after they came back from some program in another district, and that's when they rang the bell."

That fit the story we'd gotten from others. "And Morrissey didn't wonder why Jack hadn't reported the fire?"

"Didn't say. I guess he figured what I did, that Jack tried to handle it on his own. He always was braver than the rest of us."

"'Courage is running toward the fire, not away from it,'" Gordon quoted darkly.

I'd heard some of the other boys mention the motto, and it always hit me the wrong way, but now it seemed especially unhelpful. "And look where that got him."

Instantly, Shorty crossed gangly arms over his chest. "Hey now, that's not fair, Miss Hightower. It was an accident. Not Jack's fault. He was a real swell guy, and you didn't even know him."

Was it true? I was Jack's older sister, only a year of age difference between us. I'd known him his whole life.

And yet Gordon, Shorty, and the others probably saw a side of him that I never had.

"You're right," I said, suddenly subdued. "I didn't."

For a moment, Gordon turned to look at me, concern in his eyes. *Please don't.* Now wasn't the time for me to fall apart.

To my relief, he focused back on Shorty. "Anything about why they took Jack to an army hospital?"

"Just said we're War Department property, and anyway, army doctors have more experience treating burns that bad. Made sense." He hitched a thumb toward the bunkhouse. "Listen, Wingtip, I've got to pack. The truck's going to be here by supper to pick me up."

Something about the timing bothered me. "One more thing," I interjected. "When did you ask Mr. Morrissey these questions?"

"Right before calisthenics—got me out of at least fifteen minutes of running." He grinned at his own brilliance.

"And when did he tell you about the transfer?"

"Just now. Which is why I'm in a hurry." Shorty tousled Gordon's hair, then bowed in my direction, all formality. "It's been fun. But hot diggity, a real basketball team!"

I watched him scamper down the trail before I turned to Gordon. "So. Shorty goes in to dig up information for us, comes up with nothing. Now Morrissey is transferring him to a different camp. What does that tell you?"

He looked reluctant but delivered the answer I'd been hinting at, the only reasonable one. "It means Morrissey doesn't want anyone asking questions. So that's a dead end."

I let out a breath of frustration, a puff of white in the air. "Isn't there any way to get more information without going straight to Morrissey? Did Jack keep a journal?"

"We thought he did. But it was just the radio plays, and I looked through all of those before sending them to your parents."

Except the one he'd sent to me. Full of clichés and bad dialogue, sure . . . but so like Jack that it had made me ache.

Stop it. There's no time for that.

"Did he write a letter to anyone where he might have mentioned something?"

Gordon shook his head. "I doubt it. He once joked that his family disowning him saved him a fortune on stamps."

"Hilarious." I made sure my tone was completely devoid of humor. Because I couldn't think about that, couldn't let the guilt come back again. I'd nearly broken down writing to my parents, telling them I couldn't come to the funeral.

"So there's no written record of anything he might have said, seen, or done before the fire?"

"I don't think . . ." Gordon paused, staring blankly, then snapped his fingers. "Wait. There's a log."

I gestured to the forest. "Something different from the thousands of other logs around us?"

He gave me a flat look. "A log like a leather-bound book, not a chunk of wood."

"When you think about it, a book really *is* a chunk of wood," I pointed out.

Gordon looked significantly less appreciative of my cleverness than my usual male audience. "Some fellow back in the thirties started an observation log up at the fire tower. Not for the weather or fire data that we put in official reports. Lookouts will write their name, the date, and . . . well, anything interesting. Some fellows will copy out a quote from a book they're reading, draw wildlife they've spotted, or even write poetry."

"You think Jack might have recorded something that would help us?"

Gordon nodded, his words coming faster. "Not everyone used the log. But Jack did. His entries were usually the philosophical sort. Musings. Quotes. Sometimes Bible verses. If something was on his mind when he went up to that tower . . ." He trailed off.

Who's the dramatic one now, Gordon?

But it was fun, seeing the light of curiosity leap into his eyes. Yes, Gordon Hooper would make a decent detective's sidekick after all.

"Fine. You've sold me. Let's convince Morrissey, and then I'll pay a social call to your crow's nest. Maybe even stay overnight."

His eyes bugged out at me. "Overnight? But . . . I don't think that would be . . ."

The stutter and unease on his face reminded me that I hadn't given him all the details of getting called in to Morrissey's office the day before. "You don't know who the lookout is, do you?"

"No," he said slowly. "Who?"

I could feel a smile spreading across my face. "Sarah Ruth Morrissey."

CHAPTER 23

Gordon Hooper

January 23, 1945

Of all things, Dorie insisted I get permission from Morrissey for her to go up to the lookout. "I get the feeling he doesn't trust me" was her explanation, which I wanted to say was pretty smart of him.

"But what if he sends me away like he did Shorty?" That would be the end of our little investigation.

She brushed my objection aside. "I'm going to be the one snooping, not you. Gollee, Gordon, loosen up. Even if he did, it might do you some good to get a change of scenery, instead of being stuck here, where . . ." She waved her hands at the trees in general. "I mean, doesn't this place remind you of him?"

Of course it did. There was the birdhouse Jack had helped Thomas put up outside the bunkhouse window. The fire pit where he presided with stories and jokes and games every Friday night. The fence where he and Shorty had held a balancing contest—and both tumbled into a snowbank. Memories of Jack were everywhere here.

Maybe it would be easier to start over with a pack of strangers who wouldn't talk about Jack or give me a pitying look whenever I passed by.

"That's the thing," I said slowly, speaking it as I thought it. "I want to remember."

Something passed over her expression that I couldn't quite read, but then she blinked it away and patted me on the arm. "Well then, just *remember* that Jack would do anything to help his sister, and you should too."

That was true enough, so I swallowed hard and set off in the direction of the ranger station, knocking on Morrissey's office and explaining Dorie's whole scheme in practically one breath.

"So," I said, clasping my hands behind my back and trying to sound casual, "will you let her go?"

Morrissey considered this, scratching the overgrown beard stubble on his usually cleanshaven face, like he had already made up his mind but was searching for a by-the-books reason to back up his answer.

Then a slight smile tilted on his face, gone in the next second like an ember blown out.

"As long as you can get Sarah Ruth to agree, I won't stand in your way." He gestured to the telephone on his desk, and suddenly the shiny black earpiece cradled there looked like a torture device.

I'd have to ask Sarah Ruth? I swallowed. "Phone lines probably have trouble in the winter, don't they? Ice and all."

"Sometimes. But it's forty-two degrees out right now, son."

Never try to best Earl Morrissey with a nature-related question. He could probably sniff the air and tell you the temperature, the atmospheric pressure, and the latest three woodland creatures to amble by.

"Sure." I traced the number used to connect to the lookout tower, written in a list by the phone, and prayed she'd be out trapping rabbits or whittling a tree limb or whatever Sarah Ruth did when she was alone on a mountain.

"Hello?" Crisp, tense, like a soldier waiting for orders. She must have thought it was her father calling with official news.

"Hi, Sarah Ruth?" *Of course it's her, who else would it be?* "This . . . this is Gordon. Hooper."

The voice on the other side turned considerably chillier. "What do you want?"

How was I going to lead into this? I'd had a plan once, but the words completely fled my mind, with Sarah Ruth snapping at me and her father staring at me. "H-how are things at the lookout?"

If her voice had been cold before, now it was like something left out overnight in a snowbank. "Don't you think I've got better things to do than shoot the breeze? This forest is under my watch. So, if that's all . . ."

"It's not all," I interrupted. *Come on. Just get the words out.* "You see, the WAC who's visiting the camp wants . . . well, she asked if she could stay the night at the fire tower."

Clearly, from the crackling silence, she hadn't expected that. "The girl with the red lipstick and heels?"

Even over the crackling line, I heard the skepticism in her voice loud and clear. "That's the one."

"Why would she want to do that?"

Finally, a question I'd prepared an answer for. "She told me she wants to get the full smokejumper experience for her report."

Though it wasn't a lie, it still felt too close to deception for me to feel comfortable, so I changed the subject. "I'm sure she won't be any trouble."

Actually, come to think of it, that was even closer to a lie.

"Isn't she already poking her powdered nose into our business?"

"Well, not *much* trouble anyway," I amended.

Sarah Ruth grunted and stayed silent for a long moment. I could practically picture her expressive eyes narrowing. "Do *you* think it's a good idea?"

Not the question I'd been expecting. "Sure," I blurted. "I mean, isn't it good to show people as much truth as we can?"

Another pause, and I glanced over to see Morrissey pretending not to listen, the way he watched me over the top of his file folders the only giveaway.

"Well . . . all right," Sarah Ruth said at last. "As long as it's only one night."

Only Morrissey's eyes on me kept me from jumping in victory. Yes! It had worked. Dorie would be thrilled.

"You'll need to tell her I'm not a tour guide or her nanny. If she wanders off and gets mauled by a bear, that's her own fault. I'm on fire watch duty."

"I'll be sure to pass that along."

For a moment, I thought she'd ended the call. Then she sighed. "Listen, Gordon, I'm sorry for being rude. It's just that, there was a time when I . . . I used to take social calls on lookout duty. But I shouldn't have. It's not right."

"I guess not." Although this deep into January, it wasn't likely she'd spot another fluke fire. "But no one doubts you're the most responsible one of all of us."

"Thanks for that, Gordon." For a moment, her voice actually softened. Then it was back to its usual gruffness. "So you're coming tonight?"

"As soon as she's packed and ready."

"I'll watch for you, then."

And with that, the line went dead.

I twisted around to see Morrissey staring at me, dumbfounded. "She said yes," I clarified.

"I gathered." He shook his head at this unexpected development, and I waited for him to make up some excuse, to tell me a meddling WAC had no place in his beloved forest. But not Earl Morrissey, dutiful district ranger and keeper of his word. "Best get started if you want to be back before dark."

"Yes, sir." I started to duck out of the office before he could ask any more uncomfortable questions, then paused.

Should I?

"Just curious, sir, but did you assign Sarah Ruth to lookout duty?"

As soon as Dorie announced it, it had made sense—after all, I hadn't seen Sarah Ruth around the camp for days. The news of Jack's death had put me in such a fog that I hadn't thought to ask why. Even if I had, with the vehement way Sarah Ruth had told Charlie and me she wouldn't be going back to lookout duty, it wouldn't have occurred to me as an option.

Morrissey barked out a laugh. "Hooper, no one 'assigns' my daughter to anything. She pretty well does what she wants—and she was dead set on this."

Strange. I'd have guessed the opposite, but who could understand women anyway?

All I knew for sure was that having Dorie and Sarah Ruth trapped together for a full night would be a sight to see.

CHAPTER 24

Dorie Armitage

January 23, 1945

By the time night fell and it was too late for Sarah Ruth to give me the old heave-ho off what you'd think was her own personal mountain, we'd completely run out of things to talk about.

When I'd huffed my way up three flights of stairs to the top of the tower and knocked on the lookout door, she was barely cordial. "Why are you here again?" she'd asked, and my cheerful explanation of the army report didn't lower her skeptical eyebrow even a twitch. Neither did my attempts at interview questions or my compliments on her knowledge of the wilderness.

Never mind. I don't have to win her over, just sneak past her.

"The stars are lovely here, aren't they?" I attempted. "Like diamonds against a black-velvet evening gown." That was the one benefit of glass houses jutting into the sky—you could see for miles in all directions.

Sarah Ruth continued to brush her auburn hair—surprisingly pretty when it wasn't tucked under her ugly, slouching hat. "They're lovely everywhere. You can just see them better from here."

"Well, yes. I suppose." And silence reigned once more as Sarah

Ruth set her brush down to clean the pearl-handled pistol she'd used to kill our supper. I'd forced a few salty forkfuls down without risking a question about what sort of meat, exactly, it was. Better not to picture it with fur on.

How could this hawkish female possibly be related to Edith "Betty Crocker" Morrissey? And how had I thought, from our brief encounter at the ranger station, that she was sweet and polite?

I tried again. "You really didn't need to leave me the cot, you know. I feel just awful about stealing your bed."

"I've slept on the ground before."

I laughed brightly. "Yes, I'm sure you've roughed it on logging expeditions with Paul Bunyan."

She stared. "Paul Bunyan wasn't real. And he lived in Minnesota and the Dakotas, not Oregon."

She clearly hadn't heard the nickname Shorty had given her. "Well, I suppose it's time to get our beauty sleep."

"You'll need a blanket." Her eyes roamed the length of me with one eyebrow cockeyed, and I realized how I must seem to her, dressed in blue silk pajamas with a bow at the waist and a pair of calfskin slippers, all against the backdrop of the rugged exposed beams of the lookout. Could I help it if having a paycheck for the first time in my life had driven me to the irresistible Bon Marché window displays in downtown Seattle?

"If you have an extra one, I'd appreciate it." I tried not to shiver. Terribly drafty, these lookout towers, with just the one potbelly stove and windows for walls.

She knelt by the cot and dragged out a wooden crate. I peered over her shoulder to take a look at the contents: a first aid kit, a coil of thick rope, a shovel, matches, a lantern—and a blanket that looked like it was made from the wool of a sheep who had lost a fight with a gully full of brambles.

"Thanks," I said, trying to sound sincere as I shook it over the cot . . . and sneezed from the cloud of dust it loosed into the lookout.

There wasn't much to use for an evening toilette, just a basin of water and an old dishcloth that I cringed to touch to my face. Oh, for the porcelain sinks and tubs of the Stratford Hotel. Thankfully, I'd remembered to toss in my tin of cold cream, which I patted on afterward.

Time to "sleep." Faking an elaborate yawn, I eased onto the cot . . . then sprang up with a cry.

"What's the matter?" Sarah Ruth said, reaching for the pistol in her belt, instantly tense and alert.

By that point, I'd made it to the wall behind the stove, which was as far away as I could get without flinging myself out onto the outside platform. I indicated the warm lump under my blanket. "S-shoot it! Something *alive* is under there."

Sarah Ruth watched where I pointed. "Did you feel it move?"

I nodded, eyeing the lump under my blanket. "Could it be a mouse? A squirrel? Or . . . or . . ." What sort of small animals did they have up in the mountains? "A vampire bat?"

"I think," Sarah Ruth said, stepping around the cot to head the thing off, "it's much more likely to belong to the rare species called a . . ." With a flick of her wrist, the blanket flew through the air. "Hot water bottle," she finished and burst out laughing.

There, nestled cozily on the cot, was the lumpiest hot water bottle I'd ever seen. "I was sure it moved," I grumbled. Or at least, it was meant to be a grumble, but in between, I'd lain down on the cot, and it was difficult to be cross when snuggled up to a hot water bottle.

"Let me know if you hear anything during the night," Sarah Ruth said, pulling her own blanket over herself and blowing out the lantern that made our lookout glow like a frontier homestead. "It might be a teakettle or a pillowcase on the warpath." She chuckled in the dark.

I huffed silently so she wouldn't hear. *We'll see who's laughing once I get what I came for.*

It was only after several minutes of scheming my next move in the dark that I realized: There had been only one hot water bottle warming near the stove. And Sarah Ruth had given it to me.

Characters were always sneaking here and there in detective novels and romances. All of them would tell you it was easy for an eavesdropper to decipher when a person's breathing shifted from "awake" to "asleep." Almost as clear as a light switching on or off, or so I'd always thought.

That was a lie.

Or at least, lying on the lookout cot with Sarah Ruth bundled up only a few feet away, I couldn't hear a single snore over the creaky floorboards as the platform groaned in the wind.

So there was nothing to do but wait for my hot water bottle to go stone cold and hope enough time had passed to be safe.

When I stood, the floor gave a loud shriek, and I stayed motionless for a few heartbeats. When the shadowed form stretched out on the floor didn't rise or call out, I breathed again.

I'd tucked my small chrome flashlight inside my slippers and drew it out, holding it like a policeman's baton but not turning it on, trying to move around the shadows based on my memory of Sarah Ruth's "tour." For a room of five yards on each side, that had mostly meant an exhaustive description of the Osborne FireFinder and how a gadget that looked like Columbus must have toted it around could determine the precise location of a blaze. I hadn't seen a logbook out in the open anywhere, but Gordon had told me it was usually kept on the bookshelf beside the door.

I placed each slippered step with care, until a sharp pain cracked through me as my toe connected with a chair left askew from the small table in the center of the lookout. I froze, biting my tongue, but no sleepy call of "What's going on?" interrupted me.

After a few agonizing moments, I moved again, this time more quickly. I flicked on my flashlight, shielding and focusing the light with a cupped hand, and aimed it at the shelves. Two different copies of the Bible, one in something that looked like German. *A Farewell to Arms. Pilgrim's Progress. Being and Time. The Conquest of Violence: An Essay on War and Revolution.* Ugh. No wonder Gordon and his fellow COs turned out so dull, if this was what they had for light bedtime reading.

Wait.

There, resting flat on the second shelf, was a brown leatherbound book. I picked it up, glancing behind me. The heap by the stove still didn't stir.

No embossed gold lettering, but on the interior flap, someone had written *Observation Log* in bold strokes. Underneath it was *Roy Winters, May 18, 1937. Share what you dare.* The creator of the log, I assumed, one of the CCC men who had lived at the camp nearly a decade ago.

Carefully, I paged through the book. Even though I knew what I was looking for—something the week before January 12—I couldn't help but pause on some of the pages. Several early love poems, a hand-drawn crossword puzzle, two terrible attempts at self-portraiture, and a five-stanza epic entitled "Ode to the Commode," signed by Shorty. A few pages later, a pencil sketch of an owl swooping in for the kill caught my eye, every detail sharp and lifelike. The tiny *GH* beneath its claw identified the artist.

Too talented for his own good, that Gordon Hooper. His drawings for the brochure had been breathtaking, capturing motion and beauty in a few simple lines. *What could he be doing right now if Japan hadn't bombed Pearl Harbor?*

Silly. War had come, and Gordon had made his choice. So had Jack. There was no sense getting sentimental about it.

I licked my finger and paged quickly to January 1945, scanning for Jack's familiar handwriting: neat, blocky capitals, because he hated trying to scrawl out cursive.

There. I'd found my bedtime story. Jack's last entry, a page of musings set off in pairs.

If we participate in evil (killing) to prevent more evil (killing), how can good triumph?

Followed by the next line: *Can we justify turning aside while innocents die?*

Jesus said, "Resist not evil: but whosoever shall smite thee on thy right cheek, turn to him the other also."

And yet, "Therefore to him that knoweth to do good, and doeth it not, to him it is sin."

And finally, all alone and centered at the bottom of the page without reply or rebuttal, the familiar words: *This is what happens when a good man does nothing.*

The very same sentence I'd scrawled on that last newspaper article.

Conscientious objector or not, he was at war, all right, my brother. Not with the Axis powers. With himself.

Maybe Jack would have torn these pages out of the logbook at the end of his shift so his fellows wouldn't know about his struggle. Or maybe he was tired of pretending and meant to let them stand.

We'd never know. Because he never came back to the tower.

"I'm sorry."

The words were spoken aloud, but only in a whisper. I breathed in deeply and blinked the tears away, thinking of the military recruitment brochure still tucked in my coat pocket. Thomas was sure Jack was on the brink of joining up. I could see upraised lines through the observation log page, showing writing on the other side. What had Jack decided?

But when I turned the page, there was no conclusion, only a headline, still in Jack's handwriting: *Spotted January 11.*

The day before the fire that killed him.

There was a drawing scrawled underneath. The only parts I could identify were rough, triangle-like trees. I turned the book to the side, trying to see what it could be. It looked like a blob of mystery meat served up at a mess hall. Jack apparently hadn't picked up any of Gordon's talent for art.

Still, I recreated it as best I could in my notebook, tucked in the waistband of my pajamas.

Underneath the sketch was this note: *Silk?* Then, *Report to Morrissey.*

Silk. In my interviews, several men had talked about "hitting the silk," referring to going on a parachute drop.

If that's what Jack had spotted, why would a parachute be hidden in the woods?

"I'll find out what really happened," I whispered to the pages, tracing Jack's handwriting. "You'll see."

"What are you doing?"

I sucked in a breath, dropping the logbook, and turned to see Sarah Ruth, blanket draped loosely around her shoulders. The dim light my flashlight threw in her direction was enough to see that she was glaring at me.

Rookie mistake. Not hearing an enemy approach over the sound of howling wind.

"I . . . I was having trouble falling asleep. So I thought I'd do some reading." All technically true. Gordon would be proud.

Sarah Ruth took a step closer and nudged the logbook with her foot, which was covered in a thick wool sock. "I *hate* that book."

Good. At least that meant her ire wasn't directed at me personally. "What, the woodpecker sketches are a bit too much?" Her face didn't soften, and I realized my joke had fallen on an unappreciative audience.

"The man who started it was a first-class cad."

"Ah," I said. Because "ah" is always the safest response where hated men are involved. If she wanted to say more about Roy Winters, she would.

"Mark my words, there's nothing worth reading in there." Before I could stop her, she bent down to pick up the book by its spine, straightening the bent corner on the page I'd been looking at—and inhaling sharply. "The parachute . . ."

Not "a parachute." "*The* parachute." One glance, without even time to read the words, and she'd known what the vague drawing was supposed to represent.

"What do you know about what Jack saw, Sarah Ruth?" In the pause, I snatched the Observation Log away from her. She didn't resist, her arms retreating into the blanket again. "And don't you dare say nothing."

It was risky. PFC Nora Hightower, army investigator, wouldn't have said that. But if this was my chance to crack the case, I couldn't worry about details like that.

She was a Morrissey. This was her forest, her mountain. And that meant she might know some of its secrets.

For a moment, we stood staring at each other. Then, instead of answering, Sarah Ruth turned, floating across the lookout, her blanket cape trailing behind her, and lit a match. The kerosene lantern glowed again, and she set it on the table next to the FireFinder, studying me in the dim glow like she was peering at coordinates through its sights.

"You're Jack's sister, aren't you?" she whispered, as if someone might hear us.

My hand seized the flashlight in a death grip before I could control my instincts. Could I lie my way out?

No. The way she stared at me, those too-large hazel eyes calm and certain, I knew there was no use. "How did you know?"

"Jack mentioned his sister once, when he asked me for . . ." Whatever she was going to say evaporated as she shook her head. "And you look like him. Not your features. But the way you gesture when you talk. Your laugh. That sort of thing."

I fought my rising panic with logic. Maybe this was good. I could use this. Yes.

I held up the log. "Jack saw something the day before the fire. Did he report it to your father? Or you?" After all, she was the national forest secretary.

Her eyes darted away. "I . . . I don't think I can answer that."

"I see. Because your father set the fire himself and you're trying to cover for him."

My below-the-belt accusation, carefully aimed, connected. "No! He would *never* do that."

"Oh?" I asked coolly, meeting her eyes. "Then convince me otherwise."

She hesitated, but I was ready for that. "I've got nothing against you or your family, I swear. But my brother died and I don't know why. You can't understand how that makes me feel," I said.

And the look in her eyes just then . . . it was like a wildcat transformed into a kitten, small and vulnerable. "Yes, I can."

Of course. William Morrissey. A fallen hero buried in some unknown overseas location.

Don't get distracted. Sympathy can wait. "I just want the truth. Please."

For a moment, she stared out of the windowed wall, as if hoping the stars would rearrange to tell her what to do.

Then she creaked the lone chair away from the table. "Sit down. I'll tell you what I know."

I didn't dare say a word and ruin the moment. Just sat, pulled my knees up to my chest for warmth, and listened.

The day before the fire, Morrissey had burst out of his office, demanding to know if all the parachutes were accounted for. Surprised, Sarah Ruth had checked the storage shed, comparing the inventory to her list. Every parachute pack was neatly lined up on the shelf in its place.

When she brought back the report, her father had immediately made a call to the regional supervisor's office, leaving his office door cracked open enough for Sarah Ruth to hear every word.

"'Our lookout's spotted something odd, Baumgartner. A downed parachute in our district.' He paused. 'No, it's not one of ours. Do you think it could have—' Another pause, longer. 'I'm sorry, I don't understand. Why would the army need to get involved? I'm sure the Forest Service can handle whatever—yes, sir. I'll tell him you're reporting it. Can you tell me anything else?'

"And then," Sarah Ruth said, shrugging, "he ended with, 'Yes, sir. I understand.' But it didn't sound like he understood. He sat there for a while, quiet. Then he called the lookout."

"Jack."

She nodded. "I heard him say, 'Armitage, under no circumstances should you investigate that parachute.' Then, 'I don't know. But it'll be taken care of. There's a time for asking questions . . . and there's a time for following orders.'"

As a WAC, I'd heard statements like that before. "You're sure?"

"Wouldn't you remember, if the next day there was . . . that awful fire?"

Of course I would. Especially if the lookout my father talked to had later died from his injuries.

"I don't know what they were talking about, but it was like . . . like someone knew what was going to happen." Sarah Ruth's voice, once steady as her trigger finger, actually shook, and she wrapped the blanket tighter around herself. "Like they could have stopped it but didn't."

"Is that what your father thought?"

The edges of the blanket rose with her shrug. "I waited for him to come home that night, after the fire. It was late." Her voice caught. "He . . . he didn't look good."

I could picture that, all right. Earl Morrissey, smelling of smoke with the hangdog look of a soldier dragged out of a failed mission. I'd met them at the hospital, men who'd woken up on a battlefield, trapped under debris and fallen bodies, who'd watched their buddies die in front of them . . . but they'd survived. Alive but marked by guilt. Maybe that was why Morrissey's shifting expression had seemed so familiar. I'd met a hundred other men like him, plagued by guilt they shouldn't have to bear.

"I asked him what happened, and all he said was, 'Something's not right, Ruthie. The army's coming. Here. To this forest.'"

That fit with what Lloyd had told Gordon, seeing the jeeps at dawn the day after the fire.

"When I asked why," Sarah Ruth continued, "he said he didn't know. Swore—which he's only done in front of me one other time that I can remember. Told me no one was answering his questions, everything was classified. 'They've got no right to keep secrets, not when it affects my forest, my boys,' he said."

"That doesn't make sense."

"I thought so too. But we Morrisseys—well, we're not the nosy sort. We stick together, do our duty, and don't ask questions. So I let it be."

The perfect motto for a mobster clan . . . but maybe one that was on the side of good all along.

If I believed Sarah Ruth's story.

"Have you learned anything since then?" I pressed.

"Dad's been working late, typing his own letters instead of dictating them to me, and making more calls than normal." Her smile was wry and brief. "Mama's going to have a fit when she sees the bill. To strange places too. Some of the other national forests, but also Washington, D.C., and Seattle and a library in Portland, plus a few newspapers and an old war buddy. I searched through the outgoing mail. Didn't have the guts to open them. I don't know how many wrote back, because that's when you showed up and I left for lookout duty."

My mind was jumping ahead. Letters. That meant documentation. Probably kept with the photographs from Charlie's camera.

How could Gordon and I get to them without raising Morrissey's suspicions?

"But you see . . ." she said, stepping back into my line of sight and snapping my attention back. Her face was somber, searching. "Whatever happened to Jack, it's not my father's fault."

I should have just agreed, to pacify her. No sense being stuck in a tower with an angry daughter. But I couldn't help asking, "Then whose was it?"

"I don't know," she said, and the frustration that colored her voice sounded like my own. "But I think . . . I think he's trying to figure out what happened too. Just like you. And I'm afraid he's going to get in trouble for it."

You'd say anything to protect your family, wouldn't you? The Morrissey gang, closing ranks. Couldn't all of this be some elaborate story meant to cover up an uglier truth?

And yet . . . the young woman before me, worry-lined features deceptively fragile in the flickering lamplight, seemed completely sincere in her belief that her father wasn't a murderer, just another detective.

So which story was true?

"I believe you," I said, trying to inject my voice with reassurance, and the way she breathed out in relief almost pricked my conscience, "but I need you to promise something: No one, especially not your father, can know who I am."

A puzzled frown flickered on her face. "I don't understand."

Now that I was found out, my only hope rested right here, in this speech. "If word gets out that I'm Jack's sister, they'll send me home. And I have to know, Sarah Ruth. I have to know what happened."

Without realizing she was doing it, Sarah Ruth glanced over toward the phone, the one that ran right to Morrissey's office. "I'm not sure I can promise that."

Ugh. Another rule follower. She and Gordon would be perfect for each other.

That's it.

"Gordon Hooper knows the truth," I said. "We've met before, and he's helping me. That's why he asked if I could come here tonight."

And just like that, her stance softened. "Well, if Gordon thinks it's all right . . ."

Bingo. Thank goodness some woman still had a soft spot for ol' Hooper.

"I just need another week, Sarah Ruth. That's all." After that, answers or no, Fort Lawton would expect me back. I held out my hand, put on my best pleading look. "Promise me? From one sister to another."

And after a moment of consideration in the flickering dark of the lookout, she shook it.

CHAPTER 25

Gordon Hooper

January 24, 1945

I lifted my axe and split the log in two, letting some of my stress burn away in the repetitive motion. "Are we sure Jack meant to draw a parachute?"

"What else could it be? The skirt of a silk ball gown?"

"Maybe Jack saw something and only thought it was silk from a distance. A tent or a discarded tarp. Because if that's to scale"—I pointed toward the crude drawing she'd copied in her notebook— "it's far too large to be a chute."

Dorie drilled me with a skeptical look, picking up the split logs and stacking them onto the pile, her breath coming in white puffs from the exertion, and hair all askew. "Gordon, he drew the pine trees as triangles with lines poking out of them. I don't think technical accuracy was first on his mind."

It was a fair point. Jack could do arithmetic in his head in seconds and spin a yarn around the campfire, but he was no artist. I set a new log on the chopping block. "Why would someone abandon a parachute? Each one costs over one hundred dollars."

"Maybe they had to hide before they were seen."

"And leave behind a giant white sign that says, 'I was here'?" I sighed and heaved the axe down again, letting two rangers pass on the way to an assignment. They barely gave Dorie more than a nod, used to her presence now, and she waved at them.

"Okay, so pretend it was a parachute." Even saying it hypothetically felt ridiculous. "Who's parachuting into an Oregon forest during wartime? And why would the army show up the next day to investigate it?"

"A spy." She jutted her chin out, as if she knew her words were absurd. "Maybe that's who you saw in the fire."

"Dorie, even if the rest of your suspicions are right, why would Morrissey try to cover for a spy? His son died serving in the army. The *American* one," I added before she could raise any theories to the contrary. "You don't get a Gold Star flag for your window and then harbor a Japanese spy."

"It isn't in their window."

The absent-minded comment caught me off guard. "What?"

"The Gold Star. They don't display one, not anywhere that I could find."

I tossed my hat down and swiped the sheen of sweat off my forehead, setting the axe aside for a moment. She was right, wasn't she? "Trust me on this: Not everyone likes talking about their deceased family members."

Wouldn't I know that better than most?

"All right, well . . . maybe there's a twist." She tapped her pencil against her temple. "Like in a Christie novel. Maybe the question isn't 'Who parachuted into the woods?' but '*What* was parachuted into the woods?' Something that an American contact like Morrissey could pick up and transport for Axis powers."

I wasn't buying it yet, but at least it was the first theory that made a lick of sense. "Such as . . ."

"Sabotage equipment, maybe." Dorie's dark curls—more disheveled

243

than the perfect pinned-up style she'd worn when she first arrived—bounced as she shook her head. "I don't know exactly."

"What would they sabotage? This isn't a Boeing factory or a munitions plant. Even our smokejumping planes come from an airfield hours away. The most advanced technology we own here is a crosscut saw."

Every answer led only to more questions, like a ball of tangled-up yarn with ends poking out in every direction. There was no good way to unknot it all.

Finally I asked what had been bothering me ever since Dorie had told me about Sarah Ruth's story. "Listen, are you sure Mr. Morrissey is guilty of anything? According to Sarah Ruth, he was only—"

"Oh please," Dorie said, blowing out a frustrated breath. "Don't go and let a pretty pair of eyes muddle your mind."

"I'm not—" Was there a point to defending myself? Dorie's smug smile told me she'd never believe me. *Whatever you do, don't blush.* "All I'm saying is, what evidence do we have against him?"

Dorie flared out her gloved fingers, touching them one by one. "The Japanese symbol in his pocket. The way he keeps dodging anyone's questions. The army jeeps investigating the night of the fire that he didn't tell anyone about. Secret photographs he took of the scene. And now this drawing of a parachute that Sarah Ruth flat-out admitted Jack reported to Morrissey the day before the fire." She faced me with hands on her hips. "We could get a pair of handcuffs custom engraved with his name for all that."

All circumstantial. "Sarah Ruth said her father didn't know about the fire."

"Wouldn't you say that too, if you knew someone was after your father?"

That, at least, I knew the answer to with certainty. "No, actually.

I'd help the police take him away." Which was a kinder fate than he'd deserved.

But also a kinder fate than he'd gotten.

Dorie ducked her head, suddenly subdued. "I-I'm sorry. I forgot your father . . . passed on."

The subject of my family had come up that Thanksgiving so long ago, though I'd given her the stock answer with none of the details. There are some things you just don't tell a girl you admire the first time you meet her. Although, since trading my home in New York for a fresh start at university in Philadelphia, I hadn't told anyone how my father had died. Some secrets were better off buried. "Don't be. I don't miss him anymore."

Had I ever, really?

I covered my response with the crack of a blow to the next log, unsure she'd heard me.

Sarah Ruth would have noticed and pressed me, narrowing those hazel eyes of hers that took in every detail. But Dorie just began to pace again. "Mark my words, Gordon: Before he died, Jack saw something, knew something, about what Morrissey was up to. And Morrissey made sure to silence him. What else could explain all this?"

I tried to square all of that with the stern, honorable man I thought I'd known. "But he was accounted for the day of the fire. You have no proof. Just suspicions."

"Which is why we need to find some. And I know where." Dorie's eyes darted to the left and right; then she reached into her pocket and pulled out a ring of keys . . . the same one I'd seen before on Sarah Ruth's desk.

I fumbled my grip on the axe, hitting the chopping block instead. "You *pickpocketed* Sarah Ruth at the lookout?"

Her eyes rolled heavenward. "Don't be silly. I'm staying in her bedroom. They were on her bureau."

She dangled the keys high, letting them glint in the cold morning light. "Oh five hundred hours tomorrow, Gordon. I'll be at the ranger station, and you're welcome to join me."

An hour before the rising bell rang. Objections swirled through my mind. I drew a breath and tried to pick the most persuasive one in an attempt to dampen that adventurous gleam lighting her eyes. "But—"

She raised a finger, cutting me off. "Just think about it, Gordon." And with that, she strolled away. "I could sure use a lookout."

CHAPTER 26

Dorie Armitage

January 25, 1945

I gripped my flashlight tightly in the darkness, just to remember that I could have light with a flick of my fingers if I needed it. Lit only by the halo glow provided by the lone light pole embedded past the ranger station, the timber-framed outbuildings threw long shadows, with corners perfect for a hundred lurking gangsters.

Even worse was the forest beyond, no longer Currier-and-Ives charming but full of strange rustling sounds and . . . was that a growl?

No. Those were just stories the COs told to scare you. According to Shorty, smokejumpers were black bears' favorite prey—"on account of we taste just like a roast that's been hanging in a smokehouse"— but they'd settle for anyone they could pounce on.

Calm down, Dorie, I scolded myself, gripping the ranger station railing tighter and remembering my fright over Sarah Ruth's hot water bottle.

I'd taken shelter on the ranger station's south porch, where twin statues of Lewis and Clark held up the gabled roof, their stern cedar faces declaring that the wilds of Oregon were only for the bold.

There. A flicker of movement caught my eye, someone headed down the path from the bunkhouse. *Well, well, well. I convinced Gordon after all.*

But wait. I didn't recognize the thick brown coat, and the walk was all wrong, bobbing to a jauntier rhythm than Gordon's proper posture. The closer the figure got, the more sure I was. . . .

Lloyd Abernathy. That's right. Hadn't Gordon said he went for an early morning walk most days?

Slowly—quick motions could be seen more easily out of the corner of the eye—I eased over a step until I was directly behind the statue of William Clark, letting the pioneer shield me from view. I held my breath and angled myself so I could watch Lloyd, his shadow long as he passed by the lamppost.

This time, though, seeing no jeeps to catch his attention, he didn't amble closer to the ranger station, just kept going over the frosty grass and into the woods.

I let out a breath of relief. It was an effective reminder that this wasn't some caper, like sneaking into the USO dance or pulling a prank on Sergeant Bloom. Jack had died. Morrissey was hiding something. And if he caught me breaking into the ranger station, who knew what he was capable of?

A few minutes more, with no one else emerging from the darkness, I faced facts. *Gordon's not coming.*

I hadn't really expected him to. I'm sure, in his mind, the chessboard battle of ethics had been making moves all during my last speech, and I was no grand champion. But something in me was forced to admit: It was nice having an accomplice. Even if mine happened to be an old fuddy-duddy out of one of the films they'd shown us in high school about good manners.

No way forward but alone. With my rucksack set on the ground, I dug in my pocket for Sarah Ruth's keys until the statue of Meriwether Lewis whispered, "Are we going to get this over with?"

I almost dropped the keys, then jammed on the button and leveled the flashlight beam at Gordon Hooper, who stepped out from behind the statue, squinting in the sudden brightness.

"How in the world did you sneak up on me?" I snapped, trying to get my heart to slow down from the sudden sneak attack.

"I've been here for an hour. Couldn't sleep." That seemed plausible enough, given his dark-circled eyes and tense, stubbled jaw.

"So you're with me, then?" I turned off the flashlight, hoping no one had seen the light. "Or are you here to perform a citizen's arrest?"

He shook his head. "Do you . . . do you really think we'll find out what happened to Jack?"

"I'm confident of it."

"You're confident about everything."

That wasn't strictly true, but it was close enough that I didn't argue.

Sarah Ruth's keys weren't labeled, so I jammed the two largest in the lock. Neither fit. "I hope I don't have to pick this." I'd tucked several sizes of hairpins into the cavernous recesses of my hurried bun just in case, but it would take longer than I liked to force the lock open.

"You have practice at that?"

I ignored him and attempted the third key. *Click.* My heart sped up like an engine turning over. "Stay here, somewhere discreet, and if you see someone coming, knock on the door. Hard."

He nodded. "And then hightail it out of here?"

"Of course not." Didn't he have any idea how a heist worked? "Stay and distract whoever it is. Talk to them."

"You mean lie?"

And *this* was why I regretted asking Gordon along. I put on my patient schoolteacher voice. "Do you have questions for Morrissey?"

"Sure. Lots of them."

"Then just ask them. And stall long enough so I can climb out a window." I eased the ranger station door open and pocketed the keys. "And yes, I've had practice at that too."

With my hand pressed against the log frame for balance, I yanked off my shoes and fished my slippers out of the army haversack. "Keep this for me, will you?"

He slung the haversack over his shoulder. "Your footwear's a little casual if you need to flee, isn't it?"

"Better than leaving muddy footprints inside." I could tell from his expression that he hadn't thought of that, which made me feel, if not a full-out criminal mastermind, at least pleased with my cleverness.

For a moment, surrounded by the total darkness of the ranger station, I breathed in deeply—the smell of dead leaves, firewood, and pine. *Time to get to work.*

I flicked on the flashlight—revealing a pair of eyes only a few feet from my face.

My beam jerked wildly, but my scream caught in my throat when I realized that underneath the eyes wasn't a nose but a beak.

Breathe, Dorie. Just one of the stuffed birds, that was all. I shivered, moving the light away from the blank stare and onto the floor, trying not to catch the gleam off of another feathered carcass stationed near the entryway.

Thank goodness for the rigid Forest Service schedule. We had a full fifty minutes until Morrissey rang the rising bell, calling the other COs to troop out of the bunkhouse for morning exercises. Still, that was no excuse for dawdling.

All of the spy novels talked about disturbing as little as possible during a covert search. My slippered feet glided silently across the wood floors, and I pressed the next key into the office door gently, so as not to leave a gouge.

It eased open with a slight squeak of hinges, and I stepped inside. The desk and chair behind it had seen decades of use, but they glowed with a fine polish. Stale cigar smoke lingered in the air, though I didn't remember ever seeing Morrissey light up. A private smoker, then, and possibly under more stress than usual.

To the east, the window—I'd checked for a screen when planning an escape route—let in a faint blueish light, but for a moment, I thought about turning on the brass banker's lamp on the desk to aid my search. Quickly, I ruled against it. *Don't get cocky, Dorie.*

My flashlight lit up a calendar on top of the large walnut desk, with appointments written in a feminine hand. Sarah Ruth's work. Nothing to see among the papers in the top drawer, unless I wanted to read up on current logging information or the regional spread of different termite species. Honestly, who knew being a district ranger involved so much paperwork? I'd always pictured them galloping on horses, stopping now and again to hack a fallen tree off a path or to bathe in a waterfall.

Each time I searched a new location, I had to memorize the placement and angle of even the smallest pen nib inside before riffling through, then return the items. When I looked at the clock above the door, I'd already wasted ten minutes, with nothing to show from it.

Where would you hide something you didn't want anyone to find?

No. That didn't matter. Where would *Morrissey*?

I tried to picture him standing here, cigar clenched in his mouth, blinds drawn, like a private eye in a noir movie, poring over secret documents. Then he hears a sound from outside. Startled, he looks up, and . . .

My eyes went to the file cabinet tucked unassumingly next to the small bookshelf in the corner.

No need to imagine. That's what he'd done when I barged in on him on Sunday. Hadn't he tucked something away in the bottom drawer?

I crouched on the floor, setting the flashlight down, and examined the label on the cabinet: *Ponderosa Pine Conservation and Regrowth Patterns.*

Perfect. The most innocuous, dead-boring name in all history, a place you could be sure no one would accidentally stumble into.

The drawer pulled open soundlessly, and I held my breath. This could be it. The truth, finally at my fingertips.

I thumbed through the files gently, keeping them in order and in place, and finding . . .

Maps of Oregon marked with pinpricks of data. Memorandum on sustainable logging numbers per acre. Even one scintillating folder labeled *The Life Cycle and Effects of the Western Pine Beetle.*

With each new file that I opened, my posture got further away from the army's ideal, until by the end, I'd slumped to the floor to have a good mope.

What now?

Did I search every one of the wooden cubbies against the wall, stuffed with letters and documents? Flip through each book on the shelf for photos pressed in an obscure chapter on shrubbery ecology?

Or maybe Morrissey had found what he wanted and burned the evidence. That would be the smart thing to do, but criminals in books never thought of it, always keeping the most crucial documents out of pride or some silly motivation.

"I told you, this isn't one of your detective stories, Dorie." That's what Gordon would say if I came out empty-handed, that knowing look in his eyes.

But what if it is? the stubborn part of me insisted. *Where would he keep the evidence?*

I traced my flashlight over the room again . . . and stopped on a glint of glass, hung on the back wall, where visitors entering the office and facing the desk wouldn't see it. But where Morrissey, seated in his desk chair, easily could.

A Gold Star Service Flag, boxed in with a wooden frame like a piece of art. The one to commemorate Wille's death.

So, they had one after all. And it was hanging just a few degrees crooked.

There was no suspense as I took the frame off the wall and turned it over. I found exactly what I was expecting: a file folder taped to the back of the frame.

Slowly, I tugged at the tape—it had lost some of its stick already and had clearly been moved before—and pulled the folder free, opening it to reveal the contents. *Be careful. Keep them in order.*

On the top, a stack of pictures, blurry, but some close-up, others far away. A letter from the Office of Censorship on eagle-embossed stationery. A newspaper article. Some handwritten notes.

Secret weapon. Incendiary. Other fires in the region. Classified.

I tried to scan for key words, knowing it wasn't safe to read it all right here, with the clock ticking toward the half-hour mark.

Gordon. Gordon needs to see this.

I stood, ready to call him inside. But it would take time to read all of the documents, more than we had without being caught at the rising bell.

We'd have to chance it, hope that Morrissey wouldn't look behind the frame before I could sneak back in and replace the documents.

Before I could reconsider, I hung the flag back up, tilted to just the right angle, locked the office door, and ran outside, where Gordon was kneeling on the cold, hard boards of the porch, staring dutifully out toward the silent camp. "Gordon!"

253

He started, clutching his chest like he was eighty years old and fit to keel over from a heart attack. Then he must have noticed my expression, because he scrambled to his feet. "Are you all right?"

I nodded, then shook my head. Was I all right? Not yet. My voice sounded strained, distant to my own ears. "I know why Jack didn't call in the fire."

"Why?"

"Because he started it."

Gordon hunched over the file folder, squinting to read in the pale light of dawn. Instead of starting with the letters like I had, he gathered the half dozen photographs from Charlie's camera, turning them over one by one. I leaned against the railing, aiming the flashlight for him.

Two showed bits of metal debris, another a close-up of a scrap of material with the same Japanese symbol Gordon had found in Morrissey's pocket, then a wide shot to show the material to scale. Even mangled and burned, it was easy to tell whatever it had been was massive, far larger than an average parachute.

And written on the back of the last photograph—one of a twisted-looking wheel studded with what looked like charges, fragments of charred rope dangling to the side—*Remains of the bomb Armitage triggered.*

"A bomb," I said, my throat tight. "A Japanese bomb."

Japan was full of surprises. First Pearl Harbor, now this. What "this" was and how it had gotten here, I couldn't say exactly, but Morrissey clearly knew.

"So Sarah Ruth was telling the truth," Gordon said, releasing a slow breath. "Jack reported this . . . thing the night before the fire.

Morrissey didn't know what it was and told him not to go near it. But the next morning, he . . ."

"He went anyway," I finished when I heard the wavering in Gordon's voice. "And when he got close enough to touch it . . . it exploded."

"And lit the forest on fire." His voice was a whisper now, like it should be when speaking of the dead.

I pictured shrapnel, fire blooming out in a circle around Jack's limp body, burning until the smoke got high enough to alert the other rangers. All because he had to examine the strange object he spotted in the woods.

"Why couldn't you leave it alone, Jack?"

It was only when Gordon asked gently, "Would you have?" that I realized I'd said it out loud.

"No." We had that in common, my brother and I: our curiosity. Only mine hadn't been fatal—yet.

"But why all the secrecy?" I asked as if the papers and photographs might speak up and answer. "If Morrissey simply wanted to understand what happened, why wouldn't anyone answer his questions? And if the army—"

"Dorie!"

That one word, hissed from his mouth, shot me through with alarm, and I guessed what I'd see when I turned around: the dim lamppost illuminating a tall figure hunched against the wind as he strode across the path.

Morrissey. Early.

Hadn't Sarah Ruth said he'd been working strange hours lately? And we only had a few moments before he spotted us.

"Hide the file," I said, fumbling with the keys. I could hear papers rustle, and when I turned around again, the ranger station door securely locked, Gordon was latching my haversack.

"Act like you belong." I held my flashlight loosely and smoothed down my hair. "And for pity's sake, let me handle this."

I probably wouldn't have needed to tag on that last part. Gordon looked about ready to die on the doormat, clutching the haversack like it was stuffed with counterfeit money.

To avoid suspicion, be proactive. That was key, and the reason I sang out, "Good morning, Mr. Morrissey!"

He jerked his head up sharply, as if wondering if he should run for a rifle to chase the riffraff from his porch. As he came closer, I took the measure of him. If Gordon had looked like the "before" part of a shaving advertisement, Earl Morrissey was the red-eyed mongrel from a pamphlet on the dangers of drink. Though there was no smell of alcohol on him, exhaustion caused his steps to weave, and a patchy beard had sprouted on his chin.

How long had it been since he'd gotten a full night of sleep?

"What are you two doing here so early?" he asked gruffly. "Rising bell's not even rung."

Gordon sputtered, and I shifted over to make sure his guilty face was blocked. "In Mr. Hooper's defense, he did try to stop me. Said you'd never agree to it, but I was determined to march over here and attempt to persuade you at the first opportunity."

He took my bait, asking the question that I'd left dangling. "Agree to what?"

"Why, to a plane ride, of course." I might as well have clocked him with a cast-iron pan, the way he stared dumbly at me. "Now, before you say a word, you have to know that Amelia Earhart was my hero growing up."

To give Gordon time to recover and stop blushing, I launched into the full saga, mostly true, of my childhood obsession. I'd just started on my favorite theory about Earhart's mysterious disappearance when he cut me off.

"Miss Hightower, unless there's a fire—and I want you to pray that there is *not*—we're not landing a plane at our airstrip. Even if we did, you wouldn't be on it."

"Why on earth not?" I raised my foot to stomp it for emphasis, then realized I was still wearing my slippers. *Please don't look down.*

"Fuel's at a premium right now, and we can't spare it for joyrides." He waved at me impatiently, and I stepped aside, letting him unlock the ranger station door. "Or don't you know there's a war on?"

He was mad now; that was good. Angry people were more likely to forget suspicions.

"Well, Mr. Hooper, you were right." I tried on a tragic face. "Guess I'll have to set my lifelong dream aside."

"I'm sure you can figure out a new dream," Gordon said sweetly, which should have annoyed me more, but I was focused on the fact that he didn't look like a bank robber caught in a searchlight anymore.

Morrissey clutched the door handle, drawing out every word. "You *sure* that's all?"

Time for another appearance of the Armitage smile. "Yes, sir. I was too excited to wait till breakfast to ask. Just ask Mr. Hooper here."

It was a mistake. I knew it as soon as Morrissey's eagle eyes turned back on Gordon. "Is that true, Hooper?"

And after a half second pause, he said, "Yes. It is."

I let the tension in my shoulders relax. *Thank goodness.*

"Huh." Morrissey rocked back a bit, stroking the dark whiskers on his chin, and I didn't like his expression one bit. "Listen, Hooper. About Sarah Ruth . . . she doesn't much care for the fire lookout."

257

All of a sudden, Gordon was back to squirming like someone had emptied an ant farm down his collar. "I . . . ah . . . had heard her say that once, sir."

I groaned inside. Pretty ranger's daughters and ethical dilemmas— Gordon Hooper's two weaknesses.

"I'd like you to go on up there and relieve her a day early. It's about time one of you CPS fellows took a turn."

What?

Gordon wasn't meeting my eyes, which was a shame, because I was throwing daggers at him. *Say no. Make up some excuse. For once in your life, just—*

"I'd rather you assigned someone else, if it's no trouble."

I almost groaned out loud. He hadn't said yes outright, but he might as well have.

Morrissey nodded emphatically. "I've already made up my mind. You're on fire watch. In fact, I'll have Jimmy hike up there with you after calisthenics. Deliver some supplies."

"But, Mr. Morrissey, I heard on the radio that there's snow on the way soon. A fire couldn't possibly—"

"If I've learned anything out here, it's that a man can never be too cautious." You could almost taste the irony in his words. "I insist."

I could see Gordon's breath coming faster in the cold air. He was panicking. He had to be panicking—*I* was panicking. Morrissey must know what we'd seen. What we'd done. Soon, he'd demand to search my rucksack and—

No. He's just suspicious of us, that's all, like he was with Shorty. Who better to get out of the way for a week than Jack's best friend, especially one caught snooping outside his office?

Besides, I hadn't gotten a good look at those papers, but unless we were far off in our guess, Earl Morrissey was no spy. Until we found out more, he might be an ally, an accomplice, or an enemy.

258

Gordon bowed his head in surrender. "Yes, sir. I'll gather my things."

Morrissey grunted his approval. "And as for you, young lady"—he turned to me—"I think you've gotten enough information for that report of yours by now."

Now it was my turn to search for the right words. "Oh, I'd have to talk to my superiors about that, sir."

"Maybe I will instead." Before I could tell him that wasn't really necessary, he turned and plodded inside, slamming the door in my face.

That's it. We're finished. If he called Fort Lawton, insisted on talking to my superior, then they'd know I wasn't in Pennsylvania comforting my grieving family after all. And everything would fall apart.

"Some accomplice you are, Gordon." I kept my voice low but without skimping on annoyance, tugging him off the steps and down the path. "Couldn't you have said you couldn't go to the tower because you sprained your ankle or something?"

"And stoop to your level? Never." He might as well have shouted it, the words sounded so loud in the early morning emptiness.

"Shh!" A glance in all directions showed no sign of any other shadows moving in the dark, so I reached for the rucksack. "Quick, give me those papers. I'll keep them safe while you're at the lookout. We'll find some way to—"

He yanked the haversack away, the canvas brushing my fingers, and hurried ahead of me, back toward the bunkhouse. "No."

"What, don't you trust me?" I joked.

But his face was stone-set serious. "How can I? All you ever do is lie. And now you're bringing me into it."

Guilt stabbed at me. It had been an instinct, that was all, but even though that was the one thing I'd promised Gordon he wouldn't have to do, I'd still asked him to lie for me. "I . . . I'm sorry. I couldn't think of any other way to—"

"No more, Dorie. No more lies. What would it feel like, do you think, to tell the truth for once in your life?"

How was I supposed to answer that? It had all been for Jack, to find out how he died.

But now we knew, and it didn't feel like the victory I had hoped for.

"I want this to be over." He yanked open the rucksack, but instead of taking out the papers, he tossed my shoes on the ground at my feet. "Once I look these over and we know what happened, I want you to go home. Tell your parents the truth. Cry a little. And let me get my life back."

He wanted *his* life back? "So, that's what this is to you?" I snatched up my shoes by the laces. "Just an inconvenience? Now that we know how Jack died, you want to forget about him and move on?"

What about the truth? What about justice?

This time, though, he didn't react with anger. "Dorie. Go home." His voice was absent of emotion.

And he walked away. Just like he had all those years ago, walking away with his high-horse convictions, looking down on everyone else. On me.

"He was going to join the army." The words came out before I realized I'd decided to say them.

Gordon stopped, then turned, his face shadowed. "Who?"

"Jack."

If I'd executed a judo kick directly to his middle, I don't think he could have looked so surprised. "I don't understand."

"Ask Thomas if you don't believe me. Or take a look at this." I drew the recruitment brochure out of my coat pocket and thrust it at him. His hands closed over it without his looking down to read the bold military headline.

"There must be a mistake."

"There isn't." Now that I'd started, I couldn't stop, the words tumbling out like a rockslide. "While you're up in the lookout, see what he wrote in the observation log. Jack may have died, but at least he died wanting to do what was right."

I'd done it. Gordon wanted the truth, and I'd given it to him. All of it.

CHAPTER 27

Gordon Hooper

January 25, 1945

My body moved mechanically through the usual pattern of laps, stretches, and arm exercises at morning calisthenics, my mind a thousand miles away. Or maybe just a few weeks away.

Jack had been planning to join the army.

The moment Dorie said it, even before she showed me the brochure, I knew it was true—not one of her screwball conjectures or an attempt to make me angry.

I'd searched through the brochure, trying to understand what had made Jack question his convictions. It was clearly from early in the war, tattered and full of outdated information. On the back, under a plea for able-bodied men to register at their local recruitment station, someone had written in neat cursive, *Ecclesiastes 3:1–8*. Not Jack's handwriting, but that didn't make me question that the brochure was his. It explained all of the doubts and heavy sighs, the half-finished meals and philosophical wonderings toward the end.

I threw myself into another round of push-ups as Richardson paced in front of us, grunting approval or disapproval in turn.

Why didn't Jack tell me?

He'd clearly been thinking about this for a long time. And I hadn't noticed, hadn't been there for him.

If I had, would he have volunteered for the lookout tower? Maybe he never would have seen the strange object that dropped the bomb into the woods, never would have moved toward it, determined to find out what had threatened his forest and his friends.

A shrill whistle burst into my thoughts. "Hooper!"

Morrissey jogged over to me, and I collapsed on the ground, breathing hard.

Had he discovered the file's contents were missing? Was he going to confront me, demand to have the documents back before I'd even gotten a chance to study them?

"Think you missed the bell for breakfast."

Sure enough, when I hauled myself to my knees, I saw the other fellows jogging down to the cookhouse. No wonder my arms felt like they'd been put through the laundry room's wringer washer. "Sorry, sir."

"Here," he said, tossing an envelope my way. "This came in for you."

I glanced at the outside. From Mother. The flap, usually sealed with careful precision, had a strip of tape slapped over it. "Did you . . . open this?"

His mouth formed a stiff line. "The army censors mail. Could've been that."

"Not ours." They never had in the past, not once, knowing that we were far away from any military secrets. Or so they'd thought.

"Times change, Hooper." He jogged away, knowing I wouldn't challenge him, that I'd meekly eat breakfast, then go back to the bunkhouse and pack like he'd ordered me to.

Instead, I tucked the letter in my pocket and rose on my burning muscles, running after him. "Wait, Mr. Morrissey."

By the time he turned, I knew what I was going to say. The benefit of being desperate, I suppose. I had nothing left to lose.

"I have to know. Did the army have anything to do with why Jack died?"

He stared at me for a long moment, then jerked his head toward the bunkhouse. "Pack up, Hooper. Those sorts of questions aren't safe around here."

"But why?"

He took a step closer, until I could smell cigar smoke lingering in the wool of his uniform. "I don't know what you've figured out—or think you have—but let me make this clear. I'm the district ranger. This is my land. And I'm responsible for what happens on it. If anyone's going to take a fall for all of this, it's going to be me."

"Yes, sir," I said, too surprised to say anything else. And when he let go of my shoulder, eyes solemn, I was sure. Whatever wild theories Dorie had spun, whatever the details of what was going on, Morrissey felt that what he knew could put him in danger—and he wanted to protect us. Protect me.

Because it was too late to protect Jack.

As far as I knew, Jimmy wasn't aware that he was supposed to be my bodyguard, an agent of his father to make sure I did my duty and went straight to the lookout after breakfast. His pack bulged with supplies, a human substitute for the mule trains they used to bring provisions to supply smokejumpers in remote locations for the fires that spanned days or weeks.

I'd gotten the lighter load, just a sack of pancake mix, a few bottles of milk packed in a box filled with sawdust, and my belongings—with the documents Dorie had stolen buried inside. Better to keep them safe and close, I'd decided. And at least at the lookout, I'd have plenty of privacy to read them all and understand what had really happened.

The cans Jimmy carried clunked softly together, a low percussion under the sounds of the forest. Soon, the ground began to incline, leading up to the mountain trail, where snow dusted the path in patches as the air cooled. In warmer months, these trails would be a haven for hikers, mushroom seekers, and bird watchers, but even now, the towering pines and exposed rock jutting into the horizon formed a vista worthy of Charlie's camera. It would be even more striking if the snowstorm the radio weatherman had predicted for the next few days blanketed this part of Oregon.

I'll miss this place if I go home when the war is over. True, unbroken quiet was hard to find in the city. There was a reason Thoreau—himself a pacifist—called the great outdoors "the tonic of wildness" in *Walden*, saying our souls needed more exposure to "untamed" and "unfathomable" nature.

Jimmy and I exchanged a few words along the way, mostly warnings of slick spots on the path where ice had formed in the shade. But it wasn't until we stopped for a water break that Jimmy looked over at me. "So," he said, tilting the canteen back into his mouth, "you sweet on Miss Hightower?"

I almost said, "Who?" before I remembered Dorie's false name.

What was the honest answer to that? Something like, "Once, a long time ago"?

For a moment, I let myself remember, picturing the Dorie I'd known three years before, cheerfully greeting guests, her dark hair in a stylish wave, smelling like pumpkin pie and evergreens and home. I'd been dazzled. Would have declared myself willing to climb the highest mountain for her. If I'd been dumb enough to write poetry, it would have rivaled the sappiest of sonnets scrawled in the lookout's logbook.

But I wasn't willing to change my beliefs for her. We were so different, the two of us. It made a fellow wonder. How many other compromises would I have had to make to court Dorie Armitage?

"That's what I thought," Jimmy grumbled, and I realized I hadn't answered him.

"No," I said quickly, "it's not like that. We might have been friends. If things were different."

Something tugged at me, saying those words out loud. It wasn't the heartbreak I'd felt when I got Dorie's last letter. But it was a sad thought, all the same, to have lost a friendship before it ever began.

Jimmy grunted, just like his father. "That's not what it looked like." Then he immediately clamped his mouth shut, chewing a gum wad.

Sure, he could have noticed the fact that we'd talked to each other during chores a few times. But I didn't think it was only that.

"You were the one we saw in the woods." I'd decided to state it instead of ask it, and his sheepish shrug confirmed my theory. "Why were you following us?"

"Dad told me to."

So it wasn't just the curiosity of a schoolboy crush. "Why?"

Jimmy muttered something, kicking at a rock until it skittered off the edge and into a ravine.

"What's that?" I prompted.

He straightened enough to look at me. "He wanted me to keep my eye on her because he doesn't like the army interfering. Says we can't trust them."

I chuckled. That was all? "Well, we agree about that at least."

He brightened, as if he'd never thought of it that way before. "Say, that's right."

I thought back to all the times he'd stood by when his friend had made fun of us for not lining right up to enlist. "Does Roger know what your family thinks about the army?"

Jimmy shook his head. "You kidding? I could never tell him."

I could understand. It wasn't so long since I'd been his age. Fatherless, awkward, wearing pants a few inches too short because Mother was gone and my uncle refused to buy new ones. Just wanting a friend. I hadn't found one, not in high school. Not until Jack.

Of course. That's why Jack hadn't told me. Just like Jimmy, Jack—the fearless one, who could give a war whoop as he fell through the air to a raging fire below—had been afraid of what I would think. Maybe even afraid I would be angry at him. So he sought out the recruitment brochure in secret.

And by now, I was fairly sure I'd guessed how he'd gotten it.

"That's why I didn't join up, even when I got old enough. Most people around here, they were raring for war from the start," Jimmy went on, passing the canteen my way. "They don't know what it's like to—"

He shrugged, and I remembered his brother again, the way Jimmy had disappeared for days after they got word of his death.

They don't understand what it's like to lose someone to it.

Well, now I did too. Because if my instinct was right, and that bomb had somehow been launched from Japan, Jack had died in the line of fire just like any of the overseas troops running into battle.

I took a swig out of the canteen before passing it back. "Looks like you're more one of us than you thought."

And instead of getting mad, Jimmy's shoulders relaxed a bit. "Yeah. Yeah, I guess I am." He put the canteen in his pack. "Anyway, if you ask me, better to stay away from that Hightower woman. She's trouble."

I couldn't quite bring myself to agree with him. Sure, Dorie was reckless, maybe even irresponsible. But she had a good heart underneath it all. "Thanks for the tip."

He grunted. "Just had to be sure, y'know? I've seen the way you smile at my sister. And we Morrisseys look after one another."

There it was, that familiar heat trickling up my neck and into my face. "Um . . . that's a good thing for a family to do." I tried to think of what Dorie might say, how she'd fill up the empty space. "So . . . read anything good recently?"

His face lit up. "Well, I went to the dime store on Saturday, and they had the new Detective Comics in. . . ."

By the time we reached the lookout, out of breath from the climb, I'd almost managed to forget the heaviness of my pack and my heart in a lively discussion of art, heroism, and how characters like Super-American and U.S. Jones were blatant rip-offs of Captain America.

Small talk. Who knew?

The fire tower stood in solidarity with the tallest pines beside it: three stories tall, with crisscrossed flights of stairs built within the stilted frame holding the platform aloft. It was flanked by a telephone pole strung with wire to its left, and a lean-to filled with firewood to its right.

At the top, Jimmy threw open the door, only to be greeted by a startled Sarah Ruth, wearing layers of bulky sweaters instead of the Forest Service uniform, her auburn hair plaited, frazzled, and fuzzed like a discarded bird's nest.

And, more important, she had an antique-looking pistol aimed right at us.

I was instantly grateful to be behind a human shield of Morrissey blood.

"It's just us," Jimmy exclaimed. "Geez, Ruthie, will you put that thing down?"

"I've got eyes." Sarah Ruth lowered the pistol—but with a reluctant expression on her face. "Isn't being a lookout supposed to be a solitary job? It's been like Grand Central Station around here, the amount of company I've had this week. Can you blame me for being jumpy?"

"What's wrong, Sarah Ruth?" Jimmy taunted. "Did'ya think we were that old boyfriend of yours?"

I saw Sarah Ruth's eyes narrow. "Jimmy, I wouldn't—"

"If you were," Sarah Ruth interrupted, her voice low and dangerous, "I'd shove you down the stairs and hope you broke both of your legs."

With that, she disappeared back into the lookout, leaving the door open, presumably an invitation for us to enter.

"A real romantic, my sister." Jimmy grinned at me, tossing his pack down beside the door.

"There was nothing romantic about Roy Winters." She spat out the name like it left a bad taste in her mouth.

I, valuing my life more than Jimmy did his, declined to comment, and instead busied myself putting the supplies away in the cabinet by the stove, where a teakettle was set to boil. The question I'd asked myself earlier this morning burned in my mind.

You could just let it go. Never ask her, never know, not for sure.

It was the coward's way out, I knew. But ever since the news of Jack's death, it felt harder to be brave.

Sarah Ruth stepped over the pack to get to the stove, shoving another log inside to counteract the cold air we'd let in. "Did you come all this way just to restock my cupboard?"

Jimmy frowned. "Didn't Dad call to tell you?"

"Would I be asking if he had?"

That was odd. Then again, Morrissey had a lot on his mind lately.

Jimmy shrugged. "He wants you back early. Don't know why. But he was sure set on it. Gordon's taking your place."

"Knowing Dad, he's got his reasons." Sarah Ruth sat down on the cot, pulling a bag of clothes from underneath it and tossing in a hairbrush and a bar of soap. No protest, no further questions. Loyal to her father, no matter what, just like all the Morrisseys were to one another. "Well, Gordon, try not to go mad from boredom up here."

Jimmy leaned against the wall behind us, so I had a direct line of sight to Sarah Ruth.

This is it.

Time to test my theory, one I'd developed back at the bunkhouse. "Don't worry. I've got some interesting reading material to pass the time." I cleared my throat to make sure she looked up at what I'd tugged out of my pocket: the army recruitment brochure.

I knew the look on her face, because I'd seen it in the mirror. Not just surprise. Recognition. Guilt.

She knew I had found her out.

In the next instant, she'd recovered, standing and waving at the metal milk pail by the door. "Hey, Jimmy, take down that water bucket to the spring and fill it up, would you? There's only an inch left."

I glanced up from my can stacking to see Jimmy scowl in true younger-brother form. "What am I, your maid?"

She snatched up a tattered dishcloth. "Either that or wash dishes. Your choice. Gordon's already making himself useful, see?"

Muttering something about tyranny, Jimmy let the door bang behind him as he dragged the bucket away, leaving the two of us alone.

Someone had to say it. So I did, standing, watching her as she wrung the dishrag in her hands, the only sign she wasn't completely at ease.

"You're the one who gave Jack the recruitment brochure."

The hands on the dishrag stilled. "I did."

Even though I'd been fairly sure of my guess, hearing her speak the words triggered a familiar sensation inside me, hot like a flame. I thought I'd beaten it, that I'd learned my lesson after the fistfight with Thomas, but there it was again, my old enemy, inherited from my father. And like him, it wouldn't truly leave me till the day I died.

"You should have left him to his own conscience." I slapped the brochure down on the table.

"He asked if he could have it." Calmly. Stating the facts, not making excuses. "Saw it on my desk one day—it was Willie's—and said he had some things to think about."

The note about Ecclesiastes 3 written in the brochure had been what tipped me off, after I'd looked the reference up back at the bunkhouse. *To every thing there is a season, and a time to every purpose under the heaven . . . a time to kill, and a time to heal . . . a time to love, and a time to hate; a time of war, and a time of peace.*

Just like what Sarah Ruth had said to me back in the empty church sanctuary: *"There's a season to everything. Maybe you're meant to come back to the scorched earth and help something grow again."*

"And," Sarah Ruth added, "he made me promise not to tell anyone, especially you."

Was it true?

Probably. It sounded like Jack, all right.

"Still, you should have . . . kept out of it," I repeated, trying—failing—to keep my voice from rising. "He was doing the right thing, and you . . . you tried to . . ."

I had to get away. Had to get out of here before I said something, did something, I regretted. But when I stumbled toward the door, there she was, blocking my path, like a mama bear staring down a hunter.

"Stop. Just . . . stop it, Gordon." And despite her size, I couldn't see how anyone could describe Sarah Ruth as delicate, seeing her there, hands on her hips and fire in her eyes. "You can't run away from this, and you sure can't yell your way out. Though I can take it if you want to try."

But I didn't want to. That's why I needed to run, like my father had always done. He either lashed out or stayed away from us, sometimes all night. Sure, it made Mother frantic with worry, but I'd always thought it was better than the alternative.

Looking at Sarah Ruth now, standing between me and escape, I wondered if I'd been wrong. "It was your fault he changed his mind."

"No, it wasn't. I lent some literature to your best friend, then kept my word not to blab about it. That's all, and you know it."

She's right, something whispered through the anger, and I took a deep breath. "Then why does it feel so . . . wrong? Why am I so angry?"

"Because Jack isn't here to be angry at."

Yes.

That was it.

And with that, the anger faded, leaving behind that dull, aching sadness again. I backed away from the door, nearly tripping over the ladderback chair, and sat in it, feeling heavy.

She tiptoed over on the groaning floorboards, but her grip on my shoulder was anything but timid. It was strong, warm, like she was trying to hold me together. "He was a good man, Gordon. This"—she pointed to the offending trifold in all its red, white, and blue glory—"doesn't change that."

"I know. But he should have trusted me enough to tell me."

"Sure. But there's a special kind of fear when you have a secret. It weighs on you. Keeps you separate from others, even ones who you know care." She let go of my shoulder and tucked her arms close to her body, a shiver passing through her.

There it was again, the certainty in her voice, even though she didn't come from a broken family, hadn't known what it was like to be called a coward at every turn. "What could you possibly know about that?"

Gordon, you idiot. That was the kind of personal question no one answered, but especially not Sarah Ruth Morrissey.

But instead of waving her pistol around and shoving me out the door, Sarah Ruth nodded. She crossed over to the stove, unpinning stiff wool socks from a makeshift clothesline we'd rigged up there, her voice taking on the lilting tone of a campfire tale-teller. "I was just seventeen the summer the CCC men came. Dad had finally let me apply as a lookout after I argued with him for six months. He made sure I was assigned to the Cutter Basin tower so I couldn't hike back home if I got lonely or scared."

I nodded. That sounded like the Morrissey I knew, believing in his daughter but also unwilling to coddle her. I pictured Sarah Ruth then, all braids and sharp elbows and hand-me-down clothes from her older brother, climbing the steps to the tower with determination.

She drew in a breath, and I added quickly, "You don't have to talk about it if you don't want to. I-I don't know why I asked."

But she looked back at me, and there was something soft under the hardness I was used to seeing. "I want someone to know."

I thought of her whispering to the cross, worn smooth from years of silent prayers. "I'm willing to listen."

She nodded, then took the steaming kettle off the stove and poured it into the tiny sink basin, likely using the dishes as an excuse to keep her back to me. "Sometimes the lookouts would call each other late at night, bored and lonely. Roy Winters happened to be on the line one time, and when we talked . . . it felt like we were inches apart instead of miles."

She attacked a metal pot, scrubbing it so hard I worried she'd grind a hole inside. "I'd met him before, of course. And I took to his words like a bear to a shank of venison, never realizing they were bait in a trap."

I remembered the love poems in the early pages of the logbook. Had Roy written those? And if so, had he meant them?

"Back at the camp, we met together in secret a few times. Of course, I knew Dad would make Roy the next stuffed trophy on the ranger station wall if he knew." She clanged the pot on the table, leaving it dripping. "At the end of the summer, after a month-long drought, we were both on duty again at our different towers. He dared me to abandon my post and visit him here."

I could see where this was going. "And you did."

"Twice. It took me six hours to hike from my lookout to this one. And the second time, I stayed . . . all night." She paused, fist tight around the dishrag, then started in again. "By the time I made it back to Cutter Basin in the morning, a fire fifty miles to the north, directly in my line of sight, had blazed out of control, enough that another lookout had called it in."

I breathed in as the doomed love story transformed into something worse, something tragic. It was every lookout's fear: not catching a fire in your area quickly enough, before the fire crowned and spread.

Sarah Ruth draped the rag over the clothesline, and when she turned back to me, she looked like the story had taken a toll in years instead of words. "Eventually, the Basin Fire—that's what they named it—jumped the mountains. Took five days to put out."

"Even if you had been there, you might not have caught the smoke early enough." Fires that started overnight were notoriously hard to spot, especially with lookouts droopy-eyed and weary in the middle of a storm.

"One of the rangers fighting it got trapped by a flare-up." Her voice broke, and she swallowed. "He didn't make it out."

I remembered the somber look on Richardson's face when he'd told me about the other death that Morrissey felt responsible for. Now I understood why.

Yes, Sarah Ruth understood regrets, all right. Maybe better than I ever would.

"Roy told me it wasn't my fault, tried to soothe me, but I knew better. And a few weeks later, he was gone, along with all of his fancy promises. I never heard from him again."

In that moment, I hated Roy Winters like I'd never hated anyone before, even if the fire wasn't his fault either. For selfishly using a young girl and breaking her heart, for not standing by her when she needed him most, for leaving her cynical and unwilling to trust others.

It didn't seem like the time to interrupt—and what would I say?—so I defaulted to silence, staring out over the trees with Sarah Ruth as she dried the dishes.

"Now, every time the fire bell rings, or we get a report of a smokejumper injured or killed, I pray at the cross in the church. Because God knows the reason I didn't see the smoke, even if my father doesn't. Or anyone else." Finally she turned to look at me. "Except you."

I kept my gaze on the mountains, asking the question that had bothered me since Dorie had told me Sarah Ruth had taken a shift of lookout duty. "If this place has so many bad memories . . . why did you come back?"

"Because Dad assigned you to the tower last week. When I saw the schedule, we argued, and I said I'd go instead. That's all."

That still didn't answer my question. "But why?"

She bent down to heft the sack I'd brought onto a shelf, then dusted the loose flour off her hands. "Because you made biscuits."

Was that some kind of code? "Pardon?"

"The day after we got the telegram telling us Willie had died, remember?"

Slowly, the memories surfaced—the whispers among the COs between calisthenic drills about what had happened, the only time I'd seen Sarah Ruth cry. Over a year ago now, wasn't it?

"Mama was sobbing her eyes out back at home, and I was try-ing . . . to be strong, I guess. Or at least make breakfast." She took a deep breath. "When you came and took over, told me to go out into the forest for a while . . . when I could grieve without having to check anything off a list . . . It helped, that's all."

"I burnt them." It was a stupid thing to say, but it made Sarah Ruth smile.

"They were awful. But I needed the woods and quiet then, and you let me have it. You need to be with your friends now, and I thought I could return the favor. But here you are anyway. Daddy doesn't understand people very well." Her voice was apologetic as she covered for the gruff veteran ranger.

I thought of the letter he'd read, the fact that he'd sent both me and Shorty away, the way he'd sent Jimmy to follow us. Whatever Morrissey knew, he wanted to keep it to himself. "I think he had other reasons for sending me up here."

"What do you mean?"

And her brown-green eyes were so wide and sincere that I al-most risked it all, almost told her what we'd found out, and how, while I was glad it wasn't the criminal behavior we'd anticipated, it still seemed serious.

But at just that moment, I heard footsteps on the porch, and Jimmy swung open the door and clunked the bucket inside. "Special delivery. Didn't even shovel in any yellow snow."

"Charming," she said at the same time that I said, "Thanks."

He looked at us—probably a bit too cozy to his wary brother's eyes—and opened the door again. "Come on, Sarah Ruth. Better start back if we want any lunch."

"Sure," Sarah Ruth said, even though the look she gave me told me she wanted to know more.

Later. I'd tell her later. Maybe try to call the ranger station and hope she, rather than Morrissey, answered.

I could hear their muffled voices as they climbed down the steps, then watched out the glass as they set off on the mountain trail toward home. And I took a moment to pray that confessing a long-kept secret would help Sarah Ruth understand something I was sure of: She'd been forgiven long ago.

Quiet settled over the lookout—the popping of the fire in the stove and the slight moan of the wind the only sounds. Finally, I was alone.

Sitting on the cot's thin mattress, I unlatched Dorie's haversack—thankfully no one had asked me why I was suddenly toting around something made of army khaki—and took out the clothes and personal items I'd stuffed on top, upending the rest of the contents on the blanket.

A plain white envelope tumbled out first. Mother's letter. I'd almost forgotten. I set it aside and opened the file, tracing the label on the tab.

Jack's Fire. That was all. Just two single, devastating words.

Whatever Morrissey knew about the bomb, soon I would too.

HANDWRITTEN NOTE AT THE TOP OF OFFICIAL DOCUMENT

December 5, 1944

Earl, this is the letter I told you about on our call. Now listen, I'll need this back or I could get into real trouble . . . worse than the Baked Bean Incident of '18, if you catch my meaning.

–Dan

FROM THE OFFICE OF CENSORSHIP TO DANIEL CLEMENT

Dear Sir:

As an esteemed newspaper editor or radio program producer, we write to you regarding a matter of national security. The Axis powers have developed a large balloon intended to be used as a weapon of war. We have received reports that several have been spotted in the Pacific Northwest region. At least one incident has been printed in a Washington-based newspaper and picked up as a mention in *Newsweek*, prompting this bulletin.

Any discovery of such balloons, or any other suspicious, unidentified objects, should be reported to the authorities, who will contact the War Department immediately. Within 24 hours, the army will send a crew to dispose of the weapon properly. UNDER NO CIRCUMSTANCES WILL YOUR NEWSPAPER OR RADIO PROGRAM BE PERMITTED TO REPORT SUCH A DISCOVERY.

We cannot provide you with any details about the balloons'

specific workings, origin, or function, only that any individual, group, or publication that publicly distributes information about them will be prosecuted to the fullest extent of the law.

Your attention is called to Executive Order No. 8381, pertaining to wartime reporting and communication, which strictly forbids the dissemination in written, photographic, or illustrated form of any information about weaponry designated "secret," "restricted," or "confidential."

This letter shall also be treated as confidential.

Thank you for your full cooperation in service to your country during a time of great trial.

Silentium Victoriam Accelerat.

The Office of Censorship

EARL MORRISSEY'S HANDWRITTEN NOTES

Call to Supervisor Wallis, Missoula, Montana

January 13, 1945

Sorry for the loss of a man at my camp. Knows how well I care for my staff, etc.

What happened? Cannot answer.

When pressed, Forest Department in "a series of intense negotiations" with the army regarding this issue. Hoping to come to an acceptable resolution.

What's the issue? Cannot answer.

Has the boy's family been told? Only that he was injured during a fire.

Advises that an agreement between army and Forestry Department should be reached by early February.

Will more details be available then? Maybe. Maybe not.

More condolences, cordial good-bye, etc.

Warns me not to speak to anyone on my staff, no matter how trusted, about any of this.

I do not agree.

EARL MORRISSEY'S HANDWRITTEN NOTES

Fūsen bakudan. Translation: balloon bomb (University of Washington foreign language department, letter from Dr. Jordan on Jan. 23.)

What material are the scraps from the scene made out of?

* Unknown—cross between stiff paper and flexible cloth
* Very durable, never seen anything like it
* Seem to be layers held together with paste
* Hydrogen gas?

How did it arrive?

* Launch within U.S. unlikely because of the scale needed to produce a bomb (couldn't be done in secret)
* Balloons either launched from somewhere in the Pacific (naval vessel?) or from Japan itself
* In theory, jet stream might make it possible to send something across the ocean (call with Pete at the National Weather Service in Portland, January 17)

280

Asked why I wanted to know, I said Edith saw a
newsreel that made her worry Japan was going to
bomb us.

Purpose of sandbags in photos?
* Likely to control the height of balloons
* No idea how they were released. Part of a mangled
  aluminum wheel in photo?

EARL MORRISSEY'S HANDWRITTEN NOTES

January 21, 1945

Possible Next Steps
* Another call to Missoula. Three calls haven't produced
  anything but warnings to stay away.
* Announce the truth only to my staff and COs. What
  would that accomplish?
* Reveal information to mayor and request to warn
  others in town.
* Convince a station/paper that withholding information
  on these balloon bombs is a menace to public health.
* Confront the army directly. Did they send the WAC
  to spy on me? Does she know about the bomb?
* What can a man do when there are no good choices?

I let out a long breath, staring at the documents in front of me.
Earl Morrissey had figured out what Dorie and I couldn't: what
had really killed Jack.

THE LINES BETWEEN US

It seemed almost unbelievable that bombs could travel so far unmanned. How many miles from here to Japan? Four thousand? Five thousand?

And yet, people had told the Wright brothers it was impossible, unbelievable, that a machine could loft a person into the sky, but they'd done it. Since then, we'd lit up screens with actors captured in full color to be projected all across the nation. Gridded a disc with lines that played a symphony's worth of music. Fashioned a new material, strong as steel and delicate as a spiderweb, to form everything from parachutes to women's stockings.

More than that, we'd built better planes, better guns, better bombs, all in the scrambling few decades since the last war. Technology often advanced because one country looked for a more efficient way to destroy another. That was the nature of the beast we humans had created. If the Japanese wanted to attack America directly and didn't have the air force to do it . . . well, they'd find another way.

And maybe they already had: hydrogen-powered incendiary bombs.

The few notes Morrissey had scribbled only brought more questions. How many bombs had been launched? How many had made it across the ocean? Had any others been killed in the explosions?

But there was no one to answer. And if Morrissey's experiences were accurate, no one I could ask—not without stirring up suspicion of treason. No wonder he'd been so jumpy lately. He was single-handedly launching an investigation into an act of war and an army cover-up from his tiny ranger station.

And the last question in the notes haunted me most of all: *What can a man do when there are no good choices?*

It shouldn't be this hard. Wasn't that why I'd turned to the Quaker faith, so I wouldn't have to be uncertain? Because God knew the right and wrong in every situation. He had told us in the Ten Commandments and Sermon on the Mount and all the other guidance for how we should live. It was supposed to be enough.

But neither Moses nor Jesus, nor Paul nor any of the prophets, seemed to have spoken about what to do here.

"Blessed are the peacemakers, for they shall be called the children of God."

But what could the children of God do when their Father had left them in the city of man, filled with war and hurt and uncertainty?

My calves ached from the climb up the mountain as I stood and poured the water Jimmy had fetched for me into the dented-but-functional kettle. Some tea would help. The all-purpose remedy Edith Morrissey and my mother both boiled up at the first sign of anything distressing.

Mother.

I looked back at the other envelope lying on the table, thin and humble. It wasn't exactly a welcome reminder of home—my childhood home had been sold when I went to live with my aunt and uncle—but at least it would be her usual everyday life, with nary a bomb or a secret in sight. Clearly, Morrissey hadn't found anything in it worth censoring or he wouldn't have given it back to me.

It would be good to read about something normal. Comforting, even.

I swirled a tea bag in my mug, letting the golden chamomile bloom outward, and opened Mother's letter.

January 22, 1945

Dear Son,

I always wondered if you'd ask about the ones that Great-Grandmother Clara couldn't help, and what I'd tell you if you did. You know I don't stand by lying, which is why I never lied

283

to you about her Underground Railroad days. I just never told you all of the truth.

I've copied out her last diary entry. Before you read it, I want you to know this. I've made some mistakes, and the one that sent me here was the biggest of all. But if you read this, you'll know what was going through my mind that night.

I'd do it differently, given the chance. I've been separated from you almost a decade now because of it. I should've waited till God struck Nelson down, like you always said on your visits to me, talking about what Quakers say about vengeance and all. Then I wouldn't have blood on my conscience.

We can't take them back, the choices we make. But we tell stories so our children know to do better.

That's what I want for you, Gordon. It'll break your heart, reading the diary entry I'm enclosing here, and I'm sorry for that too, but you've got to know. I made a wrong choice, but maybe Clara did too.

Somehow, you've got to find a better way, son.

Your mother

TRANSCRIPT OF CLARA HOOPER'S DIARY

July 29, 1853

They are gone. Irrevocably gone, whether only from this region or from life itself, I cannot say. How badly they were bleeding when they were dragged off, beaten like Christ himself, innocent before their accusers.

But am I innocent?

I do not know.

I knew something was wrong when I heard shouts at the door. Hiram answered them so gently I couldn't hear his words, but they were not satisfied and pushed past him into the kitchen, where I was preparing for the evening meal, well knowing that below my feet were the two men who had seen our signal in the window and taken shelter during last night's storm.

The sheriff knew our secret. Had one of our neighbors betrayed us? I wondered.

He set his rifle down on the floorboards and knelt next to the cellar door, pulling the rug aside and reaching for the handle.

His weapon was there, within my reach. Had I shot it, had I even struck the sheriff with it, not to kill, but to harm . . .

But instead I stood still and prayed for a miracle.

And the God who blinded the Syrian army allowed him to see. The God who spared Daniel from the den of lions watched as our two fugitives were beaten. The God who sent an angel to deliver Peter from prison did not raise a hand as they were dragged away to become property once more, amid my weeping and cries.

I cannot understand why.

O Almighty God, thy ways may be higher than mine . . . but even my human eyes know the enslavement of our brethren to be the basest evil. How could thou have allowed it?

The sheriff cursed and his men dragged the fugitives out of our door, promising to return to arrest us. Whether they will make good on this threat or not, I know not, but Hiram and I are prepared. Anything would be better than this awful silence, this terrible waiting, with only these pages and my tortured prayers.

That weapon, soiled though it was with blood shed in evil, might have been my miracle. And I let it be.

It may be my greatest regret.

CHAPTER 28

Dorie Armitage

January 26, 1945

Morrissey was punishing me, or at least trying to keep me out of trouble. I was sure that was why he put me on Gordon's Saturday work detail—window washing. But there was something satisfying about scrubbing away a layer of winter grime from the laundry building's front panes, seeing the clear water in my bucket turn dull.

Besides, it gave me time to think. And there was a lot to think about.

Now that we knew what had happened to Jack, what was left for me to do?

Only a few days remained in my furlough, and then I'd need to beat it to the train station to get back to Fort Lawton, back to Violet and Bea and the comforting routines of garage work and Friday night dates.

Which was fine, except for one thing:

If you leave now, you won't get to say good-bye to Gordon.

After a full day and night to think about it, I knew it had been rotten of me, springing the news that Jack was planning to enlist on him like I had. We'd fallen into old patterns, both of us delivering cutting words that stung and then quickly dissolved into regret, like the crystals of ice flinging themselves at my face as I worked.

Now that there was no murderer to bring to justice, it would be easier to walk away. But was it the right thing to do?

"There she is!"

Given the limited female population at Flintlock Mountain, the "she" gave me enough of a clue to look up from my work. Four of the COs, with Thomas Martin bringing up the rear, stormed down the path toward me, dressed in dark winter wear that made them stand out against the flurries of snow filling the air. While I couldn't see any pitchforks or torches, they managed to be as intimidating as a mob of pacifists could be, armed with angry faces and voices.

This can't be good. I wrung out my rag, shook some feeling into my red fingers, and waved at them. Since they were too close for me to run away, honey instead of vinegar couldn't hurt. "Hello, boys."

As Hank, Charlie, one of the Bontrager brothers, and Thomas surrounded me, their words overlapped with one another.

"What did you say in that report of yours?"

"They can't really do this to us, can they?"

"It's not fair!"

"They ought to at least give us a choice."

"*Quiet!*" When we all turned, it was Thomas who stood, stern and commanding. "She doesn't know what you're talking about."

Thank goodness for Thomas. A sentiment I never thought I'd have. "Will someone—*one* person, if you don't mind—please explain what's going on?"

Hank stepped forward, scowling in accusation. "Mr. Morrissey told us he called the army yesterday, and they're sending some officers to inspect the camp tomorrow."

"And what's more," the Bontrager brother interjected, ignoring my "one person" request, "they expect we'll be out of a job soon."

"Why? Is the war over?" It was a joke, but no one laughed. True, we were in the middle of nowhere, but Edith snapped on the radio

THE LINES BETWEEN US

in the evenings, and most of the fellows gathered to hear the latest news. We'd all know by now if they'd wrangled a peace treaty out of the Axis powers.

Charlie shook his head somberly. "Sounds like the army might be taking over smokejumping this summer and sending us all to different camps."

Oh no. I thought of the documents we'd found, the indications that the unusual fires this winter had been set by bombs. Of course the army would want to get involved. It made sense on paper . . . but looking at the crestfallen faces of the young men around me, it was as if the army had canceled Christmas and Easter and everyone's birthday.

"I'm sorry, boys, but this is the first I've heard of it. Why, I haven't even filed my report yet." The fact that it was the honest truth must have shown on my face, because they went from being mad to just plain disappointed.

"Come on now," I said, trying to inject a bit of pep into my voice. "Cheer up. Aren't you itching to get out of this wilderness?"

"Nah. I'll miss this ol' place." Hank almost sounded surprised, like he'd only just realized it.

"It's something to be proud of, you know?" Charlie said, and the others nodded, even Thomas. "We're doing something nobody else can do, keeping the country from going up in flames. It *matters*."

"All work matters." I passed off the stock line with the confidence of a war-bond-drive organizer, but it was clear none of them would step up to buy it.

Charlie shook his head. "Not like this. During the summer, you'd get up in the morning, go out to those forests, and you thought . . . you thought, 'Maybe today will be the day we save America.'"

And I saw, in Charlie's sincere face, a reflection of myself three years before, coming home from the theater, where starlet Loretta

Young had looked at me from the movie screen under a fringe of dark lashes and proclaimed, "There is a job for each and every one of us, and it is our duty to find that job. Because every task we complete is a pledge that our homes—and our nation—will not be destroyed."

I'd found my job . . . and Charlie and the others had found theirs. And now the army was going to take it away from them.

"When *they* come," Thomas said, clearly unwilling to speak the words *army officers*, "would you talk to them on our behalf?"

How to answer that? Because when the army representatives arrived, whatever their agenda, I needed to be out of sight, or they'd smell a rat for sure. "I don't think I'll have much influence, Mr. Martin."

Even though his expression didn't change, something in his eyes seemed to issue a challenge. "But we're your neighbors."

I had said something about loving your neighbors, hadn't I? Bother those morals. Whenever you try to dispense them on someone else, they get turned back on you. "If there was anything I could do, I . . . well . . ."

"But aren't you in the army, Miss Hightower?" Charlie pressed.

The earnest way he looked at me made the dog tags tucked underneath my blouse burn against my skin.

"All you ever do is lie."

Maybe Gordon was right.

Really, though, what was the point anymore? Jack hadn't been murdered after all. Oh, Morrissey was hiding something, but nothing close to foul play. None of the secrets we'd uncovered could bring my brother back.

"What would it feel like, do you think, to tell the truth for once in your life?"

Well, Gordon. I guess we're about to find out.

"Yes," I said, hooking the chain near my collar and pulling it over my head, "I am in the army. But the army didn't send me here, and my name isn't Nora Hightower. It's Doris Armitage."

The dog tags dangled from my fingers, clinking together in the wind with my real name stamped on them, but Jack's friends didn't so much as glance at them to verify my story. They just stared at me.

Confused, for sure. And shocked. Thomas certainly looked like he had a half dozen scriptures in mind about how taking up a false identity was a sin.

Or so I thought. The first words out of his mouth were actually "That's why you asked all those questions about him."

I nodded, suddenly tired and empty.

"He told us he had a sister," Charlie said, darting a glance at me, like he was trying to see Jack's face in mine. "Just not that she was . . . well . . ."

"A soldier?"

He dipped his head in a sheepish nod, like he'd accidentally insulted me, even though I was as proud to be a WAC as Jack had been to be a conscientious objector.

"You don't look like him," the Bontrager brother said. "Except maybe your nose is crooked in the same way."

"I'm flattered, thank you." It wasn't crooked so much as one nostril was slightly larger than the other, but now wasn't the time to get into that.

"Why?"

I expected Thomas to add more to the question that they were surely all wondering, but he just stood there, arms crossed, waiting.

Why had I come? Because the vague description of what had happened to Jack made me suspicious. Because Gordon's letter gave me some direction, something I could *do* instead of sitting at Fort Lawton, waiting for another awful telegram.

Because Gordon had sent me the detective screenplay Jack had written, and I'd read one line from it over and over, until I had it memorized: *"I'm not gonna give up on her. Not that easy. Not until I make sure she's all right. We've got to find my sister. Whatever it takes."*

I breathed in the January air and tried to force out something that would make sense. "I thought maybe . . . if I could find out where he was, if I knew what happened to him, maybe we could . . ."

I felt a sudden similarity to the rag draped over my bucket—limp, cold, the life squeezed out of me. Before my knees could buckle, I sank down on the stoop of the laundry building steps, arms wrapped around my knees to guard against the cold, not wanting to meet their eyes.

I can't cry. Not right now. Not in front of them.

But the sadness finally hit me, cold and cutting, and even the pain of biting my cheek couldn't keep back a sob.

The four men didn't sit down beside me or lay a hand on my shoulder. They didn't speak a word. But they gathered closer, like a platoon forming ranks before a charge. Alone, there was nothing to say or do, but together, at least they could shield me from the wind.

I tucked my head and focused on breathing in and out. Over the wind, I could hear someone—Charlie?—hum a low, sad song I'd never heard before. Somehow, I felt like I knew the words, or at least what the words meant. There was a bone-deep sadness to them, but here and there, a note of hope.

After a few moments, I started to breathe easier. Surrounded by these men of peace, I felt a bit of peace myself for the first time in a long time. Enough to make me stand, straighten my shoulders, and angle myself toward Morrissey's office.

They parted for me, but Charlie stood in my path, looking uneasy. "You all right, Miss . . . Armitage?"

It was nice, hearing my real name. "No," I answered calmly.

"And I probably won't be for a long time." I'd been honest enough in these past minutes—why not keep it going?

"We miss him too." His dark eyes were solemn, and the others nodded, even—I was surprised to see—Thomas.

"Thank you." I dusted the snow and dirt off my coat. "Well, boys, it's been fun. But I think it's time I turned myself in. I'm sure you've figured out by now that I'm not supposed to be here."

As I walked away, I couldn't help but think that Gordon would be proud. If he ever found out. Maybe I'd just disappear from his life forever.

"Miss Armitage!"

I stopped to see Thomas running after me, boots crunching on the path, snowflakes white against his dark beard. *Ah, of course. Now* it was time for the Bible-thumping judgment. I braced myself. "Yes?"

"I've been thinking about what you said. About whether I was too harsh with Jack."

"And?"

"I . . . I don't know."

From the surprised look on his face, it seemed like Thomas had very few occasions when he was anything but fully certain.

I patted him on the shoulder as I passed. "That makes two of us, Thomas."

As I marched over to the ranger station, I realized I had an answer now for Gordon, if he ever spoke to me again. Telling the truth for once in my life felt like freedom.

I beat my fist on Morrissey's desk, something Nancy Drew would never dream of doing, and I couldn't bring myself to care.

When I'd found the ranger station empty—locked, no lights

on, no sign of Morrissey anywhere—I'd decided to let myself in and talk to the only person who might be able to tell me what to do next.

But when I picked up the receiver and tried to contact the look-out tower, the line was dead. Here, only flurries filled the air, but I supposed it would be worse in the mountains.

"It's always the weather," I muttered, slumping down in the creaky chair, comfortable enough even though the indentations in the cushion were fitted to Morrissey's larger frame. Detectives were constantly struggling against the elements, although usually it was a dark and stormy night, with flashes of lightning that gave the English country home a dash of the sinister, rather than a plain old Oregon snowfall.

Now what?

According to the calendar on Morrissey's desk, he was in town in a meeting with the mayor for the next hour. The framed ser-vice flag didn't seem to have been moved, so Morrissey might not know we'd found his secret stash, or that Gordon had it with him up in the fire tower.

I stared at the receiver. No way to get word to Gordon and warn him about the army delegation. To ask him what to do. To tell him I'd decided to turn myself in, or even to say good-bye.

An unexpected sound cut into my worried thoughts: a knock at the door.

"Mr. Morrissey," a muffled male voice said from outside. "Are you there? I'd like to speak to you."

I gripped the keys in my hand. The ranger station door was unlocked.

The options flew through my head. Pretend to be Morrissey and order the visitor to go away? No, even at my best, my imitations could only sink to a respectable tenor, not Morrissey's growly bass.

Come up with some reason why I had broken into Morrissey's office? No, that would look even more suspicious. Climb out the window? No time.

The only option left was to duck under the desk, hold my breath, and hope the CO outside hadn't heard me.

I heard the creak of the ranger station door. Footsteps sounded on the floor cautiously, like someone unsure of being invited in, and I pictured him eyeing the eerie stuffed birds swooping from their perches on the wall. "Mr. Morrissey? Sir? Are you there?"

Just in time, I bit my lip to keep from breathing in sharply. I recognized that voice.

Of course I'd left the office door ajar and—I cursed myself for not thinking about it—the desk lamp on. The footsteps got louder. Stopped in front of the desk.

I held my breath, because that always worked in books, but no one clicked off the lamp, said, "Strange, I thought for sure I heard something," and walked right back out the door.

Instead, the tall black boots—I could see the toes of them from my hiding place, covered in slushy mud—remained firmly planted. "I know someone's under there," the voice said. "You can come out."

The floorboard underneath me squeaked, ratting me out, and I gave in. I tried to clamber up with dignity by using Morrissey's desk chair like a ladder, putting on a brave face for the tall, shadowed figure to see.

"Well, if it isn't PFC Doris Armitage. How did I know it would be you?"

I straightened my cap and saluted at the crisply uniformed man in front of me, trying to smile. "Hello, Lieutenant Leland. Fancy meeting you here."

CHAPTER 29

Gordon Hooper

January 26, 1945

I dreamed of fire and woke up to ice. Not literal ice—the lookout floor creaked here and there, but it had been solidly built only a decade before. Even under three layers of blankets, though, I could feel an invasive chill, unbroken by the light streaming in on all sides.

The stove had gone out during the night—I hadn't stocked it with enough wood in the hours of early morning when I'd finally slumped into a restless sleep. Slowly, I sat up, my legs sore from the mountain climb, keeping the blankets wrapped tightly around me . . .

And remembered.

Jack had been about to enlist in the army. A bomb had started the fire that killed him. Morrissey was considering treason. Even Clara had doubted pacifism in the end.

It was enough to make a fellow want to roll over and go back to sleep.

Last night, I'd done what Dorie suggested and read Jack's last entry in the observation log. She'd been telling the truth for once. Seeing the worries and wonderings there in Jack's own handwriting took the last bit of strength I had. Numbly, I'd tucked Morrissey's incriminating papers underneath the observation log on the bookshelf, with a hope that it would be better in the morning.

But it never worked that way.

From the glimpses we'd gotten, I expected the papers describing the balloon bomb. But Mother's letter and Clara's journal entry . . .

Think about something else. And I tried, savoring the first sip of coffee after brewing a pot, the feeling of warmth crawling back through my limbs as I edged closer to the relit stove. I wondered if Morrissey had found his folder missing, and what lies Dorie might tell to cover for us. I planned what I would draw next for the trail guide, even took out my sketchbook, looking out at the birds swooping past the tower for inspiration.

Every time, though, my mind drifted back to the faces of two enslaved men, terrified, as light shone down into their hiding place. Sometimes I imagined what would have happened if Clara had picked up the sheriff's gun.

Should she have?

No. Violence was always wrong. That was the one thing I'd been sure of from the time I was a child. After all I'd seen, it had to be true.

When Nelson overindulged in drink and shouted at or hit my mother, that was wrong.

But when my mother found him passed out drunk in our garage at midnight, a tire iron clutched in his hand, when she'd turned on the car's engine and left him there . . . that was wrong too.

She'd worried about what he would do to us when he woke up, so she'd made sure he never would. That was how she explained it to me the next morning. "But . . . you shouldn't have . . . why—" I'd stammered, trying to push past her to the garage to see my father's body, but she grabbed my arm in a vise grip.

"I was protecting you," she countered, her voice eerily calm. "It was what Clara would have wanted."

"I'm fifteen years old." My voice, strained under pressure, had cracked as I said it, mocking me. "Almost a man."

And she'd looked at me, with those dark, serious eyes like mine. "What sort of man would you have become, with a father like that?"

A better man, I wanted to promise her. But how could I be sure?

Because she pled guilty to second-degree murder when she could have easily made Nelson's death look like a suicide, the court gave her a lenient twelve years. She'd served ten. Maybe, by the time she was free again, the war would be over.

"It was what Clara would have wanted." At the time, I'd been far too shocked to ask what she meant, but I'd asked her later during my first visit to Bedford Hills Correctional Facility. She had only smiled wearily and changed the subject.

Now I knew.

My pencil flew over the page, shading it heavier, darker than my usual sketches.

How was it possible to feel betrayed by someone who lived and died decades before you were born?

And yet . . . why had God let two men be captured, beaten, and hauled back into bondage if Clara had followed the way of righteousness? Shouldn't he have rewarded her with a miraculous escape?

That was how it was supposed to work. When a forest burned because of Sarah Ruth's teenage carelessness, that was justice: terrible consequences following a wrong action, just like Thomas was so fond of talking about. But what happened to Clara's fugitives . . . that didn't seem just. Neither was Jack's death or the German camp from Dorie's article where the Nazis killed women and children.

When I looked down at my sketchbook, I saw that I'd traced the soft curves of a mourning dove—Clara's favorite bird, because, according to my mother, *"its song could break your heart."* But the dove wasn't roosting contentedly on her nest. No, her wings were a flurry of motion, striking out at whatever predator I had yet to add to the scene. A snake, maybe. A hawk. Something attacking the ones she loved.

Violence, but for a good purpose.

Was there such a thing?

The old coals of anger were burning again, deep inside me. Only this time, there was no one to direct it at, just like Sarah Ruth had said. No one to punch or curse or shout at. Jack and Clara were both dead now. There was no reasoning with them.

They're wrong. They have to be wrong. I crumpled up the drawing of the mourning dove, tossing it in the tinderbox to burn. The edges caught and curled in a satisfying glow.

Only four steps to cross the room. I yanked Mother's letter and the copy of Clara's diary entry from within the pages of the observation log, leaving Morrissey's documents alone. Then I knelt by the stove and slid them inside too.

There. I'd done it. I'd burned away the inconvenient information, tossed my doubts into the stove and slammed the cast-iron door.

So why didn't it make me feel any better?

"Courage is running toward the fire, not away from it."

Bending down with a lurch, I jabbed the poker into the fire, trying to save a scrap of the letter, but it was too late. There was nothing left but ashes.

CHAPTER 30

Dorie Armitage

January 26, 1945

"Do you realize what you've done?"

They were the first substantial words, other than clarifying questions, that Lieutenant Leland had spoken during my entire story. He sat with hands clasped in his lap and an unreadable expression on his face.

When I didn't respond, he named my misdeeds for me. "You lied to your commanding officer about your furlough, impersonated an army representative, swindled your way into the Forestry Department under false pretenses, and dug up information about a bomb no one is supposed to know about."

"But I *was* honest about it," I said, trying to find some scrap of redemption. He continued to look at me skeptically. "To you. Right now. And the reason I'm here was because I was trying to confess to Morrissey."

It was clear from his expression that he didn't believe me. How was I supposed to convince him?

"What are you doing here anyway?" So far, I'd done all the talking, but now it was time to get some answers. "I thought the army wasn't coming until tomorrow."

He grudgingly allowed the change of topic, though I could tell it wasn't finished in his mind. "Our official appointment is tomorrow. But on the train here, Major Hastings mentioned that Morrissey had asked about a WAC reporting on camp conditions, which he thought was a waste of time and resources."

"And you knew it was me," I finished.

"I wondered. Which was why I hoped to speak to Morrissey today to ask. Only to find you snooping around his office."

"Guilty as charged." I studied him, his uniform neatly pressed whereas mine was wrinkled and in need of a good laundering, his slush-caked boots the only unpolished thing about him. "The army's after Morrissey, aren't they? To shut him up about the bomb. That's the real reason you came."

He looked like he was going to offer up the magic word "classified" again, but then sighed long and hard. "We were supposed to visit some of the spike camps anyway, to see a demonstration, meet some of the training instructors. But yes, we want to speak to him. After the accident, Major Hastings knew there might be trouble."

"That 'accident,'" I said, glaring at him, "killed my brother."

Leland ducked his head, looking properly chastised, but I wasn't done. "I saw what Morrissey found." Enough of it anyway. "If the army knew about all this, if Jack had been told what he saw in the woods was a bomb, none of this would have happened."

"And then what? The whole nation would be talking about it, from the president to the soda jerk at the drugstore. Everyone would be afraid."

Unease crept into my stomach. So far, America had been safe, secure with an ocean between them and any of the Axis powers. "And then Japan would hear about it."

Leland nodded. "Right now, for all they know, every single

balloon bomb fell harmlessly in the ocean. How many more, better bombs might they send if they knew some of them made it?"

I didn't like it, not one bit, but he had a point. And yet . . .

"But what if others like Jack stumble across those balloons, never
knowing what they've found? Bird watchers. Travelers. Children
on a Sunday afternoon picnic."

That made him flinch. "That's why the army wants the Triple
Nickles to take over the smokejumping. So no more civilians get
hurt. But until then, I need your promise of silence."

I thought for a minute, leaning back in my chair and lacing my
fingers together like I'd seen Captain Petmencky do once.

No. I couldn't give that. Not yet. "Who are the Triple Nickles,
Lieutenant?" I held up a hand. "And don't say you can't answer.
Because I won't agree to keep quiet about the bomb until I have
the story."

He stared at me. "You're serious."

I stared right back and let him figure out the answer on his own.

"Fine." He reached into his pocket, pulled out a photograph,
and tossed it onto the desk.

I picked it up and inspected the line of black men standing tall
and proud and wearing paratrooper gear.

"Back in the summer of '43, you might not have recognized
me." He paired a smirk with a limp salute. "Vince Leland, less-
than-proud member of the service corps of the Jump School at
Fort Benning. Most nights, you'd find me leaning against the jump
platform while on guard duty, nodding off in the Georgia heat
soon as the white troops marched out in stick formation and we
took over."

It was hard to picture, but I tried. "What happened?"

"We were only support staff, you see. No black men were allowed
to actually be paratroopers. But our leader, a lowly first sergeant,

figured there weren't any *White Only* signs around, and that as long as we were guarding the place, we might as well train on it."

"A bold move." Although I hadn't admitted it outright, Charlie was right: The army wasn't known for being progressive about race.

He nodded in acknowledgment. "Well, General Gaither heard about it before long. And he called us in, asked what we thought about starting an all-black airborne infantry unit."

There was a whole battalion of black paratroopers? And one started in Georgia, no less.

"I got trained as an officer, seeing as they'd need some fellows to run things and I was dumb enough to volunteer. After four weeks of paratrooper training, they gave me these." He rubbed the gleaming wings pinned to his uniform, unable to keep back a proud smile. "And just like that, I went from the laziest loafer you ever did see to a proud member of the 555th Parachute Infantry Battalion."

"The Triple Nickles. I see." I applauded. "Well, Lieutenant, I'd say if Hollywood's ever looking for a blockbuster, that'll do it." It checked every box of a classic underdog story: an inspiring leader, secret training under cover of darkness, and eventually, hard-earned triumph.

He smiled—briefly, but it seemed genuine. "Now listen, PFC Armitage, wouldn't you say those men would be the ones you'd want to call in if you had an unsolvable problem?"

Even I had to admit they seemed to be perfect for the job. "Wouldn't your men rather be fighting Hitler overseas?"

"You bet." The answer was instant, delivered with a wry smile. "Every last one of us. We've been waiting months for orders to fly into a combat zone. But if this is what America gives us, we'll take it." His hand was in a fist, I noticed, his jaw set in a determined line. "And maybe, if we fight in this war, if we can do anything the white soldiers can, when we come back, they'll have to treat us equal."

It was a fair enough answer, but I could still think of problems with it. "There's a black CO here—a man named Charlie Mayes— who says only a fool would think you could change the country from the inside like that."

He leaned back in his chair, as if considering. "Do you think it's easy, Private Armitage? Figuring out the best way to fight hate that's been around for hundreds of years? Knowing what to do, what will make a difference, how to be heard?"

That wasn't the reaction I'd expected. "No, but . . . but don't you think you're doing the right thing?"

"Yes, ma'am, I do." He nodded firmly. "So do all of us in the Triple Nickles, or we wouldn't have joined up. But if a brother of mine thinks and prays and decides he's going to take a stand in a different way, I understand. It's hard to know."

But was it? It had always been easy for me, right and wrong and what to do next.

Until now.

"What if I said the same thing? That it's hard for me to know whether or not to keep quiet about these bombs?"

There wasn't a note of challenge in my voice anymore. I couldn't manage to make a joke or even look up. Jack was dead and a Japanese bomb had killed him and nothing made sense anymore. Instead, I studied the picture in my hand, the faces of the Triple Nickles standing at attention, tall and proud.

"Well. I guess I'd ask you to trust that we'll take care of them."

And I looked up from the picture to see Lieutenant Vincent Leland himself. Maybe he'd started out an unambitious security guard, but that's not the man I saw before me now.

He really means it. Whatever he and his men could do to prevent more deaths, they'd do it, no matter the cost. "Okay."

"Because if you don't—" He paused, realizing what I'd just said, and the shocked look on his face almost broke through my heavy mood to make me laugh.

"I promise I won't tell anyone about the papers, or about the bombs. Not a single soul." I stuck my hand out, and he shook it, warm and firm.

"Thank you." Tentative, like he wasn't sure if he could trust me.

All of a sudden, I felt exhausted, the way I did when I made it safely inside after a date where I'd put on a cheerful front to entertain a fellow about to ship off to war. I rubbed my temples, willing away the headache I could feel coming on. "All I wanted was a simple solution. Someone I could bring to justice. When we found the papers, Gordon said—"

Oh no.

I'd done it. Like the villains in books during interrogations. Let my emotions get a hold of me and make me say just a bit too much. *Maybe he won't notice.*

But Leland's eyes focused in on me. "Who's Gordon?"

So much for that hope. "He was my brother's best friend. One of the COs."

"And he knows about the bomb too."

If I'd thought quicker, if I'd pulled out my innocent smile, if I wasn't so gosh-darn tired, I could have salvaged my mistake. Maybe.

Or maybe I didn't try because I wanted to drag Gordon into it with me.

All I know is that I sighed a sigh it felt like I had been holding in since Pearl Harbor and said, "Yes. He does."

His mouth tightened in a frown, and I guessed what he was thinking: *More loose ends for the army to deal with.* "Then how about you track him down for me, PFC Armitage? I'd like to tell him the same thing I just told you."

"That's going to be tough." I explained about lookout duty and the downed phone lines, and the same frustration I'd felt on learning that news flashed over Leland's face.

"We can't wait a week. If anyone leaks information about the bomb, they could be tried for treason or espionage against the United States."

Treason and espionage? Those were strong words, meant for black-cloaked criminals with a hatred for their country, certainly not me or Gordon or Morrissey. "That's absurd. None of us have done anything wrong."

"Oh?" He raised his brows. "Based on what you told me, Earl Morrissey deliberately violated an order from his superior to let this matter rest."

I thought about the papers I'd seen, the warnings and official seals and the word *confidential.*

"And if you're telling the truth about those documents you found, then a court could find him guilty of intention to commit treason."

But, I wanted to protest, *Morrissey isn't a traitor.*

Still, I couldn't deny that, by the laws of the land, he might be.

It was all so complicated. Did Morrissey deserve to be punished? Was keeping quiet about the bomb the right decision?

Words. Words and ethics and philosophy and everything else I hated. And that's when something clicked into place in my mind. "You need to talk to Gordon."

"You're right," Leland said at last. "I think I do. If his story matches yours, I'll report to my superiors back at the hotel tonight . . . and Earl Morrissey and the United States Army will need to have a reckoning tomorrow."

Leland stood, and I stood with him, turning off the lamp and, by habit, adjusting each chair so it matched the angle it had faced when we came in. Just in case.

"It's a little over an hour to hike up to the lookout." I glanced at the clock. Just after 1400 hours. "If you leave now, you'll be back by nightfall."

He followed me into the ranger station proper, shuddering at the owl perched beside Sarah Ruth's desk. "Will the snow affect anything?"

As he opened the outer door, I could see an inch had accumulated on the ground. "Not if you're careful."

"And I assume the trails to the lookout are marked?"

"Ha!" a voice burst out, and we both turned to stare. Jimmy Morrissey leaned against the railing of the ranger station porch, his sharp-featured face spread with a cocky smirk. I braced myself for an interrogation about what we'd been doing in the ranger station alone, but Jimmy just shook his head. "You must be a city slicker for sure to say that."

"I'm sorry, who are you?" Leland asked, frowning.

He reached into the wheelbarrow beside him, stacking firewood on his arms. "My name's James. I'm one of the smokejumpers around here."

James? That must be his given name—no one named their child Jimmy on his birth certificate—but it was the first time I'd heard him use it.

"Ah, one of the COs." Leland nodded in greeting. "Good to meet you. Lieutenant Vincent Leland."

"If you want, I could take you there," Jimmy said, all teenage bravado.

So that was it. "James" was trying to sound grown-up in front of the army man. Typical.

"He does know the mountains better than anyone else around here," I added, and Jimmy's chest seemed to expand another few inches.

Leland seemed to weigh this, snow landing on his collar in a pattern of lace. Then he nodded. "All right. Let's go."

It's for the best, I reasoned. Gordon would hear Leland's story and know what to do, whether to give up the documents or protect Morrissey. Gordon always knew what to do, with that rock-solid certainty of his.

Feeling generous, I even took the armful of logs from Jimmy so they could get started. When I stooped down to the hole cut into the stone fireplace, though, it was already full to the brim with logs, so I opened the grate to toss in some of the ones Jimmy had brought, prodding the coals with the poker to spur them on. He'd clearly been restocking the wrong building.

I flipped through my notebook, reading some of the interviews, looking over what Gordon and I knew, trying to decide if I'd done the right thing. It was so hard to tell.

And something seemed . . . wrong.

I sat on the wood floor in front of the fireplace, lost in the flickering glow of the growing flames, thinking through what might feel off.

"James," he'd said. Not Jimmy Morrissey. No mention of his last name at all.

And when Leland had assumed Jimmy was one of the conscientious objectors, Jimmy hadn't protested.

It did seem like a bit of a coincidence that he'd arrived when he had. Was it a godsend . . . or had he been eavesdropping? And if he had, did he hear Leland accusing his father of treason?

The ranger station door banged open, and Sarah Ruth burst in, snow swirling around her feet as she tramped the excess off her boots, muttering to herself like an eccentric mountain hermit. She craned her neck past me to the office, dark and still. "Where's my father? And what are you doing here?"

307

"Out," I said, figuring that was the safest answer. "And I came to use the telephone."

She seemed about to question that, then shook her head, displacing droplets of melting snow, and hurried into the office. I followed.

Her finger skimmed the surface of the calendar splayed on Morrissey's desk. "January twenty-sixth . . . meeting with Mayor Simmons?" She shook her head. "I never scheduled that meeting."

"Maybe it came up while you were at the lookout," I offered. "Anyway, if it's an emergency and you need a ride into town, I'm an ace driver."

"No time. I'll have to go after them myself."

Go after them? "It's Jimmy, isn't it?"

She looked astounded at my deductive insight, which should have made me feel smug, but nothing could overpower that prickling unease that now grew stronger. "Is something wrong? I know Jimmy was taking Le—an army officer to the lookout. But surely the snow isn't bad enough to worry you."

She paced the floor, her boots tracking muddy prints in all directions. "It's not that. He came back to the house to get his thicker coat. But the way he talked on the way out the door . . ."

No one had told me that a detective could correctly identify the clues and still feel a sick feeling in their stomach when someone confirmed them. "What did he say, Sarah Ruth?"

Her voice changed in imitation of her younger brother. "'I'm going to protect Dad. Just like Willie told me to.' And then when I asked him what he was talking about, he said, 'When the greater good is at stake, you've got to do anything you can to get there. Anything.'"

I forced a laugh through tightness in my throat. "Is that all? I've said things like that before." *To Jimmy, actually.* "I'm sure it doesn't mean anything."

But what if it did? What if I'd sent Leland out with a hotheaded teenager, completely loyal to his family, who had just learned that his father might be accused of treason?

"He seems to be taking it seriously." Sarah Ruth stopped pacing, desperation in her eyes. "I don't know what's going on, but I'm worried Jimmy's going to do something he will regret."

CHAPTER 31

Gordon Hooper

January 26, 1945

Sometimes, when Nelson woke up hungover and apologetic on a Saturday morning, he'd let Mother "rest" and would make soup. Not out of a can, but hearty meat-and-potato stew, bursting with flavor, the kind that would weigh your spoon down and warm your body up. Even so, Nelson's soup always tasted like boiled-over guilt to me.

The stock of tomato soup at the watchtower mostly tasted like tin, but heating it up in the saucepan still brought back memories I'd rather forget. I tried to crumble them up with a handful of crackers on the top. At least preparing an early supper gave me something to do other than stare at the forest for hours at a time.

Outside, the snow had gotten worse, and with lookout windows all around, it was like I was trapped in a souvenir snow globe. I blew on a spoonful of soup and let the warm steam rise toward my face.

Creak. Creeeeeak.

Strange. It almost sounded like someone was climbing up the wooden steps to the platform.

But that didn't make sense. It was the wind and my imagination, picturing the escaping slaves who made the perilous journey to Clara's door and . . .

Knocked.

Yes, someone was really knocking. Now I knew how Sarah Ruth felt, startled by visitors to her lonely forest outpost.

I dribbled soup on my hand in my hurry to stand. Throwing the door open, I saw Jimmy Morrissey next to a stranger swaddled to the upper lip with a scarf that might have doubled as a blanket. Above that, I could see that his skin was darker than even Charlie's.

"Gordon Hooper?" the man asked, his voice stern in a way that reminded me of my gym teacher asking me why I had bruises on my legs again.

"That's me." As if he might have gotten the wrong fire tower by accident.

Behind him, Jimmy shook his head. Or maybe he was just knocking snow off his knit cap.

"I'm Lieutenant Vincent Leland of the US Army."

So that was it. Dorie had been found out, and they'd sent someone after her.

But why was he here?

The question must have been on my face, because the lieutenant added, "I wanted a chance to talk to you privately about a . . . sensitive matter."

He looked beyond me into the lookout, and I threw the door open wide. "Sorry, Lieutenant Leland. I don't mean to be rude. I'm just not used to company here. Come on in."

They performed the usual buffalo-stampede tromp of snowy winter days on the braided rug, and I shut the door behind them, shivering from the cold they'd let in.

"I can make more soup if you're interested," I said, noticing Lieutenant Leland eyeing my bowl. I'd figure out soon enough why they were here, so why not all pretend this was a social call in the meantime?

"We're hoping to head back to the camp shortly, before the snow gets worse." Instead of looking at me as I spoke, the lieutenant's eyes roamed the small room, like he was taking in every detail. "Any chance of a wildfire with a storm like this?"

"It's highly unlikely," I admitted. "But Earl Morrissey—that's our district ranger—is always cautious."

"Hmm," he said, and his expression told me he didn't buy my halfhearted explanation.

Trouble was, neither did I. This wasn't caution. It was an exile.

"My fingers are near frozen," Jimmy piped up, fumbling at his collar. "Help me get this off, will you, Gordon?"

Strange. Jimmy had never asked me for help with anything, not even his parachute gear.

"Sure." I came closer and reached for the clasps on his coat. He caught my arm and gripped it tightly.

His voice tickled my ear with a harsh whisper. "Do you have the papers?"

My first thought was to play innocent and say, "What papers?" But of course, if he knew about them, Dorie must have told him for some reason, so I nodded.

"Hide them." His voice was so urgent that I felt like Clara with a runaway slave to stow in the root cellar. "Better yet, get rid of them. You can't let him find them."

Before I could ask what was going on, Lieutenant Leland stood from where he'd been stooped to remove his black boots. They were taller than most, with thick, stiff leather . . . the kind all the smokejumpers had been issued for fire drops to protect our ankles from twisting on landing. "Not much of a place, is it?"

Jimmy let go of me and peeled his coat off just fine on his own. I wondered if the lieutenant noticed.

Destroy the papers? After his father had gone to all the work of gathering them? And why would this officer want them, or even know about them?

Something wasn't right here.

I realized Lieutenant Leland was waiting for me to answer, or at least react. "It fits what we need." With a scrape of old wood, I yanked the bench near the south observation window and pulled it nearer the fire for him to sit on.

Jimmy stayed standing, shifting from side to side like a fellow on fence duty with a powerful need to use the latrine.

I glanced at my watch. Almost four o'clock. During the summer, there would still be another four full hours of daylight, but January squeezed out even the dusky twilight that had leaked through the snow clouds. Nothing but steadily graying skies and a whirl of snow out the window. "It's going to be hard for you to get back down safely tonight. I can't imagine what would be so important that you'd have to come all the way up here just to talk to me."

"Oh, I think you might." And there was that tone again, even down to the way the lieutenant leaned just slightly closer. "I need to know what you know, Mr. Hooper. *Everything* you know."

CHAPTER 32

Dorie Armitage

January 26, 1945

They should have sent me to Alaska.

That's where we WACs thought we were being sent at first, traveling by train all the way across the country. We had heard of the Aleutian Islands campaign, making attacks on Japan and protecting the cities of the West Coast, and the daring exploits and perilous weather had sounded like the best sort of lark. If they'd shipped me another leg of the journey north, I'd be used to struggling through the snow.

But no, I'd been rolled under the carriage of jeeps in Seattle instead of developing my survival skills in the sunless winter of Alaska. Skills I now found I desperately needed.

While Sarah Ruth and I had been hiking in the forest, the boughs had sheltered us, blocking the wind and filtering the worst of the snow through their branches. The mountain trail, though, left us unobstructed, to be flayed by stinging pellets of ice.

"Are you sure this is the way?" I called to Sarah Ruth ahead of me, even though I knew Lewis and Clark probably hadn't nagged their guides about things like that.

The wind, aimed bracingly against our backs, must have carried my voice well enough. "Just keep moving. We've got to hurry."

To convince Sarah Ruth to let me come along, I'd told her everything. About the papers we'd found. The bomb. Leland and the army's involvement. Gordon and the evidence up at the lookout.

Earl Morrissey was still in town, for all we knew telling the mayor about the bomb and committing treason to boot. The phone line was down, so we couldn't send a warning to Gordon that way. Running to the barracks to tell the other smokejumpers would only complicate the situation.

It was up to us.

Which is a sentiment far more exiting and noble when you're watching it play out in a movie while clutching a box of Cracker Jack and not while stumbling up a mountain in a blizzard. I hadn't reckoned on the smell of mothballs heavy on the collar of my borrowed coat, or the raw rubbing of wet wool socks in boots, or the growling of my stomach—it was nearing time for supper, wasn't it?

But on we pressed. While I knew Leland and Jimmy had gotten a head start on us, I couldn't say for sure how much. Thirty minutes? Forty? More?

"How much farther?" I called out, unable to help myself.

"We're more than halfway."

Halfway. That meant there would be no turning back. I pulled my roomy coat tighter against the onslaught of snow pellets.

Every now and then I'd look down, trying to find footprints, but even though there were only a few inches of snow on the ground, it was constantly shifting in the wind. A herd of elk might have trampled up the mountain ten minutes before us, and we wouldn't see a trace.

Though we weren't high on the mountain, we'd reached the section where the path narrowed. When I'd hiked up to the lookout with Gordon to visit Sarah Ruth, I'd almost refused to keep going, and that was in full sunshine, without a flake of snow in the air.

I'd managed then by keeping one hand to the mountain wall, rubbing it reassuringly over the rock as I edged forward, so I tried the strategy again now.

That, of course, wouldn't keep me within pace of Sarah Ruth, who seemed to be trying to beat a Kentucky Derby record, even without the horse. She looked back every few minutes with what I'm sure was—half blind though I was by my scarf—an exasperated expression.

"I'm doing the best I can," I wanted to grouch at her. We couldn't all be Paulette Bunyan.

We plowed on, winding along the trail, and soon Sarah Ruth got far enough ahead of me that she no longer heard my shouted questions about how far we'd gone. Either that or she just ignored them.

I shivered, stumbling toward a bend in the path. Maybe there we'd have a few moments of shelter from the punishing wind.

And just then, a human shriek joined the howling wind.

I can't describe the feeling any better than ice the whole way down. Not like someone had shoved a handful of snow down the collar of my pilfered overcoat to slowly melt. Like a flash freeze down my spine.

And by the time I scrambled around the bend, pressed against the side of the trail for balance, all I saw was a place where snow had scuffled over the edge. Sarah Ruth was gone.

CHAPTER 33

Gordon Hooper

January 26, 1945

"Well," I said, pacing a groove in the lookout floor past the cot and stove and back again, "that's quite a story, Lieutenant."

I'd refused to answer questions until I learned everything I wanted to know: why the army had pretended Jack's death was an accident, how many people knew about the incendiary bombs' existence, and why spreading information about the bombs was considered treason.

"War is full of complicated stories."

I glanced at the windowed wall, where the gray sky grew darker and Jimmy was shivering by the door, looking out over the mountain. Leland had insisted on a private conversation, even if that meant exposing Jimmy to the harsh wind three stories in the air. Now I understood why.

"So why did the army come to Flintlock Mountain the night after the fire?"

He dipped a slice of bread into his near-empty bowl, sopping up the remains with the crust. "I wasn't involved with that, but I imagine they took away the remains of the bomb to study them. Maybe disarmed any explosives that didn't detonate."

That explained the muddy boot prints we'd seen at the site of the fire. Too bad they didn't know Morrissey had already captured the evidence with Charlie's camera.

I rested my head on my hand for a moment, then sat on the bench I'd pulled over to the table, shivering as a cold draft brushed against my back. We'd cleared away the Osborne FireFinder to make room for our makeshift dinner, but my soup remained un-eaten in front of me. "Where does that leave us?"

"I've got to convince you and PFC Armitage that, in this case, speaking the truth could cost hundreds, maybe thousands, of in-nocent lives—and the destruction of the forests."

"What's that supposed to mean?" We both turned to see Jimmy standing in the doorway, face pale and snowflakes melting away to drops on his face.

When had he come inside? "The forests," he prompted when it looked like Lieutenant Leland wasn't going to say more. "What do you mean about the forests being destroyed?"

"I thought I asked you to wait outside."

Jimmy stomped over to the stove, shaking off snow and not both-ering to remove his shoes. "I heard most of what you said anyway. Thin walls."

That excuse didn't hold, not with the howling wind. The only way Jimmy could have heard was if he'd cracked the door open to listen intentionally. Maybe I hadn't imagined the chill on the back of my neck.

Lieutenant Leland watched the boy warily, then looked at me, as if waiting for me to vouch for him.

Could I? Whatever he meant about those papers, Jimmy was involved in this through his father, like it or not. He deserved to know. "Go on," I finally said. "You can tell us both."

The lieutenant inclined his head in a shallow nod. "If Japan finds

318

out their balloons actually worked, they'll start launching better, more effective balloons in spring and summer, when the ground dries out. And this whole country could burn."

"Not on your life," Jimmy said, smacking the table, causing our bowls to rattle. "We could fight those fires. Us smokejumpers. That's what we do."

"Calm down, Jimmy." How many times had Mother or Jack said the same words to me? And it rarely helped.

Anger. I could spot it in almost anyone like I had a birdwatching guide with illustrations detailing its every form. First Jimmy's father, now the forests and his beloved smokejumping job. Leland was threatening everything he loved.

Lieutenant Leland shook his head wearily. "The army has been going back and forth with the Forestry Department for weeks now. I've been listening in, heard all the arguments. The rangers are short-staffed as it is, which is why they had to bring in COs like you two."

"Jimmy isn't a—" I began.

"We've got plenty enough to put out the fires," Jimmy interrupted, folding his arms and defying Leland to challenge him.

Lieutenant Leland pushed his empty bowl away and sat back in the chair, eyes thoughtful. "And what happens if the COs refuse to continue, given . . . new information?" He turned to me. "Think about your friends, Mr. Hooper. Tomorrow, if Major Hastings tells them that this summer, they'd be putting out fires set by Japanese bombs and would have to undergo military training to defuse them . . . would they accept?"

I thought about it, repeated what he said in my mind. Disabling enemy bombs and fighting the fires they caused was purely defensive . . . and yet, we had chosen the path of absolutism, had refused to serve as noncombatants like medics, because we believed anything associated with the war was wrong.

What would someone like Thomas do if he knew he suddenly was doing war work?

What would I do?

I didn't know, but the lieutenant and Jimmy were waiting for an answer. "You'd get a mix of responses," I finally said. "Some would stay. Others . . . would request a transfer. Maybe many others."

Lieutenant Leland nodded. "That's what the War Department thought. That's why they didn't tell you the truth, even after Mr. Armitage's death. They didn't want you to protest and see over half of their smokejumpers organize 'some kind of Gandhi hunger strike' for the 1945 fire season. Their words, not mine."

It wasn't farfetched. Many of the men in the CPS had been inspired by tales of nonviolent resistance. Over in Wyeth, the camp Shorty was sent to, they'd threatened to stop work when one of their men, a Japanese American, was slated to be sent to an internment camp, and several protests against segregation or overworking in other CPS camps had nearly gotten some of the fellows arrested.

I met his eyes. "That's what we do, Mr. Leland. We follow our consciences. We resist."

"I know, and I respect that." He raised a finger to stall my protest. "To a point. But we can't have you fellows on this job anymore. We've got to bring in the army, and above all, we've got to keep news of the bombs silent."

Silent. I remembered the list of options in the notes Dorie had lifted from Mr. Morrissey's office. He was considering making information about them public. Maybe he already had.

Lieutenant Leland looked earnestly across the table at us. "Listen, Mr. Hooper, this isn't personal. But we're concerned about the fact that Earl Morrissey violated direct orders to investigate this bomb. If he's reckless with that information—or if you are—it could ruin everything we've tried to protect."

320

My eyes darted to the observation log, where the documents rested, full of incriminating information. Across the table, Jimmy looked at me pleadingly.

"I've put all my cards on the table, Mr. Hooper. Now I can only ask, appealing to your love for this country: Do you have those documents?"

I didn't answer right away. What would Dorie do? Or better, what would Jack do?

That's not the right question. What sort of a Quaker was I? I was supposed to be thinking of what Jesus would do. But he seemed so far away, in his robes and sandals, teaching about lost sheep and hidden talents instead of bombs and censorship.

He hadn't helped Clara decide what to do. What made me think he would help me?

"Ye shall know the truth, and the truth shall make you free." That was something, anyway. All I had to go on.

I may have made mistakes—not being there for Jack when he needed me, punching Thomas in anger, bullying Dorie to cover my own shame—but I always told the truth. It was what made me different from my father. It was who I was.

I stood, almost ready to go to the bookshelf and take out the folder. But there was one thing I needed to know first. "You're going to arrest Morrissey for this, aren't you?"

"No. You won't."

The voice was almost unfamiliar and so cold and hard that I was surprised, when I turned, to see Jimmy holding the antique pistol in shaky hands, aimed at Lieutenant Leland.

CHAPTER 34

Dorie Armitage

January 26, 1945

Dizziness, panic, and fear made a cold braid down my spine as I squinted into the dark through the falling snow, down who knows how far.

"Sarah!" I shouted again. "Sarah Ruth, you answer me right now or I'll . . ."

What was I doing? Threatening someone who was injured? *Please let her just be injured and not . . .*

I closed my eyes, straining to hear. Yes. A weak groan.

The edge was already too close, a yard away. But there was no way to avoid it. I fell to my knees and crawled nearer, fumbling for the flashlight in my pocket with glove-wrapped fingers, then aiming the beam down.

There. Thank God, it wasn't a bottomless abyss over the edge of a sheer cliff like I'd been trained to expect from movies. Sarah Ruth had fallen, sure, but only about nine feet down, to a rocky, snow-covered ledge. Her right leg was splayed out awkwardly to the side at a painful angle.

"Did you break anything?"

She shifted, and I could see pain on her face. "I don't . . . don't think I can stand."

Not unexpected, but not good either. Heroines were always twisting their ankle in stories, but usually when there was a muscular man around to lean on. At that moment, I actually looked around as if one might materialize out of the blizzard.

No such luck.

"I'll come down for you," I declared.

"You can't . . . carry me back up. You need to get—" she paused, as if struggling to say the word—"help."

My shoulders, squared nobly, sagged in relief. Help. Yes. I could do that. Mr. Morrissey would know what to do. Wasn't that what rangers did? Rescue people and such? "I'll find your father, I promise. Once I get back to the camp, I'll drive into town if he's not back yet."

"We're closer to the fire tower than the camp."

Why would that . . . ?

She couldn't be serious. "Yes, but that's . . . *up.*"

"It's the best way."

The only way, she might as well have said. "But what if I get lost?"

"Follow the path."

What I wanted to say was, *"Right, the path that's completely covered in snow?"* But there was nothing for it, so instead, "Don't worry, I'll come back for you." Because if you said things forcefully enough, they must come true.

I could do this.

"Get Gordon. Please." Sarah Ruth's voice, once all gruffness, sounded surprisingly weak, and that worried me more than anything.

"I will. And I'll hurry too."

Though not too much. After all, that's what had caused Sarah Ruth's fall.

"*Gordon,*" she'd said. Not Jimmy, her own brother. Maybe she figured he'd be too agitated over Leland to be of much help. Or maybe there really was something going on between the two of them. At the moment, I'd accept help from just about anyone I could find in this storm.

I pulled my borrowed coat tighter, and the flecks of ice that had been stinging my neck melted down my collar, burrowing the cold deeper. There was only one thing left to do: persevere in the direction that seemed most likely to lead to rescue . . . and pray that I hadn't been on the wrong path from the start.

CHAPTER 35

Gordon Hooper

January 26, 1945

I'd faced down that pistol once already, when Sarah Ruth held it the day before, but that was different. She'd only been frightened, a woman startled into defending herself, and had lowered her weapon as soon as she recognized us.

Jimmy was angry down to his bones. A seething anger that, I'd learned with my father, you didn't reason with—not if you were smart. You ran from it.

But unlike with Nelson, here there was nowhere for me to run or even hide.

"You can't ruin my father's life," Jimmy said, spitting out the words. "I won't let you."

And I could tell from the way the lieutenant's eyes widened, enough that I could see the whites, that he hadn't known Jimmy was a Morrissey. In the next moment, though, he recovered, his voice completely unrattled, his eyes trained on the barrel of the pistol. "James, this won't end well. Not for you, not for your father."

"What am I supposed to do? Let you run down the mountain, call in your army buddies, and arrest Dad for treason? They hang people for that, you know."

Leland almost chuckled, catching himself so barely with a cough that Jimmy must have noticed. "No one is getting hanged."

Clearly, he didn't understand how serious this was, probably thinking Jimmy was just a nervous kid who had watched too many gangster movies.

I tried to interject. "Why don't you listen to him, Jimmy? He just wants to talk."

"I don't want to hear it, Hooper. His kind doesn't care if people like us get hurt. Remember? You agreed with me. You said we can't trust them."

There it was, the language of us versus them, Jimmy trying to keep me on his side against Lieutenant Leland.

"Before I do anything, I want all the facts. That's all." The lieutenant started to slowly stand. "That's why I want to see any documents your father found."

"Don't move," Jimmy burst out, and Leland froze. I tensed too. Sweat streaked Jimmy's pockmarked forehead, but he didn't move to wipe it away, keeping both hands, slightly unsteady, on the gun.

Does he know how to use it?

Of course he does. He and Sarah Ruth regularly supplemented our dinner with game from the forest.

"Take out your weapon," Jimmy ordered. "Slowly. And set it on the ground."

His weapon?

Of course. An army officer would be armed.

Leland complied, moving sunrise slow toward his army-issue holster, drawing out the sidearm. "All right. But you have to understand that—"

"Shut up!" Jimmy said, and I heard the desperation in his voice. He had no plan for what to do next, did he? His gaze flitted around the room like a bird searching for a place to land, then turned to me. "Gordon, pick it up."

No hesitation. He knew the gun would be safe with me, safer even than slid across the floor or flung out the door into the snowstorm. I was his ally, and more important, a pacifist.

"I don't want—" I began but was cut short by a slice of a glare from Leland. *Take it,* he seemed to be saying.

Jimmy wanted me to hold the pistol. But so did Leland, a man I'd just met, an army man.

My mind couldn't answer why, not fast enough, and while it puzzled over that, my hand reached down and accepted the gun.

I'd never held one before, unless you counted the Brown Bess musket carried by a reenactor on the Revolutionary War float of a Fourth-of-July parade. Leland's military sidearm was different. It wasn't a prop or a tool. It was cold steel, made to tear through flesh and blood. Maybe it already had.

Now both Lieutenant Leland and I were facing Jimmy, with him standing between us and the door. Leland was still trying to explain. "The other officers and I came because we wanted your father to know why we can't have newspapers across the nation reporting the bombs. If he's a reasonable man, he'll understand that."

But the glazed look in Jimmy's eyes told me that, even if he heard what Leland was saying, he didn't believe him.

He's not going to listen. Dear God, he's going to shoot.

I could feel my heart thumping in my chest, so loudly I thought Jimmy would whip around and shoot me instead.

You could stop it. Like Clara wished she had done. You could save a life.

By taking one?

No. Firing a bullet didn't mean killing a person. Of course not. There were nonlethal places I could shoot.

But is it the right thing to do?

I felt the gun shake in my hand. Could I even aim?

Leland looked at me briefly, not long enough for Jimmy to turn and notice. But somehow he saw the struggle and . . . nodded.

Do what you have to, he seemed to be saying.

What I wanted was to run out the door and down the ladder, storm or no storm.

"Love thy neighbor as thyself," Jesus had said. But there was no battered Samaritan on the side of the road to make it clear who most needed my help.

"Go, and do thou likewise."

There was no likewise here, nothing that remotely resembled any story in Scripture.

Dogging the panic, anger irrationally filled me again. As if it were God's fault for not telling me how to respond to this, for not making it clear to me. Just like Clara.

"And who is my neighbor?"

I. Don't. Know.

"What are you going to do now?" Leland asked, his voice low and level.

Jimmy opened his mouth, then closed it, uncertainty in his eyes, his hand slightly unsteady on the gun, and I felt a pang of sympathy. That was the question, wasn't it?

For both of us.

CHAPTER 36

Dorie Armitage

January 26, 1945

I'd expected to see the lookout from afar, like the illustration of Rapunzel's tower in my childhood storybook with the jam-print stains, rising like a sentinel out of the mists. A beacon of hope, easily visible to the one questing after it.

But the only things I could see past my frosty lashes were rocks, snow, trees, and the swirling darkness beyond, while behind me, Sarah Ruth was hurt and huddled against the mountain, waiting for my promised rescue.

Stop being dramatic. That's what Gordon would say. I'd wandered slightly off the path in a national forest during a snowstorm, and soon enough, the wind would die down and I'd see the fire tower.

Yes. Everything was going to be fine. If only Jimmy hadn't foolishly decided to protect his father, we wouldn't be in this mess.

But who told him anything was justified as long as his motive was right? the critical part of my brain argued back. *You practically argued him into this.*

I was the ignition, the first step in the chain that got the engine roaring to life. Never the last step, so I could always claim, with complete sincerity, that I wasn't to blame for what happened next.

"You didn't kill him, Dorie, but you sure did make him want to die a hero's death. Can you blame him for taking his chance?"

It wasn't true—it couldn't be. Jack made his choices, him and his stupid conscience he was always going on about. And my choices, why . . . I hadn't thought them through quite so much. Didn't take the time to follow them to their logical ends like my overly studious brother. *But that's no crime.*

Suddenly I wasn't so sure of that.

Keep going. I couldn't get distracted, not now.

Sarah Ruth was born and raised in these mountains, made of sterner stuff than I. She'd be fine. She'd have to be.

Unless she lied about how badly she's injured. Unless the loose rock falls again, this time on top of her. Unless you can't find your way and she freezes to death, alone.

No.

In the frozen silence, I prayed and tried to ignore my fears as I kept taking one step forward after the other, my boots aimed in an upward direction. It was all I knew to do.

And then I heard it—a *crack* pitched just above the wind—and I turned. Was that a twinkle of light?

I chose to believe it was, directing everything I had in the direction of the sound. But even as I took a few steps, something in me faltered. That sound . . . the wind had distorted it, but it had sounded an awful lot like a gunshot.

Maybe one of them is shooting into the air as a signal to us from the fire tower. Cheered by that thought, I forged ahead, visually marking the direction where I'd heard the gunshot, determined that their efforts to alert us wouldn't be wasted.

Until I remembered that no one knew Sarah Ruth and I were coming, not even Jimmy and Leland.

Oh no.

Jimmy and Leland. Together. With the evidence of Earl Morrissey's treason just within reach.

Instead of a deeper chill at the realization, it felt more like a fire lit inside me, pushing me on toward that beautiful light and that terrible sound.

And then, before a prayer had even made it past my lips to crumple into a puff of steam, the sound cracked through the air again.

Dear God. Not one gunshot.

Two.

CHAPTER 37

Gordon Hooper

January 26, 1945

After years as a smokejumper at Flintlock Mountain, I was used to smelling smoke.

But never from the barrel of my own gun.

The bullet had lodged over Jimmy's shoulder, into the door, where I'd meant it to. Just to get his attention.

Which I most definitely had, along with the direction of the gun's barrel.

I thought he'd swear a blue streak, the way he looked at me, betrayal in his eyes. Instead, he hissed, "I thought you were on my side."

Was he crazy? "I can't let you do this, Jimmy."

If possible, his eyes narrowed even further. "You're all 'peace on earth' until the chips are down. I see how it is."

Beside me, I thought I saw Leland take a step forward. Would he try to rush Jimmy, tackle him . . . with a gun still pointed at me? "We can talk about this. I wasn't going to—"

"There's been enough talking, Hooper." Jimmy cocked the pistol, his hands less shaky now. "More than enough. Put the gun down, or I'll shoot you."

I thought about it for a second too long, keeping the pistol raised, because a slow smile wavered on Jimmy's feverish face. "No. Wait." And I knew what he was going to say as his eyes shifted away from me back to Leland, closer now. "You put it down, or I'll shoot *him*."

In that second, with Jimmy swiveling toward Leland, his arm not yet in position, I lunged forward, wrapping him in a tackle like the football players I'd watched on campus from afar.

In that moment, I felt a sudden certainty. *What can a man do when there are no good choices?*

Protect.

Jimmy twisted, trying to squirm free of my hold and, failing that, trying to pry me off, his arms corded from hours of smoke-jumper training. But I'd done those same exercises, pounded in just as many fence posts, dug fire line after fire line, until I'd become strong enough for this moment.

There were no words, just heavy breathing and struggle, cold metal and warm flesh, my finger on the trigger . . .

And an explosion of sound as another gunshot split the air.

Jimmy's body tensed, his face inches from mine.

I shot him.

"It was an accident!" I wanted to scream, but the words didn't come. I could only look at him, now limp in my arms.

God and Mother and Great-Great-Grandmother Clara all held their breath—but Jimmy's eyes didn't close. He didn't slump to the ground, bleeding on the tower floor.

Why not?

A sharp realization cut into my wondering, and I looked down to see blood staining my pants just below the knee.

My blood.

The gun had gone off. Who had pulled the trigger, we might never know, but the shot had hit me.

And then, so did the pain. I cried out, stumbling backward on my good leg. Still alive? Yes. If I wasn't, it wouldn't hurt like this.

Everything felt foggy, distant. I collapsed on the cot, propped against the wall, watching Jimmy stare at me like I was a ghost.

Leland had his pistol back, but he wasn't pointing it. "Give me the gun, James," he ordered. He had a tone that reminded me of someone. Who?

Oh yes. Jesus. The voice he might have used when he told the storm to be still or demons to be gone or Lazarus to come forth out of the grave. Commanding miracles from people and creatures and forces that ordinarily wouldn't obey.

"Give me that gun," he repeated.

And of all things, Jimmy did, surrendering it with a look of horror on his pale face, his hand outstretched toward me, toward the wound in my leg. "Is he . . . what did I . . . ?" And then he was bent, retching over the pot in the corner we used as a makeshift latrine when we didn't want to climb down to do our business in the woods.

Leland was in front of me in an instant, blocking the sight. "Lie down now."

I couldn't do that. I'd bleed on the cot, on the sheets that Mrs. Edith washed with sprigs of lavender so they'd smell nice, even up here in the middle of nowhere.

But gravity and the force of a hand on my shoulder lowered me without my consent, and I was looking up at the rough beams of the ceiling. Dark splotches filled my vision, crowding out the heat, the pain, the light. . . .

"Focus, Mr. Hooper," that miracle voice boomed again. "Stay with me now. This is going to pinch."

Dimly, I remembered this terminology from childhood doctor's appointments and had only drawn a breath to ask what he was doing when every nerve in my body spasmed at once, starting from my leg. I gurgled out a yelp, then clamped my mouth closed again.

"You got any bandages here, or do I have to tear up the sheet?"

"Crate," I managed. Full sentences took too much work. "Under cot."

He rummaged around, and I tried to think of something, anything, other than the pain.

Counting. Yes. Counting good things. Like Mother had told me to.

The smell of earth after a rain. The sound of Mother's laugh, rare and beautiful as a diamond. The elk I'd spotted looking proudly out over the forest, as if it secretly ruled it all.

Through the throbbing, I felt a sudden tightness. Something was cinching my leg. Good. There was too much blood already. I tried to sit up to see how bad it was, but Leland's firm hand pressed me down again. "Don't you move."

So I didn't. I just tried to breathe. In. Out.

A swirl of cold air filled the room, giving me sudden clarity. I turned my head to the door, visible past Leland's broad shoulders hunching over me.

I could have sworn that there, wrapped in scarves and a man's coat, was Dorie Armitage.

No. Surely I'd passed out from the pain, and now I was just hallucinating. She couldn't . . . Why would she . . . ?

The throbbing in my leg intensified, and I closed my eyes.

Her voice. She was saying something, but what? Something important. I heard Sarah Ruth's name.

Which, all things considered, wasn't the worst choice for the last thing I heard before passing out.

CHAPTER 38

Dorie Armitage

January 26, 1945

All I could think of as Jimmy led Leland and me through the driving snow was Gordon, pale and wrapped in bloodstained sheets, lying back at the lookout.

Where we'd left him. Alone.

Everything in me had protested, but Leland assured me he'd be fine.

"How can you say that?" I'd demanded.

"Because I went through four weeks of Advanced Tactical Division Training, and I know the difference between a glancing flesh wound to the leg and somebody shot through the stomach."

That sounded convincing. And yet . . . "He's unconscious."

"Because of shock, exhaustion, and blood loss, which I've stopped." He explained it as calmly as he'd listened to my story about Sarah Ruth's fall. "Trust me, Dorie. We're not going to leave him long . . . but we have to leave him, or that woman out there hasn't got a chance."

Still, I had stood, eyes fixed on the bloodied bandage. "Jack never woke up."

A pause, and when Leland spoke again, his tone had been less clinical. "I'm sorry. Sorry Jack didn't know what he was doing, sorry we couldn't find a way to warn him. Sorry he had to die because of this awful war."

It wasn't his fault, and yet, in that sharp-looking uniform of his . . . maybe he represented something that was to blame. I didn't know anymore.

Jimmy had urged us on, told us we had to hurry. He'd wanted to leave Leland behind too, but Leland insisted on coming, partly because he knew we might need three to rescue Sarah Ruth, partly because he didn't want Jimmy "out of his sight for one moment."

Neither of them had explained what happened, except for Leland's Dick-and-Jane simplification: "There was a struggle. One of the guns went off." It would have to do for the moment, although my imagination did a fair job of filling in the details.

I tried to focus on the next snow-slick step in front of me instead. *Bring them to Sarah Ruth*. If Gordon was really going to be all right, that's what mattered now.

"Are you sure we're going the right way?" I called to Jimmy, who claimed he could find the path amidst snow and could tell one patch of trees or rocky outcropping from another. The wind had died down, or maybe it was just that following the two men sheltered me from it more than struggling through alone.

"As long as you were on the path," he replied.

We had been . . . at least while Sarah Ruth was leading.

But then we got to a place where the path narrowed by a stand of three scrappy pine trees. "There!" I shouted, and Jimmy and Leland stopped. "Down there. That's where she fell."

Instantly, Jimmy knelt down on the ground, not waiting for Leland and me to come over with our army-issue flashlights. "Sarah Ruth! Ruthie!" he bellowed over the wind.

And when a thin voice called back, "Here," I felt like I could give

God a pass for all of the selfish childhood prayers he'd declined to answer. She was still alive.

Leland knelt in the snow, taking out the coil of rope we'd brought from the lookout. "Is it just one leg that hurts, or both?" he called.

"Just . . . the right one."

"Good," Leland muttered, which seemed overly optimistic to me. Did he hear how weak her voice was?

"Hang on, Sarah Ruth," Jimmy called, "we'll get you up." But the confidence in his words didn't follow through to his face, drawn in fear.

I'd seen enough adventure sequences in Westerns—people falling down mine shafts and wells—to know how it was supposed to work. "So," I said as soon as Leland stood to join the huddle we'd formed against the mountain, "will all three of us haul her up?"

Jimmy shook his head. "Won't work. Look at the angle."

"You mean straight down?" With outcroppings jutting here and there, it wasn't quite as sheer as a manmade wall, but it was no gently sloping incline either.

He nodded. "We'd smash her against the mountain if we tried that. Even if she's strong enough to hold on, she'd get all cut up."

"At least she'd be alive." To me, that seemed like the priority of the moment.

"No," Leland said slowly, staring over the edge and running the rope through his hands. "Here's what we're gonna do. We tie that rope to a tree trunk," he pointed to the three pines, "and I climb down and hoist her to my shoulders. She can grab the rope, then the two of you pull her a few feet until you can grab her arms and haul her the rest of the way."

"Why do you get to go down?" Jimmy demanded.

"Because I'm a head taller than you, and I have emergency medical training."

338

That sounded convincing to me, and even Jimmy hesitated, worry curving his eyebrows down. "You . . . you don't think she needs it, do you?"

"She might. And this way, you'll be pulling her up at the top."

Jimmy looked doubtful, and I wanted to shout at him, tell him we were wasting time, that he couldn't let his precious ego interfere with his sister's rescue.

Let them handle it. Whatever had gone on at the lookout, it hadn't created trust. So for once in my life, I held back, though I had to bite the inside of my lip to do it.

"I'm gonna have your sister's life in my hands at one end or the other," Leland pointed out.

The way Jimmy and Leland sized each other up, they might have been boxers circling in the ring. Finally Jimmy, clearly unable to think of another way, nodded. "I'll pull her up." He snatched the end of the rope from Leland, stalking toward the tree.

"We'll do it together." I wouldn't add much—tinkering with jeeps and typewriters hadn't exactly given me Rosie-the-Riveter muscles—but it was something.

Choosing the thickest trunk of the lot, Jimmy wrapped the rope around the pine, his hands moving and twisting the rope so much I expected to see a half-woven basket instead of a knot when he stepped away.

Leland gave it a yank. "That'll hold."

"Of course it will." Jimmy punched a warning finger in Leland's face. "If anything happens to Sarah Ruth—"

"James, I promise, if there's anything I can do to keep your sister safe, I'll do it." And the way he looked just then, swear-on-a-Bible serious, I would have believed anything he said.

Jimmy grunted—if not satisfied, at least accepting the inevitable.

Pushing off the mountain with his feet, his arms tight with

effort, Leland edged down the rope. He angled his head at the ground to land next to Sarah Ruth, huddled in a half-slumped position. Despite the wind, I could hear him pass on the instructions, calmly and clearly. Then I saw her nod and reach out for his hand, putting all her weight on her left leg as she stood.

Leland took his hands, with those long, strong fingers clasped together, and held them at stepstool height. Sarah Ruth stepped on, gripping his shoulder for balance as he hefted her up.

Beside me, Jimmy was tense and still, never taking his eyes away from the two of them. "Come on," he whispered, nearly in my ear.

Her hand stretched out for the rope, and she tugged on it, getting enough leverage to step on Leland's shoulder.

And as she did, I watched in horror as a fist-sized rock broke loose, stirred up by the rub of the rope, headed right at them. Jimmy and Sarah Ruth cried out at the same time, but I barely had time to draw in a breath before Leland, eyes pointed up, grabbed on to Sarah Ruth to steady her and twisted away.

The rock thudded against his opposite shoulder, and he grunted in pain as it glanced off and fell down the mountainside. I aimed the flashlight at him. "Are you all right?"

"We're fine." Which could be anywhere at all on the spectrum from lie to truth, but I saw him wince as he shifted Sarah Ruth back into position. "Try again. Just watch for anything loose before pulling."

In my flashlight beam, Sarah Ruth looked about as capable of following complex instructions as the average GI Joe rushed into the base hospital, but she reached out and grabbed the rope again. This time only a clod of snow shook loose.

"Ready?" Jimmy asked, and she nodded, bracing herself. "Then hang on."

We pulled together in slow, steady tugs, until Sarah Ruth's head appeared over the edge of the outcropping. Then I held the rope taut with everything in me so Jimmy could wrap his arms around his sister and help her scramble up. Once she was resting on the ground, he stood, stripping off his coat.

"You'll freeze," I said.

"She needs it more." He knelt down beside Sarah Ruth, tucking the coat backward around her.

"Jimmy," she said before getting cut off with a cough.

"I'm here, Ruthie. I'm right here. We've got you now."

"You came." Her drawn face managed a smile, which then faded as she looked at the two of us, blinking. "Where's Gordon?"

To his credit, Jimmy didn't try to give a half-truth answer like "He stayed at the lookout." Instead, he looked away and said nothing, face flushing with shame.

Letting them have privacy for their reunion, I stepped over to the edge again. Leland was climbing the rope hand over hand, the strain clear on his face.

When he crawled onto the path, I reached down as if he might need help standing after scaling a small cliff. He looked over at Jimmy and Sarah Ruth huddled together and lowered his voice. "That's no sprained ankle. I'd bet my last buck on a broken leg. We'd better get a splint on that as soon as we can."

I tugged off my gloves to join Leland at working out the knot. Once it was free, I looped it back into a neat coil. "You, sir, are going to have quite a bruise."

He gathered a handful of snow and pushed it under his coat to rest against his shoulder. "All that movement, it was bound to happen. It'll heal."

"Mm-hmm." I knew bravado when I saw it. I also knew bravery. "You know, the Triple Nickles—heck, the army in general—should

341

be proud to have you as an officer." He looked up, surprised. "I'd follow you into combat any day, Lieutenant."

He smiled wryly. "I think you just did, PFC Armitage. But it's not over yet." He raised his voice and turned toward Jimmy, who had stood silent, watching our exchange. "Come on. We've got to get her back to the fire tower and warmed up."

That tiny lookout stove never sounded so good.

Wait a minute.

It didn't take long to do that math. Two treasonous ranger's children, the army officer who wanted to arrest their father, a WAC running a long con, and a wounded pacifist. All trapped during a blizzard in a 225-square-foot tower with a dead phone line.

It was going to be a long night.

CHAPTER 39

Gordon Hooper

January 27, 1945

Someone was humming.

My eyes flickered open, and I saw the lookout, lit faintly orange in the dull glow of the stove and the brighter glow of the lantern set by the window.

I frowned, my thoughts cotton padded and vague. Had I forgotten to put out the lantern before drifting off to sleep?

Got to get to it. Could start a fire.

I tried to roll off the cot, but my leg stabbed me with a thousand needles of pain.

Now I remembered all of it. The documents—still in the observation log as far as I knew—the shouting, the pistols, the wound.

That's when I saw Sarah Ruth Morrissey, stretched out on the floor only a foot away from the cot, her ankle elevated and her auburn hair loose around her head, the tips of it wet and clumped. *But why . . . ?*

When I braved the pain to shift slightly, I could see Dorie slumped in a chair, her head tilted to the side, snoring slightly, as if she'd tried to stay awake and failed.

So I hadn't been hallucinating.

Jimmy was curled in a heap close to the stove, while the lieutenant sat on the bench by the door, his weapon safely holstered, watching the snow blow past the windows.

It didn't take much conjecture to figure out the basic plot. Somehow, Dorie had worked out what Jimmy bringing Leland here would mean, and she'd dragged Sarah Ruth into coming with her to stop him. Impulsive, as usual.

As I watched, Sarah Ruth's eyes twitched, then opened, blinking a few times and catching me staring before I could pretend to be asleep. "You're awake," she whispered. Her voice sounded softer in that register, or maybe it was just the flickering lamplight on her flushed face.

"You're hurt."

"Just a sprain," she said, which didn't convince me, because she'd probably say the same if she lost her foot to a rusty bear trap.

"Listen, I wanted to say . . ." It wasn't exactly the time, with her brother and Dorie asleep nearby and the lieutenant standing watch, but I'd learned from Jack that you didn't always get a second chance. "I was wrong to yell at you like I did. About giving the recruitment brochure to Jack. You were only trying to help."

"I didn't take it personally." She tried to smile. "You saw me after Willie died. I was a cold, rude mess. Pushing people away, like I always do."

That's not how I remembered her. Sure, she'd snapped at me a few times when I tried to offer condolences, but I hadn't seen anger, only grief.

Maybe that's what she saw in me too.

And maybe someday, if I stayed in Oregon, I'd tell her everything. About my father in a New York graveyard and my worn-down mother who put him there. About growing up the son of a drunk, then of a murderer and jailbird. About fleeing to the Quaker faith to keep myself from becoming like either of them.

Because something told me Sarah Ruth would listen. And she wouldn't run away.

"You know—" she paused to yawn—"I swore once I'd never spend another night here."

"I'm sorry you had to." I looked at the others—her misguided but fiercely loyal brother, Dorie in all her impulsive love of justice, Leland, faithfully standing watch. "But you're safe here now."

"I think I am." A smile lit the corners of her mouth, then faded as she looked over at Jimmy, who whimpered in his sleep. "What are you going to do about Jimmy?"

So. She knew he'd shot me. Or at least, that it was his fault I'd been shot.

What would we do?

I returned to the only place I was sure of, one the COs returned to whenever someone tried to argue with them about pacifism. "I don't know for sure. But the Scriptures say, 'Be ye therefore merciful, as your Father also is merciful.'"

Saying it, I realized that Mother shouldn't have worried about my future, all those years ago. I had another Father I could imitate.

Sarah Ruth's eyes fluttered sleepily. "He is, isn't he?"

"Yes," I said, and meant it, even if I couldn't understand how it worked, why Jack died and I lived. "There's always mercy if we reach out for it."

She yawned again . . . and then stretched her hand up toward me.

I braved the pain of movement to roll to the edge of the cot and grasp it, holding it lightly as she closed her eyes, feeling her pulse tick a rhythm of peace and rest.

By the time morning came, I had eased myself up to a sitting position, clinging to the frame of the cot and ignoring a throbbing like someone was using my leg as an anvil. Thankfully, the cot was pushed against the wall, so I rested my head against it until the dizziness passed.

I'd woken hours before the others—except Lieutenant Leland, who didn't seem to have slept the whole night—which gave me plenty of time to think. We had to make the journey back to the camp for medical treatment, but there was no way on God's green earth I was putting weight on my bum leg. *Maybe I could get by with a pair of crutches.*

I could practically hear Sarah Ruth's mountaineering scoff. *"Down a snowy mountain? Don't you try it, Gordon."*

"Morning." Dorie appeared at the head of my cot, keeping her voice low so as not to disturb Sarah Ruth or Jimmy. Her hair stuck out wildly in all directions, and I tried not to stare at it. "How are you feeling?"

"I can think of times I've been better. Any day when I wasn't shot, for instance. Which is—" I pretended to think—"all of them."

"Hmm," she said, unconvinced, and poked my leg experimentally, shooting pain through me.

"Stop that," I snapped, making Sarah Ruth stir. I lowered my voice. "Listen, we need to talk."

"Do we?" she said dubiously, clearly judging from my expression that it wouldn't be her favorite topic.

I let her have it anyway, all the conclusions I'd made in the predawn hours. "Once everyone wakes up, Sarah Ruth is going to need help to walk." I gave her a moment to let that sink in. "And, unless I'm suddenly healed, the other two of you will probably have to carry me along narrow mountain trails."

She narrowed her eyes at me, traces of smudged makeup giving them an owl-like appearance. I couldn't wait until she found a mirror. "What's your point?"

"I'd feel a lot better about that journey if Jimmy wasn't trying to shove Leland off a cliff."

"He wouldn't do that."

"You weren't here earlier. You didn't see him." I remembered the crazed look in his eyes, the way his hands shook on the pistol. "He's scared, Dorie, and a scared man can be dangerous. That's why I need you to talk to him."

She actually took a step back, nearly stepping on Jimmy's hand, sprawled out behind her. "Oh no. Listen, I don't talk things out, Gordon. I don't reason or debate with anyone. That's you. That was Jack and all of your CO buddies. I'm the last one you'd want to do this."

"You're also the last one we have." Her arms, held out as if to ward off my idea, went slack, and I pushed ahead. "Jimmy's clearly not going to listen to me—he tried to shoot me the last time I tried. His sister is exhausted and feverish, and you know Leland has even less of a chance of getting through to him."

She bit her bottom lip. "I . . . I can't."

Come on. Where was the Dorie who joined the army, who barged her way into our camp with nothing but a hunch and some moxie?

This Dorie was rumpled, scared, and . . . real.

She has fears too. No matter how confident she looked, there were evidently times when Dorie Armitage, private eye, was at a complete and total loss.

"If you can't, it's going to be awfully hard to get all five of us away from here safely." When she didn't move, I added, "Leland seems like a good man."

She glanced over at him, and I wondered how much he could hear of our conversation. "He is. So is Jimmy, deep down."

"Then you've got to do all you can to make peace between them. You know what the Scriptures say, 'Blessed are the peacemakers—'"

"—for they're hated by everyone but God. That's what it *should* say, you know." I wasn't sure if her scowl was directed at me or the situation in general.

"Dorie . . ."

She sighed. "I know, I know. I don't have a choice."

"I was going to say, I believe you can do it."

Her skepticism was easy to read, and could I blame her? Even when we were on the same side, we'd acted like mortal enemies. "Really?"

I nodded. "What this situation needs is someone who's determined and full of life."

And I could see her stand straighter. "It does, doesn't it?" She turned and stared down at Jimmy, and for a moment I was afraid she was going to try kicking him awake—never a good start.

But instead, she looked back at me and smiled. Not the high-watt manipulative smile or even the carefree, charming smile. This one was slight, tired . . . and genuine. "Thanks, Gordon."

I leaned back against the pillow, the throbbing in my leg a little more distant. Maybe, despite what I'd told Jimmy, Dorie and I ended up as friends after all.

CHAPTER 40

Dorie Armitage

January 27, 1945

Fortunately for me, a legion of past lookouts seemed to have agreed with my priorities: coffee, first and always.

The aluminum percolator might have been antique, but at least it hadn't been sacrificed to a scrap drive. By the time it filled the tower with a soft bubbling and the rich scent of roasted coffee, Jimmy was awake and desperate enough for a mug to fall prey to my claim that I wanted him to come examine the telephone wire with me. "Just in case it's something easy to fix," I said, searching my memory for an appropriate electrical term to drop and finding none. I widened my eyes instead. "Please?"

"All right," he muttered, draining the mug, "but it's not going to help."

Leland stood as we approached the door, opened his mouth to say something—probably, "Are you sure this is a good idea?"—before I silenced him with a shake of my head.

No. It wasn't a good idea. But Gordon was right. I had to try.

Out on the platform, the view was even more breathtaking, the rosy glow of the sunrise reflecting off forests and mountains covered in white like sifted sugar.

The fresh air seemed to jostle Jimmy awake a bit, or maybe it was the coffee. Either way, he pointed to a thick wire running from the tower to the ground. "That absorbs lightning. Up here, all exposed, the tower's a magnet for it. And it'd sure be embarrassing if a fire lookout burnt down."

We picked our way around the platform, shuffling snow out of the way in our wake, until we could see the pole on the south side of the lookout, where the wire sagged loosely instead of its usual clothesline-taut.

"There you go," Jimmy grumbled. "Looks like wind and ice took it down. Nothing we can do about that, other than call an electrician once we get back to the ranger station."

He frowned at the last part, and I followed the path his mind must be traveling. Back to the ranger station. Back to his father. Back to whatever consequences would be waiting for him.

"We should go back in."

He tried to pass by me, but I caught his arm. "We need to talk, Jimmy."

"So, this *was* a trap." He scowled at me. "If you're mad at me because of Gordon, he shot at me first. My gun went off when he tackled me, that's all. Might've even been him who pulled the trigger."

Whether or not that was technically true, it wasn't the whole story, and we both knew it.

"I did what I had to do." He squared his shoulders, but I could hear the desperation under it. "You said that's how it's got to be when you know you're doing the right thing."

I took a deep breath. "I was wrong."

He looked shocked. "What?"

"Don't make me say it again." Humble pie, it turns out, is made out of unripe blackberries and arsenic, and this was my first slice, as far as I could remember. "It doesn't work, Jimmy. I've tried it here and most of my life, so I should know."

I thought of every lie I'd told and every person who had trusted me. All of Gordon's lectures about honesty. Thomas and Charlie and the other COs finding out they'd been interviewing with Jack's sister all along. Leland's disappointment when he'd heard what I'd done. What my mother would say when she found out I'd deceived her.

"You think your good intentions will be enough to even out the harm you've done to get there. But they aren't."

When I got the courage up to look at him, Jimmy was clutching the railing like he was afraid that, otherwise, he might plummet to the ground. "I was trying to protect him, that's all. Dad isn't a traitor."

"I know. And we'll make sure the army knows. Then Lieutenant Leland and his paratroopers will take over the bomb-related fires to keep civilians safe. They're going to make this right, and—"

Jimmy's laughter, broken by a snort, was forced and bitter. "Don't you get it? Your brother died because the army didn't tell anyone about the balloon bombs."

My brother. Jack. So, however he'd eavesdropped on my conversation with Leland, he'd heard that much.

"They knew about those bombs—knew all about what they looked like and how dangerous they were—and they kept it a secret. And my brother . . ." He slammed his mouth shut and looked away.

So. There was something more to this. Something even more personal than the charges against his father.

Now was the time to press, to ask questions.

"What happened to your brother, Jimmy?"

"We don't know." He finally looked me straight in the eye, but his gaze was unfocused and dull, somewhere far away. "That's the worst part of it. They won't tell us. He was an OSS man."

I knew what that particular can of alphabet soup meant. Office of Strategic Services. Their overseas agents were spies, saboteurs, resistance leaders, assassins. "I see."

"No, you don't see. I didn't want him to go. Didn't even say good-bye, just locked myself in the room we used to share and turned up *The Green Hornet* on the radio to full blast. He knocked for a long time."

Just like Jack had with me.

"When I finally opened the door after I heard the truck pull away, I found a box filled with his whole Action Comics collection. And this note."

He fumbled inside his coat, unbuttoning his shirt pocket—over his heart—and passed me a fuzzed and faded paper. When I opened it, I read, *Hey, Sport. Sorry I had to go, but here are some heroes to keep you company till I'm back. It's your job to protect the family while I'm gone, all right?*

By the time I got to the signature—*Your brother*—the lump in my throat nearly choked me.

"Dad tried to find out what country Willie was operating in. No one would answer his questions."

"I'm sure they'll tell you all they know after the war." I hoped that would be true . . . that peace would mean no more secrets.

"What does it matter? He's dead." The way Jimmy leaned over the railing, I was almost afraid he was going to jump, but instead of looking down, he looked up, over the snowy mountains stretching into the distance. "It wasn't fair. Everything he learned here made *them* want him."

I pictured William as a younger version of his father, with broad shoulders and serious brows, climbing, cutting trails, moving

352

soundlessly through the forest, trying to best Sarah Ruth at marksmanship. And then enlisting and being recruited to an elite division of the army.

As an OSS man, William wouldn't have been wearing a US uniform. The codes of war didn't apply to special operatives. No Red Cross to register him or to intervene on his behalf. No limit to any starvation, deprivation, or torture the Germans could inflict on him. No requirement to send his body home or even bury him.

"I could have joined up too, last year when I turned eighteen. But I didn't. Got an exemption for smokejumping. Maybe I was mad at the army. Or maybe I was just plain scared."

"This is your chance, Jimmy," I said in the silence that followed, trying to think like Gordon, make my voice persuasive. "But you don't have to be a hero. You just have to be—"

"'Defender of law and order, champion of equal rights, valiant, courageous fighter against the forces of hate and prejudice who fights a never-ending battle for truth, justice, and the American way.'" He practically said the whole thing in one breath.

I cracked a smile. "I wouldn't go all *that* far."

"That's Superman's mission." Even discussing his favorite hero, his voice was leaden and devoid of spark. "But you're right. I'm not a hero. I won't ever be. Not like Willie was. And it's their fault he's not here today."

Now, that I wasn't going to let stand. "Lieutenant Leland and the others didn't kill your brother, Jimmy. Or mine."

"Then who did? The Axis powers? The war? God?"

As the circles got bigger, the hopelessness of it all grew. Willie and Jack had died, and it wasn't right . . . but there was no one to blame. I'd seen my share of revenge dramas, a favorite Hollywood plotline. But what if the Count of Monte Cristo couldn't find the villainous trio who put him in prison, or a betrayed Heathcliff had no Edgar or Cathy to torment?

We were on the Orient Express with no one to stab. Something was rotten in the state of Denmark, but no ghost could tell us how to right it. It was all evil systems and blind forces, espionage and balloon bombs, domino chains of events beyond our control, and we were so very small next to it.

"Dear God . . . what do we do?"

Jimmy shifted, and I realized it hadn't been a thought. He'd spoken out loud, just as uncertain as I was.

"What do we do now?" he repeated.

"I don't know." Something else I'd never said before, but this admission felt better. Honest. Like parachuting out of a plane into the unknown, praying you'd make it safely to the ground.

As I drifted in that silence, I found a few more words and spoke them. "But maybe it's not about making anyone pay. Maybe . . . maybe we have to start by letting go of that."

His voice was hoarse. "I can't. It's all I've got."

That, at least, I knew how to answer. "That's not true. I saw what you've got, Jimmy, back on the cliff. You would have died to save Sarah Ruth."

"She's my sister." As if nothing was more natural in all the world.

Wouldn't Jack have said the same thing?

I swallowed hard, tried to keep my composure. "You're a good brother, Jimmy."

But he was shaking his head so forcefully I was afraid he'd tip off the platform. "No, I wasn't."

You have to tell him.

I swallowed hard. "You knew that Jack is—was—my brother."

Jimmy swiped at his runny nose with his sleeve, giving me that same calculating look Sarah Ruth had. "Yeah."

No time to stop now. "I never wrote to him after he left, except sending him angry newspaper clippings to call him a coward. The last thing I said to him was 'I hope I never see you again.' And now I won't."

"I'm sorry," he said, but what he meant was *"I understand."* He was probably the only one who did, who felt the awful weight of unspoken good-byes and buried regrets.

I'm still not sure which one of us opened our arms first, but I huddled against his thick corduroy coat, and I wept without trying to hide it. My tears mixed with the windblown snowdrifts, but Jimmy held me tight. Maybe he was crying too.

When he let go, it felt like someone else had taken up the burden, the guilt from leaving Jack the way I had, and whether it was Jimmy or God or both of them, I couldn't say. But it felt good.

Jimmy looked down at the ground, a sheepish kid again. "About Gordon—I didn't mean to . . . I didn't want . . ."

"I believe you. And we'll work it out." Just like I had in the blizzard, we'd move toward the light, one step at a time. "Right now, we need you, Jimmy. Leland and I don't know the path. Gordon and Sarah Ruth are hurt. That leaves you. You've got to get us down from here safely."

Gripping the railing, he turned away from the snowy horizon and back to me, and when he set his jaw, he looked every inch the mountain pioneer from days gone by. "All right," he said, "we'll do it."

CHAPTER 41

Gordon Hooper

January 27, 1945

"I always imagined," Dorie said, pausing to huff a bedraggled lump of hair out of her eyes, "that my return after acts of heroism would be more . . . heroic."

I tried to smile but winced instead as Lieutenant Leland tripped on a rock, jostling me. I'd refused to look when he'd changed my bandages before we set out, but I knew the wound needed a real doctor—and fast. Which was not how I'd describe our progress down the trail back to the national forest headquarters. What should have taken an hour had already stretched into two.

Sarah Ruth limped along beside us, using the makeshift crutch the lieutenant had fashioned for her out of a sturdy fallen branch but needing to lean against Jimmy to walk. Her mouth was still plenty free, though, and she made good use of it to tell us what we were doing wrong along the way.

"*Three* canteens of water? It'll weigh us down, and besides, there's fresh snow if we need more."

"We need to remember to tell Dad to keep more blankets stocked in the tower, just in case."

"Make sure to keep the stretcher level and watch your feet—we'll be going downhill."

That last one felt important to my well-being since I was the one trussed up in the "stretcher"—a fancy word for the canvas and frame of the cot that we took off its legs.

It had been a long trek down the mountain, our progress slow, even in the blinding sunlight glinting off the snow. Still, whatever Dorie had said to Jimmy must have worked, because he didn't make a single complaint, not even when I gave Leland the papers we'd found in Morrissey's office for safekeeping. Once, when we'd stopped to eat some of the bread from the cupboard—a poor midmorning snack, but welcome all the same—Jimmy had brought me my share. "And," he said, glancing over his shoulder to make sure the others were occupied with the packs, "thanks."

I tried to laugh. "For what? Shooting myself in the leg?"

He didn't crack a smile at my poor attempt at a joke. "For keeping me from doing something worse."

And I wondered if maybe my other Father had helped me find Mother's better way after all.

By the time we reached the base of the mountain, where the trees grew thicker and the path became blessedly flat, we made a straggling group indeed. Leland had to stop several times to scoop a handful of snow on his shoulder, streaked purple with bruising, and Dorie strained to keep her side even, her breathing coming short and labored.

But the end was in sight. Just another mile through the forest to the camp. "Almost there," I said, trying to work enthusiasm into my tone.

"Easy for you to say," Dorie said, glaring over her shoulder at me. "Once we get back, you're going on a diet of Jell-O, cottage cheese, and celery, mister." She and Sarah Ruth burst out laughing at the disgusted face I made in response.

"I'll let Mama know about the change in menu." Sarah Ruth shifted her crutch to pat me condescendingly on the arm.

I considered delivering a good fake grumble but instead said what I was really thinking. "It's been a long time since I've seen you laugh."

She hesitated, swiveling to look around, and I realized how stunning Oregon in January could be, branches white and bowed, tracks skittered here and there across the path. "Will this be normal again someday, do you think?"

Helping two injured people down a mountain after a blizzard?

But of course, that wasn't what she meant. She was talking about fresh air and sunshine gleaming against the fallen snow, about being able to make jokes and laugh at them without feeling a shadow. About remembering the ones who wouldn't come home—but loving them enough to keep on living anyway.

"Yes," I said. "I think it will. Soon enough, things will start to grow again. And we'll be there to help them along."

The beautiful smile that appeared on Sarah Ruth's face, slowly at first, like a sunrise, made me hope that some things were already blooming. Maybe even in places where fire had once passed through.

On the other side of her, Jimmy stopped, hunched over with Sarah Ruth's arm around his shoulder, his breathing heavy. "Maybe you should all rest here and let me go on ahead. I could—"

And then, one of the sweetest sounds I'd ever heard: a distant voice calling out, "Hallo! Who's there?"

All of us shouted until tree branches crashed aside with calls of "Hey, we've found 'em, fellows!"

"Gordon!"

"Where have you been?"

"We've been searching for you all morning."

"Some snowstorm, eh?"

"Someone radio back to Morrissey and tell him to call in the others!"

Four of the COs, including the Apostle Tom, surrounded us, all talking at once and asking for explanations we could hardly give. Leland and Dorie didn't set me down, knowing how much the jostling hurt me.

At this point, I'd take any pain. We'd made it back to safety and friends excited to see us alive and, hopefully, a meal more substantial than cottage cheese.

While the other COs swarmed Jimmy and Sarah Ruth, asking questions, Thomas strode over to us.

"Gordon," he said, his deep voice emotionless.

"Thomas."

I braced myself for something snide, like "All they that take the sword shall perish with the sword." Instead, he turned to Dorie. "I'll take your place the rest of the way."

Uncertainly, she turned to me, waiting for permission.

Sure, Dorie needed a break, but why Thomas? Was it his over-developed sense of duty? Maybe this was a ruse so he could "trip" and dump me to the ground the first chance he got. "Why would you do that?"

"Because," he said, and for some reason he was looking at Dorie, not me, "loving your neighbor means more than just not killing him."

With that, Thomas bent to take up the front of the pallet, like the battlefield stretcher-bearers he'd refused to join.

Maybe we'd all learned a thing or two this terrible winter.

That left Dorie to walk by my head, beside Leland, with some of the other COs helping Sarah Ruth pick our way back toward the camp. "I guess we've made it, then. They'll take you to a hospital."

"I sure hope so." Since Leland was standing right there, quietly keeping pace beside us, I didn't say it, but his reassurances that I wouldn't lose a leg or get a fatal infection would have been a lot more convincing if they'd come with a stiff painkiller.

"Well, once you're gone . . . if I don't get the chance to say it again . . ." She huffed out a breath, still looking more at the snowy ground than me. "It takes real courage, putting on a uniform and fighting for your country. I still believe that."

"I know." She'd said the same thing three years ago, when the subject had come up at Thanksgiving, wearing that red scarf and arguing away with Jack and me into the late hours of the night. I'd known all along where she stood.

"But maybe it takes courage to stand up to people making fun of you for what you believe, or to jump out of planes, or to fight a trigger-happy kid to save a man you barely know." To avoid looking at me, she pretended to kick away a rock from the trail.

"Dorie . . ."

"You were braver than I realized, that's all." She looked down at me then, and I saw the track of a lone tear down her face. "You and Jack both."

Sure, there were still things unspoken between us, battles we'd fought and won and lost, questions that wanted answers.

But maybe this was enough. "Thanks. That means more than you know."

She nodded briskly, brushing the skirt of her uniform as if she could get rid of the mud stains spattered on it. "Now, you'd better rest until we can get you to a doctor to heal up. You've still got a debt to your country to pay off, you know. The war's not over yet."

But it felt like one war, anyway, was as good as done. And I was thankful.

CHAPTER 42

Dorie Armitage

January 27, 1945

I learned, over a hearty stack of flapjacks in the near-empty cook-house, that Mr. Morrissey hadn't committed treason.

"I'm not sure what he was thinking when he planned that meeting with the mayor," Leland said, "but all he said was that he wanted permission to give a safety demonstration to the town before spring. Major Hastings contacted the mayor to confirm the story. Apparently he mentioned wanting to warn people to report unidentified objects to the proper authorities, but that was all."

I knew a loophole when I saw one, and my mind began spinning. "Doesn't sound like a half-bad idea, if you ask me."

Leland drizzled more syrup over his pancakes. "Once we explained things to him and promised we were training a specialized crew to handle incendiary bomb fires, he agreed to keep things quiet. Major Hastings is satisfied with that."

"So, no treason trial?" He shook his head, and I was surprised by the relief I'd felt. I'd only known the Morrisseys for a little over a week, but their little gang was one worth knowing and protecting.

The faint strains of a hummed "Oh My Darling Clementine" made me look over to see Edith bustling in from the kitchen, a platter extended toward us. "More bacon?" Since Gordon had been taken to a hospital and the local doctor had set Sarah Ruth's fractured ankle and told her—three times—to stay still and get some rest, Edith was free to mother over two of her daughter's rescuers. Five pancakes and about a month of butter rations in, I didn't feel like objecting.

Leland smiled broadly. "The answer to that question is always yes, ma'am."

Even I took another slice. To heck with a girlish figure and the army's concern over fitness. I'd survived a harrowing experience, and that entitled me to all the bacon I could hold.

"You're welcome," she said, beaming at both of us. "After all you did for my Sarah Ruth, I'd give you a whole hog roast if meat wasn't so scarce these days."

"I'm afraid we won't be staying long enough for that, ma'am."

And that comment triggered another bout of looming dread, a familiar emotion for me these days. We'd solved the mystery. Now it was time to go back to Seattle. I tried to think of happy things, of Bea's record collection and the upcoming Valentine's Day talent show and writing letters for Howard at the base hospital. But it all seemed so far away now.

Once Edith had disappeared into the kitchen again, Leland turned serious. "In case you're wondering, I'm not going to report you, PFC Armitage."

I cut off a delicate piece of pancake and swirled it around in syrup. "Well, I should hope not. Because if you did, you'd rob me of the chance to report myself."

His fork clattered to his plate, and I continued before he had a chance to say anything. "Don't try to talk me out of it. I plan to give Captain Petmencky a full report the second I set foot back in Seattle."

"But that's . . ." He shook his head. "You didn't tell *Jimmy* he needed to turn himself in."

Leland and Gordon had decided together not to press charges against Jimmy. Their official story—strictly true—was that a fight had broken out, and a gun accidentally went off. The shocked look on Jimmy's face when they'd told him that neither he nor his father would be going to jail had been something to witness.

I'd had a long mountain hike to think on it and decided this was different. "Jimmy is a teenager who acted on impulse to protect his father. I, on the other hand, swore the oath of a Women's Army Corps soldier and still plotted an extended deception, using my uniform as a cover. It was . . . wrong."

It turns out the second slice of humble pie only tastes like lemon juice and crushed gravel. Maybe, if I kept this up, I'd eventually be able to stomach it on a regular basis.

Leland stroked his moustache, his face grave. "You'll be dishonorably discharged."

"Most likely. But I think it's worth it, for a clear conscience, don't you?"

He stared at me, then burst into a laugh. "You might be just the right amount of crazy, PFC Armitage."

I stood and bowed. "Why, thank you." I stacked my syrup-covered dishes to bring them back to Edith. "And another thing. I'd like to speak to Major Hastings. I have an . . . idea to run past him."

Leland tilted his head at me when I didn't add anything more. "Should I be worried?"

I gave a dazzling smile. "Always."

He chewed thoughtfully on his last piece of bacon. "Well, we *are* going back to Seattle from here. Maybe you could come with us."

"Perfect," I said. "Nothing like a train ride to give you a captive audience."

"Actually," Leland said, and a sudden grin spread across his face, the widest I'd seen from him, "it won't be a train."

I held back a squeal of excitement, but only barely, as our plane tilted sharply to miss the trees . . . and then we were off the ground and into the wild blue yonder, to borrow a phrase from my air force compatriots.

Major Hastings gave me a jowly *"For heaven's sake, be dignified"* sort of look from across the way, but Leland, next to me, only smiled. Like he'd felt the same way on his first airplane flight.

As we rose, I plastered my face to the small window, watching the trees and mountains get smaller, looking for one area in particular. There. It was easy to see from this height, broken trees and patches of charred black showing through the melting snow.

The bomb. The fire. Jack.

I stared at it, the dark ruins rising out of the ashes. *Good-bye, brother.*

It would be a meadow someday. Gordon and Sarah Ruth had promised.

In a moment, it was gone, and I could only see clouds all around me, wispy and pure white. The view looked like one of the illustrations of heaven in the children's Bible picture cards I'd been given for coming to church on Easter.

I miss you.

Beneath me, the floor of the plane tilted, jolting me against the canvas strap holding me in, and I gasped out loud.

Leland cleared his throat, and I straightened. "Sorry."

"Don't be." He grinned, his voice pitched above the engine's roar. No posh commercial liner for us—we were being toted back to Seattle in one of the smokejumpers' smaller planes, where you could feel every turn and jostle. "There's nothing like it, is there?"

"There sure isn't." I'd always thought the idea of soaring through the air sounded like a grand adventure, but I hadn't been prepared for something that managed to be both effortlessly weightless and noisily, jarringly physical. Swing dancing and engine repair had nothing on this.

Knowing the plane itself wouldn't be ideal for conversation, I'd spent the time while we waited by the landing strip to give Major Hastings my initial pitch.

My plan was simple: If the army was afraid of running stories about balloon bombs in the national press, why not distribute safety flyers to local communities in city halls and schools? That way, citizens would be able to identify and report any bombs they found, but the scale would be small enough that Japanese interceptors wouldn't know about them.

Hastings's aide put forth a dozen objections, but Hastings himself seemed interested, and I intended to persist on that interest no matter what it took. He was about to learn how relentless a WAC could truly be.

Leland's voice cut through my thoughts. "Can you imagine jumping out of this tin can?"

I tried to picture it, to feel what it would be like, teetering on the edge of that door, ready to topple into nothingness with only a scrap of silk keeping you from near-certain death.

This time, when I looked out the window, I felt what Gordon and Jack must have felt on their first jump, a sickening lurch and desire to run away—the same way I felt when thinking about the conversation I'd need to have with Captain Petmencky where I explained everything I'd done.

But I'd do it. Yes. There was no going back now. It was the only right thing to do.

Maybe, after all this, I was a little braver too.

Epilogue

May 11, 1945

Dear Mother,

I've had a lot of time to think this spring, but I haven't told you much about it, sticking to safer things like Mrs. Edith's gingerbread or the latest flowers to bloom. But it's time.

Thank you for sending Clara's journal entry in January. Reading her words might have been exactly what I needed. They also made me realize I never really forgave you for letting Father die. For killing him.

Maybe I understand more, reading what Clara wrote. It was wrong, but you know that—you've told me that yourself a hundred times. I've learned something this year about grace too. And if you've asked God for forgiveness, who am I to withhold it?

Because of my injury, I'll probably never go back to strenuous physical labor like construction or smokejumping. There's an open position here at the national forest for the summer: clerk/ secretary. The young woman who previously held it decided to take shifts as a lookout instead, since they're worried about increased fire activity right now.

Mr. Morrissey's given the job to me as a temporary role with CPS. If the war ends soon, like most are saying it will now that Germany's fallen, I'm thinking of taking it permanently. But before I start, I have one last special assignment as a smoke-jumper for a week. A training mission, so don't worry, I'll be able to stay off my leg.

I hate to admit it since it was the War Department who forced me here, but I've come to love Oregon. Among the mountains and trees is a raw beauty, a stillness I couldn't even find in Quaker meetings, and underneath it all, a sense of purpose. I came looking for peace—and I found it. I don't think I could go back to New York again after this.

Maybe, once you've served your sentence, you'll want to come visit. You're welcome to, you know. Sarah Ruth once told me, "The West has always been for people looking to start over. The sun comes up over those mountains fresh and new every day," and I think she's right. (There's another reason for you to visit—so you can meet her.)

Your son,
Gordon

TO DORIE FROM LIEUTENANT VINCENT LELAND

May 18, 1945

Dear Dorie,

Your story about applying as a USO junior hostess made me laugh out loud. I bet those ladies' eyes just about bulged out of their heads when you gave an army officer as your reference. Guess they saw soon enough that you're qualified. I hope you *spend the rest of the war swing dancing till your feet are sore. And now that Germany's out of the fight, it won't be long, thank God.*

Today I learned how to safely collect and dismantle a bomb. Not a bad day's work, eh? The War Department's got some detailed pictures from recovered ones they reverse engineered. Let me tell you, it's a wicked mechanism: an aluminum wheel hung with sandbags and several dangling incendiary bombs that look like small stovepipes, plugged with demolition charges.

They're keeping a crew of us with know-how ready to be sent up in a plane headed to any fire. Most of them will be regular summer blazes, but if we need the bomb squad, the Triple Nickles will be there.

Maybe I shouldn't write to you about things like that, seeing as one of them killed your brother. But I want you to know that we're not gonna let it happen again. Not one more civilian death.

They brought in the crew from Flintlock Mountain to start training yesterday for Operation Firefly, as they're calling it. Classified, and all that, but since you already know what we're doing out here, I guess it doesn't spoil much.

That James Morrissey fellow might be hotheaded, but the boy's a mountain man, sure enough. He took us on a hike through the hills, and while we were all panting and out of breath, he jumped from rock to rock like a cat. Charlie's been giving us tree-climbing lessons for any time we get tangled up on a jump. And Gordon, he's got an eye for details, teaching map reading and showing us which spring mushrooms are edible and which could kill you.

They'll be gone by the end of the week, leaving us with just the Pendleton folks. The reception's a tad chilly here toward us fellows, but we've found one place at least that'll serve us, and they make an all right burger, so that's something.

I've stuck in the latest war bond poster—would you look at that? I don't know if you've heard of the Tuskegee Airmen, but you can bet all of us Triple Nickles have. The first (and only) black pilots the air force's got. They're putting the poster up in all the colored parts of town to drum up support . . . except in the corner drugstore in my neighborhood in Detroit, because my mother got so excited to see it that she tore it down and sent it to me. I told her that defeats the purpose, but she wanted to know when I'm gonna get on a poster.

Probably not anytime soon. Firefighting isn't as dramatic as flying escort for bombers over Italy. The rest of the Triple Nickles are disappointed we won't be going into combat, but I keep telling them this is combat of a different kind.

I'm passing the Tuskegee Airman poster along to you to remind you: If you want something bad enough, you can go get it. Sure, you'll have to wait till the war's over, but if you're not first in line for flying lessons after Japan surrenders, I'll eat my hat. (And right now my hat's a helmet with a metal face guard, so don't you make me do that.)

Hope all's well in Pennsylvania. You take care of your family, and don't go making too much of a menace of yourself as a civilian.

Lieutenant Vincent Leland

FROM GORDON TO DORIE

May 25, 1945

Dear Dorie,

I hope you don't mind me writing you now, because I have good news to pass along. I'll get to that later.

Since the Triple Nickles are taking over smokejumping for the summer season, they're sending some of the men away to other camps. About six of us are staying, including me—even if we're not responding to fire calls, someone's got to repair fences, maintain the trails for tourist season, and, of course, man the fire lookouts.

Speaking of which, they're talking about some sort of memorial to Jack at the site of the fire: The only civilian killed by enemy action on US soil. I don't know if Jack would've wanted all the attention, but I like the idea. We won't ever forget him.

But that's not all. Before I tell you the rest, I should remind you that I'm an artist, not a storyteller, but some of the other men are, as you likely gathered from your interviews with them.

You should have seen us, sitting cross-legged on the bunkhouse floor on Sunday afternoons with Jack's notebook pages fanned out between us. Turns out, a lot of his ideas were all right—some of the crimes were actually interesting—but they were just like any other hackneyed detective stories. Something had to be done. Something different. The idea for that was my main contribution, but Jimmy did most of the actual writing. He said that it wasn't much different than those Detective Comics he's always burying his nose in. Sarah Ruth typed it out for us, which I hope you understand was a sacrifice, since she hates paperwork.

I'll let the other letter I've included do the rest of the explaining for me. I hope it means as much to you as it did to all of us.

Sincerely,
Gordon

FROM KENNETH S. WHITE TO GORDON

May 21, 1945

Dear Sir (or should I say Sirs):

Thank you for the submission of your short story, "A Matter of Arson," to Black Mask *magazine. I'm delighted to inform you that we are accepting it for publication in our January 1946 issue.*

I see in your letter that you would like to use the pen name Jack Armitage. A good choice, as I can't imagine we'd have the space to write out all eighteen of your cowriters' names. Quite extraordinary.

A check for the standard article rate will be made out to your name. It is up to you to decide how to disburse it amongst your team.

I will add that your story particularly caught our eye because of its unusual protagonist. A female private eye added just the twist we love here at Black Mask.

It should be noted that our secretary and first reader, Miss Hattie McDermott, brought the manuscript directly to my desk in the middle of my lunch and demanded that I read it straight through. She—who is taking dictation on this letter—would like to know how you came up with the idea for Nora Hightower, and if you're planning on writing any more stories with this character.

Should you choose to do so, our staff would certainly be interested in considering them.

Thank you again for your time, and I look forward to working with you and your fellow writers on any revisions.

Kenneth S. White
Editor, Black Mask

FROM DORIE TO GORDON

May 28, 1945

Dear Gordon,

I'm so excited I could just die. Jack's story in Black Mask? *I can't stand the fact that I'll have to wait half a year to read it. You must send me a copy of the manuscript at once.*

I thought when you asked for Jack's notebooks back in February that you wanted them for purely sentimental reasons. I bet Thomas hated that you wrote the story on Sundays, didn't he? Did Shorty come back to help? Tell me everything.

And a female detective! Well, I'm glad Nora Hightower was a hit. I'm certainly not going to be trotting that name out again anytime soon, since using it got me expelled unceremoniously from the WAC.

As for me, I'm nearly dying of boredom. Father's burying himself in his work as a way of coping. Mother finally went to church with me last week, dressed all in black like a Victorian dowager, but it was a step. I told her what you said about church being the place to go when you're grieving. I think it helped. We'll get through this together.

I've managed to wrangle a job as a stenographer at a finishing school that probably wouldn't have accepted me as a pupil, and I've got a fund started for flying lessons. (It's a canning jar, actually, but I've taped a photo of Amelia Earhart above it, so that makes it official.) Turns out, there's a regional airport twenty miles away. At the moment they're running only government jobs—I checked—and not taking on new students.

When the war's over, you'll be able to keep your feet firmly on the ground every day for the rest of your life. But me? I plan to fly.

And somehow, I think we'll both end up right where we're meant to be.

Your friend,
Dorie

Author's Note

Although they're very real in my imagination, Dorie, Gordon, and their friends are fictional, as is Flintlock Mountain National Forest and the Basin Fire. However, the daily routine of life is modeled on the actual spike camps throughout the Pacific Northwest where conscientious objectors were stationed as smokejumpers during the war. Their headquarters at Missoula is real, and if you're ever there, check out the Missoula Smokejumper Visitor Center to learn more about the history and responsibilities of smokejumpers. I'm grateful for the many historians who have collected written and recorded interviews with WWII COs that I used to form my characters and some of their ethical dilemmas.

Dorie's experiences in the Women's Army Corps at Fort Lawton are also drawn from accounts of WACs serving there at the time. Some USO clubs welcomed WACs into their programs and dances; others worried about the rumors that the WACs were "loose women," a common prejudice at the time.

Starting in November 1944, Japan really did send hydrogen-powered incendiary bombs over the jet stream, intending to cause mass chaos with fires all across the Pacific Northwest. Many of the balloon bombs were lost in the ocean, but dozens landed. Some ignited fires; a few were spotted and reported to law enforcement before they exploded. (The latest dormant balloon bomb to be discovered at the time of this writing was in British Columbia in 2014.)

After one leaked article, the Office of Censorship determined that no American newspaper, radio station, or individual would be permitted to report a balloon sighting, which is why most people have never heard of this strange tactic in WWII history. As in the novel, they relaxed this ban once the first civilian deaths convinced them that citizens needed to be able to recognize the danger, causing them to provide local instruction to recognize the bombs like Dorie suggested. However, the real deaths were not of a conscientious objector, but a pastor's wife and five young people from her church on a picnic in Bly, Oregon. This tragedy—the only civilians killed by enemy action on US soil—inspired the mystery storyline of this book.

In response, the Triple Nickles—the 555th Parachute Infantry Division—were called in to take over a looming 1945 fire season that the Forestry Department feared would be made worse by even more incendiary bombs. All of the enlisted men and commanding officers of the Triple Nickles were proudly Black. The Triple Nickles put out over three dozen fires during the unusually dry summer 1945 season, protecting America's forests, though it's likely that few were caused by incendiary bombs. To everyone's relief, Japan didn't launch another round of them, thinking they had failed to land on American soil when they heard no reports about them.

One liberty I took in *The Lines Between Us* was that the officers of the Triple Nickles didn't know the details of their mission and hadn't been involved in the negotiation process for what was called Operation Firefly. I wanted readers to have the chance to hear directly from one of the brave men who fought for a prejudiced country, so I included Lieutenant Vincent Leland as a character. He is fictional, but many of his experiences are based on reading interviews with and books about Triple Nickle officers. If you're interested in learning more about these men, I recommend *Courage Has No Color* by Tanya Lee Stone.

For more details on the fact versus fiction of this novel and recommendations for further reading, visit amygreenbooks.com and click on the History tab. I'd love to see all of you research lovers there!

I'd also like to take this time to thank those who helped this book arrive to you (and to keep its author sane, a more difficult task). First, my Bethany House family. Dave Horton and Dave Long, thank you for your guidance and championing all along the way. Rochelle and Elizabeth, I so appreciate the insightful editorial queries and corrections that made this story from the mess it was to the finished product it is today. Jenny, as always, your cover art is lovely and evocative, and thanks also to Paul for directing it through the process. I'm so glad to have the fiction marketing team behind me, including Noelle, Brooke, Rachael, Chris, and Serena—thanks for being fantastic. And of course, I'm grateful to the Bethany House authors (and others) who have graciously welcomed this newcomer with open arms. Special thanks to Christina Suzann Nelson for sending me some descriptions of the natural beauty of her home state of Oregon to use in my story.

Outside of my publishing team, I'd also like to thank my writing buddy, Ruthie, for all of the feedback and check-ins (on my book and on me). Much love to my parents and sister, Erika, for being so excited for my books, now and always, and cheering me on all the way—and the rest of my extended family as well. A special award this time goes to my husband, Jake, for allowing my work on, and occasional complaints about, this book to dominate our first year of marriage, during a pandemic, no less. He brainstormed and meal prepped and deprived me of my fun board games when I was behind on my deadline to make sure this book got written—and took good care of me along the way.

Finally, I'm so thankful for all of the readers who have supported me, leaving reviews, sending me words of encouragement, and loving my characters as much as I do. It means so much to me.

Reading Group Guide

1. What were some of the main differences that you felt came between Dorie and Gordon throughout the story? Did you see them as irreconcilable, or did you hope that they might get back together?

2. Why do you think conscientious objectors like Gordon and Jack were treated with such contempt during WWII? What do you think of the choice they made and the reasoning behind it?

3. Early on, Lieutenant Vincent Leland tells Dorie that "People are never simple." What are some ways Dorie learns this throughout the story? How about Gordon?

4. What did you think of the sections of letters and other documents throughout the book?

5. At what point did you wonder if the fire and resulting "accident" that injured Jack wasn't really an accident? Did you have any suspicions about the cause? As Dorie and Gordon investigated, did your theories change?

6. When asked for her opinion on pacifism, Sarah Ruth tells Gordon, "Men like my brother William are called to raise

barricade lines to keep the fire of evil from spreading. . . .
Maybe you're meant to come back to the scorched earth
and help something grow again." Do you agree or disagree
with her?

7. The conscientious objectors in the book, like the ones in
real life, protested both segregation and the internment
of Japanese Americans. Why do you think they were so
"ahead of their time" when it came to issues like this?

8. When the secret of Jack's accident—and the resulting
cover-up—was finally revealed, was it satisfying to you as a
reader?

9. Both Gordon's mother and Clara were faced with a violent
man threatening harm to people they cared about. Both
felt that they made the wrong choice in their actions—or
inaction—against those men. Do you agree? What do you
think Clara should have done when facing the sheriff?
How about Gordon's mother when confronted with her
abusive husband?

10. After reading the real-life historical background in the
Author's Note, do you think it was right in this case for the
US government to suppress and censor information for the
greater good?

11. Do you feel that, in the end, Jimmy faced appropriate consequences for his actions? What about Mr. Morrissey?
Dorie? Is there anything you wish the characters had done
differently?

12. Morrissey claimed that the smokejumper's motto should
be "Courage is running toward the fire, not away from
it." In what ways did Dorie and Gordon show this kind of
courage throughout the novel?

Amy Lynn Green is a publicist by day and a novelist on nights and weekends. History has always been one of her passions, and she loves speaking with book clubs, writing groups, and libraries all around the country. She and her husband enjoy playing board games, trying new recipes, and hiking near their home of Minneapolis, Minnesota. Write her a note or sign up for the updates and bookish fun in her quarterly newsletter at www.amygreenbooks.com.

Sign Up for Amy's Newsletter

Keep up to date with Amy's latest news on book releases and events by signing up for her email list at amygreenbooks.com.

More from Amy Lynn Green

In this epistolary novel from the WWII home front, Johanna Berglund is forced to return to her small Midwestern town to become a translator at a German prisoner-of-war camp. There, amid old secrets and prejudice, she finds that the POWs have hidden depths. When the lines between compassion and treason are blurred, she must decide where her heart truly lies.

Things We Didn't Say

You May Also Like . . .

After promising a town he'd find them water and then failing, Sullivan Harris is on the run, but he grows uneasy when one success makes folks ask him to find other things—like missing items, or sons. When men are killed digging the Hawk's Nest Tunnel, Sully is compelled to help, and it becomes the catalyst for finding what even he has forgotten—hope.

The Finder of Forgotten Things by Sarah Loudin Thomas
sarahloudinthomas.com

After a deadly explosion at the Chilwell factory, munitions worker Rosalind Graham leaves the painful life she's dreamt of escaping by assuming the identity of her deceased friend. When RAF Captain Alex Baird is ordered to surveil her for suspected sabotage, the danger of her deception intensifies. Will Rose's daring bid for freedom be her greatest undoing?

As Dawn Breaks by Kate Breslin
katebreslin.com

As the nation's most fearless travel columnist, Augusta Travers explores the country, spinning stories for women unable to leave hearth and home. Suddenly caught in a scandal, she escapes to India to visit old friends, promising great tales of boldness. But instead she encounters a plague, new affections, and the realization that she can't outrun her past.

Every Word Unsaid by Kimberly Duffy
kimberlyduffy.com

❦ BETHANYHOUSE

More from Bethany House

When a renowned profiler is found dead in his hotel room and it becomes clear the killer is targeting agents in Alex Donovan's unit, she is called to work on the strangest case she's ever faced. Things get personal when the brilliant killer strikes close to home, and Alex will do anything to find the killer—even at the risk of her own life.

Dead Fall by Nancy Mehl
THE QUANTICO FILES #2
nancymehl.com

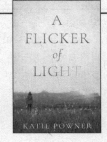

Widower Mitch Jensen is at a loss with how to handle his mother's odd, forgetful behaviors, as well as his daughter's sudden return home and unexpected life choices. Little does he know Grandma June has long been keeping a secret about her past—but if she doesn't tell the truth about it, someone she loves will suffer, and the lives of three generations will never be the same.

A Flicker of Light by Katie Powner
katiepowner.com

After an abusive relationship derails her plans, Adri Rivera struggles to regain her independence and achieve her dream of becoming an MMA fighter. She gets a second chance, but the man who offers it to her is Max Lyons—her former training partner, who she left heartbroken years before. As she fights for her future, will Adri be able to confront her past?

After She Falls by Carmen Schober
carmenschober.com

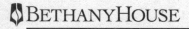